point of hopes

Also by Melissa Scott and Lisa A. Barnett

The Armor of Light

point of hopes

Melissa Scott
and
Lisa A. Barnett

A Tom Doherty Associates Book / New York

This is a work of fiction. All the characters and events portrayed in this novel are either fictitious or are used fictitiously.

POINT OF HOPES

This book is printed on acid-free paper.

Edited by David G. Hartwell

A Tor Book
Published by Tom Doherty Associates, Inc.
175 Fifth Avenue
New York, N.Y. 10010

Tor Books on the World-Wide Web:
http://www.tor.com

Library of Congress Cataloging-in-Publication Data

Scott, Melissa.
Point of hopes / by Melissa Scott & Lisa Barnett.
p. cm.
ISBN 0-312-85844-2
I. Barnett, Lisa A. II. Title.
PS3569.C672P65 1995
813′.54—dc20 95-35364
CIP

First edition: December 1995

Printed in the United States of America

0 9 8 7 6 5 4 3 2 1

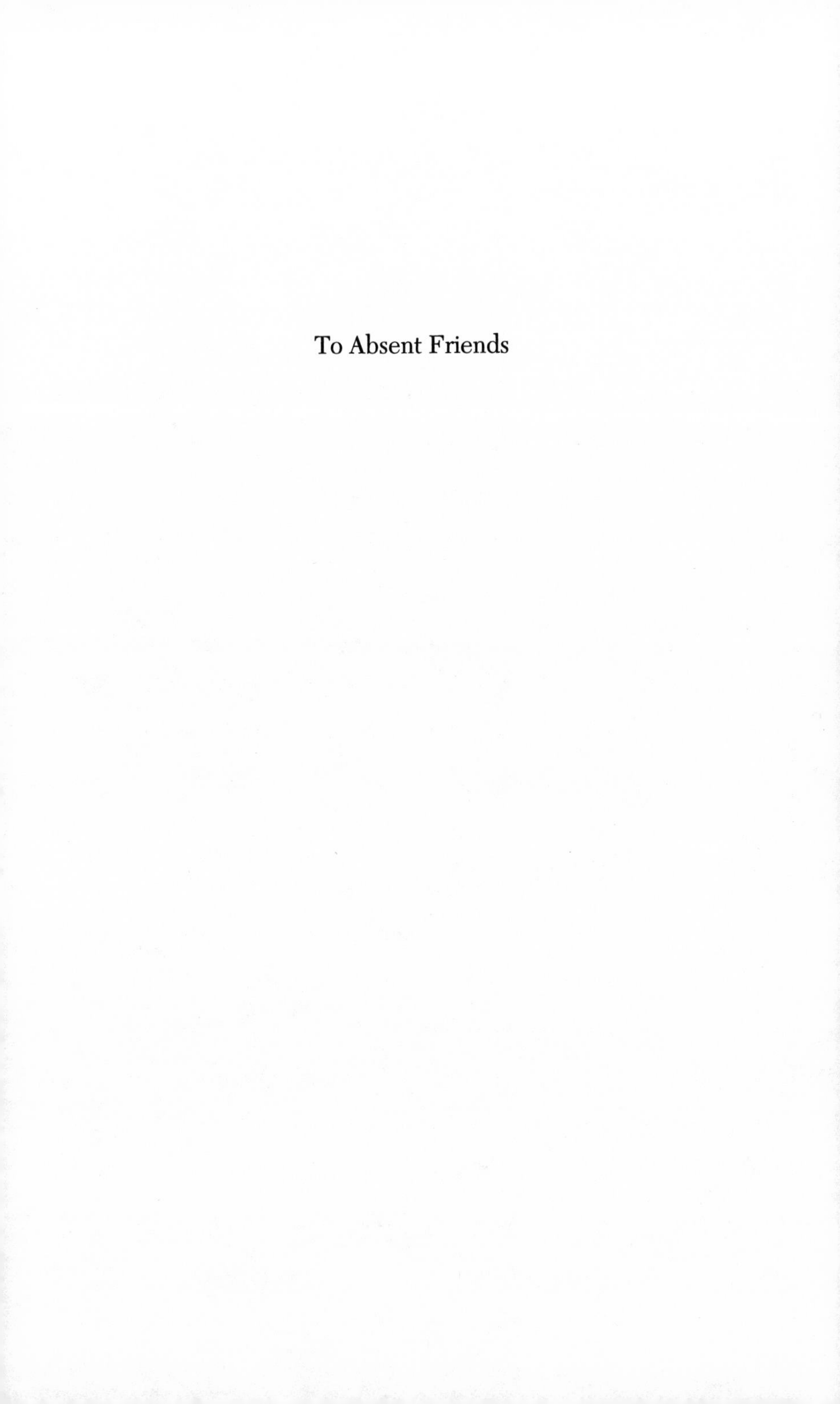

To Absent Friends

point of hopes

Prologue

The long room was cool, and very quiet, not even the sound of a house clock to disturb the silence. The magist who sat in the guest's chair by the empty fireplace was very aware of that unnerving quiet, and folded her hands in her wide sleeves to stop herself fidgeting with her rings. The room smelled of sour ash, as though the fire hadn't been lit in a week or more, for all that it was only the last day of Lepidas and the Rat Moon. The spring came late and cold in the Ajanes; she would have been glad of a fire to cut the chill that clung to the stones of floor and walls. The heavy tapestries and the one paneled wall did little to warm the room. She looked around the room again and was reassured by the sight of silver on the sideboard and wax candles in the carved-crystal holders, though she could have sworn there had been a case-clock by the window the last time she'd come to Mailhac.

The landame of Mailhac—who had been plain Jausarande d'Orsandi, one of five daughters with sixteen quarterings and no prospects, before she had made her bargain with the magist's employer—saw that look from the doorway, and knew it instantly for what it was. To see a shopkeeper's daughter, or worse, presuming to judge her own financial standing, to count the value of silver that had belonged to this estate for generations, was intolerable. Still, it had to be tolerated, at least a little longer, and she smoothed her skirts, displaying long, fair hands against the rich green silk, and swept forward into the room.

The magist rose to her feet, the drab black of her gown falling in easy folds over a plain travelling suit, the wine-colored skirt and bodice dull even in the doubled sunlight that seeped in through the flawed glass of the single window. "Maseigne."

"Magist." The landame acknowledged the other woman's greeting with a nod, deliberately did not sit, and was pleased to see the magist stifle a sigh at the reminder of her place. "What brings you here?"

What do you think? The magist swallowed that response, and said more moderately, "We are concerned about the terms of your loan. About your meeting them."

Her voice was common, the sharp vowels of the capital's poorer districts barely blunted by her education. The landame achieved a sneer. "I'm surprised to see you here on such an errand, magist. I thought you were concerned with more important parts of your master's—business."

The magist shrugged, shoulders moving under the heavy fabric. "You can take it as a compliment to your rank, if you like. Or you can assume—if you haven't already heard—that it's just because Douvregn was arrested for dueling, and we haven't found a knife to replace him yet. As you please, maseigne."

The landame caught her breath at the insult—how dare she suggest that her employer would send a common street bully like Douvregn to deal with an Ajanine noble?—but controlled herself with an effort that made her hands tremble. She stilled them, stilled her thoughts, reminding herself that she, they, needed time to finish the work at hand, time to get all the pieces into place, but once that was accomplished, neither she nor any of her rank would ever have to crawl to folk like the magist again. "Douvregn was getting above himself, then," she observed, and was annoyed when the magist grinned.

"No question, maseigne, one prefers to leave blood sports to the seigneury. However, that's hardly the matter under discussion." The magist let her smile fade to the look of grave inquiry that had intimidated far less cultured opponents. "We expect the gold at Midsummer—by the First Fair, maseigne, not like last year."

The landame met the other woman's stare without flinching, though inwardly she was cursing the impulse that had made her delay the previous year's payment. That had been petty spite, nothing more, but it seemed as though it would haunt her dealings now, interfering with her current plans. She said, "But the payment was made by Midsummer, magist, as agreed in our bond. I cannot be held responsible for the vagaries of the weather."

The magist's mouth tightened fractionally. She knew perfectly well that the other had held back the previous year's payment until the last possible moment, though she doubted that the landame had any real conception of the effects that delay had had on her employer's business. "Of course not, maseigne, but, as one who is experienced in such matters, may I suggest you allow more time for bad weather this year? The roads between Astreiant and the Ajanes can be difficult even at the height of summer."

The landame bent her head with a passable imitation of grace, hiding her anger at the condescension in the other's voice. "I'll take that suggestion to heart, magist. As you say, I'm not as familiar as you are with the proper handling of trade."

"How could you be, maseigne?" the magist answered, and the landame was suddenly uncertain if her insult had even been recognized.

"When will you be leaving us?" she asked abruptly, and wondered then if she'd spoken too soon.

"In the morning," the magist answered. "As soon after second sunrise as we can manage, I think. Enjoyable as your hospitality is, maseigne"— the flicker of her eyes around the chilly room pointed the irony of the words —"we have business to attend."

"Of course," the landame answered, hiding her rage, and the magist moved toward the door.

"Then if you'll permit me, maseigne, I'd like a word or two with your steward."

The landame bit back her first furious answer—how dare the woman interfere in the running of a noble's household?—and waved a hand in gentle dismissal. "As you wish."

"Thank you, maseigne," the magist answered, and bowed before slipping from the room.

The landame swore as the door closed behind her, looking around for something to throw, but controlled her temper with an effort. This was not the time, was too early to tip her hand—but when the time came, she vowed silently, when my kinswoman sits on the throne, then you will pay, magist, you and your employer both. That thought, the reminder of her plans, steadied her, and she turned toward the chamber she used for her private business. The catch was hidden in the paneling, hard to find even for someone who knew where to look, and she had to run her thumb over the carved clusters of fruit before she found it. She unlatched the door and went on into the little room. It smelled of stale scent and windows that had been closed too long, and she made a face and flung open the shutters. The air that rushed in was chill despite the sunlight—the estate lay in the high hills, and the manor had been built for defense rather than gracious living—and she considered for a moment calling a servant to relight the fire in the stove. But that would take too long; she had come here only to calm herself with the reminder of her plans, and would be gone again before anyone would hear the summons bell. She went to the case that held the estate's books instead, unlocked it, and reached behind the cracking volume that held the estate's charter to pull out a thin, iron-bound box. She set that down on the table, fumbling beneath her bodice for its key, and unlocked it, stood looking with satisfaction at the papers that nearly filled it. The handwriting was her own, laborious and old-fashioned—these were not matters that could be trusted to any secretary, no matter how discreet—and the words, the plans they outlined, were frankly treasonous. But the starchange was almost upon them, the Starsmith, ruler of monarches and astrologers, was about to pass from the Shell to the Charioteer, and that meant that times were ripe for change. The Queen of Chenedolle was getting old, was childless, and had little prospect now of bearing an heir of her own body; with no direct heir, the succession was open to anyone within the far-flung royal family who possessed the necessary astrological kinship. Law and simple prudence demanded that she name her successor before the starchange, before the events that shift portended actually came to pass. The landame allowed herself a slight, almost rueful smile, studying the jagged letters. In practice, there were only a handful of possible candidates—the queen's first cousin, the Palatine Marselion chief, among them; then the palatines Sensaire and Belvis, both granddaughters of the previous monarch's sister; and finally the Metropolitan of Astreiant, who was only the daughter of the queen's half sister but was rumored to have the queen's personal favor, as well as a favorable nativity. Her own chosen candidate, the Palatine Belvis, to whom she was related by marriage as well as the more general kinship among the nobles of the Ile'nord and the Ajanes, was rumored to be deeply out of favor at court, for all that her stars were easily as good as Astreiant's. The landame's smile widened then. But that would change, she vowed silently. She had taken the first steps toward ensuring Belvis's accession at the Spring Balance; the next step was well in hand—as long as the magist's employer could be kept at arm's length until after Midsummer.

She sorted through the top layer of papers—letters to her agent in the capital, blotted accounts, guarded letters to Belvis herself, and the palatine's equally guarded replies—and finally found the sheet she wanted. It was not her own, but from her agent: an accounting of the money already spent and a request for more, along with its proposed uses. Most of it would go to the half dozen astrologers who were at the heart of her plan; the rest would go to the printers who sold the broadsheets that promoted Belvis's cause and to the dozen or more minor clerks and copyists who carried out her agent's business at court and in the tangles of the city bureaucracy. She looked at the total again, grimacing, but copied the number onto a slip of paper, and closed the box again, pressing hard on the lid to make sure the lock caught.

"Maseigne?" The man who peered around the edge of the door tipped his head to one side like one of the fat gargoyles that infested the manor's upper stories. "I hope everything's all right—she, that so-called magist, is hardly a cultured person. Hardly someone one would choose to handle such a delicate business. . . . " He saw the landame's eyebrows lift at that, and added, "If one had had other options, of course. I thank my stars I've been able to offer some assistance there."

"And I'm grateful," the landame said, with only the slightest hesitation. She placed the box back into the cabinet, set the estate's charter back against it, then closed the double door and relocked it.

The man straightened his head. He had discarded his usual robe for the duration of the magist's visit, wore a slightly out-of-fashion suit, his linen fussily gathered at neck and sleeves, cravat fastened in a style too young for his sixty years. "I take it all went well, maseigne? She had no suspicions?"

"I don't think so." The landame shook her head, her lip curling. "No, I'm sure not. All she wanted was the money."

The old man nodded, his ready smile answering her contempt. "Good. Excellent, maseigne, and I understand she's leaving tomorrow?"

"Yes."

"Better still," the man said, and rubbed his hands together. "And she said nothing? No mention of the clocks, or the—well, of your investments?"

The things she had sold to finance his work, he meant, and she knew it perfectly well. A faint frown crossed her brow, but she said only, "No, nothing. As I said."

"Of course, maseigne, forgive my concern. But things are delicately balanced just now, and I wouldn't want to take any unnecessary chances—"

"No," the landame said firmly. "No more do I. But she said nothing." Fleetingly, she remembered the way the other woman had looked around the outer room, the way her eyes had run over the silver and the wax candles and the blown glass, but shook the memory away. The magist had seen only the proper signs of wealth and standing; there was nothing to make her suspicious.

"Even about the clocks?" the man continued. He saw the landame's frown deepen to a scowl, and spread his hands, ducking his head in apology. "Forgive me, maseigne, but she is a magist, and that is the one thing that might rouse her suspicions. And we cannot afford that, not yet."

"She said nothing," the landame said, again. "And I didn't see any indication that she'd noticed anything." In spite of herself, her eyes strayed to the empty spot on the shelf, imperfectly filled by a statue of a young man with a bunch of grapes, where her own case-clock had once stood. "My people aren't exactly pleased by that, you know. The clock in Anedelle is too far away, they tell me, they can barely hear the chime unless the wind's in the right quarter—"

The man held up his hand, and the landame checked herself. "Maseigne, I know. But it is necessary, I give you my word on it. To have clocks in the house now would—well, it would offer too many chances of revealing our plans ahead of time, and that would never do."

The landame sighed. She was no magist, knew no more of those arts than most people—less, if the truth were told; her education had been neglected, and in her less proud moments, she admitted it. If he said he couldn't work while there were clocks in the house, well, she would have to rely on him. "Very well," she said, but the man heard the doubt in her voice.

"Maseigne, what can I do to convince you? I only want what you want, the accession of a proper queen to the throne of Chenedolle, and an end to the erosion of noble privilege. And I assure you, if the clocks—and very fine clocks they were, too, which is part of the problem—if they had stayed in the manor, our plan would be betrayed as soon as I begin the first operations. They cannot remain—and none can be brought back into the household, not by anyone, maseigne. Otherwise, I cannot offer you my services."

His tone was as deferential as always, eager, even, but the landame heard the veiled threat beneath his fawning. "Very well, I said. There will be no clocks in the house."

"Thank you, maseigne, I knew you would understand." The man bowed deeply, folding his hands in front of him as though he still wore his magist's robes. "I think, then, that I can promise you every success."

"I trust so," the landame said, grimly.

"I assure you, maseigne," the man answered. "The time is propitious. I cannot fail."

1

It was, they all agreed later, a fair measure of Rathe's luck that he was the one on duty when the butcher came to report his missing apprentice. It was past noon, a hot day, toward the middle of the Sedeion and the start of the Gargoyle Moon, and the winter-sun was just rising, throwing its second, paler shadows across the well-scrubbed floor of Point of Hopes. Rathe stared moodily at the patterns thrown by the barred windows, and debated adding another handful of herbs to the stove. The fire was banked to the minimum necessary to warm the pointsmen's food, but the heat rolled out from it in waves, bringing with it the scent of a hundred boiled dinners. Jans Ranazy, the other pointsman officially on this watch, had decided to pay for a meal at the nearest tavern rather than stand the heat another minute, and Rathe could hardly blame him. He wrinkled his nose as a particularly fragrant wave struck him—the sharp sweet scent of starfire warring with the dank smell of cabbages—but decided that anything more would only make it worse.

He sighed and turned his attention to the station daybook that lay open on the heavy work table in front of him, skimming through the neat listing of the previous day's occurrences. Nothing much, or at least nothing out of the ordinary: this was the fair season, coming up on the great Midsummer Fair itself, and there were the usual complaints of false weight and measure, and of tainted or misrepresented goods. And, of course, the runaways. There were always runaways in the rising summer, when the winter-sun shone until midnight, and the roads were clear and open and crowded enough with other travelers to present at least the illusion of safety. And the Silklanders and Leaguers were hiring all through the summer fairs, looking for unskilled hands to man their boats and their caravans, and everyone knew of the merchants—maybe half a dozen over three generations, men and women with shops in the Mercandry now, and gold in their strongboxes, people who counted their wealth in great crowns—who'd begun their careers running off to sea or to the highways.

Rathe sighed again, and flipped back through the book, checking the list. Eight runaways reported so far, two apprentices—both with the brewers, no surprises there; the work was hard and their particular master notoriously strict—and the rest laborers from the neighborhoods around Point of Hopes, Point of Knives, Docks' Point, even Coper's Point to the south. Most of them had worked for their own kin, which might explain a lot—but still, Rathe thought, they're starting early this year. It lacked a week of Midsummer; usually the largest number took off during the Midsummer Fair itself.

A bell sounded from the gate that led into the stable yard, and then another from above the main door, which lay open to the yard. Rathe looked up, and the room went dark as a shape briefly filled the doorway. The man stepped inside, and stood for a moment blinking as his eyes adjusted to the light. He was big, tall, and heavy-bellied beneath a workingman's half-coat, but the material was good, as was the shirt beneath it, and as he turned, Rathe saw the badge of a guildmaster in the big man's cap.

"Help you, master?" he asked, and the big man turned, still blinking in the relative darkness.

"Pointsman?" He took a few steps toward the table. "I'm here to report a missing apprentice."

Rathe nodded, repressing his automatic response, and kicked a stool away from the table. "Have a seat, master, and tell me all about it."

The big man sat down cautiously. Up close, he looked even bigger, with a jowled, heat-reddened face and lines that could mean temper or self-importance bracketing his mouth and creasing his forehead. Rathe looked him over dispassionately, ready to dismiss this as another case of an apprentice seizing the chance to get out of an unsatisfactory contract, when he saw the emblem on the badge pinned to the man's close-fitting cap. Toncarle, son of Metenere, strode crude but unmistakable across the silver oval, knives upheld: the man was a butcher, and that changed everything. The Butchers' Guild wasn't the richest guild in Astreiant, but it was affiliated with the Herbalists and the scholar-priests of Metenere, and that meant its apprentices learned more than just their craft. An apprentice would have to be a fool—or badly mistreated—to leave that place.

The big man had seen the change of expression, faint as it was, and a wry smile crossed his face. "Ay, I'm with the Butchers, pointsman. Bonfais Mailet."

"Nicolas Rathe. Adjunct point," Rathe answered automatically. He should have known, or guessed, he thought. They weren't far from the Street of Knives, and that was named for the dozen or so butcher's halls that dominated the neighborhood. "You said you were missing an apprentice, Master Mailet?"

Mailet nodded. "Her name's Herisse Robion. She's been my prentice for three years now."

"That makes her, what, twelve, thirteen?" Rathe asked, scribbling the name into the daybook. "Herisse—that's a Chadroni name, isn't it?"

"Twelve," Mailet answered. "And yes, the name's Chadroni, but she's city-born and bred. I think her mother's kin were from the north, but that's a long time back."

"So she wouldn't have been running to them?" Rathe asked, and added the age.

"I doubt it." Mailet leaned forward, planting both elbows on the table. A faint smell rose from his clothes, not unpleasant, but naggingly familiar. Rathe frowned slightly, trying to place it, and then remembered: fresh-cut peppers and summer gourds, the cool green tang of the sliced flesh. It was harvest time for those crops, and butchers all across the city would be carving them for the magists to preserve. He shook the thought away, and drew a sheet of paper from the writing box.

"Tell me what happened."

"She's gone." Mailet spread his hands. "She was there last night at bedtime, or so Sabadie—that's my journeyman, one of them, anyway, the one in charge of the girl-prentices—so Sabadie swears to me. And then this morning, when they went to the benches, I saw hers was empty. The other girls admitted she wasn't at breakfast, and her bed was made before they were up, but Herisse was always an early riser, so none of them said anything, to me or to Sabadie. But when she wasn't at her bench, well . . . I came to you."

Rathe eyed him warily, wondering how best to phrase his question. "She's only been gone a few hours," he began at last, "not even a full day. Are—is it possible she went out to meet someone, and somehow was delayed?"

Mailet nodded. "And I think she's hurt, or otherwise in trouble. My wife and I, after we got the prentices to work, we went up and searched her things. All her clothes are there, and her books. She wasn't planning to be gone so long, of that I'm certain. She knows the work we had to do today, she wouldn't have missed it without sending us word if she could."

Rathe nodded back, impressed in spite of himself. Even if Mailet were as choleric as he looked, a place in the Butchers' Guild—an apprenticeship that taught you reading and ciphering and the use of an almanac, and set you on the road to a prosperous mastership—wasn't to be given up because of a little temper. "Had she friends outside your house?" he asked, and set the paper aside. "Or family, maybe?" He pushed himself up out of his chair and Mailet copied him, his movements oddly helpless for such a big man.

"An aunt paid her fees," Mailet said, "but I heard she was dead this past winter. The rest of them—well, I'd call them useless, and Herisse didn't seem particularly fond of them."

Rathe crossed to the wall where his jerkin hung with the rest of the station's equipment, and shrugged himself into the stiff leather. His truncheon hung beneath it, and he belted it into place, running his thumb idly over the crowned tower at its top. "Do you know where they live?"

"Point of Sighs, somewhere," Mailet answered. "Sabadie might know, or one of the girls."

"I'll ask them, then," Rathe said. "Gaucelm!"

There was a little pause, and then the younger of the station's two apprentices appeared in the doorway. "Master Nico?"

"Is Asheri about, or is it just you?"

"She's by the stable."

Asheri was one of half a dozen neighborhood children, now growing into gawky adolescence, who ran errands for the point station. "I'm off with Master Mailet here, about a missing apprentice—not a runaway, it looks like. I'm sending Asheri for Ranazy, you'll man the station until he gets here."

Gaucelm's eyes widened—he was young still, and hadn't stood a nightwatch, much less handled the day shift alone—but he managed a creditably off-hand nod. "Yes, Master Nico."

Rathe nodded back, and turned to Mailet. "Then let me talk to Asheri, Master Mailet, and we'll go."

Asheri was waiting in the stable doorway, a thin, brown girl in a neatly embroidered cap and bodice, her skirts kilted to the knee against the dust. She listened to Rathe's instructions—fetch Ranazy from the Cazaril Grey where he was eating, and then tell Monteia, the chief point who had charge of Point of Hopes, what had happened and bring back any messages—with a serious face. She caught the copper demming he tossed her with an expert hand, then darted off ahead of them through the main gate. Rathe followed her more decorously, and then gestured for Mailet to lead the way.

Mailet's house and workshop lay in the open streets just off the Customs Road, about a ten-minute walk from Point of Hopes. It looked prosperous enough, though not precisely wealthy; the shutters were all down, forming a double counter, and a journeyman and an older apprentice were busy at the meat table, knives flashing as they disjointed a pair of chickens for a waiting maidservant. She was in her twenties and very handsome, and a knife rose into the air, catching the light for an instant as it turned end over end, before the apprentice had snatched the meat away and the knife landed, quivering, in the chopping board. He bowed deeply, and offered the neatly cut chicken to the maidservant. She took it, cocking her head to one side, and the journeyman, less deft or more placid than his junior, handed her the second carefully packaged bird. She took that, too, and, turning, said something over her shoulder that had both young men blushing and grinning. Mailet scowled.

"Get that mess cleaned up," he said, gesturing to the bloodied board. "And, you, Eysi, keep your mind on your work before you lose a finger."

"Yes, master," the apprentice answered, but Rathe thought from the grin that he was less than chastened.

Mailet grunted, and pushed past him into the shop. "Young fool. And the pity of it is, if he makes a mistake with that trick, it'll be Perrin who loses a finger."

"How many people do you have here?" Rathe asked.

"Four journeymen, two boys and two girls, and then a dozen prentices, six of each. And my woman and myself. She's co-master with me."

"Do they all live here?"

"The apprentices, of course," Mailet answered, "they've two big rooms under the roof—with a separate stairway to each, I'm not completely a fool—and then the senior journeymen, that's Perrin whom you saw, and Sabadie, they each have a room at the head of the stair.

And Agnelle and myself live on the second floor. But Mickhel and Fridi board out—their choice, not mine."

The door that gave onto the main hall opened then, and a dark-skinned woman stepped through, tucking her hair back under her neat cap. She was close to Mailet's age, and Rathe was not surprised to see the keys and coinpurse at her belt.

"Agnelle Fayor, my co-master," Mailet said, unnecessarily, and Rathe nodded.

"Mistress."

"You're the pointsman?" the woman asked, and Rathe nodded again.

"Then you'll want to talk to the girls," Fayor said, and looked at Mailet. "They're almost done, I don't think it'll cause any more stir if he does."

Mailet grinned, rather wryly, and Rathe said, "I take it the apprentices were upset, then?"

Mailet nodded.

Fayor said, "They didn't know she was going to run, I'd stake my life on that." She looked at Mailet, seemed to receive some silent signal, and went on, "We've had prentices run away before now, everyone has, but they've always told us first, given some warning."

"Not in so many words, you understand," Mailet interjected. "But you know."

"Did Herisse have any special friends among the apprentices?" Rathe asked. "A leman, maybe? Somebody she might've confided in?"

Fayor's mouth turned down at the corners. "I don't hold with that. It causes all sorts of trouble."

"You can't stop it, though," Mailet said. It had the sound of a long argument, and out of the corner of his eye, Rathe saw Fayor grimace expressively. "And it keeps their minds off the opposite sex." Mailet looked back at the pointsman. "Sabadie would know if she had a leman. You can ask her."

"Thanks. I'd like to talk to her. But right now, can you give me a description of Herisse?" Rathe had his tablets out, looked from Mailet to Fayor. The two exchanged looks.

"She's an ordinary looking girl, pointsman, pretty enough, but not remarkable," Fayor began.

"Tall for her age, though," Mailet added, and Rathe noted that down, glancing up to ask, "And that's twelve, right?"

Mailet nodded and took a breath, frowning with concentration.

"She has brown hair, keeps it long, but neat. Not missing any teeth yet. Brown eyes?" He looked at Fayor, who sighed.

"Blue. She has a sharp little face, but, as I said, nothing out of the ordinary."

"What was she wearing, last time anyone saw her?"

"Last time I saw her, she was wearing a green skirt and bodice. Bottle green, the draper called it, and it's trimmed with ribbon, darker. She had the same ribbon on her chemise, too, she liked the color. And that's probably what she was wearing when she went missing, her other clothes are still in her room," Fayor said. She spread her hands. "I don't know what else I can tell you."

Rathe closed his tablets. "That's fine, thanks. Right—can I speak with Sabadie now?"

Mailet nodded. "I'll take you to her. Mind the shop, Agnelle? And make sure Eysi doesn't hurt himself with his fancy knife tricks."

Fayor muttered something that did not bode well for the apprentice, and Rathe followed Mailet through the door into the main hall. The room was filled with the sunlight that streamed in through the windows at the top of the hall, and the air smelled sharply of vegetables. A dozen apprentices, conspicuous in blue smocks and aprons, stood at the long tables, boys on the left, girls on the right, while a woman journeyman stood at the center of the aisle, directing the work from among baskets of peppers and bright yellow summer gourds. Another journeyman, this one a woman in the black coat and yellow cravat of the Meteneran magists, stood toward the back of the room, one eye on the clockwork orrery that ticked away the positions of the suns and stars, the other on the sweating apprentices. From the looks of things, the piled white seeds and discarded stems, and the relatively small number of baskets of whole vegetables, the work had been going on for some time, and going well. The journeyman butcher turned, hearing the door, and came to join them, wiping her hands on her apron. Rathe was mildly surprised to see a woman in charge—butchery was traditionally a man's craft—but then, the woman's stars probably outweighed her sex.

"Just about done, master," she said. "We've another two hours yet, and this is the last load for Master Guilbert."

Mailet nodded, looking over the hall with an expert eye. "I brought the pointsman—his name's Nicolas Rathe, out of Point of Hopes. Sabadie Grosejl, my senior journeyman. Can you spare Trijntje to talk to him?" He glanced at Rathe, and added, "Trijntje was probably Herisse's closest friend."

"She's not much use to me today," Grosejl said, rather grimly, and Rathe glanced along the line of girl-apprentices, wondering which one it was. She wasn't hard to pick out, after all: even at this distance, Rathe could tell she'd been crying, suspected from the hunch of her shoulder and the way she glared at the pepper under her knife that she was crying still.

"I'd like to talk to Sabadie as well," he said, and the journeyman hesitated.

"Go on, I'll take over here," Mailet said. "Fetch him Trijntje when he's done with you, and then you can get back to work."

"Yes, Master," Grosejl answered, and turned to face the pointsman, jamming her hands into the pockets of her smock beneath her apron. She was a tall woman, Leaguer pale, and her eyes were wary.

"So you're in charge of the girl-apprentices?" Rathe asked.

Grosejl nodded. "For my sins." She grimaced. "They're not so bad, truly, just—"

"Young?" Rathe asked, and the journeyman nodded.

"And now this has happened. Master Rathe, I don't know what Master Mailet told you, but I don't think Herisse ran away."

"Oh?"

"She liked it here, liked the schooling and the work and the people—she didn't tell Trijntje she was going, and she'd have done that for certain."

"Was she Trijntje's leman?" Rathe asked.

Grosejl hesitated, then nodded. "Master Mailet doesn't really approve, nor the mistress, so there was nothing said or signed, but everyone knew it. You hardly saw one without the other. If she'd been planning to run away, seek her fortune on the road, they would have gone together."

Rathe sighed. That was probably true enough—runaways often left in pairs or threes, either sworn lemen or best friends—and it probably also told him the answer to his next question. "You understand I have to ask this," he began, and Grosejl shook her head.

"No, she wasn't pregnant. That I can swear to. Mistress Fayor makes sure all the girls take the Baroness every day."

"But if it didn't work for her?" Rathe asked. The barren-herb didn't work for every woman; that was common knowledge, and one of the reasons the guilds generally turned a blind eye to the passionate friendships between the apprentices of the same gender. Better barren sex than a hoard of children filling the guildhalls.

Grosejl hesitated, then jerked her head toward a child of six or seven who was sweeping seeds into the piles of rubbish at the center of the hall. "That's my daughter. There'd have been a place for her, and the child, if she was pregnant. More than there would have been with her family."

"A bad lot?"

Grosejl shrugged. "Useless, more like. I met them once. The mother's dead, the father drinks, the other two—boys, both of them, younger than her—run wild. I don't know where they came up with the indenture money. But Herisse was glad to be away from them, that's for sure."

Rathe paused, considering what she'd told him. They all seemed very certain that Herisse Robion was no runaway, and from everything they said, he was beginning to believe it, too. And that was not a pleasant thought. There was no reason to kidnap a butcher's apprentice—or rather, he amended silently, the only reasons were of the worst kind, madmen's reasons, someone looking for a child, a girl, to rape, to hurt, maybe to kill. He could see in Grosejl's eyes that she'd thought of the same things, and forced a smile. "There may be a good explanation," he said, and knew it sounded lame. "Can I talk to Trijntje now?"

"Trijntje!" Grosejl beckoned widely, and the girl Rathe had picked out before put down her knife and came to join them, wiping furtively at her eyes with the corner of her sleeve. "This is Trijntje Ollre, pointsman. She and Herisse were best friends."

"She was my leman," Trijntje interjected, with a defiant glance at the older woman. "And something's happened to her, pointsman. You have to find her. I've money saved—"

"I'm looking into it," Rathe said. "We can talk fees if there's extra work to be done." And there won't be, he vowed silently. I don't take money from poor apprentices. But he had learned years ago that telling people he didn't want their money only bred more distrust and uncertainty: what kind of a pointsman was he, how good could he be, if he didn't take the payments that were a pointsman's lot? Rathe dismissed that old grievance, and took Trijntje gently through her story, but there was nothing new to be learned. Herisse had gone to bed with the others, and had risen early and gone out, missing breakfast, but had not come back when Mailet opened the hall for work. She had taken neither clothes nor books nor her one decent hat pin, and had said nothing that would make Trijntje or anyone else think she wanted to run away.

"We were planning to run a workshop together," Trijntje said, and gave a hopeless sniff. "Once we'd made masters."

That would probably have come to nothing, Rathe knew—he remembered all too well the fierce but fleeting passions of his own adolescence—but he also remembered the genuine pain of those passing fancies. "I—we at Point of Hopes—will be treating this as more than a runaway," he said. "We'll do everything we can to find her."

Trijntje looked at him with reddened eyes and said nothing.

Rathe walked back to Point of Hopes in less than good humor. Trouble involving children was always bad—of course, by law and custom, apprentice-age was the end of childhood, but at the same time, no one expected apprentices to take on fully adult responsibilities. Herisse had been only in her second year of apprenticeship; she would have had—would have, he corrected himself firmly—six more to go before she could be considered for journeyman. It was still possible that she'd simply run away—maybe run from Trijntje Ollre, if she, Herisse, had grown out of that relationship, and been too softhearted, still too fond, to end it cleanly. Twelve-year-olds weren't noted for their common sense, he could see one running away because she couldn't find the words to end a friendship. . . . He shook his head then, rejecting the thought before it could comfort him. Trijntje had spoken of their plans as firmly in the present tense, though that could be self-deception; more to the point, the journeyman Grosejl had treated the relationship as ongoing, and she, if anyone, would have known of an incipient break. He would ask, of course, he had to ask, but he was already fairly confident of Grosejl's answer. And that left only the worst answer: if Herisse hadn't run, then someone had taken her. And there were no good reasons—no logical reasons, reasons of profit, the understandable motive of the knives and bravos and thieves who lived in the rookeries of Point of Sighs and Point of Graves—to steal a twelve-year-old apprentice butcher.

He took the long way back to the points station, along the Customs Road to Horse-Copers' Street, smelling more than ever of the stables in this weather, and dodged a dozen people, mostly women, a couple of men, bargaining for manure at the back gate of Farenz Hunna's stableyard. Horse-Copers' Street formed the boundary between Point of Hopes and Point of Sighs, though technically both points stations shared an interest in the old caravanserai that formed a cul-de-sac just before the intersection of the Fairs Road and Horse-Copers'. The 'Serry had long ago ceased to function as a market—or at least as a legal market, Rathe added, with an inward grin—and the seasonal stables that had served the caravaners had been transformed into permanent housing for sneak thieves, low-class fences, laundry thieves, and an entire dynasty of pickpockets. What the 'Serry didn't do was trade in blood—they left that to the hardier souls in Point of Graves—and he turned into the enclosed space without wishing for back-up. But there had been trouble of that kind there once before, a child rapist, not officially dealt with, and he had questions for the people there.

The 'Serry was as crowded as ever, a good dozen children chasing each other barefoot through the beaten dust while their mothers gossiped in the dooryard of the single tavern and the gargoyles clustered on the low roofs, shrieking at each other. Below them, the low doors and windows were open to the warm air, letting in what little light they could. Another group was gathered around the old horse-pool. Women in worn jerkins and mended skirts sat on the broad stone lip, talking quietly, while a chubby boy, maybe three or four summers old, waded solemnly in the shallow basin, holding the wide legs of his trousers up while he kicked the water into fans of spray that caught the doubled sun like diamonds. Rathe recognized at least one of them, Estel Quentier, big, broad-bodied—and, if he was any judge, at least six months gone with child—and at the same moment heard a shrill whistle from one of the blank doorways. He didn't bother to turn, knowing from experience that he would see no one, and saw heads turn all across the 'Serry. He was known—the people of the 'Serry knew most of the senior points by sight—and was not surprised to see several of the women who had been sitting by the fountain rise quickly and disappear into the nearest doorways. More faded back into the tavern, but he pretended not to see, kept walking toward the fountain. Estel Quentier put her hands on her hips, belly straining her bodice, but didn't move, squinted up at him as he approached.

"And what does Point of Hopes want with us? This is Point of Sighs."

"Just a question or two, Estel, nothing serious." He nodded to her belly. "I take it you're not working this fair season."

Quentier made a face, but relaxed slightly. She was the oldest of the Quentier daughters, all of whom were pickpockets like their mother and grandmother before them; there was a brother, too, Rathe remembered, or maybe more than one, also in the family business. Estel had been effective mistress of the 'Serry since her mother's death three years before, and she was a deft pickpocket, but a pregnant woman was both conspicuous and slow. "I'm an honest woman, Nico, I have to work to live."

"So you'll sell what they take?" Rathe asked, and smiled.

Quentier smiled back. "I deal in old clothes, found goods, all that sort of thing. I've my license from the regents, signed by the metropolitan herself if you want to see it."

"If I'd come to check licenses," Rathe said, with perfect truth, "I'd've brought a squad."

"So what did you come here for, Nico?" Quentier leaned back a little, easing her back, and Rathe was newly aware of the women behind her, not quite out of earshot. He knew most of them: Quentier's sister Annet, the third oldest, called Sofian for her ability to charm or fee the judges; the dark-haired singer who was Annet's favorite decoy; Cassia, another Quentier, thin and wiry; Maurina Tacon, who was either Annet's or Cassia's leman—it was hard to unwind the clan's tangled relationships. They were dangerous, certainly, he knew better than to underestimate them, but if there were a fight, he thought, the immediate danger would come from the hulking man loitering in the tavern dooryard. He had a broom in his hand, and he drew it back and forth through the dirt, but his attention wasn't on his job.

"There's a girl gone missing, a butcher's apprentice over in Point of Hopes," he said simply, and was not surprised to see Quentier's face contort as though she wanted to spit. Behind her, Cassia—LaSier, they called her, he remembered suddenly, for the length of her river-dark hair—said something to her sister, who grinned, and did spit.

"What's that to me, pointsman?" Estel Quentier said. "Apprentices run away every year."

"She didn't run," Rathe answered. "She didn't take her clothes or anything with her, and she liked her work. No cause to run, no place to run to."

"So why do you come to me?" Quentier's eyes were narrowed, on the verge of anger, and Rathe chose his words carefully.

"Because I remember four or five years ago, in your mother's time, there was trouble of that sort out of the 'Serry. We knew who the man was, raped two girls, both apprentice-age or a little older, but when we came to arrest him, he was gone. Your mother swore he'd been dealt with, was gone, and we didn't ask questions, being as we knew your mother. But now . . . "

He let his voice trail off, and Quentier nodded once. "Now you're asking."

Rathe nodded back, and waited.

There was a little silence, and then Quentier looked over her shoulder. "Annet."

Sofian took a few steps forward, so that she was standing at her sister's side. She was a handsome woman—all the Quentiers were good-looking, dark, and strong-featured, with good bones—and her clothes were better than they looked. "I remember. Rancon Paynor, that was. He lodged here, he was Joulet Farine's man's cousin, or something like that. A farmer, said he was running from a debt he couldn't pay."

She looked down at her sister, and seemed to receive some kind of confirmation. "He's not your man."

"You're very sure."

Sofian met his gaze squarely. "I helped carry his body to the Sier."

Rathe nodded slowly, not surprised. He remembered the case all too well, remembered both the victims—both alive and well now, thank Demis and her Midwives—and the frustration, so strong they could all almost taste it, when they'd come back to Point of Sighs empty-handed. It was one of the few times they'd all agreed the chief point shouldn't have taken the fee. But when Yolan Quentier said she'd deal with something, it stayed dealt with, and they'd all had to be content with that, much as they would have preferred to make the point and watch Paynor hang. It was good to know that he wouldn't be cleaning up an earlier mistake, even if it meant he was back where he'd started.

"You'll be going, then?" Quentier asked, and Rathe snapped back to the present.

"I told you, that was my business here. This time."

Quentier nodded. "The runaways are starting early this year, or so they say. Girls running who shouldn't. Is there anything we should be watching for, Nico?"

For Quentier to ask for help from a pointsman, even so obliquely, was unprecedented, and Rathe looked warily at her. *What do you know that you're not telling me?* he wanted to say, but knew better than to ask that sort of question without something solid to trade for her answers. It was enough of an oddity—and maybe a kind of answer—for her to have asked at all. "Nothing that I know of, Estel. I don't have anything to go on right now—the complaint came to me, oh, maybe an hour ago." He shrugged. "You know what I know, right now. She walked out of the hall last night or this morning early, leaving her goods behind, and she hasn't come home. Her master's worried, and her leman's distraught, and I don't think she ran. Until we know more, yeah, keep an eye on your kids."

Quentier nodded thoughtfully. "I'll do that. Will you let me know if there's more?"

"I will if you will," Rathe answered, and Quentier grinned.

"As far as I'm able, Nico." The smile vanished. "Anything about the girl, though—what's her name?"

"Herisse Robion, not that that would help, necessarily. They said she was tall for her age—she's just twelve—and still pretty skinny." He reached into his pocket and pulled out the tablet where he'd scrawled the description. "Brown hair, blue eyes, sweet-faced, good teeth, wearing a bottle green suit, linen, bodice and skirt trimmed to match with darker green ribbon."

"There are a hundred girls like that in Astreiant," Sofian said, shaking her head, and Rathe nodded.

Quentier said, "If I hear anything, I'll send to you, Nico."

"Thanks." Rathe tucked his tablet back into his pocket, then wondered if he should have betrayed its usual place in this den of pickpockets. But it was too late to do anything about it; he shrugged inwardly, and turned away, retracing his steps to Horse-Copers' Street.

"Oy, Nico!" That was a new voice, and he turned to see LaSier striding after him, her long hair flowing behind her like a horse's tail. "Wait a minute."

Rathe paused, suppressing the instinctive desire to put his hand on his purse, and LaSier fell into step beside him. She was younger than he by a year or two, slim and pretty, with a gait like a dancer.

"This butcher's girl," LaSier began, "she's not the only child who's gone missing who shouldn't."

"Oh?" Rathe stopped, already running down the list of missing persons they'd received from Point of Sighs. Not that that was always reliable, as every station guarded its prerogatives and points jealously, but he couldn't remember anything out of the ordinary. Runaways, certainly, and more than there should have been, or usually were, but nothing like Herisse.

LaSier made a face, as though she'd read his thoughts. "It hasn't been reported, I don't think. But there was a boy here, learning the trade, and he went out to the markets to watch the crowds and he never came home."

"No one made a point on him, then?" Rathe asked, already knowing the answer—if it were that simple, the Quentiers wouldn't be worrying; prison was an occupational hazard for them—and LaSier spat on the dust at her feet.

"We checked that first, of course, though he'd been here just long enough to learn how much he didn't know, and I didn't think he was stupid enough to try lifting anything on his own. But he's not in the cells at Point of Sighs or anywhere southriver. And I'm worried. Estel's worried."

There was no need to ask why LaSier or Quentier hadn't gone to Point of Sighs with the complaint. The Quentiers had always kept a school of sorts for pickpockets, their own kin and the children of friends and neighbors—Rathe sometimes wondered if there were some secret, hidden guild organization for illegal crafts—and he wasn't surprised to hear that Estel was keeping up that part of the business. But she would have no recourse when one of her "students" disappeared, not without giving Astarac, the chief at Point of Sighs, an excuse to search the 'Serry and in general look too closely into Quentier business. "Are you making an official complaint to me?"

LaSier shook her head, smiling. "If it were official, we'd've gone to Point of Sighs, they're the ones with jurisdiction. But I thought you ought to know. He didn't have any place to run, that one. Gavaret Cordiere, his name is, his family's from Dhenin."

"Would he have run back to them?" Rathe asked. "If he—forgive my bluntness, Cassia—if he decided he didn't like the business after all?"

"It's possible," LaSier answered. "But I don't think he did." She smiled again, a sudden, elfin grin. "He liked the trade, Nico, and he had the fingers for it. I'd've put him to work soon enough."

Rathe sighed, and reached into his pocket for his tablet. "I'll make inquiries northriver, if you'd like, see if he's in cells there. And you might as well give me a description, in case—anything—turns up."

A body, he meant, and LaSier grimaced and nodded in understanding. "He's fourteen, maybe shoulder height on me, dark-skinned—not as dark as me, but dark enough—brown hair, brown eyes. There's a touch of red in his hair, maybe, and it's curly. He cut it short when we came here, he looks like any apprentice."

"Your stock in trade," Rathe murmured.

"Exactly." LaSier squinted, as though trying to remember, then shook her head. "That's about all, Nico. He's a bright boy, but not memorable looking."

"I'll keep an eye out," Rathe answered, and scrawled the last note on the face of the tablet, stylus digging into the wax. He was running out of room on the second page: not a good sign, he thought, and folded the tablet closed on itself. "And I'll check with the cellkeepers northriver. Would he give his right name?"

LaSier smiled again, wry this time. "He's a boy, fourteen. Maybe not."

"I'll get descriptions, too," Rathe said.

"Thanks," LaSier said. "And, Nico: I—and Estel—we'll take this as a favor."

Rathe nodded, oddly touched by the offer. Besides, this was the kind of fee that he didn't refuse, the trade of favor for favor within the law. "I'll bear that in mind, Cassia, thanks. But let's see what I find out, first."

"Agreed," LaSier said, and turned away. She called over her shoulder, "See you at the fair!"

"You'd better hope not," Rathe answered, and started back toward Point of Hopes.

Monteia was waiting for him, the youngest of the runners informed him as soon as he stepped through the courtyard gate. The duty point, Ranazy, repeated the same message when he opened the hall door, and in the same moment Monteia herself appeared in the door of the chief point's office.

"Rathe. I need to talk to you."

Rathe suppressed a sigh—it was very like Monteia to make one feel guilty even when one had been doing one's duty—but shrugged out of his jerkin, hanging it on the wall pegs as he passed behind Ranazy's desk. "And I need to talk to you, too," he said, and followed Monteia into the narrow room.

It was dark, the one narrow window looking onto the rear yard's shadiest corner, and crowded with the chief point's work table and a brace of battered chairs. The walls were lined with shelves that held station's daybooks and a once-handsome set of the city lawbooks, as well as a stack of the slates everyone used for notes and a selection of unlicensed broadsides stacked on a lower shelf. The latest of those, Rathe saw, with some relief, was over a moon-month old: hardly current business.

"Have a seat," Monteia said, and waved vaguely at the chairs on the far side of her table.

Rathe took the darker of the two—the other had been salvaged from someone's house, and mended, not reliably—and settled himself.

"I hear you had another runaway today," Monteia went on. She was a tall woman, with a face like a mournful horse and dark brown eyes that looked almost black in the dim light. Her clothes hung loose on her thin frame, utterly unmemorable, if one didn't see the truncheon that swung at her belt.

Rathe nodded. "Only I don't think it was a runaway. The girl seemed happy in her work."

"Oh?" It was hard to tell, sometimes, if Monteia was being skeptical, or merely tired. Quickly, Rathe ran through the story, starting with the butcher's arrival, and ending with his visit to the 'Serry and the Quentiers' missing boy. When he had finished, Monteia leaned back in her chair, arms folded, long legs stretched out beneath the table. Looking down, Rathe could see the tip of her shoe protruding from beneath the table, could see, too, the string of cheap braid that hid the mark where the hem had been lengthened for her. Monteia might be chief point, but she was honest enough, in her way, and had children and a household of her own to keep.

"How many runaways is that so far this season?" she asked, after a moment.

"I could check the daybook to be sure," Rathe answered, "but I'm pretty sure we've had eight reported. Nine if you count Herisse, but I want to treat that as an abduction. And of course the Cordiere boy, but that's not our jurisdiction."

Monteia nodded.

"Of the eight, then, two were apprentices, both brewers, and the rest ordinary labor," Rathe continued. "That's a lot for so early—the first of the Silklands caravans are only just in, and the trading ships haven't really started yet."

Monteia said, "We had the points' dinner last night."

Rathe blinked, unsure where this was leading—the chief points of the twelve point stations that policed Astreiant dined together once every solar month, ostensibly to exchange information, but more to help establish the points' legitimacy by behaving like any other guild. The points were relatively new, at least in their present form; it had been the queen's grandmother who'd given them the authority to enforce the laws, and not everyone was happy with the new system.

Monteia smiled as though she'd guessed the thought, showing her crooked teeth. "We're not the only station to be seeing too many runaways, too early. I went planning to ask a few discreet questions, see what everybody else was doing this season, and, by the gods, so was everyone else. So we did a little horse-trading, and I got some useful information, I think."

Rathe nodded. He could imagine the scene, the long table and the polished paneling of a high-priced inn's best room, candles on the table to supplement the winter-sun's diminished light. The chief points would all be in their best, a round dozen men and women—six of each at the moment, all with Sofia, Astree, or Phoebe, the Pillars of Justice, strong in their nativity—sitting in order of precedence, from Temple Point at the head of the table to Fairs' Point at the foot. He had met all of them at one time or another, as Monteia's senior adjunct, but really only knew Dechaix of Point of Dreams and Astarac of Point of Sighs, the jurisdictions that bordered Point of Hopes, at all well. And Guillen Claes of Fairs' Point, he added, with an inward smile. Claes was a solid pointsman, had come up through the ranks, and took no nonsense from anyone, for all that he had the unenviable job of handling the busiest and most junior point station in the city. Most of the southriver points got to know Claes well over the course of their careers, as the professional criminals who lived southriver, pickpockets like the Quentiers and horse-thieves and footpads and the rest, tended to do their business in Fairs' Point.

"Everyone's got an unusual number of runaways this year," Monteia said. "What's more to the point, there are as many, or nearly so, missing from City Point as there are from Fairs' Point."

Rathe looked up sharply at that. City Point was one of the old districts, second in precedence only to Temple Point itself; children born in City Point were among the least likely to be lured away by the romance of the long-distance traders—or, if they were, they had mothers who could afford to apprentice them properly. Fairs' Point children, on the other hand, had not only the proximity of New Fair and Little Fair to tempt them, but good cause to want to better themselves.

Monteia nodded. "Aize Lissinain, she's chief at City Point since the beginning of Lepidas, was asking if we'd had any increase in the brothel traffic."

"Trust northriver to think of that," Rathe said, sourly.

"She was also asking Huyser how the workhouses were doing," Monteia went on, and Rathe made a face that stopped short of apology. Huyser was chief of Manufactory Point; as the name implied, most of the city's workhouses and manufactories lay in his district, and there were always complaints about the way the merchant-makers treated their day-workers. It was a good question—as was the one about the brothels, he admitted—so maybe Lissinain would be better than her predecessor.

"What did Huyser say?" he asked. "I was thinking that myself. Children are cheap."

"But I wouldn't want them working with machinery," Monteia answered. "Too much chance of them breaking something. Anyway, Huyser said he was having as much of a problem with runaways as anyone, though not from the manufactories proper. He hadn't heard of any of the makers letting workers go, or hiring new, for that matter, but he said he'd look into it." She smiled, wry this time. "And Hearts and Dreams and I said we'd take a look round the brothels, just to be sure."

Rathe nodded again. "It's a reasonable precaution. We might even find one or two of them, at that."

"Mmm." Monteia didn't sound particularly hopeful, either, and Rathe sighed.

"Does anyone know just how many children have gone missing?"

"Temple's asked us each to compile a list for her, children missing and found, to be cross-checked by her people just in case we've found some of them and don't know it, and then circulated around the points for general use." She made a face. "I can't say I'm particularly happy with the idea, myself—Temple's always looking for an excuse to stick her fingers in the rest of us's business—but I think she's probably right, this time."

"It could help," Rathe said. "As long as everyone gets listed. Did she say just the missing, or all the runaways?"

"Anyone reported missing," Monteia answered. She grimaced. "I know, you're thinking the same thing I am, some of them won't list everyone—it's embarrassing, gods, I'm embarrassed myself. But it's a start."

"Agreed," Rathe said. "But then what?"

Monteia shook her head. "I wish I knew. This isn't right, Nico. It feels . . . I don't know, all wrong somehow. Kids disappear, sure, but not like this, not from everywhere. I was junior adjunct here when Rancon Paynor raped those girls, took them right off their own streets at twilight—it was spring then, right at the end of Limax, the suns were setting together. I remember what it felt like, and it wasn't like this."

"No," Rathe said, and they sat in silence for a moment. He remembered the Paynor case, too, though he always counted the year by the lunar calendar, remembered it as the middle of the Flower Moon. There had been the victims, for one thing, the girls themselves; they'd disappeared for a day, two, but appeared again—and we were just lucky they weren't bodies, he added to himself. People had been afraid. The women and girls had traveled in groups for weeks, even after it became clear that Paynor had disappeared, but it had been clear that something had happened. Not like this, when they couldn't even put a name to what was happening. "I suppose no one's found any bodies," he said aloud, and surprised a short, humorless laugh from the chief point.

"Not so far. Though if they went in the Sier . . . the river doesn't give up its dead easily."

"But why?" Rathe shook his head again. "One madman, another Paynor, making his kills, yeah, I could believe it, but not with so many kids gone from so many districts. One man alone couldn't do it."

"Or woman, I suppose," Monteia said, "if her stars were bad."

"But not one person alone," Rathe repeated.

Monteia sighed. "We don't know enough yet, Nico, we can't even say that for certain." She straightened, drawing her feet back under the desk. "I want you to draw up the report—get in a scrivener to do fair copies, I don't want to waste any more of your time than I have to, but get it done by tomorrow. We'll know better where we stand once the compilation comes in."

"All right." Rathe stood up, recognizing his dismissal. "With your permission, boss, I'll make a few inquiries northriver, just in case the Quentiers' boy ended up in the cells there."

"Go ahead," Monteia said. "That'd be all we need, to get the 'Serry really roused against us."

"People are going to talk," Rathe said.

"They're already talking," Monteia answered. "At least, northriver they are. Oh, when you go back to the butcher's, get the girl's nativity from him."

Rathe stopped in the doorway, looked back at her. "You're going to go to the university?"

"Do you have any other leads?"

"No." Rathe sighed. "No, I don't." Usually, a judicial horoscope was the last resort, something to be tried when all other possibilities had been exhausted; even the best astrologers could only offer possibilities, not certainties, when asked to do a forensic reading.

"And I'm going to talk to the necromancers, too, see if any ghosts have turned up. You've a friend in their college, don't you?"

Rathe winced at the thought—bad enough to be a necromancer, constantly surrounded by the spirits of the untimely dead, worse still if it were children's ghosts—but nodded. "Istre b'Estorr, his name is. He's very good."

Monteia nodded. "I've got a nasty feeling about this one, Nico," she said, her voice almost too soft to be heard.

"So do I," Rathe answered, and stepped back into the main room to collect the station's daybooks and begin the list of missing children.

2

The last muster was nearly over. Philip Eslingen eyed the lines at the rickety tables set up by the regimental paymasters, making sure his own troopers got their proper measure, and mentally tallied his own wages. His pay, a single royal crown, rested in his moneybag beneath his shirt, a soft weight against his heart; he was carrying letters on the temples of Areton that totaled nearly four pillars, his share of the one raiding party: enough for a common man to live for a year, if he were frugal. It should certainly last him until spring, when the new campaigns began—unless, of course, someone reputable was hiring. Whatever he did, it would mean taking a lower place than the one he'd had.

His eyes strayed to the temporary platform, empty now, but bright with banners and heavy patterned carpets, where the Queen of Chenedolle had stood to receive the salute of Coindarel's Dragons and to release them from her service. Even from his place at the front with the rest of the regiment's officers, Eslingen had been able to see little more of her than her elegant suit of clothes, bright and stiff as the little dolls that stood before the royal judges in the outlying provinces, visible symbols of the royal authority. The dolls were faceless, for safety's sake; for all Eslingen had been able to see, the queen herself might have been as faceless, her features completely hidden by the brim of a hat banded with the royal circlet. He had watched her when he could, fascinated—he had never seen the Queen of Chenedolle—but she had barely seemed real. Only once, as he brought his half of the company to a perfect halt, had he seen her move, and then she had leaned sideways to talk to the Mareschale de Mourel who was her leman and acknowledged favorite, a gloved hand lifted to her shadowed face, as though to hide—a smile? A frown? It was impossible even to guess.

"Eslingen."

He turned, recognizing the voice, hand going to his hat in automatic salute. "Captain."

Connat Bathias nodded in response and looked past his lieutenant to the last half-dozen troopers lined up at the paymasters' table. A royal intendant stood with them to supervise the payout, conspicuous in her black-banded judicial robe, and there were three well-armed men—back-and-breast, short-barreled calivers, swords, and daggers—at her back, guarding access to the iron-bound chest that held the money. "How goes it?"

"Almost done," Eslingen answered. "No complaints so far." Nor were there likely to be: Bathias's company was made up mostly of experienced troopers, who knew what their pay should be, and the royal paymasters were generally honest, at least under the queen's eye.

"And the horses and the weapons?"

Eslingen looked away again. "As agreed. The Horsemaster took the mounts in hand, and we let the people who wanted to buy back their weapons. Those who didn't already own them, of course." Which was well over half the troop, and those that didn't had mostly paid the captain's inflated price to keep their calivers: most of them would want to hire out again as soon as possible, and this late in the season most captains would want people with their own equipment. There was still plenty of fighting to be done, along the Chadroni Gap and north past the Meis River, and Dragons were always in demand, particularly for the nasty northern wars, but there was no time to outfit a man.

Bathias nodded. The horses were part of his perquisites, to sell or keep as he chose, and Eslingen suspected he would sell most of them: with the troop disbanding, there was no point in keeping half a hundred animals, and there were other captains who would be willing to buy. Coindarel had persuaded Aimeri de Martreuil to add an extra company to his Auxiliary Horse, and to take most of the gentleman-officers, the commissioned officers; he would probably buy the horses, as well. "I'm willing to let you purchase your mounts, Eslingen. There's no point in seeing you unhorsed."

Eslingen hesitated, tempted and rather flattered by the offer, but shook his head. He couldn't afford to pay for stabling in the city for more than a month or two, and he had no way of knowing how long it would be before he found work he liked. "Thank you, sir, but I'll have to pass."

Bathias nodded again, and looked uneasily toward the empty platform. He was a young man, the fourth child, Eslingen understood, of an impoverished Ile'nord noble, with two older sisters and a brother between him and whatever income the family estates provided: a commission and an introduction to the Prince-marshal de Coindarel would be the best his mother could do for him. Not that an introduction to Coindarel was the worst she could have done, Eslingen added, with an inward smile. Bathias was young, and very handsome in the golden Ile'nord fashion; his hair, long and naturally curling, glowed in the double light of sun and winter-sun like polished amber, and his skin had taken only delicate color from the spring campaign. Coindarel notoriously had an eye for a pretty young man, and was inclined to indulge himself in his officers. He picked his juniors, the sergeants and lieutenants who did the real work, with more care, but, all else being equal, a handsome man could go far in Coindarel's service. Eslingen had earned his sergeancy the hard way, but his promotion to lieutenant, and the royal commission that came with it, had come by way of Coindarel's roving eye.

"Will you be going with Martreuil, Eslingen?" Bathias asked, and the older man shook himself back to the present.

"No, sir. There are plenty of other companies still hiring, even this late in the season." It was a sore point—Eslingen had lost any claim to gentility when he lost his commission, and Martreuil, it had been made very clear, was taking only Coindarel's gentleman-officers—and he was relieved when Bathias merely grunted, his mind already clearly elsewhere. Probably on the palace, Eslingen thought. Bathias was of noble birth and could claim board and lodging from the queen on the strength of it, and he could do worse than to be seen at court, too.

"I'm sorry to hear it," Bathias said. "You're a good officer, and could do well in the royal service."

"Thank you, sir." Eslingen kept his face still with an effort, waiting for the dismissal. The line at the paymaster's table had dwindled to a single trooper, a skinny, huge-handed former stable boy whom Eslingen had signed on at an inn outside Labadol because he'd needed someone who could handle the major-sergeant's bad-tempered gelding. Then he, too, had accepted his pay and made his mark on the muster list, and turned away to join his fellows waiting at the edge of the

Drill Ground. The taverns and inns where most of the recruiting officers did their work lay only a few steps away, along the Horse-Gate Road.

"You've served me well," Bathias said, and held out his hand. Eslingen took it, startled at this presumption of equality, and then Bathias had released him, and was reaching into his own wide sash. "And, Eslingen. I know you're not a sergeant anymore, but I also know we didn't serve out the season. Will you take this from me, as a token of my appreciation?" He held out a bag the size of a man's hand. It was embroidered—not expensively, Eslingen thought, probably by one of the farm-girls we took on at Darnais—with Bathias's arms and the regimental monogram.

Eslingen took it, stiffly, and felt, through the linen and the coarse threads of the monogram, the square shape and weight of at least a pillar. That was more than he could afford to refuse, and he tucked the purse into his own sash. "Thank you, sir," he said again, stiff-lipped, saluted, and turned away.

The rest of the company's sergeants were standing by the sundial that stood at the city end of the Drill Ground, and Anric Cossezen, the senior sergeant, lifted a hand to beckon him over. Eslingen came to join them, and Maggiele Reymers said, "You've come up in the world, Philip, if the captain deigned to give you his hand."

"He gave me drink-money, too," Eslingen said, before any of the others could point it out, and Saman le Tamboer laughed.

"Betwixt and between, Philip, neither fish nor fowl."

Eslingen shot the other man a look of dislike—le Tamboer had a sharp tongue on him, to match his sharp Silklands eyes—and Cossezen said, "Have you given a thought to Ganier's offer? It's decent money, and a good chance for plunder."

"If," le Tamboer added, honey-sweet, "the lieutenant doesn't mind serving with us peasants again."

Eslingen ignored him, said to Cossezen, "I've thought about it, yes, and I've wondered why a man with Ganier's reputation is still hiring, so late in the year."

Reymers laughed. "That had crossed my mind, too."

"Ganier always hires his dragons last," Cossezen said.

Eslingen shook his head. "I've fought in the Payshault, Anric. I've no mind to do it again, not this year. I'll see who else is hiring."

"No one," le Tamboer said.

"Then I'll wait until someone is," Eslingen answered.

"How nice to have the money," le Tamboer muttered.

Eslingen ignored him, and Reymers said, "If you need lodging, Philip—"

"I don't have any place in mind," Eslingen said.

"There's a tavern in Point of Hopes, south of the river. It's called the Old Brown Dog, off the Knives' Road." Reymers cocked her head. "Do you know Astreiant at all?"

"I can find it," Eslingen answered. *Or if I can't, I can ask at the Temples when I change my money.* "So I can get lodging there?"

Reymers nodded. "A woman named Aagte Devynck runs it—she's from Altheim, but she served Chenedolle as well as the League during the War. She's always glad to house a fellow Leaguer, and the place is clean and cheap enough."

Eslingen grinned. "How's the beer?" Chenedolle, and Astreiant in particular, were known for their wines; the measure of a League tavern was its beer.

"Good enough," Reymers answered. "She buys it from a Leaguer brewer—and he's got enough custom that he hasn't had to change his ways."

"Thanks, Mag," Eslingen said. "I'll look her up."

There was a little silence then, and Eslingen looked away. Parting was always awkward—you never knew who would die on campaign, or, worse, come home maimed or blinded—and there was always that moment of recognition, as quickly put aside. "Good luck with Ganier, then," he said aloud, and turned away, lifting a hand to wave to the cluster of boys who had been hovering at the edges of the Drill Ground to see the soldiers mustered out. Half a dozen came running, and Eslingen pointed to the first two who looked big enough. "You, there, and you. A demming each if you'll carry my gear to the Aretoneia."

The older of the boys scraped a hasty bow, and answered, "Yes, sir, to the Aretoneia."

The younger said, "May I carry your piece, please, sir?"

"You may not," Eslingen answered, striding to the last cart—almost emptied now—where his baggage was waiting. He tossed the bigger boy his heavy saddlebags, and the smaller locked case that held his pistols. The boy slung the bags over his shoulder and stood waiting, but Eslingen judged he had about as much as he could carry. He handed the smaller boy his cased swords, also locked, and the pouch that held his own supply of powder and lead, and slung his caliver across his shoulder. It felt odd to be without the engraved gorget of his rank, or the royal monograms on the caliver's sling, and he ran his thumb across the darker spot where the split-silver disks had been removed. But there was no point in regrets, not yet; he lifted a hand to the other sergeants, still standing by the sundial, and started down the Horsegate Road, the two boys following at his heels.

There were pointsmen on duty at the Horsegate itself, two men in the heavy leather jerkins that served them for rough-and-ready armor, crowned truncheons at their belts. At the sight of the little party, the older of the pair stepped into the gate, holding up his hand. "Hold it, soldier. Those are well outside the limits." He pointed to the caliver, and then to the cased swords. "You'll have to leave them, or pay a bond."

Eslingen sighed ostentatiously—he had been through this routine before, every time he came to Astreiant—and slipped his hand into his purse. "I'm taking them to the Temple for safekeeping, pointsman, surely that's allowed."

"They're still oversized," the older man said. "And that means a bond. A horsehead a piece, that's the law—that's two seillings, Leaguer, our coin."

Eslingen bit back his first answer—there was no point in antagonizing the points on his first day in Astreiant—and pulled two of the silver coins from his purse. "Two seillings, pointsman. May I pass?"

The pointsman stepped back, bowing too deeply, his plumed hat nearly brushing the ground. "Have a pleasant stay in our city."

Eslingen ignored him, and walked through the sudden cool of the gate, almost a tunnel in the thick wall, to emerge into the bright doubled sunlight and the bustle of the city's center. He took the easiest route toward Temple Fair and the Aretoneia, down the broad expanse of the Horsegate Road to the Horsefair itself. No one sold horses there anymore, of course—Astreiant was too large, too prosperous, to buy and sell horses within its richest districts—but the law still kept the space open and beaten flat, the dust damped three times a day by water-carriers in city livery. At this hour, it was busy with the afternoon merchants, selling everything except food from vividly painted pushcarts. Eslingen sighed to himself, seeing the rolls and figures of lace laid out on the black carts clustered in front of the Laciers' Hall, but turned resolutely away. It would be apprentices' work—masters' work was sold within the hall, free of the dust and dirt of the street—but it was still beyond his means to have lace at his cuffs and collar.

He turned instead toward College Street, slowing his steps so that the boys could keep up with him in the press of people. The younger boy was breathing hard, but he and his fellow seemed to be managing their burdens well enough. Still, it was a relief to step into the shadow of the overhanging buildings of College Street, out of the cheerful bustle of the Horsefair. This was another of the old neighborhoods, not as rich as Riversedge or the Mercandry, but prosperous enough. The shop signs were freshly painted, some showing touches of gilt and silvering, and more than half displayed the snake-and-gargoyle design of the Merchants-Venturer above the doorframe, promising goods brought to Astreiant by the long-distance traders. He smelled Silklands spices as he passed one open door, and saw a woman emerge from a side door carrying a string of bright red peppers; at the next door, an apprentice sat in the sunlight outside the door, a tray of polished stones balanced on her lap. It was a nice display, Eslingen acknowledged silently—the stones were rivvens from Esling, gaudy enough to catch the eye, but not worth stealing—and touched his hat as he passed. The girl—young woman, he amended—looked up at him, a smile lightening her intent face, but then went back to her work.

The Aretoneia lay on the western edge of Temple Fair, at the mouth of a street where most of the buildings still carried the wrought iron lanterns that meant they belonged to the university. Most of them were rented out, either to shopkeepers and craftsmen, but here and there the lanterns were still lit and once he saw a scholar in an ochre-banded gown leading a class in recitation. A toddler clung to her skirts, and she stooped, lifted it without missing a beat. Temple Fair was as busy as ever, travellers clustering around the Pantheon, the broadsheet sellers doing a brisk business at their tables under the awnings along the east side of the square, the book-printers and their apprentices trying to look aloof beyond them. Eslingen hesitated, tempted by the tables of broadsheets and the sample prophecies displayed on the sun-faded boards, but turned instead into the narrow door of the Aretoneia: business, after all, before pleasure. He nodded to the senior of the two soldiers on duty at the door—both older men, past the rigors of a campaign season but not too old to put up a decent defense, not that anyone would be stupid enough to attack the Aretoneia—and shouldered past them into the temple.

Tapers blazed in half a dozen hanging candelabra, and stood in rows in sconces along the walls. More candles, smaller votive lights the length of a man's finger, flickered at the foot of the central statue of Areton, the god of war and courage, throwing odd shadows across the statue's archaic leg armor and making the base of his long spear seem to waver. This was not Eslingen's favorite incarnation of the god—he preferred the younger shape, dancing, before he turned to war—but he touched his forehead dutifully anyway before turning toward the money changers.

Their booths lined the side walls of the temple, each one marked with familiar symbols—the cock-and-hens of Areill, the rose and wine-cup of Pajot Soeurs—but he made his way to the biggest booth, the one marked with the ram's head of Areton's own priesthood. Enough of Areton's old servants retired from soldiering into banking, drawing on the sense of value and exchange gained over a lifetime's fighting in every kingdom from the petty lands west of Chadron to the Silklands themselves; their commissions might be higher than some of the others who rented space in the temple, but the rates of exchange tended to be better.

"Wait for me here," he said to the boys who were standing wide-eyed, staring at the thanks-offerings of guns and swords pinned like trophies to every pillar, and took his place in line at the table marked with the ram's head. The clerk at the next table, a pretty, dark-skinned boy, smiled at him.

"I can offer good rates, sir, and no waiting."

Eslingen shook his head, but returned the smile. The clerk's hands were painted with a pattern of curving vines, black picked out with dots of red and gold, vivid in the candlelight. If that was the fashion in Astreiant now, Eslingen thought, it was a handsome one, though hardly practical. Then the man ahead of him had finished his business, and he stepped up to the table, reaching into his pocket for one purse, and under his shirt for the other. The clerk—greying, one-eyed, ledger and tallyboard in front of him, abacus laid ready to a hand that lacked part of a finger—looked up at him shrewdly.

"And what do you have for me—sergeant, isn't it, from Esling?"

"From Esling, yes, but I earned my commission this season," Eslingen answered, and set the purses on the table.

"Congratulations," the clerk said, busily unfolding the letters of credit, and Eslingen allowed himself a sour smile. Words were cheap; the ephemeral commission was unlikely to get him an improved exchange rate for the Leaguer coins. The clerk poured out the small horde of coins—the gold disk of the royal crown that had been this season's wages, warm in the candlelight; the heavy silver square of the pillar that was Barthias's gift; a pair of Altheim staters hardly bigger than sequins, but bright gold; a scattering of miscellaneous silver, Chadroni, League, and Chenedolliste equally mixed. The clerk grunted, fingering them neatly into the holes of the tallyboard, then spread the letters of credit beside them, bending close to read the crabbed writing. He grunted again and flicked the beads of his abacus, the maimed finger as deft as the others, then chalked something on his slate and flicked the abacus again.

"You have four crowns and three pillars by my reckoning, sergeant—lieutenant—all good coin of Her Majesty. Do you want it now, or do you want to bank it here and gamble on the exchange?"

Eslingen sighed. One did not bargain with the ram's-head bankers the way one bargained with other merchants; if one tried, the clerk was as likely to push the coins back to you and send you searching for another broker. The only question now was whether he would take the cash—and its attendant worries, theft and loss—or take a letter of credit on the Astreiant temple and hope that the exchange between the written amount, the monies of account, and actual coin shifted in his favor. And when one thought about it, it was no choice at all.

"How's the exchange been so far?" he asked, without much hope, and wasn't surprised when the clerk shrugged.

"Up and down, sergeant, up and down."

"Give me two pillars in coin," Eslingen said, "and a letter for the rest."

The clerk nodded, put two fingers—the undamaged hand—into his mouth and whistled shrilly. A junior clerk came running, carrying a case of seals. Eslingen waited while the letter was drafted, signed, and sealed, then put his own name to it and folded it carefully into the purse around his neck. He tucked it back under his shirt, and watched as the clerk counted out two pillars for him. The coins rang softly against the wood, the heavy disks of heirats, bright with Heira's snake, the lighter disks of seillings, marked with Seidos's horsehead, and a handful of copper small-coin, spiders and demmings mixed. He had been born under the signs of the Horse and the Horsemaster; he tucked a selling with the coppers in his pocket for luck, and knotted the rest securely in his purse.

Turning away from the table, he waved to the waiting boys—they came quickly enough, a little intimidated, he thought, by the bustling soldiers and long-distance traders—and led them over to the locked door of the armory. He gave the keeper his name and the details of his weapons—Astreiant limited the length of blade a person could carry in the streets, and utterly prohibited locks except to their pointsmen—and waited while the old woman laboriously inscribed them in the book. Then he handed them through the narrow portal, first the caliver and then the swords and finally the locked case of pistols. That left him with a long knife, just at the limit, and, tucked into the bottom of his saddlebag, a third pistol with its stock of powder and lead. The keeper gave him the sealed receipt, which he slipped into the purse beneath his shirt, and he turned away, working his shoulders. He felt oddly light without the familiar weight of caliver and swords—freer, too, with money in his purse, and for an instant he considered looking for lodgings north of the river. Then common sense reasserted itself: the northriver districts were too expensive, even with four crowns in the bank. He would take himself south of the river—the Old Brown Dog lay in Point of Hopes, Reymers had said, which meant doubling back west along the Fairs Road and across that bridge—and be sensible.

He looked back at the boys, reached into his pocket for the promised demmings. "Does either of you know a tavern in Point of Hopes called the Old Brown Dog?"

The younger boy shook his head at once; the older hesitated, obviously weighing his chances of another coin or two, then, reluctantly, shook his head, too. "No, sir, I don't know southriver very well."

Eslingen nodded—he hadn't really expected another answer—and handed over the coins, the doubled moon, the old in the curve of the new, glinting in the candlelight. The older boy handed back his saddlebags, and he and his friend scurried for the door. Eslingen followed more slowly, looking around for fellow Leaguers. If anyone would know how to get to the Old Brown Dog, it would be League soldiers—provided, of course, that Reymers was right about the quality of the beer. There were plenty of Leaguers in Chenedolle, for all that League and Kingdom had fought a five-year war twenty-five years before; he should be able to find someone. . . . Even as he thought that, he saw a familiar flash of white plumes, and Follet Baeker came into the light of the candelabra, showing teeth nearly as white as the feathers in his broad-brimmed hat. As usual, he had a knife with him, a sullen looking, leather-jerkined man who looked uncomfortable inside the Aretoneia—as well he might, Eslingen thought. Baeker was almost the only broker based in the city who took weapons and armor in pawn; despite Baeker's generally decent reputation, his knife might well worry about protecting him from dissatisfied clients. After all, it would only take one of them and a moment's carelessness to end Baeker's career permanently.

"Sergeant!"

"Lieutenant," Eslingen corrected, without much hope, and Baeker continued as though he hadn't heard.

"Back so soon? I heard Coindarel was disbanded."

Eslingen nodded. "Paid off this noon."

Baeker's expression brightened, though he didn't quite smile openly. "Pity that. Should you find yourself in need of funds, of course—"

"Not at the moment," Eslingen answered. "Tell me, do you know a tavern in Point of Hopes, called the Old Brown Dog?"

Baeker nodded. "I do. Aagte Devynck's house, that is, and I heard she needs a knife, this close to Midsummer and the fairs."

"I was looking for lodging," Eslingen said, a little stiffly—knife to a tavern-keeper, bodyguard, and bouncer all in one, was hardly a job to which he aspired. "A friend recommended it."

"Well, she rents rooms," Baeker said, with a shrug. "Do you need the direction?"

"All I know is it's in Point of Hopes."

"Which it is, but that won't get you there," Baeker said. "Take the Hopes-point Bridge, and when the road forks at its foot, take the left-hand road. Then it's no distance at all to the Knives' Road—that's the Butchers' quarter, you'll know it by the signs—"

"And the smell," Eslingen said.

Baeker grinned. "It's mostly vegetables this time of year. Autumn, now. . . . But the first road to the right off that, take it to the end, and the Old Brown Dog's the last house. You'll see the sign."

Eslingen nodded. "Thanks."

"Give my regards to Aagte," Baeker answered. "And keep me in mind, sergeant. Should you need coin . . . " He let his voice trail off, and Eslingen sighed.

"I'll keep you in mind."

He turned toward the door, drew back as it swung open almost in his face. A thin, sharp-faced woman in a drab green suit of skirt and bodice—better material than it looked at first glance, Eslingen thought, but cut for use, not show—stepped past with a nod of apology. The candlelight glinted from the gargoyle-and-snake pinned to her neat cap, and Eslingen glanced curiously after her. The vagabond professions were traditionally men's, and the Merchants-Venturer were more vagabond than most—but then, enough women had masculine stars and followed mannish professions, just as there were any number of men who claimed feminine stars and worked at the fixed professions. He watched her as she made her way to the door of the central counting room—the long-distance traders generally changed their money and letters through the temple networks; letters on the temples of Areton were good throughout the world—and then went on out into the sunlight of the Temple Fair.

Baeker's directions were better than he'd expected, after all. He crossed the River Sier by the Hopes-point Bridge, dodging the two-wheeled barrows that seemed to carry most of Astreiant's goods, and followed the left-forking road toward the Butchers' quarter. Southriver was busier than the northriver districts, the streets crowded not with neatly dressed apprentices and their seniors, guild badges bright against their blue coats, but shopwives and carpenters and boatmen and sailors and members of a dozen other unguessable trades, all in aprons or working smocks over ordinary clothes. It was louder southriver, too, voices raised over the rumble of carts and the shriek of unoiled wheels from the docks, the shrill southriver accent sharpening their words. The smell of kitchens and shop fires warred with the stink of garbage. If anything, it reminded him of the back streets of Esling where he'd been born, and he found himself walking a little faster, unsure if he liked the memories.

At the corner of the next street, a crowd had gathered—largely children just at apprentice-age and younger, but there were some adults with them, too, and Eslingen paused, curious, to look over the bobbing heads into the manufactory yard. It was a glassblowers', he realized at once, and the pit furnace was lit in the center of the open yard, waves of heat rolling off it toward the open gates. A young woman, her hair tucked under a leather cap, skirts and bodice protected by a thick leather apron that reached almost to her ankles, leather gauntlets to her elbows, spun a length of pipe in the flames, coaxing the blob of glass into an egg and then a sphere before she began to shape it with her breath. He had seen glassblowers at work before, but stared anyway, fascinated, as the sphere began to swell into a bubble, and the woman spun it deftly against a shaping block, turning it into a pale green bowl like the top of a wineglass. One had to be born under fire signs to work that easily among the flames; he himself had been born under air and water, and knew better than to try. He became aware then that another woman, an older woman, also in the leather apron but with her gauntlets tucked through the doubled ties at her waist, was watching him from the side of the yard. Her face was without expression, but the young man in the doorway of the shed was scowling openly. There were still plenty of people in Astreiant who thought of the League as the enemy, for all that that war had ended twenty-five years earlier; Eslingen touched his hat, not quite respectfully, and moved on.

Knives' Road was as busy as the other streets, and narrowed by the midden barrels that stood in ranks beside each butcher's hall. Outside one hall, a barrel had overflowed, and gargoyles scratched and scrabbled in the spilled parings, quarreling over the scraps. Eslingen gave it a wide berth, as did most of the passersby, but as he drew abreast of the hall a boy barely at apprenticeship came slouching out with a broom to clean up the mess. The gargoyles exploded away, shrieking their displeasure, some scrambling up the corner stones of the hall, the rest lifting reluctantly on their batlike wings. Eslingen ducked as a fat gargoyle flew straight at him; it dodged at the last minute, swept up to a protruding beam and sat scolding as though it was his fault. The creatures were sacred to Bonfortune, the many-faced, many-named god of travelers and traders, but if they weren't an amusing nuisance, Eslingen thought, someone would have found justification for getting rid of them centuries ago. Their chatter followed him as he turned onto the street Baeker had mentioned.

The Old Brown Dog stood at its end, completely blocking the street. It was a prosperous-looking place, three, maybe four stories tall, if there were servants' rooms under the eaves. The sign—a sleeping dog, brown with a grey muzzle—was newly painted, and the bush that marked the house as Leaguer tavern was a live and flourishing redberry in a blue and white pot. A gargoyle was rooting among the dropped fruit but took itself off with a shriek as he got closer. The benches to either side of the door were empty, but the main room seemed busy enough for mid afternoon, half a dozen tables filled and a waiter sweating as he hauled a barrel up through a trap from the cellar. Light poured in from an open door on the opposite side of the room—a door that gave onto a garden, he realized. The air smelled of beer and pungent greenery and the first savory whiffs of the night's dinner.

The waiter got the barrel up onto its stand behind the bar, and let the trap door down again. He wiped his hands on the towel tied around his waist, and nodded to Eslingen. "Can I help you, sir?"

"I understood you rented rooms," Eslingen answered.

The man gave him a quick, comprehensive glance, taking in the heavy soldier's boots and the saddlebags slung over his shoulder, but never took his hands from the towel. "That's up to the mistress," he said. "And if we have a room. Adriana!"

A moment later, the top half of the door behind the bar opened—

the kitchen door, Eslingen realized—and a young woman leaned out. She had taken the sleeves off her bodice while she cooked, and her shirtsleeves were pinned back to the shoulder, showing arms as brown as new bread; her tightly curled hair and broad nose were unmistakable signs of Silklands blood. "Yeah?"

"Is Aagte there?"

"Mother's busy."

"There's man come about a room."

"Oh?" The woman—she was probably about twenty, Eslingen thought, not precisely pretty but with a presence to her that wasn't at all surprising in the tavernkeeper's daughter and heir—tipped her head to one side, studying him with frank curiosity. "Who are you, then?"

Eslingen stepped up to the bar, gave her his best smile. "My name's Philip Eslingen, last of Coindarel's Dragons. Maggiele Reymers said the Brown Dog rented rooms."

"We do." The woman—Adriana, the waiter had called her—returned his smile with interest, showing perfect teeth. "I'll fetch Mother." Before he could answer, she popped back into the kitchen, closing the door behind her.

Eslingen set the saddlebags at his feet—the floor looked clean enough, and he was glad to be rid of their weight—and leaned against the bar. The waiter had vanished in response to a shout from the garden, but he was aware of the tavern's regulars watching from their tables, and did his best to ignore their stares. Reymers had said that Devynck kept a Leaguer house; her regulars must be used to the occasional, or more than occasional, soldier passing through.

The kitchen door opened again—both halves, this time—and a stocky woman came out, pushing her grey hair back under the band of an embroidered cap. She wasn't very tall, but she had the familiar sturdy build and rolling walk of the longtime horse trooper, and Eslingen touched his hat politely. "Sergeant Devynck?"

The rank was a guess, but he wasn't surprised when she nodded and came forward to lean on the bar opposite him. "That's right. And you're—Eslingen, was it?"

"Philip Eslingen, ma'am, just paid off from Coindarel's regiment. Maggiele Reymers told me you rented rooms."

Devynck nodded again. She had a plain, comfortably homely face, and startlingly grey eyes caught in a web of fine lines. The daughter, Eslingen thought, had obviously gotten her looks from her father.

"That's right. Three seillings a week, all found, or one if you just want the room. How long would you want it for?"

"That depends. Maybe as long as the fall hirings."

"I see. No taste for the current season—what rank, anyway, Eslingen?"

"I had my commission this spring," Eslingen answered. "Before that, I was senior sergeant."

"Ah." This time, Devynck sounded satisfied, and Eslingen allowed himself a soundless sigh of relief. She, at least, would understand the awkwardness of his position; it would be a reason she could sympathize with for sitting out a campaign. Hearing the change in her voice, he risked a question.

"Three seillings a week all found, you said. What's that include?"

"Use of the room, it's a bed, table, stove, and chair, and clean linen once a week. The boy empties your pot and rakes the grate, and the maid'll do the cleaning, Demesdays and Reasdays in the morning. You haul your own water, there's a pump out back." Devynck's eyes narrowed, as though she were considering something, but she said only, "I suppose you'll want to see the room first."

"Please," Eslingen answered.

Devynck glanced over her shoulder, as though gauging whether she could afford to leave the kitchen, then came out from behind the bar. "Stairs are through the garden."

Eslingen followed her out the back door. The garden was bigger than he'd realized, stretching almost twice the length of a normal city plot, and there were fruit trees along one wall, the hard green apples little bigger than a child's fist. There were tables nearer the door and the ground around them was beaten bare; beyond that area, rows of woven fence kept the drinkers out of plots crowded with plants. Pig apples ripened on their sprawling vines, yellow against the dark green leaves, and he thought he recognized the delicate fronds of carrots in the nearest patch. The pump, as promised, was by the door, a spout shaped like Oriane's Seabull roaring above a cast-iron trough; the pump handle was iron, too, and looked nicely weighted. A well-worn path led between the fences to an outhouse by the back wall.

The stairs ran up the side of the tavern, and Eslingen followed Devynck up past the first floor landing, wondering if he would be offered a space under the eaves with the servants. She stopped at the second floor, however, producing a bunch of keys from her belt, unlocked the door and stood aside to let him past. Eslingen glanced surreptitiously at the lock as he went by, and was relieved to see a sturdy double bolt.

"First on the right," Devynck said, and Eslingen went on down the well-scrubbed hall.

The door she had indicated stood ajar. Eslingen pushed it open—it too had a solid-looking lock attached—and went on into the room. It was surprisingly bright, the light of the twin suns casting double shadows: the single window overlooked the garden, and there was glass in the casement rather than the cheaper oiled paper. The bed looked clean enough, the mattress lying bare on its rope cradle, the plain curtains knotted up to keep away the dust; as promised, there was a table big enough to seat two for private dinners, and a single barrel chair. A ceramic stove was tucked into the corner by the window, its pipe running out the wall above the casement. It was small, Eslingen thought, but would at least keep off the worst of the chill in winter, and let him make his own tea and shaving water. It was all ordinary furniture, clearly bought second- or thirdhand, or relegated to the lodgers' rooms when Devynck's own family had no further use for them, but still perfectly serviceable. He could, he thought, be reasonably comfortable here.

As if she had read his mind, Devynck said, "I offer lodgers a break on the ordinary. Two seillings more a week, and you can have two meals a day below, dinner and supper. You take what we're serving, but it's generally good, though I say it myself."

The smell that had come from the kitchen was tempting enough, Eslingen admitted. He looked around the room again, pretending to study the furniture, and added up the costs. Five seillings a week wasn't bad; that came to two pillars a lunar month—twenty-one months, if he bought nothing else and earned nothing else, neither of which was likely, and in practice he should only have to stay in Astreiant until the spring, thirteen months at most. He glanced at the whitewashed walls, the well-scrubbed floorboards, and nodded slowly. "It sounds reasonable, sergeant. I'll take it."

Devynck nodded back. "Meals, too?"

"Please."

"Wise man. You won't find it cheaper unless you cook for yourself." Devynck smiled. "I'll need the first week in advance."

"Agreed." Eslingen reached into his pocket, took out his purse, and searched through the coins until he found a single heirat. The snake coiling across its face gleamed in the sunlight as he handed it across. Devynck took it, turned it to check the royal mint-mark, and slipped it deftly into her own pocket.

"Make yourself at home, Eslingen. I'll send someone up with your linens and your key. We lock the main door at midnight, mind, but one of the boys will let you in if you come back later."

"Thank you," Eslingen answered, and the woman turned away, skirts rustling. Eslingen shut the door gently behind her, and stood for a moment contemplating the empty room. As always when he moved into a new place, either quartered on some stranger or in lodgings of his own, he felt an odd thrill, half apprehension, half anticipation; the room, the city, the air, and the sunlight coming in through the open window, felt somehow thick, heavy with potential. He set his saddlebags beside the bed—he would need a clothes press, or at least a chest, he thought, and wondered if he could borrow something suitable from Devynck—and went to the window, leaned out into the scent of the fruit trees and spilled beer, grateful for that note of commonality.

To his surprise, it was Adriana who appeared with the sheets and blankets, followed by a pair of waiters carrying a battered storage chest. At her gesture, they set it down inside the door, and headed back to their other jobs. Adriana nodded cheerfully and began to make up the bed.

"You're from Esling, then?" she asked.

Eslingen nodded, watching her work—the sheets were mended, but looked impeccably clean, and the blankets were only minimally patched—said, "I left some years ago, though."

"Mother left Altheim when she was sixteen." Adriana loosened the curtains, slapped them smartly to loosen what little dust had been allowed to gather, then stooped to the chest, dragging it further into the room. Eslingen bent to help her, and found himself looking down the front of her bodice, at the cleavage between two nice breasts. He smiled, realized she was aware of his stare, and looked quickly away.

"Where do you want this?" Adriana asked.

"Oh, under the window would be fine," Eslingen answered, more or less at random, and together they carried the heavy chest across the room.

"So you were with Coindarel's regiment," Adriana went on, and lifted the chest's lid to reveal a squat chamberpot, an equally unpretentious kettle, and a washbasin and jug. "One hears a great deal about Coindarel."

I wouldn't be surprised, Eslingen thought. He said, "I doubt all of it's true."

"Oh?" She smiled, a not quite openly mischievous expression that started a dimple in one dark cheek. She seemed about to say something, but then changed her mind, her smile still amused and secret. "I brought a candle-end for you, but after that, you'll buy your own."

"Thanks." Eslingen watched her out of the corner of his eye, wondering just which of the many rumors she had heard. Probably the one about Coindarel choosing his officers for their looks, he thought, and didn't know whether to be regretful or relieved. She was pretty—more than pretty, really, and Devynck's daughter would have a substantial share in her mother's business, if not the whole of it, since he'd seen no other sisters—but he would be wise to keep hands off until he knew her intentions. Not that he would be so lucky as to attract an offer of marriage—I think well of myself, he admitted, with an inward smile of his own, and with reason, but there's not a woman alive who'd think I have enough to offer her to make that contract worth her while. But there were other obligations, other degrees of interest and desire, and until he knew more about her, it would be wise to step warily. She was certainly of an age to be thinking about children.

Adriana's smile widened briefly, as though she'd guessed what he was thinking, but she said only, "That's your furniture, sergeant—and Mother does charge for damage. The kitchen's open from six o'clock to first sundown, you can eat any time then. I've told the waiters not to charge you."

"Thank you," Eslingen said again, and Adriana answered, "My pleasure, sergeant."

"Certainly mine," Eslingen replied automatically, and wondered if he'd been entirely wise. Adriana flashed him another quick grin, showing teeth this time, and let herself out in a flurry of skirt and petticoat.

Left to himself, Eslingen leaned out the window to check the sundial that stood in the garden below. Past four, he guessed, from the length of the shadows, but couldn't see the dial itself. He would want a timepiece of some sort, he thought, frowning—one needed to keep rough track of the hours; even the least observant did their best to avoid their unlucky times—and then a tower clock sounded from the direction of the Street of Knives, a strong double chime marking the half hour. There would be no missing that sound; probably the real difficulty would be learning to sleep through it every night. He allowed himself a small sigh of relief, and began methodically to unpack his belongings.

He had traveled light, of necessity. It didn't take long to arrange the borrowed furniture to his satisfaction, and to fold his spare clothes neatly into the bottom of the chest. The locked case that held his pistol went beneath his clean shirts: in the morning, he thought, I'll buy a lock for the big chest, too. There would be other errands to run, as well—find the nearest bathhouse and barber, buy candles of his own, and herbs for the chest, to keep the moths out, and find a laundress, too, and a decent astrologer, I'll probably have to go back to the university for that—but he put those plans firmly aside for the moment, and reached into the bottom of the right-hand saddlebag for the carved tablets that were his portable altar. Like most rented rooms from the League to Cazaril in the south, this one had a niche set into the wall beside the door, and he walked over to examine it. It was typical, except for the lack of dust—Devynck was clearly a ferocious housekeeper—just a space for an image or two and a shallow depression to hold the hearth fire, but it was certainly more than adequate for him. He unfolded the hinged diptych, Areton, painted ochre since Eslingen couldn't afford gilt, dancing on the right-hand panel, Phoebe as guardian of health in solar splendor on the left. He should probably honor Seidos, too, he thought, not for the first time—he had been born under Seidos's signs, the Horse and the Horsemaster—but Seidos was patron of the nobility, not of common soldiers. Maybe I'll ask the magist when I have my stars read, he thought, but he hadn't done it yet. He tilted his head to once side, studying the altar. He would need to buy a candle for the Hearthmistress, along with the ones for his own use, but those would be easily enough found at any chandler's shop. He added that to his mental list, and stretched out on the bed, settling himself for a nap before dinner.

The tower clock woke him at five, and again at half past, and at six. He sighed then, swung himself off the bed, and began to tidy himself for dinner. The sun was very low as he made his way down the stairs into the garden, but he guessed it would be another hour at least before it actually set. The air smelled of the cooking food, rich with onions and garlic, and he realized suddenly that he was hungry. Very hungry, he amended, and hoped Devynck's portions were generous.

The main room was only moderately crowded, and he guessed that Devynck made most of her profit from her beer. He found an empty table beside one of the streetside windows, and lifted a hand to signal the nearest waiter. The man nodded back, but took his patron's orders before coming over to Eslingen's table.

"You're the new lodger—Eslingen, isn't it? I'm Loret."

"That's right." Eslingen eyed him curiously, recognizing a wrestler's or blacksmith's breadth of shoulder beneath the loose smock, and wondered if Devynck often had trouble here.

"Then you get the ordinary. Do you want beer with that? It's a demming extra for a pitcher."

"That's fine."

Loret nodded, and Eslingen watched him walk away, dodging tables on his way to the kitchen hatch. Loret had the look of country boys who enlisted out of ignorance and deserted after their first battle, good boys with all the wrong stars, more often than not—which was hardly fair, he told himself, considering that Loret was probably born and bred in Astreiant. And big men weren't all gentle; he'd learned that the hard way, years ago.

It wasn't long before Loret returned with the tray of food and the sweating pitcher of beer. He set them neatly down, and waited until Eslingen had paid for the beer before answering the next customer's shout. Eslingen made a face at the caution, but had to admit it was probably justified. Devynck's clientele would be no better than the average. The food was good—a thick stew, Leaguer style, with a decent serving of beef to supplement the starchy roots that made up the bulk of the dish, and half a loaf of good wheat bread with a dish of soft cheese on the side—and the beer was better. It had been a while since he had eaten Leaguer food—Coindarel's quartermasters had been mostly Chenedolliste, like their men—and he took his time, savoring the rich meat broth.

"Philip! Philip Eslingen!"

The voice was unexpectedly familiar, and Eslingen looked up, startled, to see Dausset Cijntien waving at him from the center of the room. Eslingen waved back, wondering what the other was doing in Astreiant—the last he had heard, Cijntien had signed on with a long-distance trader, leading a caravan-guard on the six-month overland journey to the Silklands. But then, that had been almost six months ago, he realized, and in any case, Cijntien was obviously back, and equally obviously looking for work. Midsummer was the hiring season for the long-distance traders, and the sea captains, for that matter; there was rarely any shortage of work for experienced soldiers.

Cijntien collected his refilled pitcher, reaching over the heads of the people at the nearest table, and then threaded his way through the crowd to Eslingen's table. The room had filled up since he'd arrived, Eslingen saw, and glanced at the wall stick. It was blind, the light no longer falling to cast its shadows, but from the look of the sky outside the windows, it was getting close to the first sundown.

"It's good to see you again," Cijntien said, and settled himself on the stool opposite the other man.

"And you," Eslingen answered, and meant it. "You're looking well."

"Thanks." Cijntien took a long swallow of his beer, and Eslingen smiled, watching him. They had served together years before—more accurately, he had served under Cijntien, had been a corporal and then a company sergeant under Cijntien, and had stepped into Cijntien's office of major sergeant when the older man had left soldiering for the less dangerous life of a trader's man. Or at worst differently dangerous, Eslingen amended. From the looks of Cijntien's hands, flecked with the dark specks of a recent powder burn, long-distance trading had its own hazards.

"I thought you were with Coindarel these days," Cijntien went on.

"We were paid off," Eslingen answered. "This morning, in fact."

"Hard luck. Or maybe not so hard, depending." Cijntien leaned forward, planting both elbows on the table. He was wearing a light jerkin over a plain shirt, and the grey brown leather matched the faded brown of his hair. "Have you another place lined up yet?"

Eslingen shook his head. "Not this season." He hesitated, but Cijntien was an old friend, and was probably one of the few who'd appreciate his promotion. "I had my commission this spring, you see. I'm not inclined to go back to mere sergeant so quickly."

Cijntien nodded in sympathy. "The stars have been against you, my Philip. Have you tried a good astrologer?"

Eslingen laughed. "Have you ever met an astrologer who could alter the stars once they're risen? Give over, Dausset."

"They can mitigate the worst effects," Cijntien answered, and Eslingen shook his head. Cijntien was old-fashioned—he had been born in Guisen, the most conservative of the northern cities, back when it was part of the League—and undereducated; no one had ever been able to convince him that even the greatest magists could work only with what the stars gave them.

"I'm planning to consult someone," Eslingen said. "Tomorrow or the next day. But, no, I don't have a place, and I wasn't planning to look until the winter season."

"As it happens," Cijntien said, and smiled. "As it happens, my Philip, I've a place for you, if you want it."

"Oh?" In spite of himself, in spite of knowing what it must be, Eslingen felt his heart quicken a little. He was a fish out of water in Astreiant, and that was frightening as well as a challenge; it wouldn't be bad to have familiar work, or to be serving with Cijntien again. . . . Then common sense reasserted itself. He had no desire to serve six months to a year in a trading company—of course a shipboard post would probably be shorter, assuming Cijntien had moved from the caravans to the more prestigious trading craft, though he himself had never sailed on anything larger than a river barge, much less fought from one.

"My principal's still hiring for this winter's caravan," Cijntien said. "It's a good trip, I've done it five times now, up the Queen's-road to Anver, cross the Marr at Breissa and then over the land bridge into the Silklands."

"I thought that was all desert," Eslingen said, but couldn't suppress a surge of curiosity. He had always liked travel—men were generally wanderers by their stars, and he was no exception.

"It is, mostly. But the rivers fill in winter, and the nomads—they're Haissa, there, mostly, and a lot of Qaidin—come to the city-sites to trade." Cijntien looked past him, not seeing the tavern crowd. "It's a sight to see, Philip. The sites, they're nothing, just the walls for houses, but then the people come in, pitch their tents, and make a city. They've a traders' peace, too, at least in the cities, so the various clans can do their business. We were early once, saw the Haissa setting up at Saatara. It was like magists' work, I've never seen anything like it. We came in at first sundown, pitched our camp, and there was nothing there, just mud brick walls and dirt. And then, just before second sundown, we heard the Haissa arrive—they'd been held up, their camp mother said, a storm or something—and the next thing we knew the city'd sprouted roofs and doors. All oil-silk, mind you, and those heavy carpets everywhere. When the light hit them, at first sunup, gods, it was like you'd fallen into a jewelbox. And there was nothing there before, nothing at all."

Eslingen shivered, caught by the picture the older man had conjured for him. He had met Silklanders before, of course, had served with any number of them, but they were mostly dark-skinned Maivi, from the center of the empire. He'd never met a true Hasiri, from one of the tribes, though like all Leaguer children he'd been raised on stories of the wild nomads who roamed the roof of the world; it would be wonderful to see.

"After that," Cijntien went on, "we take it by easy stages down the imperial roads to Tchalindor. My principal's factor is there. And then we come back by sea."

And that, Eslingen thought, was the rub. It would be a glorious journey, certainly, but it would take the rest of the year and well into the next spring to reach Tchalindor—the land bridge was only passable in the winter, when the rivers were full—and by the time he could get a ship back to Chenedolle or the League, the best captains would have filled their companies for the spring campaigns. Still, if the pay was good enough, he could afford to wait for the winter season. . . . "What's your principal offering?"

"Two pillars a lunar month, paid at Tchalindor, plus bonuses. And of course food, mounts, and shot and powder are his business—and weapons, too, if you don't want to bring your own."

Which wasn't enough, not even if he skimped—and besides, Eslingen told himself firmly, he'd always been a soldier, not some caravan guard. He shook his head. "I'm sorry, Dausset. I can't afford it."

"Can you afford to have your head blown off, somewhere up in the Ile'nord? Or your throat slit some dark night, more likely?"

Eslingen laughed. "But I'm good, Dausset. Besides, if it's in my stars, it's in my stars. By all accounts, you can get your throat cut just as neatly on the caravan roads."

Cijntien shook his head, the smile fading from his lips. "I wish you'd come with me, Philip. This is not a good time for Leaguers in Astreiant."

"What do you mean?" Eslingen reached for the pitcher, found it empty, and lifted a hand to signal the nearest waiter. The room had definitely filled while they'd been talking, a mix of Leaguers, marked by their lighter skin and hair and the wide hats they wore even in the tavern, and soldiers and former soldiers, equally marked by their boots and the various scars. But there was a small knot of people whom he couldn't identify immediately sitting close together at the tables by the door, and another larger group—this one with the leather aprons and pewter Toncarle badges of the Butcher's Guild—at the big table closest to the bar. Locals, all of them, and they didn't look particularly happy. The waiter—not Loret, this time—brought a second pitcher, and Eslingen paid, waving away Cijntien's perfunctory and insincere offer of coin. "So what do you mean, this is a bad time for Leaguers?"

"Haven't you heard?"

"I got into the city two days ago," Eslingen answered. "Not even Astreiant proper, the camps out along the Horse Road. And I wasn't paid off until this morning. So whatever it is, no, I haven't heard."

Cijntien leaned forward again, lowering his voice. "There's something very wrong in this city, Philip, let me tell you that. And the Astreianters are being very quick to blame everybody else before they'll look in their own stars."

Eslingen made a noncommittal noise.

"Their children are disappearing," Cijntien said, leaning forward even further. "Lots of them, just vanishing, no one knows where or why. They say—" He jerked his head toward the doorway, the city beyond it. "—they say it's Leaguers, or maybe the caravaners and Silklanders, needing hands for the road. But I say it's a judgment on herself, for being childless."

Eslingen caught his breath at that, barely kept himself from looking over his shoulder. "Have a care, Dausset."

"Well, she should have an heiress by now," Cijntien said, stubbornly. Neither man needed to say who he meant: the Queen of Chenedolle's childless state had been the subject of speculation for years. "Or have named one. The Starsmith is moving, it'll enter the Charioteer within the year—"

"Or next year, or the year after," Eslingen interrupted, his voice equally firm. Anyone in Chenedolle—in the known world—knew what that meant: the Starsmith was the brightest of the moving stars, the ruler of death, monarchs, and magists, and its passage from one sign to the next signaled upheavals at the highest levels. The current queen's grandmother had died during such a transit, and the transit before that had been marked by civil war; it was not unreasonable to fear this passage, when the current queen was no longer young, and childless. But the tertiary zodiac, the one in which the Starsmith moved, as opposed to the zodiacs of the sun and winter-sun, was still poorly defined, its boundaries the subject of debate even within Astreiant's university. The Starsmith might well pass from the Shell to the Charioteer this year, or not for another four or five years; it all depended on who you asked.

"At least you don't say never," Cijntien muttered. "Like some godless Chadroni."

"Whatever else you may say about me, you can't call me that."

"Godless?"

"Chadroni."

Cijntien laughed. "I have missed you, Philip, and I don't deny it'd be good to have you along this trip, if only for the company. But I mean it, this is not a good time to be a Leaguer here."

"Because of missing children," Eslingen said. "Missing, you said, not dead?"

"No one's found bodies, at any rate," Cijntien answered.

"So how many of them have just decided to take to the roads?" Eslingen asked. "It's Midsummer, or nearly, fair season—hiring season. When did you leave home, Dausset, or did you start out a soldier?"

"As it happened, yes, and I left home at the spring balance," Cijntien said. "But that's not what's happening, or so they say. It's the wrong children, not the southriver rats and rabble, but the merchants' brats from north of the river. Those children don't run away, Philip. They've got too much to stay for."

Eslingen made a face, still skeptical, but unwilling to argue further. In his experience, the merchant classes were as likely to run as any other, depending on their stars and circumstances—he'd served with enough of them in various companies, even with a few who had taken to soldiering like ducks to water. "Still, there's no reason to blame us. It's past the campaign season—gods, if I couldn't find a company hiring, how will some half-trained butcher's brat? If they're looking to blame someone, let them blame the ship captains."

"Oh, they're doing that," Cijntien began, and a hand slammed down onto the table.

"And what do you know about butcher's brats, Leaguer?"

Eslingen swallowed a curse, more at his own unruly tongue than at the stranger, looked up to see one of the butchers staring down at them. He was a young man, probably only a journeyman yet, but he held onto the table as though he needed its support. Which he probably does, Eslingen added silently, wrinkling his nose at the smell of neat spirit that hung about him. Drunk, and probably contentious—there's no point in being too polite with him, but I don't want a fight, either.

"Little enough," he said aloud, and gave the youth his best blank smile, the one he'd copied from the Ile'norder lieutenants, sixteen quarterings and not a demming in his pocket. "A—figure of speech, I think it's called, an example, a part standing for the whole."

"There's a butcher's brat gone missing," the journeyman went on, as though he hadn't heard a word the other had said, and Eslingen was suddenly very aware of the quiet spreading out from them as people turned to look and listen. "This morning—last night maybe. And I want to know what you know about it, soldier."

"This morning," Eslingen said, speaking not so much to the drunken boy in front of him but the listeners beyond, the ones who were still sober and could cause real trouble, "I was with my troop at the Horse Road camps, being paid off by Her Majesty's intendants—and I was there the night before, too, for that matter, making ready for it. There's a hundred men who'll witness for me." He could feel the tension relax—he wasn't likely quarry anyway, was too new to the city to be the real cause—and pushed himself easily to his feet. "But no harm done, my son, let me buy you a drink."

He came around the table as he spoke, caught the journeyman by the arm and shoulder, a grip that looked a little like linked arms but made the slighter man gasp sharply. He started to pull away, and Eslingen tightened his hold. The journeyman winced, subsiding, and Eslingen propelled him toward the door, talking all the while.

"No? Well, you're probably right, you've probably had all you want tonight. I hope you have a pleasant sleep and not too hard a morning."

Out of the corner of his eye, he saw the other young men from the table of butchers all on their feet, but hesitating, not quite certain what to do, and he favored them with a broad, slightly silly smile. "I think he was just going, don't you? And one of you should probably see him home, there's good chap, thank you. Devynck would want it that way, I'm sure."

The senior journeymen exchanged glances, and then the older of the two nodded. "I'll see him home, thanks."

Eslingen nodded and smiled, but kept his grip on the younger man until he was actually in the doorway. The senior journeyman followed him, the rest of the butchers trailing after him, pausing opposite Eslingen. The wind from the street was cool and smelled of the middens outside the butchers' halls, the sharp green scent of vegetables.

"You were paid off today? Sergeant, is it?"

"Lieutenant," Eslingen answered. "I was. I give you my word on it."

The senior journeyman looked at him for a moment longer, then, slowly, nodded. "Come on, Paas, let's get you home."

Eslingen released the journeyman's arm, and let the rest of them file out past him into the street. They went quietly enough, embarrassed more than anything, and he was careful not to say or do anything more. Let them forget as quickly as possible that Paas disgraced himself, he thought, and that'll do more to keep the peace than any threats or arguing. As the last of them left, he turned back into the tavern, glancing around the room more out of habit than because he expected more trouble. The conversations were already returning to normal, nearly everyone more concerned now with their drinks or a last order of food. He'd pulled it off, then, and as neatly as he'd ever done. He allowed himself a slow breath of relief, and Devynck said, "Not bad."

Eslingen blinked, startled—he hadn't seen her there in the shadows, or the big waiter, Loret, who was tucking a cudgel back under the strings of his apron—and Devynck went on, "I don't suppose you'd care to make a habit of it? Defusing the trouble, not starting it, that is. I'd pay you or take it off your rent."

Whatever else happened, Eslingen thought, he had not been expecting an offer of employment, but he wasn't stupid enough to turn it down, not when he'd already decided to stay in Astreiant for the summer. He nodded slowly. "I'd be interested, sergeant, but I'd rather talk terms in the morning."

"Good enough," Devynck said, and turned away. "Your beer's on the house tonight."

"Thanks," Eslingen answered, and allowed himself a wry smile. It was a cheap enough gesture: he wouldn't be drinking that much now, not if he wanted to impress her. And he did want to impress her, he realized suddenly. He wanted this job, wanted to stay in the city, though he couldn't entirely have said why. He shook his head, accepting his own foolishness, and started back to his table and Cijntien.

3

The list of missing children reported to all the points station arrived within three days—a measure in and of itself of the seriousness with which all the Points were taking the problem, Rathe thought—and was enough to silence even the most skeptical of the pointsmen. There were eighty-four names on the list, a little less than half of them from the five northriver points—no, Rathe realized, more than half, if you counted Point of Hearts as northriver. Which it was, technically; the district lay on the north bank of the Sier between the North Chain Tower and the Western Reach, but it was southriver in population and temperament. Still, he thought, that was not what any of them had expected. Logically, if children were going missing, either as runaways or because they were taken, they should come from southriver, where there were fewer people of influence to protest their vanishing. Or else, he added silently, turning over the last closely written sheet, I would have expected to hear of someone paying out money for the return of an heiress. And there had been none of that; just the opposite, in fact, merchant parents coming to the points stations to report the loss of daughters and sons, and to demand that the points find their missing offspring. There hadn't been much of that in Point of Hopes, yet; the majority of their complainants had admitted, however grudgingly, that their children might well have run away—except, of course, for Mailet and the Quentiers.

Rathe sighed, set the list back in its place—Monteia had ordered it pinned in a leather folder chained to the duty desk, to keep the names and descriptions ready to hand—and reached for his daybook, moving into the fall of light from the window to skim through the pages of notes. There had been no sign of Gavaret Cordiere in any of the northriver cells—he had even made a special trip across the river to Fairs' Point to ask Claes in person, but the man had just shaken his head. Not only hadn't they arrested any boy matching Cordiere's description, they hadn't made point on any pickpockets for nearly four days. And it wasn't that the pointsmen and women were taking fees, Claes added, with a quick grin; it was more that the pickpockets had stopped working. And that, both men agreed, had to be a bad sign—doubly bad, Claes had said, when you matched it with the new band of astrologers who were working the fairgrounds. The arbiters had declared they could stay, but no one needed any more mysteries just now. Rathe had agreed and left Cordiere's description in the station, but he wasn't relishing telling Estel Quentier of his failure.

"Rathe? Have you gotten the Robion girl's stars yet?"

Rathe looked up to see Monteia standing just outside the wedge of light, a thin, dark-clad shadow against the dark walls. "I was going this afternoon. I wanted to check everything else first."

"No luck, then."

Rathe shook his head, barely stopped himself from glancing again through the pages of notes as though he might find something new there. He had been to the local markets, and to every early-opening shop on the Knives Road, as well as searching out the rag-pickers and laundresses who served the street, all without noticeable result. "A woman who does laundry for the Gorgon's Head says she thinks she saw a girl in green going down Knives toward the Rivermarket, but she can't remember if it was Demesday or Tonsday that she saw it—or last year, for that matter. And a journeyman sneaking in late thinks he might have seen a girl in green going south, away from the river, but he says freely he was too drunk to remember his mother's name."

"That's all?"

"That's all."

"Nothing at the Rivermarket?" Monteia went on.

"Not so far. I've been through once myself, no one remembers her, but it was a busy morning. I've asked Ganier to keep an ear out, though." Ganier was the pointswoman who had semiofficial responsibility for the complaints that came from the district's markets.

Monteia nodded. "On your way back from Mailet's—or to it, I don't care—I'd like you to stop in the Old Brown Dog. I hear Aagte Devynck has hired herself a new knife, and I'd like to see what you think of him. And make sure he understands our position on troublemakers."

Rathe frowned, and Monteia shrugged. "I'm sending Andry to collect his bond, unless you want the fee."

You know I don't, Rathe thought, but said only, "Thanks anyway. I'll talk to him."

"It's not like Aagte to hire outside help," Monteia said, her voice almost musing. "I hope we're not in for trouble there. Not right now."

"So do I," Rathe answered, and slipped his book back into his pocket. He collected his jerkin and truncheon from their place on the wall behind the duty desk, and stepped out into the afternoon sunlight. The winter-sun hung over the eastern housetops, a pale gold dot that dazzled the eye; the true sun, declining into the west, cast darker shadows, so that the street was crosshatched with lines of dark and lighter shade. He threaded his way through the busy crowds, turned onto the Knives Road without really deciding which job to do first. Mailet's hall was closest; better to get it over with, he told himself, and crossed the street to Mailet's door.

There were no chopping blocks on the street today, or apprentices showing off for the servant girls, though the shutters were down and he could see customers within. He paused outside the doorway to let a matron pass, a covered basket tucked under her arm, then stepped into the shop. The journeyman Grosejl was working behind the counter, along with a boy apprentice. She looked up sharply at his approach, hope warring with fear in her pale face, and Rathe shook his head.

"No word," he said, and she gave a visible sigh.

"Enas, finish what you're doing and run tell Master Mailet that the pointsman's here." She forced a smile, painfully too bright, to Rathe's eyes, and passed a neatly wrapped package across the countertop. "There you are, Marritgen, that'll be a spider and a half."

The woman—she had the look of a householder, gravely dressed—fumbled beneath her apron and finally produced a handful of demmings. She counted out five of them, Grosejl watching narrowly, and slid them across the countertop. Grosejl took them, gave a little half bow.

"Thanks, Marritgen. Metenere go with you."

The woman muttered something in answer, and slipped out through the door. The other customers had vanished, too, and Grosejl made a face.

"They'll be back," Rathe said. He was used to the effect he had on even honest folk, but the journeyman shook her head.

"It's a sad thing, pointsman, when they're half blaming us for Herisse vanishing. There's regular customers who won't come near us, like it was a disease, or something."

There was nothing Rathe could say to that, and Grosejl seemed to realize it, looked away. "I'm sorry. There's still nothing?"

"Nothing of use," Rathe answered, as gently as he could. "We're still looking."

"No body, though," she said, with an attempt at a smile, and Mailet spoke from the doorway.

"That just means they haven't found it. Well, pointsman, what do you want this time?"

"I need some more information from you," Rathe said, and took a tight hold of his temper. "And for what it's worth, which is quite a lot, in actual fact, we don't have ghosts, either. Which means they're probably not dead."

"They?" Grosejl said.

Mailet grunted. "Hadn't you heard, girl? We're not the only ones suffering. There're children missing all over this city." He looked at Rathe without particular fondness. "Come on back, if you want to talk. My records are within."

"Thanks," Rathe said, and followed him through the narrow door into the main part of the hall. This time, Mailet led him into the counting room, tucked in between the main workroom and the stairs that led to the living quarters on the upper floors. It was a comfortable, well-lit space, with diamond-paned windows that gave onto the narrow garden—not much of a garden, Rathe thought, just a few kitchen herbs and a ragged-looking stand of save-all, but then, a dozen apprentices would tend to beat down all but the most determinedly defended plants. There were candles as thick as a woman's ankle on sturdy tripod dishes, unlit now but ready for the failing light, and an abacus and a counting board lay on the main table. A ledger was propped on the slanting lectern, and there were more books, heavy plain-bound account books and ledgers, locked in the cabinet beside the door.

"You said you wanted information," Mailet said, and lowered himself with a grunt into the chair behind the table. An embroidered pillow, incongruously bright, lay against the chair's back, and the butcher adjusted it with an absent grimace, tucking it into the hollow of his spine. A bad back, Rathe guessed, an occupational hazard, leaning over the chopping blocks all day.

"That's right," he said aloud. "My chief wants to know if you have Herisse's nativity in your records."

Mailet's head lifted, more than ever like a baited bull. Rathe met his gaze squarely, and saw the master swallow his temper with a visible effort. "I have it," he said at last. "I take it this means you don't have the faintest idea what's happened."

"I've found two people who might have seen her," Rathe said, and took tight hold of his own temper in his turn. "But their stories don't match, and I don't have a way to test who's mistaken."

"Or lying."

"Or lying," Rathe agreed. "But I don't have reason to think that yet, either. We're not giving up, though."

"Well, I have some news for you," Mailet said. "Some oddness that's come to my ears. My neighbor Follet brought me the word yesterday, I've been trying to decide what to do with it. But since you're here . . . " He shook himself, went on more briskly. "Follet knows Herisse is missing—everyone does, we passed the word through the guild—and he told me one of his journeymen was out drinking the other night, at the Old Brown Dog. Do you know the place?"

Rathe nodded. "I know it."

Mailet grunted. "Then you know the woman who runs it, too."

"Devynck's not a bad sort," Rathe said, mildly. "Honest of her kind."

"Which isn't saying much," Mailet retorted. He leaned forward, planting both elbows firmly on the tabletop. "But that's neither here nor there, pointsman. What is important is what Paas—that's Follet's journeyman—heard there. There were two soldiers drinking, Leaguers, and they were talking about the missing children. And one of them was saying, if he couldn't find a company, how could some half-trained butcher's brat?"

"He'd heard of the disappearance, then?" Rathe asked, after a moment. It was an interesting remark, and certainly suggestive considering how most of Devynck's neighbors felt about the League, but hardly solid enough to be called evidence, or even a lead.

"If he had, would I be bothering you with it?" Mailet said. "He couldn't've done, you see, he swore he'd just arrived in the city today."

"So this Paas confronted him," Rathe said.

Mailet looked away. "He was drunk, Follet said, the soldier put him out—and neatly, too, I'll give him that, no violence offered." He looked up again. "And that, pointsman, is why I didn't come to you at once. But since you're here, I thought I might as well tell you. Devynck's a bad lot, and there are worse who drink in her house."

"I'll make inquiries," Rathe said. And I will, too: convenient, being bound there anyway. It's not much to go on, but it's something. I wonder if he's the new knife Monteia was talking about?

"And you still want Herisse's nativity," Mailet said. He sighed and pushed himself to his feet, crossed to the cabinet that held the hall's books. He fished in his pocket for his keys on their long chain—gold, Rathe noted, from long habit, a good chain worth half a year's wages for a poor woman—and unlocked the cabinet, then ran his finger along the books' spines until he found the volume he wanted. He brought it back to the table and reseated himself, folding his hands on top of the cover. "And what do you want it for?"

"We intend to ask an astrologer to cast her horoscope for us," Rathe answered. "For her on the day she disappeared, and for her current prospects." Knowledge of the girl's stars would also be helpful if they had to locate a body, or to identify one long dead, but there was no need to mention those possibilities just yet. Mailet would have thought of them on his own, in any case.

"That's not likely to do you much good," Mailet grumbled. Rathe said nothing—he knew that as well as anyone; it was axiomatic in dealing with astrologers that as the focus of the question narrowed the certainties became smaller—and the butcher sighed, and opened the book. He flipped through the pages, scowling now at the lines of ink that were fading already from black to dark brown, finally stopped on a page close to the end. "Here. This is her indenture, her chart's there at the bottom of the page."

Rathe pulled out his tablet, and swung the ledger toward him to copy the neat diagram. It was, he admitted silently, almost certain to be an exercise in futility. Most southriver children knew the date and the place of their birth, but were less clear about its time. Not many common women would have the coin to pay someone to keep track precisely, and their midwives would have enough to do, tending the birth itself, and after, to make it unlikely that the time would be noted with the quarter-hour's accuracy the astrologers preferred. He himself knew his stars to within a half hour, and counted himself lucky at that; most of his friends had known only the approximate hour, nothing more. He incised the circle and its twelve divisions with the ease of long practice—even the poorest dame schools taught one how to construct that figure—and glanced at the drawing in the ledger. The familiar symbols were clear enough, the planets spread fanlike across one side of the wheel, but to his surprise there were numbers sketched beside each of the marks, and along the spokes that marked the divisions of the houses. He looked up.

"It's very complete. Is it accurate?"

Mailet shrugged. "I suppose—I assume so. She was born on the day of the earthquake in twenty-one, and she told me her mother heard the clock strike five the moment she was born. Her aunt, the one who paid her indenture, had the chart drawn for her as an apprenticeship gift."

Rathe nodded. He remembered the earthquake himself, the way the towers of the city had staggered; it hadn't done much damage, but it had terrified everyone, and untuned all the city clocks so that the temple of Hesion had been jammed for a solar month afterward, and the grand resident had built a new tower from the offerings. No one would forget that date, and the astrologers would know the stars' positions by heart. "This was copied from that chart, the one her aunt bought her?" he asked, and Mailet nodded. "Did she take it with her, or would it be in her room?"

"She carried it around with her like a talisman," Mailet answered. "You'd think it named her some palatine's missing heiress."

Rathe sighed. He would have to hope that whoever copied it into the indenture had been accurate—or pay to have the chart drawn again, which would be expensive. He drew the symbols one after the other, then copied the numbers, checking often to make sure he had it right. Nothing looked unusual, there were no obvious flaws or traps, and he sighed again and closed the tablets. "Thank you," he said, and pushed himself to his feet.

"For all the good it does you," Mailet answered, but his expression softened slightly. "Let us know if you find anything, pointsman. Send to us, day or night."

"Of course," Rathe answered, and let himself back into the hall.

The Old Brown Dog lay just off the Knives Road, on the tenuous border between Point of Hopes and Point of Dreams, and neither station was eager to claim it. In practice, it fell to Point of Hopes largely because Monteia was able to deal with Devynck woman to woman. Or something, Rathe added silently, watching a flock of gargoyles lift from a pile of spilled seeds beside a midden barrel. Maybe they'd simply settled on an appropriate fee between them.

The main room was almost empty at midafternoon, only an ancient woman sitting beside the cold hearth, her face so wrinkled and shrunken beneath her neat cap that it was impossible to tell if she were asleep or simply staring into space. A couple of the waiters were playing *tromps*, the table between them strewn with cards and a handful of copper coins, and a tall man sat in the far corner reading a broadsheet prophecy, feet in good boots propped up on the table in front of him. Good soldier's boots, Rathe amended, and his gaze sharpened. Devynck liked to hire out-of-work soldiers, and this just might be her new knife. The stranger looked up, as though he'd heard the thought or felt Rathe's eyes on him, and lowered the broadsheet with a smile that did not quite reach his eyes. He was handsome, almost beautiful, Rathe thought, with the milk white Leaguer complexion that was so fashionable now, and long almost-black hair. In the light from the garden window, his eyes were very blue, the blue of ink, not sky, and he'd chosen the ribbons on his hat and hair to match the shade. And that, Rathe thought, recalling himself to the job at hand, bespoke a vanity that, while not surprising, was probably not attractive.

"I'm here to see Aagte," he said, to the room at large, and the handsome man's smile widened slightly. One of the waiters put his cards aside with palpable relief—he'd been losing, Rathe saw, by the piled coins, and scurried through the kitchen door. He reappeared a moment later, held the door open with a grimace that wasn't quite a smile.

"She says, come on back," he said, and Rathe nodded, and stepped through into the hall that led to the kitchen. The smell of food was much stronger here, onions and oil and garlic and the distinctive Leaguer scent of mutton and beer, not unpleasant but powerful; through the open arch he could see Devynck's daughter Adriana helping to scour the pans for the night's dinner. She saw him looking, and grinned cheerfully, her hands never pausing in their steady motion. Rathe smiled back, and a side door opened.

"So, Rathe, what brings you here?" Devynck's eyes were wary, despite the pleasant voice. She beckoned him into the little room—another counting room, Rathe saw, though a good deal smaller than Mailet's—and shut the door firmly behind him.

"A few things," Rathe answered easily. "Nothing—complicated."

"That would be a first." Devynck leaned against the edge of her work table, which looked as though it had seen service in the kitchens, the top scarred with knife marks. There was only one chair, and Rathe appreciated the delicate balance of courtesy and status. She wouldn't sit, and keep him standing, but neither would she stand when he sat.

"I understand you have a new knife," he went on.

Devynck nodded. "You probably saw him when you came in. His name's Philip, Philip Eslingen. Just paid off from Coindarel's Dragon's."

"Is that a reference?" Rathe asked, with exaggerated innocence, and Devynck gave a sour smile.

"To some of us, anyway. Coindarel's no fool, and he doesn't hire fools."

Rathe's eyebrows rose, in spite of himself. Coindarel was known to choose his junior officers for their looks, and the man in the main room was easily pretty enough to have caught the prince-marshal's eye.

Devynck sighed. "Not for his sergeants—not for the men who do the real work, anyway. And Philip came up through the ranks."

"It wasn't his sleeping habits that worried me," Rathe answered. "I hear you had a little trouble here the other night."

"We did not," Devynck answered promptly, "and that's precisely why I hired the man. There could've been trouble, easy, but he nipped it in the bud."

"What I heard—what's being said on the Knives Road," Rathe said, "is that he was talking about missing butcher's brats before he could've known about it."

Devynck sighed again, and shook her head. "Paas. He's a bad lot, that one, be a journeyman all his life—if he doesn't drink himself right out of the guild."

"So what happened?"

"You'd have to ask Philip for the details," Devynck answered, "but what I saw was, Paas came over to their table—Eslingen was drinking with a man, looked like an old friend. I don't know his name, but he's a Leaguer, too, works for one of the caravan-masters. But anyway, they were drinking, and Paas comes over their table, says something I don't hear except for the tone." She smiled suddenly. "And the next thing I know, Philip's got him by the arm and is leading him gently out the door. The rest of the butchers' boys went with him, pretty well abashed. Everyone knows Paas drinks too much."

Rathe nodded. "I'll want to talk to Eslingen, of course—Monteia wanted me to be sure he understood the situation, anyway, with the fair and all."

"Reasonable enough," Devynck answered.

"And I wanted to say, if you hear anything, anything at all, that might have to do with the missing children, I expect to hear from you."

Devynck's eyes narrowed. "Did you think otherwise, Rathe?"

Rathe shook his head. "No. But people are starting to talk, up on the Knives Road. If you have any trouble, I also expect to hear from you."

"That you certainly will," Devynck said. "Who'll be taking Philip's bond?"

"Andry. You don't mind if I talk to him?"

"Philip? No."

"Thanks, Aagte."

Devynck nodded, pushed herself away from the table. "I hope I won't be seeing you, at least not by way of business, Nico."

"So do I," Rathe answered, and went back out into the main room. Eslingen—it had to be Eslingen, with those looks—was standing with the remaining waiter, flipping idly through the cards left on the table. "You're Eslingen, I presume. Can we talk?"

The dark-haired man nodded, letting the gesture serve for both answers, moved toward the windows. Rathe looked back at the waiter. "I think you're wanted in the kitchen." The man made a face, but moved slowly away, closing the kitchen door behind him. Beside the hearth, the old woman stirred slightly, then subsided again. "The chief point asked me to have a word with you, seeing that you're new in Astreiant—and seeing that it's fair time."

"Ah." Eslingen smiled, the expression consciously cynical. "How much?"

"You might hear me out," Rathe answered.

"Sorry." Eslingen reseated himself at the corner table, flipping the skirts of his coat out of his way, and gestured vaguely to the stool opposite. Rathe accepted the invitation with a nod, and leaned both elbows companionably on the table.

"What Monteia—she's the chief at Point of Hopes—what Monteia wants is for this fair to go off peaceably. Like last year, if not better, in point of fact, which, since you weren't here, you might want to ask Aagte about. And to that end, seeing as Aagte's felt the need to hire a new knife—" Eslingen flushed at that, the color clear on his pale skin. So he thinks himself above that title, Rathe thought, but went on without comment. "—she, Monteia, has asked me to tell you that we don't get a lot of trouble in Point of Hopes. Devynck's is a soldiers' place, true enough, but it doesn't get what you might call soldiers' business." Rathe paused, eyeing the other man's politely impassive face. "Which means, in plain words, if you run into trouble, send a kid to Point of Hopes. That's the only way we can guarantee everyone will get treated properly, when it's soldiers' troubles, is taking the points and letting us bear witness."

"And the fee for the service?" Eslingen asked, but he sounded less cynical than the words implied.

Rathe shrugged. "I don't generally take fees." He smiled suddenly, unable to resist. "You see, I like my points too much, or so they tell me—I get a great deal of satisfaction out of my job, and taking money to let someone go, well, that would spoil it, wouldn't it? And there's not much point in feeing me when it won't buy you off, and when I already enjoy my work. You can ask Aagte for the truth of it, or anyone in the point, they'll tell you."

"I'll probably do just that," Eslingen said.

"A wise move." Rathe leaned forward again. "I do have some questions for you, though."

Eslingen made a face. "That butcher's journeyman, right?"

Rathe nodded, not surprised that the man had guessed. He didn't seem stupid, and it would be a stupid man who failed to make that connection. "You want to tell me what happened?"

Eslingen shrugged. "Not much."

He went through it quickly, concisely—he told the story well, Rathe thought, plenty of detail but all in its place. It was the same story Devynck had told, the same that Mailet had recounted, barring the butcher's automatic suspicion of the Leaguer woman. And it sounds to me, Rathe thought, as though he handled an awkward situation rather well. He said aloud, "So why'd you pick a 'butcher's brat' for your example?"

Eslingen's mouth curved into a wry smile. "I wish to all the gods I'd picked anything else. I don't know—there were, what, near a dozen of them, butchers, I mean, sitting by the bar. I suppose that made it stick in my mind. That and being near the Knives Road."

Rathe looked closely at him, but the Leaguer met his eyes guilelessly. It was a plausible explanation, Rathe admitted. And I have to say, I think I believe him. Stealing children, for whatever cause—it's just not Devynck's style, and she'd never put up with that traffic in her house. He nodded. "Fair enough. But remember, if you have trouble here, send to Point of Hopes. It'll pay you better in the long run than feeing me."

"I'll do that," Eslingen said again, and this time Rathe thought he meant it. He pushed himself to his feet, and headed for the door.

Eslingen watched him go, impressed in spite of himself. Rathe wasn't much to look at—a wiry man in plain-sewn common clothes, hands too big for his corded arms, with a scar like a printer's star on one wide cheekbone and glass grey eyes with a Silklands tilt to them—but there was something in his voice, an intensity, maybe, that carried conviction. He shook his head, not sure if he was annoyed with himself or with the pointsman, and crossed to the kitchen door, pushing it open. "Oy, Hulet, you can come out now."

"Thanks," the waiter answered, without notable conviction. "Aagte wants to see you."

"What a surprise. So who is he, the pointsman?"

The other man shrugged, and went to pick up the coins that lay still untouched on the table among the scattered cards. "Nicolas Rathe, his name is. He's adjunct point at Point of Hopes."

"How salubrious," Eslingen murmured.

"Oh, Point of Hopes isn't bad," Hulet answered. "Monteia's reasonable, for a chief point."

Or bribeable, Eslingen thought. His experience with the points had been minimal, but unpleasant; for all their boasting, Astreiant's vaunted points seemed to make a very good thing out of the administration of justice. He nodded again, and stepped through the kitchen door.

Devynck was waiting in the doorway of her counting room, arms folded across her chest. She jerked her head for him to enter, closed the door behind him, then seated herself behind the table. "So Point of Hopes is already taking an interest in your exploits. Did he tell you about Andry?"

Eslingen shook his head.

Devynck snorted. "Andry's one of the pointsmen. He'll be along to collect your—bond, he'll call it. Tell me what he charges, I'll pay half."

Eslingen lifted an eyebrow, but said, "Thanks. Is this trouble?"

"Not the bond, no," Devynck answered, "but these kids . . . that could be."

Eslingen nodded at that, thinking about his own brief explorations in the neighborhood. The people hadn't been precisely unfriendly, the bathhouse keeper and the barber had been glad of his custom, but he'd been aware of the eyes on him, the way that people watched him and any stranger. He'd walked across the Hopes-point Bridge that morning to the Temple Fair, to visit the broadsheet vendors who worked there, and the talk had been all of this child and that one, gone missing from their shops or homes. Half the prophecies tacked to the poles of the stalls had dealt with the question, and the lines had been five or six deep to read and to buy. "People are worried."

"And ready to blame the most convenient target," Devynck said, sourly. She shook her head. "I can't see the recruiters bothering, damn it. There're usually too many people wanting a place, not the other way round."

"Do you suppose it's the starchange?" Eslingen asked, and Devynck looked sharply at him.

"I don't see how it could be, these are common folks' kin who are going missing."

Eslingen lowered his voice, despite the closed door. "The queen is childless, and the Starsmith is about to change signs. There is talk—" He wasn't about to admit it was Cijntien's idea. "—that that might be the cause."

Devynck winced, looked herself toward the closed door. "That's dangerous talk, from the likes of us, and I'll thank you to keep it to yourself." Eslingen said nothing, waiting, and the woman shook her head decisively. "No, I can't think it. If the queen were at fault—well, there would have been some sign of it, surely, some warning, and she wouldn't have ignored it. Besides, the gossip is, she's barren. She couldn't be blamed for that."

Eslingen nodded. He was less convinced by the benevolence of the powerful—though Devynck was a skeptic by nature, certainly—but he acknowledged the wisdom of her advice. This wasn't speculation to be voiced openly, at least not now.

"In any case," Devynck went on, "I want to make sure we don't have any trouble here for a while. I'll tell Hulet and Loret, too, of course, but I'd like you to keep a special eye on the soldiers, especially any newcomers. If they haven't heard what's going on, they may do something stupid."

"Like I did?"

Devynck smiled. "Not everyone has your—tact, Philip."

Eslingen laughed. "I'll keep an eye on things."

"It's what I pay you for," Devynck said, without heat, and Eslingen made his way back into the main room.

The broadsheets he had bought that morning still lay on the table by the garden window, and he collected them, shuffling them back into a tidy pile. The one on top caught his eye. It was a petty thing, one of the two-for-a-demming sort, offering predictions for the next week according to the signs of one's birth. He had been born under the signs of the Horse and the Horsemaster, and the woodcut that covered half the page—the most professional thing about the sheet, he acknowledged silently—showed a horse and rider, and the rider held a gambler's wheel, balancing it like a top in the palm of his outstretched hand. The fortune lay crooked across the page beneath it: CHANCE MEETINGS

ARE JUST CHANCE AND CHANCY, BRING CHANCES, TAKE CHANCES. CHANCE WOULD BE A FINE THING! Eslingen allowed himself a smile at that, wondering if his encounter with the pointsman, Rathe, was covered in that prediction, then headed for the garden stairs and his own room.

Rathe took the long way back toward Point of Hopes, through the Factors' Walk, with its maze of warehouses and shops and sunken roads and sudden, unexpected inlets where the smaller, river-bound lighters could tie up and discharge their cargoes in relative privacy. He was known here, too, was aware of people slipping out of sight, staying to the edges of his vision, but they weren't his business today, and he contented himself with the occasional smile and pointed greeting. Some of the factors dealt in human cargo—there would always be that trade, no matter what the law said or how many points were scored—but they had been the first to be searched and questioned, from the first report of missing children, and all their efforts, both from Point of Hopes and Point of Sighs, had turned up nothing more than the usual crop of semiwilling recruits. A few of the more notorious figures, the ones who'd overstepped the bounds of tolerance bought with generous fees, were spending their days in the cells at Point of Sighs, but Rathe doubted the points would be upheld at the next court session.

"Rathe!"

He looked up at the shout to see a tall woman leaning over the edge of one of the walkways that connected the warehouses at the second floor. He recognized her instantly: Marchari Kalvy, who made her living providing select bedmates for half the seigneury in the Western Reach, and owned a dozen houses in Point of Hearts as well. He admired her business sense—how could he not, when she'd had the sense to provide not just bodies but the residences where a noble could keep her, or his, leman in comfort, taking their money at all stages of the relationship—but couldn't like her, wished he'd had the sense to pretend not to hear.

"Rathe, I want to talk to you." Kalvy bunched her skirts and scrambled easily down the narrow stairs that led to the wooden walkway that ran along the first-floor windows of Faraut's ropewalk. "Will you come up?"

She was more than capable, Rathe knew, of coming down, and making a scene of it, if it suited her. "All right," he said, and found the nearest stair leading up again.

The smell of hemp was strong on the walkway, drifting out the open windows of the ropewalk, and he could hear the breathless drone of a worksong, and the shuffle of feet on the wooden floor. There was a smell of tar as well, probably from the floor below, and he wrinkled his nose at its sharpness. Kalvy watched his approach, hands on her hips.

"So what is it you want?" Rathe asked.

"Do you want to discuss it in the street?" Kalvy returned.

"It was you who wanted to talk to me," Rathe said. "I've business to attend to. It's here, or come in to the station."

"Suit yourself, pointsman." Kalvy leaned against the rail, looking down onto the cobbles a dozen feet below. "It's about Wels."

"I assumed." Wels Mesry was Kalvy's acknowledged partner and the father of at least two of her children—though not, malicious rumor whispered, of the daughter who bade fair to get the family business in the end. Mesry had been arrested for pandering to a landame from the forest lands north of Cazaril. The boy in question, a fifteen-year-old from Point of Hopes, had claimed he was being held against his will, though Rathe personally suspected that he'd exaggerated the degree of force Mesry had used while his mother was listening.

"You know the point won't hold," Kalvy said. "The boy wasn't half as unwilling as he claims—hells, how could he be, gets the chance to live in luxury for a moon-month, maybe two, and it's not like she was that unattractive."

"Old enough to be his mother," Rathe muttered.

"Sister, maybe." Kalvy shook her head. "I tell you, Rathe, the brat was glad of the chance, losing his virginity that way."

"She paid extra for that?" Rathe asked, and shook his head in turn. He would have liked to claim a point on the landame as well, but Monteia had flatly refused to countenance it, saying it was a waste of time and effort. She was probably right, too, but it didn't make it any better.

Kalvy glared at him. "The landame's childless, poor woman, that hits high as well as low. The boy had the right stars to be fertile with her, and he was well paid."

"Practically a public service," Rathe said, and Kalvy nodded, ignoring the irony.

"Just so."

Rathe shook his head. "I won't release him til the hearing—and neither will Monteia, so you needn't bother walking all the way to the station. Think of it this way, Kalvy, I'm doing you a favor, keeping him in. This way, he can't be blamed for any of the other kids who've gone missing."

"That's not my trade, and you know it," Kalvy said. "You can't blame that on me."

In spite of herself, her voice had risen slightly. Rathe glanced at her, wondering if it meant anything, but decided with regret it was probably just the general climate. Anyone would be nervous, these days, at the thought of being linked to the missing children. "See you keep out of it, then," he said aloud, and pushed himself away from the rail. He thought for a moment that she was going to follow him, or call after him, but she stayed where she was, still staring down at the cobbles. He went down the far stairs, past the ropewalk's lowest doors where the smell of tar was strongest, mixing with the damp of the river.

The Factors' Walk ended in the crowds and noise of the Rivermarket, where the merchants' carts and pitches had spilled out onto the gentle slope of the old ferry landing. There was no ferry anymore—no need for it, since the Hopes-point Bridge had been built fifty years before, in the twenty-fifth year of the previous queen's reign—but a number of the merchants brought their goods in by boat, and the brightly painted hulls were drawn up on the smooth damp stones at the bottom of the landing, watched by apprentices and dogs. Rathe skirted the edge of the market, watching with half an eye for anything out of the ordinary, but saw and heard only the usual cheerful chaos. Except, he realized, as he reached the top of the low slope, there were fewer children than usual in sight. There were a couple by the boats, a third buying vegetables at one of the cheaper stalls, and a fourth, a slight boy in patched shirt and breeches, stood talking to a man in a black magist's robe. The magist wore neither hood nor badge, unusually, but then a man with a handcart trundled by, blocking Rathe's view. When he had passed, the magist was gone, and the boy was running back down the slope to the river, wooden clogs loud on the stones. Rathe shook his head, wishing there were something he could do, and lengthened his stride. It was past time he was getting back to the station.

As he turned down Apothecary's Row, he became aware of a new noise, low and angry, and a crowd gathering in front of one of the smaller shops. Squabbling among the 'pothecaries? Rathe thought, incredulously. It hardly seemed likely. He started down the street toward the commotion, and was met halfway by a woman in the long coat of a guildmaster, open over skirt and sleeveless bodice.

"Poinstman! They're trying to kill one of my journeymen!"

Swearing under his breath, Rathe broke into a run, drawing his truncheon. The guildmaster kilted her skirts and followed. Outside the shop—one the points knew well, sold more sweets and potions than honest drugs—a knot of people had collected, hiding the group, maybe half a dozen, scuffling in the dust. With one hand, Rathe grabbed the person nearest him, and hauled back. "Come on, lay off. Points presence."

His voice cut through the confused noise, and the people on the fringes of the trouble gave way, let him through to the knot at the center. They—mostly men, mostly nondescript, laborers and clerks rather than guild folk—stopped, too, but at least two of them kept their hands on the young man in a blue shortcoat who seemed to be at the center of the trouble. His lip was split, a thread of blood on his chin, but he glowered at his attackers, jerked himself free of their hold, not seriously hurt. Rathe laid a hand on his shoulder, a deliberately ambiguous grip, and one of the men, tall, sallow-faced, in an apothecary's apron, spat into the dust at his feet.

"Almost too late to save another child, pointsman, or is that part of the plan?"

Rathe set the end of the truncheon in the the man's chest and pushed. He gave way, glowering, and Rathe looked round. "Get back, unless you all want to be taken in for riot. Now—one of you—tell me what in hell is going on. You, madam"—he pointed to the guildmaster—"is this your journeyman?"

"Yes," the woman answered, and glared at the crowd around her. "And there's no theft here. One of my apprentices stole off this morning in the middle of his work. When children are being stolen off the streets, what master wouldn't worry, wouldn't send someone to try to find that prentice? Only this lot took it on themselves to decide that my journeyman was the child-thief."

"Maybe you both are," a woman's voice called, from the shelter of the anonymous crowd.

"Well, there's one way to find out, isn't there?" Rathe snapped. He looked around, found a boy, thin and dark, his blue coat badged with Didonae's spindle: no mistaking him for an apothecary, Rathe thought, that was unambiguously the Embroiderers' Guild's mark. He nodded to the woman who had him by the shoulder. "If you don't mind, madam. What's your name, child?"

The boy glowered up at him, half sullen, half scared—frightened, Rathe realized suddenly, as much by what he'd unleashed as by being caught. "Dix."

"Dix Marun, pointsman, he's been my apprentice for little more than a year now. . . . " The guildmaster broke off as Rathe held up a hand.

"Thank you, madam, I want to talk to the boy." He looked down at Marun, feeling the thin shoulder trembling under his hand. "Are you her apprentice? Think carefully, before you answer. If you've been mistreated in your apprenticeship, you might want revenge. But it won't be worth it, because there are laws in Astreiant to deal with lairs who send innocent people to the law."

The child's dark eyes darted to the journeyman who was nursing his lip and would have a badly bruised face in a few hours. That young man was damned lucky, Rathe thought, and looked as though he knew it. And if it was him the boy was running from, well, maybe it would be a salutary lesson for all concerned. He fixed his eyes on the apprentice then, his expression neutral, neither forbidding nor encouraging, refusing either to condescend or intimidate. Finally, Marun looked up at him, looked down again.

"All I wanted was to go to the market," he said, almost voicelessly, more afraid now of the crowd that had come to his 'rescue.' "It's almost the fair, I wanted my stars read, before the others. I needed to see my fortune."

"Does your master mistreat you?" Rathe asked, gravely, and Marun shook his head.

"No. Not really. She's hard. Sometimes she's mean."

"And the journeymen?"

The child's lip curled. "They can't help it. They think they're special, but they're not masters, not yet. They just think they are."

"Do you want to return to your master's house, then?"

"I wasn't running away, not really." This time, the look Marun gave the journeyman was actively hostile. "I would've traded my half day, but he wouldn't let me."

Rathe sighed. "I see. And you see these people just wanted to make sure you weren't harmed. But are you willing to go back with them?"

Marun looked at his feet, but nodded. "Yes."

Rathe glanced around him, surveying the crowd. It was thinning already, as the people with business elsewhere remembered what they'd been about. "I take it no one here has problems with that?"

"Give him a good hiding, madame, for deceiving people like that!"

It was a man's voice this time, probably one of the carters at the edge of the crowd. Rathe rolled his eyes, looked at the guildmaster.

"Then, madame, there's the question of harm done your journeyman. There is a point here, if you want to press it."

"It was the boy's fault, surely," a woman called from the doorway of a prosperous-looking shop, and Rathe shrugged.

"You should have sent to Point of Hopes, mistakes like this happen more easily when you don't know the questions to ask. It wasn't Dix here who beat the journeyman." He looked back at the guildmaster. "It's up to you, madame."

The woman sighed, reached out to take Marun by the shoulder of his coat. "No, pointsman. An honest mistake. Let it go, please."

"As you wish." Rathe slipped his truncheon back into his belt. "I'll see you to the end of the street, madame, if you want."

"Thank you, pointsman." She was reaching for her purse, and Rathe shook his head.

"Not necessary, madame. Despite what some think, it's what I'm paid for."

"Probably not enough," she retorted, assessing shirt and coat with a practiced eye.

Rathe managed a smile in answer, though he was beginning to agree with her. "A word in your ear, madame. Keep an eye on your journeyman there."

She nodded. "I'd a mind to it, but thank you." They had reached the end of the street, where a pair of low-flyers had pulled up to let the drivers gossip. She lifted a hand, and the nearer man touched his cap, slapped the reins to set the elderly horse in motion. "I count myself in your debt, though, pointsman."

"I'll bear that in mind," Rathe answered, and stepped back as the low-flyer drew to a halting stop. The journeyman hauled himself painfully into the cab, and Marun followed. The guildmaster hesitated on the step.

"I meant it, you know," she said.

"So did I," Rathe answered, and the woman laughed. She pulled herself into the low-flyer, and Rathe turned back toward Point of Hopes.

The rest of his walk back to the station was mercifully uneventful, and he turned the last corner with a sigh of relief. The heavy stone walls turned a blind face to the street—the point stations, especially the old ones like Point of Hopes, had originally been built as militia stations, though they had lost that exclusive function a hundred years ago—and the portcullis was down in the postern gate, barring entrance to the stable court. He pushed open the side door, the bells along its inner face clattering, and walked past the now-empty stable to the main door. No one at Point of Hopes could afford to keep a horse; Monteia used the stalls for cells when she had a prisoner to keep.

"The surintendant wants to see you, Rathe," the duty-point said the moment the man stepped into the station. "As soon as you returned, the runner said. Of course, that was over an hour ago. . . . "

"Yeah, well, some of us had work to do," Rathe muttered, but grinned. Barbe Jiemin at least had a sense of humor, unlike some of their colleagues. "And if it was over an hour ago, another few minutes won't kill him. Is Monteia in?"

"Trouble?" Jiemin asked, and Rathe shrugged.

"A—disturbance—over a runaway apprentice that could easily have gotten someone killed." Rathe ran his hands through his hair, feeling the sweat damp beneath the curls. It was still hot in the station, and the air smelled more than ever of someone's inexpert cooking. "Guildmaster set a journeyman to bring the runaway home, and the good citizens along Apothecary Row decided this was our child-thief."

"Not good, Nico." Jiemin looked down at the daybook, trained reflex, checking the day's events. "You managed all right, though?"

"This time." Rathe shook his head again. "Next time, I'm not so sure."

Jiemin nodded, soberly. Before she could say anything, however, the door of Monteia's office opened and the chief point looked out. She had removed her coat and neckcloth and loosened her shirt, but still looked hot and irritable, a few strands of hair straggling across her forehead.

"Didn't the surintendant send for you?"

Rathe suppressed a sigh. "I just got in. And I need to talk to you. We nearly had a riot in the Apothecaries Row over a runaway apprentice."

Monteia grunted. "Can you say you're surprised? Come on in."

Rathe followed her into the little room, sweltering despite the wide-open window. There was little breeze in the back garden at the best of times, and the river breeze never reached this far into Point of Hopes.

"So what's this about a riot?" Monteia asked.

Rathe told the story quickly, but wasn't surprised when Monteia grunted again.

"Guildmaster should take better care of her apprentices, if you ask me. Bah, it's not good, any way you look at it."

"No. And there's more."

"There would be," Monteia muttered.

"The butchers are blaming Devynck for their missing children," Rathe said, bluntly. "No cause for it, I don't think, but they've never liked having a League tavern on their doorstep." He ran through that story quickly, too, and Monteia muttered something under her breath.

"Chief?"

She shook her head. "Never mind. So, you think this knife—what was his name, Eslingen?"

"Philip Eslingen, yes."

"You think he was telling the truth there, about what he said?"

Rathe nodded. "I do." I rather liked him, he added, silently, almost surprised by the thought, but said only, "He seems to be sensible."

"He'd better be," Monteia said. She sighed. "Well, we expected this, didn't we? Or should have done. And you shouldn't be keeping the surintendant waiting, though I wish to all the gods he wouldn't keep drawing off my best people when they're supposed to be on duty." She reached under her skirts, flipped a coin across the desktop. Rathe caught it, surprised, and she went on, "Take a low-flyer. Doesn't do to keep the sur waiting, does it?"

Jiemin had anticipated the order, and the youngest of the runners arrived with word that a cart was waiting as Rathe stepped out into the main room. Rathe tossed the boy a half-demming—not that he could spare it easily, but that was how the runners earned their bread, taking tips from the pointsmen—and went out to meet the driver. She was a woman, unusually, but as she leaned down to take the destination, Rathe saw she had the wide-set, staring eyes that often marked someone born when Seidos was in his own signs of the Horse and Horsemaster. That made her stars not merely masculine but ideal, and he stepped up onto the iron bracket that served as a step with a slight feeling of relief. The low-flyers didn't have a wonderful reputation—half of the drivers drank the winters away just to keep warm, and the other half earned their charcoal-money in less than legal ways—and it was somewhat comforting to think the driver had been born to her position.

"The Tour de la Cité, please," he said. The woman nodded, straightening easily, and Rathe climbed into the narrow cab behind her, wondering if it wouldn't ultimately have been faster to take a boat. She threaded her way through the traffic that jammed the Hopes-point Bridge quite competently, however, and then through the maze of the Old City, drawing up at last in the cleared square in front of the Tour in no more time than it would have taken him by the river ways. He climbed out, handing over the spider Monteia had given him, and made his way across the court to the main gate.

The Tour had been built five hundred years ago as the gatehouse of the then-walled city, and no matter how much the city's regents and the various royal and metropolitanate officials who had inhabited it over the intervening years had tried to change it, the building still had the feeling of a fortress. Rathe's heels echoed on the stone floors, and even the red-coated judiciary clerks seemed chastened by the heavy architecture. At least it was cooler inside the massive walls, Rathe thought, as he made his way through the narrow, badly lit halls, and at least the regents had the sense to use mage-fire lamps instead of oil or candles. Or maybe it was the judiciary: he didn't have clear idea who paid for what inside the Tour.

The surintendant's rooms were at the midpoint of the south tower and boasted two narrow windows overlooking the city square. Rathe gave his name to one of the hovering clerks and settled himself to wait. To his surprise, however, the surintendant's voice came almost at once from behind a half-open door.

"Ah, Rathe, good. Come in and sit down."

Rathe did as he was told, his eyes on the surintendant. Rainart Fourie was a merchant's son from the Docks by Point of Sighs, had begun by buying his place as an adjunct point, but had risen to chief on his own merit, as even the most grudging critics were forced to admit. His appointment was still something of a novelty—until him, the surintendancy had generally been held by gentry, the sons of landames and the like whom the queen owed favors—and he was sometimes more aware of the politics of his situation than Rathe felt was good for either him or his people. At the moment, Fourie was dressed very correctly, the sober tailored black of the judicial nobles, his haircut as close as a Sofian renunciate's. Though that, Rathe added silently, probably had less to do with devotion or politics than with the fact that his mouse brown hair was thinning rapidly, and the fashionable long wigs would have looked ridiculous on his long, sharp-boned, and melancholy face. Fourie lifted an eyebrow, as though he'd guessed the thought, and Rathe schooled himself for whatever was to come.

"Your former patronne sent for me this morning," Fourie said. "It seems one of her clerk's apprentices is missing, and she wants you to handle the case."

Rathe exhaled. One thing about Fourie, he reflected, he always was direct. "You mean Maseigne de Foucquet?"

"Do you have another patronne?"

Rathe shook his head. He had begun his working life as a runner for the court, before he'd been a pointsman; Naudin de Foucquet had been a young intendant then, and as a judge she'd taken a benevolent interest in his career. It never hurt to have well-placed connections, but he had not been entirely sorry when Foucquet had been assigned to the courts at Point of Hearts. Friends in the judiciary could be a liability, as well as an asset, in his line of work. "That would be Point of Hearts' business, surely."

"She asked for you specifically," Fourie said.

Rathe sighed, acknowledging the ties of patronage and obligation, wondering, too, why Fourie, who usually defended his people's autonomy, seemed willing to countenance this interference. "So who is—he, she? How old, what's the family?"

"He's thirteen, and his name is Albe Cytel. His mother is assizes clerk at Point of Hearts."

So it really isn't my business at all, Rathe thought. He said, "When did he go missing?"

"Yesterday afternoon, according to Foucquet, and I would imagine her people keep a keen eye on their apprentices," Fourie answered.

Rathe nodded.

"He had the morning off, it was his regular half-day, which he was supposed to use in studying. When he didn't show up for the afternoon session, they sent a senior clerk around to his room. He wasn't there, but nothing of his was missing, either." Fourie looked up from his notes, and gave a thin smile. "Under the circumstances, they felt it was a points matter."

Rathe nodded again. "It sounds like half a dozen cases I know of, two I'm handling personally. Does maseigne know how many cases there are like that in the city right now?"

"I imagine she does," Fourie answered. "I daresay that's why she wants you. It makes no difference, Rathe. The judge-advocate wants you handling this case, and so do I. Can you tell me honestly you don't want it?"

Rathe made a face. He owed Foucquet for patronage that had been very useful when he was starting out; more than that, he liked and respected her, and beyond that still, any missing child had claim on him. "No, sir, it's not that, of course it isn't. It's just . . . " He paused and ran a hand through his hair, wondering just how far he could go. "Gods know, yes, I owe maseigne in any case, and at least she's not asking me to drop any southriver cases for some clerk's apprentice—" He had gone too far there, he realized abruptly, and stopped, shaking his head. "Sorry, sir. It's been a bastard of a day."

Fourie inclined his head in austere acceptance of the apology, but said nothing. Rathe watched him warily, not quite daring to ask the question in his mind, and Fourie leaned back in his chair, steepling his fingers. "What's your theory on it all, Rathe?"

"I haven't got one," Rathe answered. *As you well know. None of us have any theories, or at least nothing solid, from the newest runner to the dozen chief points.* "With respect, sir, why are you taking this case out of Point of Hearts? I'm not unwilling, but they're not going to like it, and I can't say I blame them."

Fourie ignored the question. "What about politics?"

"Politics?" Rathe repeated, and shook his head. "I don't see it. I mean, I know this is a tricky time, with the starchange and all, but—what do these children have to do with that? They're not well enough born for blackmail—they don't have anything in common, as far as I can see."

"I know," Fourie said. "I'm not—fully—sure myself. Maybe nothing. But there are factions seeking to influence Her Majesty's choice of a successor. Too many things are happening at once for it all to be a coincidence, Rathe." He leaned forward, as though he had reached a decision. "I want you to check out Caiazzo's involvement."

"Caiazzo?" Rathe leaned back in his chair. Hanselin Caiazzo was—officially, at least—a long-distance trader, an up-and-coming merchant-venturer who had almost escaped the taint of his southriver origins. He was also, and less officially, the paymaster for or master of a good dozen illegal businesses both south and north of the Sier, with interest that ranged from the Court of the Thirty-Two Knives to Point of Graves to the Exemption Docks. No one had yet proved a point on him, and not for want of effort. Customs Point was doing very well from his fees, or so the rumor had it. "I don't see it. . . ."

"Caiazzo has a good many business interests in the north," Fourie said. "Especially in the Ile'nord."

"That's not illegal."

"Not in and of themselves, no," Fourie agreed. "But when one of the likeliest choices for the succession is Palatine Marselion, for whom Caiazzo has acted on more than one occasion . . ." He let his voice trail off, suggestively, and Rathe shook his head.

"I don't see a connection with the missing children, sir."

"Caiazzo's been known to bankroll unlicensed printers," Fourie said. "Well known for it, in fact, even if we've never proved the point. And astrologers. If Marselion is up to something, what better way to distract the city, and by distracting the city, the queen's government? If that's the plan, you have to admit, it's working. What have all the broadsheets been talking of for the past week? The nobility? The succession? Politics or ordinary predictions at all? No—it's these missing children."

It's very thin. Rathe bit back the instinctive response, said, more carefully, "Look, politics just isn't a game Caiazzo's interested in playing, he never has been. Frankly, sir, the return just isn't good enough."

"Backing the next Queen of Chenedolle is bound to have a sizeable return, Rathe, whether it be in immediate wealth or favor and influence."

"Sir, is this really about the children, or is this just a chance to get Caiazzo?"

The surintendant gave another thin smile. " 'Just' a chance to get Caiazzo, Rathe? The man's behind at least half the illegal activities in Astreiant. We—you personally—have been after him for, what, three, five years now? If we can get him on treason and trafficking in children, he won't get free of it."

It made a kind of sense, Rathe knew, but couldn't pretend he was happy with it. He hesitated, searching for a diplomatic way to say what had to be said, then shook his head. "I won't find evidence that isn't there, sir."

Fourie nodded. "I know. That's why I picked you for the job." It was, Rathe supposed, meant as a compliment, however backhanded. "But I want you to look into this—Foucquet's more important than her rank would suggest, she has a great deal of influence with the judiciary, and so far she hadn't said who she supports. This apprentice of hers could have been taken to force her hand. Look into it, Rathe, with particular attention to Caiazzo."

Rathe stared at him with some frustration. This wasn't Caiazzo's style, he'd fenced with the man long enough to know that; Caiazzo stayed away from politics and political business as only a commoner would. And Caiazzo was southriver born and bred, he of all people would know better than to risk stirring up the smouldering angers there. Unless he was a Leveller? Rathe added silently, but dismissed the thought as soon as it was formed. Caiazzo was no Leveller: society suited him very well in its present form, and he'd be the first to say as much. But there was no ignoring the surintendant's direct order. "Very well, sir," he said, and made no effort to keep the skepticism from his voice.

Fourie ignored it, nodded in dismissal. "And keep me informed."

Rathe walked back from the Tour to Point of Hopes, grumbling that he had better things to spend his money on. He was tempted to avoid the station entirely, tell Monteia about this new case and the surintendant's new interpretation of the old one in the morning, but his mother had always said that unpleasant duties were best dealt with as quickly as possible. He sighed, and went on through the courtyard into the station.

Jans Ranazy was on duty again, and Rathe made a face, quickly concealed. He wasn't fond of the other man, and knew the feeling was mutual; Monteia had done her best to keep them working apart, but the station staff was too small to make her efforts completely effective. Ranazy's dinner sat on a tray on top of the daybook, and Rathe grimaced again, recognizing the Cazaril Grey's horsehead stamped into the cheap pottery. Only Ranazy, of all the points, including Monteia herself, managed to afford to have his dinner brought over from the inn. All the others, fee'd or not, brought cold dinners when they had the night shift, or cooked over the stove. But that didn't suit Ranazy's opinion of himself.

Ranazy looked up then, and smiled, not pleasantly. "Still on duty, Nico?"

"It's been a busy afternoon," Rathe answered. "Is the chief in the office?"

"She's out back, in the yard." Ranazy would clearly have loved to ask more, but Rathe ignored his curiosity, and pushed open the back door of the station.

The space behind the points stations was, more properly, open ground intended as defensible space, but forty years of civil peace had turned it into a back garden, lightly fenced, and sporting a few haphazardly tended garden plots. Monteia was sitting on a bench under a straggling fruit tree in the reddened light of the first sunset, the wintersun's shadows pale on the ground around her. She held a lit pipe negligently between her first two fingers, and the air was redolent of the mixed herbs. She looked up as the back door closed.

"Dare I ask what the sur wanted?"

"You won't like it. It seems Judge-Advocate Foucquet has lost one of her clerk's apprentices. It's the same as the others. No sign that the boy ran. He just—disappeared, yesterday afternoon. His mother is assize clerk in Point of Hearts." He took a breath. "And the judge-advocate and the surintendant both want me to take the case on my book."

"Oh, that's just marvelous, Rathe. As if you haven't enough to do. . . . " Monteia broke off. "And how am I supposed to justify your poaching to Hearts?"

"It was the sur's direct order," Rathe answered. "And aside from that, I do feel as though I owe this to maseigne." He had kept his tone as respectful as possible, but from the look she gave him, Monteia was not appeased.

"For a southriver rat, you certainly have a lot of friends in high places." She picked up a sheaf of papers that had been lying at her feet, weighted with a slate against the nonexistent breeze. "Well, then, since you're taking on extra work, you can look into these. The whole city's getting a rash of these unlicensed sheets, and they're not helping things. About half of them are blatantly political—hells, they've backed every possible candidate for the succession, including a couple I've never heard of—and the rest of them are passing hints about the children, but they're none of them operating under a bond license. You can add these to your daybook."

Rathe took the papers mechanically. If Monteia's assessment was correct—and it would be, he had no doubt of that—then Caiazzo could well be connected at least to the printing. He would take these home with him, and tomorrow he would begin the delicate job of tracking down their source. After, he added mentally, after I've spoken to Maseigne de Foucquet and found out exactly why she doesn't want to go to Point of Hearts.

Along with the papers, he took a batch of nativities Salineis had collected for him out through the station onto the front steps, unwilling to intrude on Monteia's quiet work in the yard, even more unwilling to remain in the still, hot air of the station—made hotter, if not stiller, he thought, by the presence of Ranazy. He sat down on the broad front step of the station, stretching his legs out with a sigh of relief, and started leafing through the nativities, settling the broadsheets under his hip. A knot of the station's runners were also playing in front of the building, despite the sun that still beat down hard in the later afternoon. Laci looked up at him from his game of jacks, a smile like the sun glinting off a bright knife blade. Jacme, a rough-boned twelve-year-old who had been thrown out of his home in the Court of the Thirty-two Knives, was sitting in the lower boughs of one of the few trees that survived in the street; Ranazy would scold him out of it, but Rathe just turned a blind eye. He'd seen few enough fruit trees ruined for being a good climbing tree as well. Fasquelle de Galhac was lazily tossing a ball back and forth with Lennar, their constant rivalry temporarily forgotten. Asheri, Rathe's favorite, sat in her usual place on the edge of the dry trough, her hands for once not busy with any needlework. He smiled at her as he sat down, and she returned the smile, lighting up her thin face. She had, he reflected, a stillness none of the others had, or rather, a capacity for stillness; Rathe had seen her fully as rambunctious as any of the others. A quiet, aloof child would have found no favor with the rest of the runners, and she had learned that quickly, despite her own personality. She was a daredevil by necessity, and a sound one, taking risks that were quickly and carefully calculated. That calculation wasn't, some of the other points thought, natural in a child of twelve. It was, Rathe thought, an attribute of a sound pointswoman.

He read through the nativities, poring over them for any similarities, anything at all that he might have missed the times he had read through his and the other points' notes, knowing it was fruitless, knowing he didn't make that kind of mistake and even if he did, it was unlikely that every other pointswoman and man in the city would overlook anything that was there. He looked at two he held in his hands—in his left, the nativity of an eight-year-old, in his right, that of a twelve-year-old.

He realized, with a sick knot in his stomach, that the station's runners were all in the age range of the children who had gone missing, from Laci, the youngest, to Jacme, the oldest. It was surely just luck that they hadn't lost any of them yet. He carefully stacked the papers, weighting them with a rock, and cleared his throat. Instantly, their attention was focused on him, on the possibility of a job to be run, of earning a few extra coins. Well, he hated to disappoint them, but . . .

"Sorry, no job at the moment, I just want to talk to you. Come on over here," he invited, and the runners, some eagerly, some warily, joined him by the table, dropping to sit on the ground beneath the tree. Jacme was still in the tree, above his head, and Rathe looked up. "Sorry, Jacme, but I'd like you down here for this, all right?"

"Right, Nico," the boy said, cheerfully enough, and dropped to the ground with a solid thud. He sat down next to Asheri. "What's up?"

These were streetwise children, for the most part, probably a lot wiser in the ways of the streets than many adults, certainly more so than most of the children who had been stolen. But like most children, they had a sense of invulnerability, despite the fact that their lives had been a great deal harder than that of most of the missing children. "All right," he said. "You lot know what's been going on, these disappearances. We're doing everything we can to find out what's happened to these kids, and, just as important, find those children who have already disappeared." He looked at them, their faces grave, but not frightened, not even worried. They were street urchins, southriver rats who faced this kind of threat most days of their lives. "And you've probably all heard all the rumors going about, maybe even some we haven't yet."

"Like the ones who say the points are doing it, Nico?" Laci chimed in, and Rathe gave him a sour look that fooled neither one of them.

"I had heard that one already, yes, thank you, Laci." He paused, not quite certain how to proceed, wanting to find the words that would reach them, and not simply send them squirming into paroxysms of impatience. "The thing is, the thing you may not have realized, is that all the missing children are between the ages of eight and twelve." He stopped, and looked at each of them in turn. They understood, he could see that, but still, he had to say it, make it explicit. "So you lot are in the exact age range of the children who have disappeared." He shrugged. "All I'm saying is, be careful. You know the city better than a lot of people, you see things other people would miss, or would dismiss as unimportant. If you see anything, no matter what you think I might think of it, let me know, or anyone else here."

" 'Cept Ranazy," Jacme muttered.

"Yes, well, just do it, all right?"

There were mumbles of assent, and looks were exchanged that made Rathe frown. "And if you've already noticed anything, now might be a good time to tell me."

Fasquelle was drawing lines in the dirt; Jacme was shredding some grass that had been struggling to exist. Rathe saw Asheri look at each of them, and then she stood up.

"I don't know if anyone else has mentioned it, Nico . . . " she began, and then frowned, closing her teeth on her lower lip in thought.

"Mentioned what, Ash?" Rathe asked, quietly, encouragingly, glancing at each of the other runners. They seemed content to let Asheri speak for them.

"I was waiting for Houssaye the other afternoon at Wicked's—he wanted me to run some of those nativities back to the station, since he was on his way home—and there were some students there. And they were complaining about these new astrologers working the fair this year."

"New astrologers?" Rathe asked, and Asheri nodded.

"The students were complaining that they're taking business away from them because they're doing readings for people for less than the students charge—a half-demming, they say. Which would be ridiculously low," Asheri added, "since you can barely buy a loaf of bread for that."

"They're not with the university, then." It was a privilege of the fair for university students to augment their stipends by working the various temple booths, casting horoscopes and doing star readings. They charged what the market would bear—not usually exorbitant, but certainly more than half a demming. "Who are they aligned to?" he asked.

Lennar burst in eagerly. "No one, Nico—they wear long robes, like a magist, but the robes are black, and they don't carry any badge or insignia, and they don't belong to any temple. They say they can offer people charms to protect their children from the child-thieves."

And at that, Rathe felt a cold anger within him. Bad enough that parents and guildmasters were worried sick about their children and apprentices, bad enough that the broadsheets were having a field day with it all, blaming any group with less influence than another, but for these hedge-astrologers to prey on these fears for the sake of coin . . . a half-demming wasn't much, admittedly, but when you multiplied it by the number of fearful adults—and adolescents—they could be making a very tidy sum. And he had seen one of them, too, he realized, at the Rivermarket. The description was too precise, a magist's robe with no insignia, and he wished he had known enough to stop the man. That was probably why he had vanished so quickly. He wondered, briefly, if this might not be Caiazzo's style, Caiazzo's hand at work, but then he dismissed the thought. Too petty, surely, for a man with the vision and ambitions of Hanselin Caiazzo. Caiazzo thought to rival the old trading house Talhafers within the next several years; it would be a fool's game to antagonize the temples.

"What else have you heard about these astrologers?" he asked, and knew that some of his anger came through in his voice, because the runners seemed to draw back. He took a breath. "No, look, I'm sorry. It's not you I'm angry with, truly. I'm glad you told me about this—if nothing else, they're probably violating bond laws, and we should look into it. But has anyone heard anything else about them? Seen them? Spoken with any of them?"

"I think I saw one of them near the fair, Nico, but I can't be sure. . . . It was a long black robe, but it might have had a badge, I just couldn't see." That was Lennar, speaking slowly, carefully. A couple of the others were nodding, Asheri included.

"Have any of them approached any of you?" he asked, and was relieved to see them all shake their heads definitively. "Right, then. It's probably nothing, they probably just don't want to pay the temple bond for casting horoscopes. But thanks for letting me know. And what I said before, I meant—be careful."

There were shrugs, looks of bravado, but these kids were smart, they wouldn't take any risks, they'd do as they were told. And that, Rathe told himself, was the best he could do, wishing that there *were* some sort of charm to protect them from danger.

4

Eslingen leaned against the bar of the Old Brown Dog, letting his gaze roam over the crowd filling the main room. It was smaller than the night before's, and that had been smaller than the crowd the night before that: Devynck's regular customers had been dwindling visibly for the past week. First it had been the butchers' journeymen and junior masters, the ones who had passed their masterships but not yet established their own businesses, who had vanished from the tap, then it had been the rest of the locals, so that Devynck was back to her original customers, soldiers and the few transplanted Leaguers who lived within walking distance in either Point of Hopes or Point of Dreams. And there were fewer of the latter every night. Eslingen looked around again, searching for familiar faces. Marrija Vandeale, who ran the brewery that supplied the Dog, was still there, holding court under the garden window, but her carter was missing, and Eslingen guessed it would only be a matter of time before Vandeale took her drinking elsewhere.

There were still a sizable number of soldiers in attendance, the half dozen who lodged with Devynck and a dozen or so others who had found rooms in the neighborhood, and Eslingen wasn't surprised to see a familiar face at the corner table. Flory Jasanten had lost a leg in the League Wars, though no one knew which side he'd served—probably both, Eslingen thought, without malice—and had turned to recruiting to make his way. At the moment, he was contracting for a company of pioneers that had lost a third of their men in a series of skirmishes along the border between Chadron and the League, a thankless job at the best of times, but particularly difficult in the summer, when the risk of disease was greatest. And given the pioneer's captain, a man generally acknowledged to be competent, but whose unlucky stars were almost legendary . . . Eslingen shook his head, and looked again toward Jasanten's table. Jasanten would be lucky to get anyone with experience to sign on.

As he'd expected, there was only a single figure at the table, a gangly blond youth with a defiant wisp of beard that only managed to make him look younger than his twenty years. As he watched, the young man nodded, and reached across the table to draw a careful monogram on the Articles of Enlistment. Well, one down, Eslingen thought, and Jasanten looked up then, meeting his eyes. Eslingen lifted his almost empty tankard in silent congratulations; Jasanten smiled, mouth crooked, and then frowned as a slim figure leaned over the table to speak to him. It was a boy, Eslingen realized, looked maybe fourteen or fifteen—just past apprentice-age, at any rate—and felt himself scowl. That was all Devynck needed, to have kids that age using the Old Brown Dog to run away to be soldiers, and he pushed himself away from the bar, intending to tell Jasanten exactly that. Before he could reach that table, however, the older man shook his head, first with regret, and then more firmly, and the boy stalked away toward the kitchen door.

Eslingen allowed himself a sigh of relief—he didn't really want to alienate any of Devynck's few remaining customers—but seated himself on the stool opposite Jasanten anyway.

"You're not looking for work," Jasanten said, but smiled again.

"Not with Quetien Filipon," Eslingen agreed. "Besides, I had my fill of pioneering by the time I was nineteen."

Jasanten grunted. "I wish you'd tell that one that." He tipped his head sideways, and Eslingen glanced casually in the direction of the miniscule gesture. The boy was back, carrying a half pint tankard, and hovering on the edge of a table of soldiers, three men and a woman who'd been paid off from de Razis' Royal Auxiliaries the same day that Coindarel's Dragons had been disbanded. The tallest of the men saw him, and grinned, edged over to make a place for him at the table.

"Who is he?" Eslingen asked. He was well dressed, for one thing, that jerkin was good linen, and the embroidery at his collar and cuffs—black and red, to hide the dirt—had cost a few seillings even second hand. Some mother had paid well for her son's keep, and would not take kindly to his hanging about here listening to soldiers' tales, or worse.

"He said his name's Arry LaNoy," Jasanten answered, "but I doubt it. He wanted to sign on—hells, he wanted to sign on with me last season, and I told him then he needed to grow. So he's back this year, and he's not much bigger."

"I doubt he took kindly to that."

"No more did he." Jasanten made a noise that was almost a chuckle. "And I'm not unaware of what's going on in Astreiant, either."

"You'd have to be deaf and blind not to be," Eslingen muttered.

"Just so. So I told him he'd need his mother's permission to sign on, Filipon wasn't taking drummers or runners without it, and he swore me blind he was an orphan."

"Not in that shirt, he's not."

"I'm not blind," Jasanten answered. "And I told him so, so he stalked off in a sulk." He nodded to the table of soldiers. "My guess is, he's trying to talk them into taking him on, and he won't be particular about what he offers them."

Eslingen sighed. "That's all we need."

"That's rather what I thought," Jasanten said, and leaned back to summon a passing waiter. "And seeing as you're Aagte's knife—"

"It's my business to deal with it," Eslingen finished for him. "Thanks, Flor, I won't forget it."

Jasenten smiled, and the younger man pushed himself to his feet, one eye still on the table where the soldiers and the boy were talking. By the look of them, it would be a while before the boy could get around to making his request; he could tell from the way the three exchanged looks that they were just showing off, enjoying an audience that wasn't all that much younger than the youngest of them. And they might have the sense not to listen—the woman, certainly, had a commonsense grace to her—but at the moment Devynck couldn't afford to take the chance.

Eslingen reached across the bar to catch Loret's shirt as the big man worked the tap of the biggest barrel. "Is Adriana in the kitchen?"

"Yes." Loret barely paused in his work. "You want her?"

"Yes. Or Aagte."

"I'll tell them," the other waiter, Hulet, said, from behind him, and disappeared through the kitchen door. Eslingen leaned his weight against the heavy wooden counter, resisting the desire to look back at the boy—LaNoy, or whatever his name really was—to be sure he was still sitting with the soldiers. At last the door opened, and Adriana came out, wiping her hands on her apron.

"What is it? Mother's busy."

"Trouble in potential," Eslingen answered. "You see the table there, the three from de Razis' Auxiliaries? Do you know the boy with them?"

Adriana sighed, the air hissing through her teeth. "Oh, I know him, all right. Felis Lucenan, his name is, his mother's an apothecary down by the river. Mother told him he wasn't welcome here anymore."

"Shall I throw him out?" Eslingen asked. "Or, better yet, take him home myself."

The kitchen door opened again before she could answer, and Devynck herself came out. "Trouble, Philip?"

"Felis Lucenan's back," Adriana said.

"Areton's—" Devynck broke off, shaking her head. "The little bastard's more trouble than he's worth."

"I'll take him home," Eslingen offered, and Devynck shook her head again.

"You will not. I don't want you accused of child-theft. No, I'll send a runner to his mother, tell her to come and retrieve him. You just keep him here." She smiled then, bitterly. "And maybe I'll post a complaint at Point of Hopes, make her keep her spawn at home."

"Good luck," Adriana muttered, and Devynck glared at her.

"You go, then, tell Anfelis he's here and I don't want him. Get on with it, it'll take you a quarter-hour to get to the shop, and then you'll have to wake the woman."

"Yes, mother." Adriana stripped off her apron, bundling it under the bar.

"And as for you—" Devynck turned her gaze on Eslingen. "See that he doesn't get away—and doesn't sign on to anything we'll regret later."

"Right, sergeant," Eslingen answered, automatically. Devynck nodded, turned back to the kitchen. Eslingen rested his elbows on the bar, let his gaze wander over the crowd again, though he kept half an eye on the boy, still sitting at the table, leaning forward eagerly to hear the soldiers' stories. A quarter of an hour to his mother's shop, Devynck had said, and the same back again, plus whatever time it took to wake the apothecary—say three-quarters of an hour, if not an hour, he thought, and heard the tower clock strike half past ten. The winter-sun would be setting soon, and he hoped Adriana walked carefully. Astreiant's streets were as safe as any, better than many as long as the winter-sun shone, and besides, he told himself, Devynck's daughter would know how to use the knife she carried at her belt. Still, he wished it had been him, or one of the waiters, to go, though that would probably have warned the boy that something was up.

He sighed, shifted his elbows to a more comfortable position on the scarred counter. At the moment, he wanted nothing more than to go lay a hand on the brat, make sure he couldn't get away before his mother arrived to claim him, but the thought of the boy's probable reaction was enough to keep him where he was. All he would need was for the brat to accuse of him of being the child-thief, and even the other soldiers would be inclined to believe it, if only to defend themselves from similar accusations. Better to wait, he told himself, do nothing unless the boy tries to leave, at least not until his mother's here.

Luckily, the boy seemed engrossed in the trio's stories. Eslingen made himself relax, stay still, counting the minutes until the clock struck again. Not long now, he thought, and in the same moment, heard the clatter of hooves and the rattle of a low-flyer drawing up outside the door. The boy heard it, too, and looked up, the color draining from his face. No one took a carriage to the Old Brown Dog, and he guessed instantly what it must be. He started up from the table, the soldiers staring after him, heading for the back door, but Eslingen stepped smoothly into his way, caught him by the shoulder.

"Hold on, son, what's your hurry?"

Behind them, the inn's main door opened, and Eslingen felt the boy slump under his hand.

"Philip?" Adriana called, from the doorway, and Eslingen turned in time to see a stocky woman sweep past her.

"Felis! How many times have I told you, I won't have you coming down here like this."

The boy rolled his eyes, and allowed himself to be transferred to her hold. Eslingen felt a sudden, sneaking sympathy for him, and suppressed it, ruthlessly. The stocky woman—Lucenan, her name was, he remembered—looked him up and down, and gave him a stern nod.

"I'm grateful for your intervention, sir."

The "sir," Eslingen knew, was more a response to the cut of his coat than to his service. He said easily, "I doubt you had anything to be concerned with, madame, no one's hiring boys this late in the season."

"It wasn't the hiring I was worried about," Lucenan said, grimly.

Eslingen nodded. "A word in your ear, madame," he said, and eased her toward the door. She went willingly, though her hand on her son's shoulder showed white knuckles, and the boy winced at her grip. "If the boy's this determined—there'll be places after the fall balance, for the winter campaigns, good places for a boy to start. Let him sign on then, til the spring. He may not like the taste of it."

"No son of mine," Lucenan began, and then visibly remembered to whom, or what, she was speaking. "Thanks for your concern, sir, but Felis—what he does when he comes of age, well, I can't stop him, but until then, I won't help him get himself killed."

Eslingen sighed, recognizing a familiar attitude, and held the door for her. As he'd expected, the low-flyer was waiting, the driver keenly interested in the proceedings. He handed them into the coach—the woman seemed surprised and pleased by the gesture, though the boy rolled his eyes when he thought she wasn't looking, and earned a slap for his presumption—and stepped back to watch it roll away.

Adriana was waiting by the bar, a glass, not the usual tankard, in her hand. As he approached, she slid it toward him, and he took it with a nod of thanks. There was a dram or so of a clear, sweet-smelling liquor in the bottom of it, and he drained it with a smile. The fiery liquor, distilled grain spirit with a strong flavor of mint, burned its way down his throat, and he set the glass down with a sigh.

"The next," Adriana said, "you pay for."

"That's all right, then," Eslingen answered. Menthe was imported from Altheim, and wasn't cheap there. He shook his head. "I hope it's done some good."

"Can't hurt," Adriana answered. "Tell me something, Philip, what do your stars say about your death?"

Eslingen's eyebrows rose. "That's a personal question, surely—or were you planning something I should know of?"

"Neither killing nor bedding you, so get your mind off it," Adriana said, but he could see the color rise in her dark cheeks. "No, I'm sorry, I know it came out wrong, but Felis—" She stopped, took a breath, looked suddenly younger than her years. "Anfelis told Mother why she won't let Felis go, aside from he's her only kid. His stars are bad for war, he's likely to die by iron."

Eslingen sighed, the menthe still hot on his tongue. "Then he'd be a fool to sign on, surely. You'd be surprised how many of us have those stars, though." It was an ill-omened thought. He smiled, and said brightly, "I, however, am like to live to a ripe age, comforting women and men to my last days."

"Comfort seems unlikely," Adriana retorted, and swung back behind the bar. Eslingen watched the kitchen door close behind her, his smile fading. Returning the Lucenan boy to his mother could only improve the Old Brown Dog's reputation—he hoped. There were a handful of butchers, the journeyman Paas chief among them, who seemed to go out of their way to find something bad to say about anything Devynck did. Eslingen sighed again, suddenly aware that it was nearing midnight, and turned to survey the thinning crowd in the taproom. Everything seemed quiet enough, the three soldiers leaning close over an improvised dice board, Jasanten limping in from the garden, his crutch loud on the wooden floor, the woman musician who worked in one of the theaters in Point of Dreams nodding over her pint and a plate of bread and cheese, and Eslingen hoped that things would stay that way, at least until tonight's closing.

Eslingen woke to the sound of someone knocking on his door. He rolled over, untangling himself from the sheets, and winced at the sunlight that seeped in through the cracks in the shutters. He could tell from the quality of the light that it was well before the second sunrise, and as if to confirm the bad news, the tower clock sounded. He counted the strokes—eight—before he sat up, swearing under his breath.

"Eslingen? You awake?"

Eslingen bit back a profane response, said, as moderately as he was able, "I am now."

"There's a pointsman to see you."

"Seidos's Horse!" Eslingen swallowed the rest of the curse. "What in the name of all the gods does he want with me?"

"Didn't say." The voice was definitely Loret's. "Aagte says, will you please come down?"

Eslingen sighed. He doubted that Devynck had been that polite—unless of course she was trying to impress the pointsman—and he swung himself out of bed. "Tell her I'll be down as soon as I put some clothes on."

"All right," Loret said, and there was a little silence. "It's Rathe," he added, and Eslingen heard the sound of his footsteps retreating toward the stairs.

And what in all the hells do I care which pointsman it is? Eslingen swallowed the comment as pointless, and crossed to his chest to find clean clothes. His best shirt was sorely in need of washing, and his second best needed new cuffs and collar, and the third and fourth best were little better than rags. He made a face, but shrugged on the second best, hoping the pointsman wouldn't notice the frayed fabric and the darned spot below the collar. He finished dressing, winding his cravat carefully, and thought that the fall of its ends would hide the worst of it. There was no time to shave, but he tugged his hair into a loose queue, and then made his way down the stairs to the tap.

Rathe was standing in the middle of the wide room, the light of the true sun pouring in through the unshuttered windows and washing over him, turning his untidy curls to bronze as he bent his head to note something in his tablets. Devynck stood opposite him, arms folded across her chest, and the two waiters were loitering behind the bar, trying to pretend they were doing something useful. Jasanten, the only one of the lodgers who had his breakfast at the tavern, as a concession either to past friendship or to his missing leg, was watching more openly from his table in the corner.

"—complaint," Devynck was saying, and Eslingen hid a grin. So she was going to go through with her threat of the night before.

"Oh, come on, Aagte," Rathe said, but kept his tablet out. "Complaint of what? You keep a public tavern, you can hardly accuse the boy of trespass for coming here."

"Felis Lucenan's been told more than once that he's not welcome here," Devynck answered. "He comes around, makes a nuisance of himself—lies to the recruiters when they're here, tries to get someone to take him on as a runner. I told him a moon-month ago not to come back, and last night, well." She fixed Rathe with a sudden stare. "I want it on the books, the times being what they are, that I don't invite him."

Rathe grinned, showing slightly crooked teeth. "I can't say I blame you, at that. All right, I'll note it down, see it's posted on the station books. And I'll send someone round to Lucenan's shop to make sure she knows you want her to keep the boy at home."

Devynck made a face, but nodded. "I suppose you have to do that, not that it'll win me friends."

"Fair's fair, Aagte. Maybe it'll make the boy a little warier, if he knows we're taking an interest." Rathe looked toward the doorway then. "Good morning, Eslingen."

"Morning." The pointsman had the look of someone who relished early rising, and Eslingen sighed. "Though I don't usually get up til the next sunrise."

"I'm sorry," Rathe said, without much sincerity.

"That was all I wanted with you, Nico," Devynck said. "People around here are starting to look sideways at me, and it's not my doing."

"I know," Rathe answered. "So does Monteia. We're doing what we can."

Devynck made a face, as though she would say something else, but visibly thought better of it. "I hope it gets results," she said instead, and went back to the kitchen, slamming the door behind her.

"So what can I do for you, pointsman?" Eslingen said, after a moment.

Rathe gave another quick grin. "I heard you had another bit of difficulty last night."

"That's right." Eslingen took a breath, preparing himself to launch into the story, and Rathe lifted a hand, at the same moment folding his tablets.

"You don't need to go through it again unless you want to, I got the bones of it from Adriana. And Felis is—known to us, as they say in the judiciary. We've had this trouble with him before."

"Then what—" Eslingen swallowed his words, went on more moderately, "What do you need me for, pointsman?"

"Why'd I get you out of bed at this hour?" Rathe asked, disconcertingly, and Eslingen nodded.

"Not to put too fine a point on it, yes."

"A couple of reasons," Rathe answered, and nodded toward one of the tables by the garden windows. "I asked Adriana if I could get a bite while I'm here, you want to join me?"

"Why not?" Eslingen settled himself on the nearest of the well worn stools, tilting it so that his back rested against the cool plaster of the wall. At the moment, the sun was pleasant on his booted feet, but he knew that within an hour or two it would be uncomfortably hot. And I should find a cobbler as well as a seamstress, he added, and shook the thought away. With things as uncertain as they were in Astreiant right now, it seemed foolish to spend money on things he didn't really need.

Rathe perched gracelessly on the stool opposite him, resting his elbows on the tabletop. "First, I wanted to ask you if you'd seen or heard anything that might have a bearing on these missing children."

"Why ask me?" Eslingen demanded, and let his stool fall forward with a thump as Adriana appeared from the kitchen.

"Bread and cheese and a good pot of tea," she announced. "That's all we've got at the moment."

"It looks lovely," Eslingen said, and meant it.

Rathe nodded his agreement, and, to Eslingen's surprise, reached into his pocket for his purse, came out with a handful of copper. "How much?"

Adriana waved away the proffered coins. "No charge—and not a fee, either."

"Aagte's not going to like it," Rathe said.

"It's on me, not the house," Adriana answered, and winked at Eslingen. "And I won't say who for."

"Fair enough," Rathe said, to her departing back, and slipped the coins back into his purse. He seemed about to say something more, reached instead for the fat teapot and the nearer of the cups. "Why ask you—lieutenant, right?"

"Right." Eslingen accepted the cup of tea, wrapped his hands around the warming pottery. "I'm practically a stranger here, Rathe."

"That's partly why," Rathe said, indistinctly, his mouth full of bread. He swallowed, said, more clearly, "There's a chance you might notice something a local might not—someone acting odd, say, when it's a change that's happened slowly enough that everyone else has just gotten used to it."

For a wild moment, Eslingen considered blaming the butcher's journeyman Paas, but put the thought aside instantly. "Not a thing, and I wish I had. The neighbors are starting to look sideways at us, and I can't find a laundress I'd trust for love nor money."

Rathe grinned at that. "I didn't really think you had, but it was worth asking."

"Then it's true what they're saying—" Eslingen broke off, tardily aware of what he had been about to say. What the neighborhood gossips were saying was that the points didn't have any more idea than anyone else of what was happening to the children.

"That we don't have a clue what's happening?" Rathe finished, and Eslingen saw with some relief that he didn't seem offended. "It's no secret. Kids've gone missing from all over the city, and no, there's nothing in common among them, and no one's found a body or seen a child being stolen, for all the talk of child-thieves. Which brings me to the other reason I'm here. You've heard the rumor that the kids are being taken by recruiters?"

Eslingen snorted, swallowed a mouthful of bread and cheese. "Yeah, I've heard it. I've heard a lot of other tales, too."

"I'm not accusing you or any soldier," Rathe said, mildly, and Eslingen grimaced at his own haste.

"Sorry. It's a sore point."

Rathe nodded. "I daresay. But my question for you is, all right, if it's not recruiters, why not?"

Eslingen stared at him for a minute, wondering where to begin, and Rathe held up a hand.

"I've never been a soldier, and we don't get much soldiers' business in Point of Hopes. Aagte's is about the only tavern that caters to your custom. Now, in other businesses I know of, children are cheap, cheaper than adults, but not for you, it seems."

"It takes strength to trail a pike," Eslingen said, "and height helps, too. The same for a piece, to stand the recoil. You want a man grown, or woman, or something close to it."

"How old were you when you signed on?" Rathe asked, and Eslingen made a face.

"Fourteen, but I joined as a sergeant's runner. And, yes, you don't need much skill or size—or anything—for that, but you don't want dozens of them, either." He took a breath. "Besides, there were three royal regiments paid off a week ago, and the recruiters can have their pick of them. No one wants kids." That wasn't quite true—there were regiments, like the pioneers Jasanten was recruiting for, that had a bad reputation, or lacked any reputation at all, that wouldn't attract any but the most desperate veterans. Even the most spendthrift wouldn't need money yet. He met Rathe's eyes squarely, and hoped the pointsman would believe him.

"There must be jobs an experienced man wouldn't take," Rathe said, and Eslingen swore under his breath. "What about them?"

"Why don't you ask Flory, there?" he asked, and heard himself turn sharp and irritable. "He's recruiting for a company like that—and it was him who turned the Lucenan boy down flat, pointsman."

"I will," Rathe answered, imperturbably. "If you'll introduce me."

Eslingen sighed, let the stool fall again. "Come on."

Rathe followed him easily, still carrying his cup of tea, and Eslingen wished for a moment he'd had the sense to do that himself. But it made Rathe look as though he rarely got a decent meal—the crumpled coat, worn to shapelessness over the pointsman's leather jerkin, added to that impression—and Eslingen refused to show himself that needy. Even when he had been close to starving, years back, he had known better than to betray himself that way.

Jasanten looked up at their approach, narrowed eyes flicking from Rathe to Eslingen and then back again, taking in the royal monogram on the truncheon tucked into Rathe's belt. He didn't move, and Eslingen said, hastily, "Flor, this is Nicolas Rathe, he's a pointsman—sorry, adjunct point—at Point of Hopes. Flory Jasanten."

Jasanten nodded, still distant, and Eslingen wished he'd kept his own mouth shut. It was too late for that, though, and he contented himself with saying, "Rathe's all right, Flor."

Out of the corner of his eye, he saw Rathe give him a quick glance, though whether it was startled or grateful he couldn't be sure, and then Jasanten grunted, and used his crutch to push a couple of stools away from his table.

"Sit down, then, why don't you."

Rathe did as he was told, his expression cheerfully neutral, but Eslingen wished suddenly that he knew what the other was thinking behind that mask. "I heard you had a bit of trouble, last night."

Jasanten snorted, looked at Eslingen. "You, too, Philip, I may want a witness of my own."

"And will you need one?" Rathe murmured. His voice was still just as neutral, but Eslingen could almost feel him snap to inward attention.

"It's all right, Flor," he said again, and settled himself on the second stool. I hope, he added silently. But Aagte seems to trust him.

Jasanten nodded once, looked back at Rathe. "I saw you talking to Aagte. If you talked to her, you know what happened, and you know I'm not hiring children. So what do you want with me?"

"The same thing I wanted with Eslingen—the same thing I want with anyone here," Rathe answered. "First, anything you might know about these kids—someone who might be recruiting them, or claim to be recruiting, anything you've heard." He paused then, and Eslingen glanced sideways to see the grey eyes narrowed slightly under the bird's-wing brows, as though the pointsman was searching for something in the distance. "The kid who's gone missing from the Knives Road—you'll have heard about that, that's the case that's got this neighborhood up in arms. She's twelve, got no family to speak of, just walked out of a good apprenticeship—left everything she owned sitting in her chest, and she was a girl who appreciated her things—and all I've got to go on is a drunk journeyman who says he might've seen her going south from the street, and a laundress who says she might've seen her, too, but going north. Now, you know as well as I do what this could mean, some madman killing or hurting for the sake of it, though so far we haven't found bodies, and no necromancer has reported a new ghost."

"They can bind ghosts," Jasanten said, almost in spite of himself, and Rathe nodded.

"So they can. It's not easy, or so I'm told. I'm not a scholar, but it can be done."

"A madman might have the strength for it," Eslingen said. "They're stronger physically than they ought to be, maybe it works the same for a magist."

Rathe looked at him, the thin brows drawing down. "Now there's a happy thought."

Eslingen shrugged, and Jasanten said, "That's right, you were with Coindarel three years ago."

Eslingen sighed—it was a subject he preferred not to think about—but nodded. Rathe cocked his head to one side in silent question, and Eslingen sighed again. "There was a man, a new recruit, out of Dhenin—he was a butcher by his original trade, in point of fact—he raped a woman and murdered her. It was pretty clear who it was, and the prince-marshal hanged him, Rathe, so you needn't look sideways at everyone who was paid off from the Dragons, either. But it took seven men to hold him, when they came to arrest him. And he was mad, that one."

"I remember the broadsheets," Rathe said. "It was a nine-days' wonder." He sighed, then. "And I hope to Demis you're wrong about madmen being magistically stronger, but I'll check that out. It's a nasty thought."

Jasanten nodded, leaning forward to plant both elbows on the table. "You'll find it's someone like that. It has to be. No one else would have cause. Areton's beard, I'm recruiting for Filipon's Pioneers, and they've had two years of hard luck now, but I can still find grown men, even experienced men, who need a place."

"The business," Rathe said, with a straight face, "just hasn't been the same since the League War ended."

"No more it has," Jasanten agreed, and then shot the younger man a wary look.

Rathe kept his expression sober, however, and said, "Eslingen here tells me you don't want kids because they're too small to handle the weapons and they don't have skills you want. What about kids who knew how to handle horses, would you want them?"

"Ah." Jasanten smiled. "Now that's another matter, I admit. If you've got kids missing from stables, Rathe, yeah, I'd look to the recruiters. A boy with the right stars and the knack for it, or a girl, for that matter, there are girls enough born under Seidos's signs, they could find a place if they wanted it. Or with the caravans, for that matter."

Rathe glanced again at Eslingen, and the dark-haired man nodded, reluctantly. "A kid would come cheaper than a trooper, and you always need people to tend to the horses. But a butcher's brat wouldn't be my first choice."

"No," Rathe agreed. He drained the last of his tea, and stood up, stretching in the fall of sunlight. "Thanks for your help, Jasanten, Eslingen—and, Eslingen, remember. If you have any trouble, anything you can't handle, that is, send to Point of Hopes."

"I'll do that," Eslingen answered, impressed in spite of himself, and the pointsman nodded and turned away. Eslingen watched him go, and Jasanten shook his head.

"I don't hold with that," he said, and Eslingen looked back at him.

"Don't hold with what?"

"Pointsmen." Jasanten shook his head again. "It's not right, common folk like him having to tend the law. That's the seigneury's job, they were born to protect us—and you mark my words, Philip, this business won't be settled until the Metropolitan gets off her ass and does something about it."

Eslingen shrugged. He himself would rather trust a common man than some noble who had no idea of what ordinary folk might have to do to live, but he knew there were plenty of people who agreed with Jasanten—and it was, he had to admit, generally harder to buy a noble. "Maybe," he said aloud, and stood, slowly. "I have to go, Flor."

Jasanten looked up at him, an odd smile on his lips, but he said only, "You don't want to waste a free breakfast."

"No," Eslingen agreed, and decided not to ask any questions. Good luck to you, Rathe, he thought, and went back to his table and the bread and cheese and the cooling pot of tea.

He finished his breakfast quickly enough, and returned to his room to shave, and to change shirts. He had errands to run, and he was not about to risk one of his two good shirts on the expedition—and besides, he added silently, he might have the good fortune to find a laundress who'd be willing to take his business. He tucked it back with the others in his chest, and shrugged himself into an older, coarser shirt, well aware that the unbleached fabric was less than flattering to his complexion. But that was hardly the point, he reminded himself, and slipped into the lightest of his coats. He should also probably find himself an astrologer as well, see what guidance she or he could provide—the broadsheets did well enough for entertainment, and for general trends, but these days, with the climate of the city less than favorable toward Leaguers, it might be wise to see what the stars held for him personally.

He went back down the stairs and through the main room, where Jasanten was drowsing over the remains of his breakfast, and ducked through the hall behind the bar. There was no sign of Devynck herself, but Adriana looked up as he peered around the kitchen door.

"Do you want me this morning?" he asked, and heard the girl who helped with the cooking giggle softly.

Adriana's smile widened, but she shook her head, and tumbled a bowl of chopped vegetables into a waiting pot. "Mother will want you back at opening, but there's no reason for you to kick your heels around here all morning. Off to fetch more broadsheets?"

Eslingen shrugged. "Probably. But I feel in need of more—personal guidance. Where does one go to get a good reading done?"

She moved away from the table, wiping her hands clean on her coarse apron. "Depends on how flush you're feeling, now that you're gainfully employed, Lieutenant. There are the temples, of course, but they're expensive, and you might not want to attract the Good Counsellor's attention just now by visiting one of his people."

"Not particularly," Eslingen answered. The Good Counsellor was one of the polite, propitiating names for the Starsmith, god of death and the unseen, as well as patron of astrologers, and no soldier wanted to draw his gaze, not even in peace time.

"You could go to the Three Nations," Adriana went on. "It's what they're there for, especially this time of year." Eslingen blinked, utterly confused, and she smiled. "The university students—they call themselves the Three Nations, every student claims allegiance to one of them, Chenedolle, the North, or Overseas."

"It sounds to me as though they're leaving out a few people."

"Oh, the students lump Chadron and the League in with the Ile'nord, though a lot of Leaguers call themselves Chenedolliste," Adriana answered. "And Overseas is the Silklanders and anybody who doesn't want to be bothered with politics. It's all political, really, a game for them and a royal pain for the rest of us." She shook her head. "Anyway, the Three—the students have always had the right to cast horoscopes at the fairs, both the little fair, which is what's happening now, and the great fair. It's supposed to just be augmenting their stipend, but they tend to charge what the market will bear."

There was a distinct note of—something—in her voice, Eslingen thought. Disapproval? Contempt? Neither was quite right. "Aren't they any good?" he asked, cautiously, and she made a face.

"It's not that, they're good, all right—they'd better be, or the university would have a lot to answer for. No, it's just that . . . well, the fees are supposed to be a supplement, but they tend to charge what they can get, which can be quite a lot, and the students—well, they're students. They think well of themselves. Extremely well of themselves, in actual fact, and not nearly so well of the rest of us." She shrugged. "They're all right, they just get my back up—get everybody's backs up, really, but it's mostly because they're young and arrogant. If you can afford it, and you want the cachet of the university, such as it is, you can go to them."

"And otherwise?"

Adriana's smile was wry. "Otherwise, of course, there are the failed students who set themselves up casting charts for the printers, they're easy enough to find, or ex-temple servants who claim they know what they're doing, or—you get the idea." She stopped then, tilting her head to one side. "Talk's been of some new astrologers working the fair—not affiliated with either the temples or the university, and the word is they're a lot cheaper than the Three Nations. Shame and all that, but a lot of people are cheering the change. It's nothing important, it's just nice to see the students taken down a peg or three. Loret had his stars read by one of them, and he seemed to think they knew what they were doing."

"But where did they train? They must be connected with some temple," Eslingen said. He'd never heard of a freelance astrologer who was any good—but then, this was Astreiant. Anything could happen here.

Adriana was shaking her head. "They don't claim any allegiance. They read the stars, they say, and the stars belong to all gods and all women—and not just to the Three Nations. The arbiters must have approved them, or they'd have been chased off. So my advice to you, my Philip, is to save your money where you can, and see if you can find one of these astrologers to read for you."

"And how do I find one?" Eslingen asked.

Adriana spread her hands, and the girl looked up from the hearth. "They say they find you, if you want them."

"Nonsense," Adriana answered, and rolled her eyes at Eslingen.

"Well, they do," the girl said, sounding stubborn, and Eslingen said quickly, "How do I tell them from the Three Nations?"

"They're older, for one thing, or so I hear," Adriana said. "I heard they dress like magists, but without badges, so look for black robes, not grey, and no temple marks."

Eslingen nodded, intrigued in spite of himself. "I think I'll look for them, then. Thanks."

It was a long walk from Devynck's to the New Fairground, almost the full length of the city, but Eslingen found himself enjoying it, in spite of the heat and the crowds. Hundreds of people jostled each other in the lanes between the brightly painted booths, or clustered in the open temporary squares to bargain over goods—spices, silks, wool cloth and yarn, dyestuffs, once stacks and stacks of beaten-copper pots—spread apparently piecemeal across the beaten dirt. It was already bigger than the Esling fairs he had attended as a boy; what, he wondered, would the real fair be like when it was fully open?

He had no idea how the booths were laid out, though it was obvious that like trades were grouped together, but let himself wander with the crowd, listening with half an ear for the chime of the clock at Fairs' Point. He would have to head back to Devynck's when it struck eleven, but until then, at least, his time was his own. He found Printers' Row easily enough, a dozen or more tables set out under tents and awnings and brightly painted umbrellas, and stopped to browse. Already he recognized some of the house names and the printer's symbols, thought, too, that he recognized some of the sellers, relocated temporarily from Temple Fair. The sheets tacked to the display boards or pinned precariously to the sides of the tents were the usual kind, a mix of weekly almanacs and sheets of predictions according to each birth sign as well as the more general prophecy-sheets. Most of the last dealt directly or obliquely with the missing children, and a good number of those blamed the League, but there was one big tent, its red sides faded to a dark rose, that seemed to deal entirely with politics. And impartially, too, Eslingen added, with an inward grin. Whoever sold or printed these sheets played no favorites; Leveller tracts hung side by side with sheets touting the merits of the various noble candidates. Among the nobles, the Metropolitan of Astreiant seemed to be the popular favorite—he could count half a dozen sheets openly supporting her, though whether that was genuine liking or mere proximity was impossible to tell. However, there were also a scattering of sheets pointing out the virtues of the various northern candidates. He picked out three of those, paid his demming, and stepped back to study them. Marselion's was the least interesting, full of more bluster than scholarship, and the one supporting Palatine Sensaire was crudely done, a mere half dozen verses beneath a stock blockprint of a seated woman. But Belvis's was something different, and Eslingen paused, frowning, to read it again. It was better printed than the others, and if the verses told the truth, Belvis certainly had the appropriate stars. He knew little about her, except that she was from the Ile'nord, but the broadsheet writer had clearly gone out of her way to reassure Astreianters wary of the old-fashioned north. Palatine Belvis, it implied, kept to the best of both worlds; besides, the stars favored her, and Astreiant should do well to accept the inevitable. Eslingen's eyebrows rose at that, and he glanced automatically for the imprimatur. It was there, if blurred, and he smiled, and tucked the papers into his cuff.

The clock struck the quarter hour, and he made a face, recalling himself to his real business. If he wanted to have his stars read, he would have to hurry, at least if he wanted the job done properly—and the way the broadsheets were running, he thought, I might do well to reconsider Cijntien's offer. He glanced at another as he passed, and controlled his temper with an effort. This one openly blamed the League cities, claiming that the children were being stolen for revenge, and possibly to form the backbone of a new army that would avenge the League's defeat. From the size of the remaining stack, it hadn't sold as well as its neighbors, but even so, it was all he could do to control his anger. The League Wars had ended twenty years before, and had been about trade; since then, League and Kingdom had been close allies, and there were plenty of Leaguers like himself who'd shed their own blood in the queen's service. He shoved past a stocky man who was reaching for another sheet, and turned down the nearest path between the stalls.

His anger cooled as quickly as it had flared, and he paused at the next intersection, looking for some sign of the astrologers Adriana had mentioned. He saw a trio of grey-gowned students clustered by a food stall, but before he could consider approaching them, an older woman tapped one of them on the shoulder, only to have her coins waved away. Apparently, Eslingen thought, the students were otherwise engaged at the moment. He turned away, too, threaded his way past a group of blue-coated apprentices, and found himself in a row of linen-drapers. In spite of himself, he sighed at the sight of the bolts of expensive fabric, wishing he could afford a shirt from them, and then, at the end of the row of shops, he caught sight of a man in a black scholar's gown. The sleeves were empty of badges, and he stood deep in conversation with a woman and a boy, a plain disk orrery held to the sunlight. One of Adriana's astrologers? he wondered, and moved closer. The man was ordinary enough looking, middle-aged, middling looks, his rusty black robe open to reveal a plain dark suit and equally plain linen. There was no temple badge at his collar, either, and Eslingen took a step closer. Even as he did, the woman nodded, and turned away. The boy followed more reluctantly, looking back as though he had wanted to ask something more. Eslingen smiled in sympathy—the woman, the boy's mother, probably, hadn't looked like the sort to spend her hard-earned coins on more than the absolute necessities, which was probably why she was consulting one of the freelances rather than a student or a Temple astrologer.

"Pardon me, magist," he said. He didn't know if the astrologer was indeed actually a magist as well, doubted it, in fact, but there was no harm in inflating the man's rank.

The astrologer gave a slight smile. "No magist, sir, but an astrologer, and a good one." He tilted his head. "Are you looking to have a reading done?"

His accent was pleasant, Chenedolliste, but without the city's sharp vowels. Eslingen smiled back, and said, carefully, "Indeed, I was wanting that, the temper of the times being what they are, but I was also wondering what temple you served."

The astrologer seemed to study him for a long moment, the smile widening almost imperceptibly. "No temple, sir, the stars are free to all. But, as we serve no one master, our fees are low—and fixed."

Eslingen hid a sigh—he had hoped to talk the price down a little, on the grounds that the astrologer had no affiliation—and said, "How much?"

"Two demmings for a man grown," the astrologer answered promptly. "In advance."

The price was much lower than he had expected, and Eslingen blinked. It probably wouldn't be a brilliant reading—in his experience, one generally got what one paid for—but at that price, he could hardly refuse. "Agreed," he said, and reached into his purse for the coins.

The astrologer accepted them calmly. "A wise course, sir—especially given that you're a Leaguer, from your accent?"

Eslingen nodded, his expression wry. "As I said, the times being what they are . . . "

The astrologer smiled again, and lifted his disk orrery. "And when were you born, sir?"

"The fifth day of Sedeion, a little past half-past ten in the morning," Eslingen answered. "In the second year of this queen's reign."

The astrologer nodded, and began adjusting the rings of the orrery.

It was double-faced, Eslingen saw; the other side would be already set to this day's planetary positions, and the astrologer would take his reading from a comparison of the two. "Do you know the time any more closely—was it closer to the half hour, or to the next quarter?"

Eslingen shook his head. "Past the half hour is all I know." His mother had lost interest in keeping precise track after her third or fourth child was born, and there had never been money for a decent midwife; he had been lucky to know this much.

"Unfortunate," the astrologer said, almost absently, and held the orrery to his eyes. "Well, I'll do what I can, but I can't promise a precise accounting."

Eslingen sighed, but said nothing. The astrologer turned the orrery from one side to the other, then went on briskly. "Well. You were born under the Horse and the Horsemaster, good signs for a soldier, and the sun is still in the Horse, which is also good for you, though it left the Horsemaster four days ago. The moon is against you just now, in the Spider and the Hearthstone, but that will change with the new moon, when it returns to the Horse. Astree stands in the Horse and Horsemaster still, which is good for seeing justice done—" He smiled at that, thinly, and Eslingen's smile in return was wry. "—but it and the sun stand square to the winter-sun. Seidos is well aspected for you, both at your birth and presently; I'd say you were due to rise in the world, possibly through your trade." He shook his head then, and slipped the orrery back into his pocket beneath the rusty gown. "With the moon and the winter-sun against you, I would advise you to stay away from lunar things for the next few days, at least until the new moon. Don't travel by water until then, and be cautious once the true sun's down. All of that should end by the new moon, and you should see a change of fortune then."

And that, Eslingen thought, was that. It wasn't much, when you boiled it down to the essentials—be careful after sundown, a reasonable enough statement in a large city, and a chance that he would change his status, possibly through his trade, with the new moon. But it was something, and the statement that Astree was placed to insure that justice would be done was a little reassuring. "Thanks," he said aloud, and the astrologer gave an odd, almost old-fashioned bow.

"My pleasure to serve," he said, and turned away.

Eslingen watched him go, and was startled at how fast the man seemed to vanish in the crowd, despite the conspicuous black robe. Still, it made sense to be inconspicuous when the trade was new, especially when they were undercutting an established group. More power to you, he thought, and heard the Fairs' Point clock strike the hour. He turned back toward the Old Brown Dog, and hoped that the astrologer's prediction was right about things changing at the new moon.

Rathe left the Old Brown Dog in an odd mood. He believed what the recruiter had said, that he wouldn't take children when he could get adults, believed, too, that he would only want the ones with Seidos in their stars, or at least practice with horses, if he were to take children. But it was quite obvious that Jasanten hadn't quite trusted him, and wondered if he should make further inquiries about the recruiter. It was probably nothing, he decided—if nothing else, he couldn't see a one-legged man having much success taking children against their will—but he made a mental note to speak to Eslingen again, find out what he knew about Jasanten. Devynck's new knife seemed a decent sort, and, more than that, he seemed to have the happy faculty of resolving potentially difficult situations without bloodshed. He'd never thought of that as a soldier's skill before, but he suspected Devynck would be glad of it.

The tower clock at the north end of the Hopes-point Bridge struck the hour, and he quickened his pace. He wanted to talk to Foucquet before she left for the judiciary, which meant, practically speaking, any time before nine o'clock. If she had been willing to ask Fourie to intervene in the matter of this missing clerk, rather than going through the usual channels, she would certainly be willing to be a little late to the courts to talk to him. And after that . . . he sighed, contemplating the day's work. After that, he would swing through Temple Fair, see if he could track down some of the broadsheets that had so annoyed Monteia. Publishing without a license was a nuisance in good times, but in bad, and these were beginning to be undeniably bad times, the unlicensed printers seemed to take positive glee in spreading predictions of disaster.

Foucquet lived in the Horsegate District, outside the city walls, an easy walk from the judiciary and the lesser courts that met at the Tour de la Cité. Rathe had been there many times before, first in Foucquet's service, and then during his time at University Point, but he always took a guilty pleasure in walking the wide, well-swept street, walled on either side by the multi-colored bricks of the grand-clerks' houses. Most of them had gardens attached, nothing as extensive as the parklands of the Western Reach, but enough to perfume the air with the hint of greenery. Rathe lifted his head as he passed under the shadow of a fruit tree. The flowers were long gone, the fruit hard green knobs among the darker leaves, but he could imagine the scent of their ripening. He heard children calling behind an iron gate, and glanced sideways to see a girl, maybe six or seven, gesturing imperiously over the head of her hobbyhorse, directing a trio of younger children as though she were a royal marshal. Their nursemaid saw him, too, and the sharpened stare and quick frown were enough to erase his pleasure. No children that young had gone missing—yet—but the woman was wise to take no chances. He moved on, never breaking stride, but he was aware of the woman's eyes on him for some time after, and looked back at the corner to see her standing in the gate, watching warily.

Foucquet's house was in the middle range, better than her mother's house had been, certainly, but far from the most expensive the Horsegate had to offer. Rathe rang the bell at the side door, the appellant's door—there was no point in alienating her household just now—and nodded to the red-robed clerk who came scurrying to answer. "Nicolas Rathe, Point of Hopes," he said. "I need to speak with Her Excellency."

The clerk's eyes widened. "You haven't—" she began, and Rathe shook his head.

"No, mistress, no word. I just need to get some information."

The clerk relaxed slightly, her disappointment evident, but held the door a little wider. She was young for her post, a bright-eyed, round-cheeked girl with a complexion like milk and roses, copper-gilt hair tucked imperfectly under her tall cap. "Come in, pointsman. Her Excellency's just dressing."

Rathe followed her down the narrow hall, past familiar painted panels, flowers, and fruiting trees that were almost invisible in the morning shadow, and then up the curved main staircase to the first floor. Foucquet was waiting in her bedroom, arms lifted to let one of her women lace the stiff corset into place over shirt and petticoats. A second woman was waiting with skirt and bodice, and a clerk sat on a low tabouret, reading from a sheaf of notes. She broke off as Rathe appeared, and Foucquet waved her away.

"All right, we can finish that later, thank you. What do you want with me this time, Rathe?" She gestured to the hovering maid, who dropped the massive skirt over her head, fastening it deftly over the flurry of petticoats. Foucquet shrugged on the bodice offered by the second woman, stood still while she fastened the dozens of buttons.

"I wanted to talk to you about this missing clerk of yours," Rathe answered.

"Ah." Foucquet nodded to the second maid, who had collected the massive scarlet robe of office and stood waiting with it. "No, leave that for now. All of you, that's all for the moment, thank you. Tefana, warn me at the half hour, if we're not done by then."

"Yes, Excellency," the older clerk answered, collecting her papers. The younger clerk and the maids followed her from the room, the last of the maids closing the double doors behind her. Foucquet crossed to her dressing table, skirts rustling, seated herself in front of the array of pots and brushes.

"You'll forgive me if I go on making ready," she said, "but I'm more than willing to answer any questions."

"Thanks," Rathe said. Her hands were painted, he saw without surprise, saw too the graceful movements with which she opened the tiny vials and began repairing blemished spots with the touch of a tiny brush. He had known forgers less deft, but then, Foucquet was always careful of her appearance.

"I would have thought you'd gotten the case from Point of Hearts," Foucquet went on, and added a dot of gold leaf to the painted arabesques coiling across her right hand. "I told them what I thought when they were here."

Rathe shook his head. "Haven't had the chance, Excellency. The surintendant only told me last night you wanted me to handle this."

Foucquet looked up sharply, her brush, laden this time with a drop of red paint bright as blood, poised in midair. "I—?" She broke off, touched the brush to its proper place in the design. "I didn't make any such request, Nico. I know how jealous the points are of their territories. Besides, as I told Hearts, I have a shrewd idea where the boy's gone."

"You didn't ask the sur to have me take the case?" Rathe asked.

"No." Foucquet's eyes narrowed, deepening the lines at their outer corners. "What's he up to, Nico?"

"I wish I knew." Rathe frowned. It was hard to see what Fourie might gain from assigning him to this particular case—if he'd wanted me to look into Caiazzo's maybe-connection to all of this, he could've just told me to do it, he added, with a feeling of genuine grievance. Or was he worried that someone would find out what I was supposed to be doing? If there's a political dimension to all of this, which he seems certain there is, then maybe he's wise to treat it this way. He put those concerns aside for later consideration, looked back at Foucquet. "You say you think you know what happened to the boy?"

Foucquet smiled, a rueful expression. "Albe's theater-mad—and talented, too, though his mother won't see it. I think he ran away to join one of the companies. It's not a bad time of year for it, they always need extra help for the fair."

That was true enough, and Rathe nodded. "How would he know where to run, though? The players aren't quite a closed guild, but they tend to stick together." And they don't much like northriver kids coming in and taking places away from their own, he added silently.

Foucquet sighed, stared for a moment at the paint now drying on her hands. "I have been—seeing—someone recently. An actress in Savatier's troupe."

"Her name?" Rathe reached for his tablets.

"Anjesine bes'Hallen. She lives in Point of Dreams."

"Chadroni, by her name." Rathe didn't bother commenting on her residence; most players lived where they worked.

Foucquet nodded. "Born there, yes, but she's lived here a long time." She looked away again. "She was here the night Albe ran, he might have gone with her."

"And you haven't asked her?" Rathe knew he sounded incredulous, and Foucquet made a face.

"We've parted ways, and not entirely happily, either. And with Albe's mother as set against it as she is, I didn't want to cause her trouble. I confess, I'm not sorry to see you handling this, even if I didn't ask for it."

Rathe nodded. "What did you tell them at Hearts, about bes'Hallen?"

"That she and I were, or had been, friends," Foucquet answered. "And I told them the boy wanted to be a player."

"Well, that should give them plenty to work with," Rathe said. "I'll make a few inquiries of my own, if you'd like, though."

"I'd be grateful," Foucquet answered. "I'm afraid Hearts will be too blinded by these other children to look closely at Albe. And he's still well under age, I suppose it's his mother's right to say what she'll have him do."

"I suppose," Rathe said, with less conviction. He had met too many mothers, and fathers, too, who seemed determined to set their children's feet on the wrong paths to agree easily with the judge-advocate. "I'll do what I can."

"Thank you," Foucquet said. "And, Nico. Do let me know what happens, whatever the hour. I won't forgive myself if he's not at the theaters."

Rathe nodded, and Foucquet reached for a bell to summon one of her servants. The younger clerk appeared almost at once, quickly enough that Rathe half suspected her of listening outside the double doors. She said nothing, however, and let him out into the rising warmth of the morning with quick courtesy.

Rathe squinted at the sky, but there was no point visiting either theaters or actors until the second sunrise, and he was unlikely to get real sense from anyone until late afternoon. That left Caiazzo and the unlicensed printers on his book: the Pantheon was closer, and more or less on his way, and he knew one or two stall-keepers in Temple Fair who should be able to give him some of the information he needed. He sighed, and started back toward the Horsegate.

It wasn't a long walk to Temple Fair. Rathe made his way across the open square, dodging travellers and the usual crowd of idlers, and climbed the three steps to the gallery that surrounded the Pantheon itself. There, he leaned against the sun-warmed stone, one booted foot braced against the wall, and tried to pretend that he was reading the crudely printed broadsheet nailed to the pillar in front of him. It was typical of its kind, obscure astrology married to bad poetry, embellished with an illustration of Areton in full armor confronting Dis-Aidones across a shield marked with a device that might have been intended to be a map of the kingdom. The dozen-plus-three couplets analyzed the position of the Areton-star in the heavens, and concluded that Chenedolle must stand adamant against unspecified enemies. It also predicted earthquakes at the equinox, but more as an afterthought. Rathe glanced automatically for the imprimatur, and found it—but then, he thought, either the printer or the astrologer had been careful to leave no grounds for refusal. Areton was a neutral god, patron of soldiers and sportsmen, and giver of courage; his worship was either specialized or cut across class and national boundaries, and his temples served as strongboxes for long-distance traders worldwide. If it had shown Seidos standing against the Starsmith, or one of the Seideian Heroes, or even Seidos's Horse, then it would have been political: Seidos was the protector of the Ile'nord and of the nobility, and the Ile'norders had been vociferous in their support for Marselion. But Areton was safe.

He let his eyes range out between the pillars, squinting a little into the sunlight of the Temple Fair. Beyond the steps that led up into the Pantheon, the flat grey flagstones were drifted with dust and debris. The booksellers' apprentices had swept it into tidy piles beside the shopfronts, but in the center of the fair the dust lay pale as straw against the bluestone flags, swirled into patterns by passing feet. Of all

Astreiant's fairgrounds, only Temple Fair was paved; the horses' hooves rang loud on the stones, and the horsebrats were busy, their shrill cries—*Horse, ma'am, hold your horse?*—greeting the passing riders. Even this early, the fair was busy, a crowd of shopkeepers and their servants clustering beneath the booksellers' bright red awnings, their bright finery shadowed here and there with the solid black of a student's gown. Another pair of scholars, thin, serious women in their dusty gowns, arms weighted with books, crossed the fair by the most direct route, heedless of the traffic: heading for the college, Rathe guessed, and an early class. A young man with a parasol, finely dressed, with painted hands and face, paused to listen to the ballad-singer on her platform in the fair's southeastern curve, joining for a moment an audience of two chubby boys and a barefoot servant girl. The woman's voice, and the fiddler's scratching accompaniment, blended into the hum of the crowd, barely audible above that general noise. The ballad sellers weren't doing their usual business, despite the singer's best efforts. Most of the customers were clustered at the line of makeshift stalls between the Queen's-road and the northern Highway where the vendors of prophecies plied their trade. Rathe let his eyes slide along the line of tables, picking out familiar faces—Ponset de Ruyr, whose wife owned two presses and a brothel southriver; the Leaguer Greitje vaan Brijx, red-faced and sweating under her wide-brimmed hat; a thin-faced boy who had to be the son of Saissana Peire, minding the store while his mother was serving her latest two months for unbonded printing; and, finally, the man he was looking for, a big man, sweating freely in the heat, his thinning hair hanging lank around his heavy face. Gallabet Lebrune had gone grey since he got his bond, Rathe noted, with a certain satisfaction, and pushed himself away from the wall.

Lebrune was doing a brisk business, and enjoying himself at it. His big hands moved deftly among the piled sheets of his stock, selecting and rolling each chosen prophecy into a tidy cylinder to be handed across the table in exchange for a demming or two quickly pocketed, as though it was beneath his and his customers' dignity to notice the exchange of coin. And I'd wager he makes a tiny sum shortchanging them that way, too, Rathe thought, and couldn't quite suppress a smile. Lebrune was a petty thief and a liar, but he had a style about him that you couldn't help admiring.

Copies of the various prophecies were tacked to the tabletop; three more, the newest or the most popular, were pinned to an upright board, and Rathe joined the crowd waiting to read them, insinuating himself neatly into the group behind a pair of blue-coated apprentices who should have known better. He peered past a feathered hat at the smeared lines of verse—Lebrune's printing skills hadn't improved, at any rate—and a crude woodcut of an astrologer hunched over a writing desk, and a woman jostled him, turning instantly in apology.

"Sorry—"

The rest of whatever she would have said died on her lips as she saw the jerkin and the crowned truncheon tucked into Rathe's belt. She smiled nervously, licked her lips, and turned quickly away. The nearer apprentice saw her abrupt departure, and glanced up and back, eyes widening as he took in the pointsman's uniform. He nudged his friend, not subtly. The second boy looked back, scowling, and the first one said, "Come *on*."

The second apprentice's eyes widened almost comically, and his friend grabbed him by the elbow, dragging him away. "Pardon, pointsman—"

That word was enough to turn heads all along the tabletop. A young gentleman—would-be gentleman, Rathe amended, with an inward grin—paused in the act of handing his demmings to Lebrune, but then drew himself up to complete the transaction with outward composure. He accepted the neatly rolled papers, and stalked quickly away, flicking open his parasol to put its shield between himself and the pointsman.

"You're bloody bad for business, you're poison, you are," Lebrune snarled, watching his customers vanish. "What do you want?"

Rathe took an idle step closer, still looking at the prophecies pinned to the standing board. "Paid your bond yet?"

"You know I have, pointsman, so I take it poorly you frightening away my customers."

Rathe shrugged, unpinned one of the sheets to look at it more closely. "If you're bonded, Lebrune, what reason did they have to be afraid of me?"

"Maybe they think you're stealing children," Lebrune muttered. Rathe dropped the sheet and reached across the table to seize Lebrune by his jerkin collar.

"That's not funny at the best of time. If you've got reason to believe there are pointsmen behind these disappearances, you tell me."

"I don't, Rathe, it's nothing more than you'll hear in half a dozen taverns!"

Rathe released the man with an oath. "North or southriver?"

"North. 'Course, southriver, they think it's northriver merchants. When it's not Leaguers. But it's all pretty ugly, and the, um, independent printers are having a field day with it." Lebrune spoke with the contempt of the recently legitimized, and Rathe acknowledged it with a sour smile.

"Caiazzo used to fee you, didn't he? Who's he fielding these days?" Rathe asked, overriding the other's inarticulate protest.

"I'm bonded, Rathe, how should I know who's printing under Caiazzo's coin?"

Rathe just looked at the other man, eyes hooded. After a moment, he said, "Just what kind of a fool do you take me for, Lebrune? No, I'm curious." He put his hands down on the table edge and leaned forward. The wood creaked slightly, and Lebrune grimaced.

"I've heard," he said, with delicate emphasis that suited oddly with his oversize frame, "that he's supporting a number of free-readers who are doubtless printing their findings."

"A name?" Rathe asked gently.

Lebrune gave him a fulminating look, but said, "One I know of is Agere. You'll probably find her working the Horsefair these days. Or she may have moved to the New Fair by now, she usually works there at Midsummer."

"So which is it?"

"How would I—?"

"Oh, Lebrune," Rathe said, and the printer sighed.

"New Fair, probably. Certainly."

Rathe nodded and straightened his back. "Thanks, Lebrune. Have a busy day."

Lebrune's response was profane. Rathe grinned and turned away.

It made sense, he thought, as he joined the traffic heading east along the Fairs' Road. The fair didn't officially open for another three days, but there were always a few dozen merchants who managed to get permission to open their stalls a day or two early in exchange for an early closing, and there were even more Astreianters eager to get a start on the semiholiday. What better place to sell unlicensed broadsheets than in the middle of that confusion?

He found the row of printers' stalls easily enough, set into the shade of a stable on the western end of the New Fair itself. At the moment, they were encroaching on the spaces generally held by the painter-stainers, but that guild's representatives had yet to make their appearance, and the fairkeepers were currently more concerned with dividing the prime space at the center of the fair to everyone's satisfaction. Administering the fair was a thankless task, falling to each of the major guilds in turn, and not for the first time Rathe was glad there was no pointsman's guild. They had enough to do to keep the peace without having to administer the fair as well.

Unfortunately, it was early enough that the broadsheet sellers hadn't collected many browsers, and Rathe was conspicuous in his jerkin and truncheon. For a moment, he considered trying to hide at least the truncheon, but put that aside as impractical. Agere, and any of the others who were printing without a bond, would be watching for just that kind of trouble; better to keep out of sight, and think of something better. Before he could think just what, however, a voice called his name.

"Rathe! I hope you're not poaching, my son."

Rathe turned to see a stocky man, his truncheon thrust into a belt that strained over his barrel-shaped body. His jerkin, white leather, not the usual brown or black, was stamped with a floral pattern that sat rather oddly on his bulk. "Chief Point," he answered, warily. Anything that brought Guillen Claes to the fair in his own person had to be of significance; Claes preferred to leave the fairgrounds to his subordinates, and concentrate his attention on the rest of Fairs' Point.

"So, if you're not poaching, what possessed Monteia to give you a day off so early in the fair season?" Claes went on.

"It's not poaching," Rathe answered. "We've had some problems with illegal broadsheets being sold in Point of Hopes; I've traced one of the printers here."

"You think," Claes said, and Rathe grinned.

"I think. But I'm pretty sure."

"Who?"

"The name I have is Agere," Rathe said.

"Franteijn Agere," Claes repeated. "It wouldn't surprise me."

"I've also heard that she's printing under Caiazzo's coin," Rathe went on, and the other man snorted.

"Also wouldn't surprise me. But I'd be astonished if you proved a point on him."

"Frankly, so would I," Rathe answered. He glanced around, seeing only the usual early fair-goers, mostly merchants, small and large, buying their goods before the general crowd. He thought he caught a glimpse of a black robe—one of the runners' astrologers?—but it whisked out of sight behind a stall before he could be sure. He sighed and lowered his voice before going on. "I came here mostly to see what she was printing, see if she is the one we're after, but there's not enough of a crowd. And I'm a little conspicuous to do my own shopping. I was going to send one of our runners, but, seeing as you're here,

I wonder if I might borrow one of yours. We'd be willing to split the point."

Claes nodded, appeased. "I trust you'll remember that when the time comes." He lifted a hand, and a skinny boy seemed to appear out of thin air. He was barefoot, toes caked with dirt, and shirt and breeches were well faded, imperfectly patched. He looked like any one of the dozens of urchins who gathered to run errands at the fairs, and Rathe nodded in appreciation of the disguise. The boy grinned back at him, showing better teeth than Rathe would have expected, but the eyes he fixed on Claes were wary.

"This is Guillot," Claes said. "He's one of our runners—not the best, not the worst."

Rathe nodded, and fished in his purse for a couple of demmings. "I'm looking for a broadsheet, printed without license, and I think you'll find it at Agere's stall. That's the one with the three gargoyles for its sign."

The boy nodded. "I know Agere. Was it a particular sheet, or will any one do?"

"The one I want shows a horse and rider, a woman rider, and a tree behind her that's full of fruit. I think they're supposed to be apples." Rathe held out the demmings, and Guillot took them eagerly. "Pick up any others that look interesting."

Guillot nodded again, and scurried away, to disappear between a pair of canvas-walled stalls. Claes watched him go, turned back to face the younger man only when he was out of sight. "How are things in Point of Hopes?"

"Nothing new," Rathe answered. There was no point in pretending to misunderstand. "Our missing ones are still missing, and the locals are blaming a Leaguer tavern."

"Which it isn't?"

"Which it isn't, at least not as far as I or Monteia can see," Rathe said. "Anything new here?"

Claes shook his head. "Not a thing. I've been keeping a watch on the caravaners, of course, but there aren't that many in yet—more coming in every day, of course, but the stalls aren't more than half filled. And we're watching the ship-captains." He shook his head again, mouth twisting into a bitter smile. "I've a pair of twins missing, I thought sure we'd find them on the docks—they're river-mad, the pair of them, but they've got Phoebe in the Sea-bull's house."

"Not good for travel by water," Rathe said, and Claes nodded.

"So you can understand they wouldn't find a riverman willing to take them on as apprentices. But then Jaggi—Jagir, his name is, he's one of our juniors, bright, too—he tells me the Silklanders don't read that configuration the same way, so I thought sure we'd found them." He sighed. "But my people have been up and down the docks and not a sign of them. No one remembers them, and you'd think someone would, a pair of identical redheaded thirteen-year-olds."

"Paid not to remember?" Rathe asked, without much hope.

"By whom? Besides, there are too many people on the docks. Someone would have noticed."

Rathe nodded. Redhaired twins would surely be noticed. "I'll have our people ask along the Factors' Walk and the Rivermarket, just in case, but I wouldn't hold my breath."

"Nor will I," Claes answered, sourly, then said, "but I would take it kindly, Rathe. Thanks. It's just—we've got these printers, and then the bloody astrologers to deal with on top of it all."

"And about those astrologers," Rathe began grimly. Claes lifted a hand.

"Freelances, no temple, no training, and they're infesting the grounds like a pack of black gargoyles," he said. "The arbiters say they're all right, but the Three Nations are getting mutinous. And that's all we need, student riots, to round out a really exciting fair."

Rathe nodded his agreement, and the boy Guillot appeared from between a different pair of stalls, a sheaf of papers in his hand. "Sir? Were these the ones you wanted?"

Rathe took the smeared pages from him, flipped quickly through them. Agere was a better printer than Lebrune, but she'd obviously worked in haste. The images—woodcuts, from the look of them, easily made and as easily burned, eliminating evidence—lay crooked on the page, and here and there a letter sat askew, or had been put in upside down. The message, however, was clear enough: the stars said the queen should name her heir, and the clear implication was that she should name Palatine Marselion. "These are the ones."

"They've all got a bond mark," Guillot said.

"Forged," Rathe said. "Look closer."

The boy did as he was told, and grinned suddenly. Rathe smiled back—it took a certain sense of humor to replace the wand of justice carried by the hooded Sofia at the center of the seal with Tyrseis's double-headed jester's stick—and looked at Claes. "As I said, we'll split the point with you, but it doesn't seem the best time to be playing politics."

Claes nodded. "Leave Agere to me, Rathe. You catch your sellers, and we'll be ready."

"Thanks," Rathe answered, and turned away. Neither man mentioned Caiazzo: proving his involvement, that it was his coin that paid for ink and paper, would require either a stroke of luck or a major mistake on Caiazzo's part, and that was more than anyone dared hope for at this point.

Caiazzo lived in a low, sprawling house in the river district of Customs Point, a new-style house, not one of the old half-fortresses. Rathe ignored the discreet alley that led to the trades' entrance and instead climbed the three broad steps that led to the main door. They were freshly washed, too, he noticed, as he let the striker fall, not just swept. But then, Caiazzo was a great believer in matching his surroundings. Rathe let his gaze run the length of the street, surveying the other houses that stood there. Caiazzo's was exactly as well kept as the rest, his brickwork as neatly pointed, the glass in his windows no better—and no worse—than his neighbors. Strictly, geographically speaking, Customs Point was southriver, and more established merchants, even the ones who had been born here, would never dream of having their houses there. These were homes of the up-and-coming, people whose fortunes were still precarious, who still feared going back to reckoning their wealth in silver rather than gold. Caiazzo was better off than that, but he made his own rules, and he chose to live at the heart of his business, a bare five minutes' walk from the wharves at Point of Sorrows. Which made a good deal of sense, Rathe thought, given how much of that business depends on the ability to slip goods and coin discreetly between one place and another. Caiazzo was southriver born and bred, and he hadn't forsaken his heritage; some of his business methods were pure southriver, the sort honed and polished to perfection in the Court of the Thirty-two Knives. Not that Caiazzo was just any court thug, Rathe added silently, and kicked a piece of mud off the freshly washed stone.

The door opened at last to reveal a young woman in a clerk's dun suit. She looked at him inquisitively, a little dubiously, and said, "Can I help you?" She bit off the honorific, seeing the jerkin, and then her eyes widened as she saw the pointsman's truncheon in his belt. Rathe hid a grin. Caiazzo's people were mostly as southriver as himself; a northriver clerk, from a family of unbroken, unblemished history of service, would have a very different attitude toward any pointsman who presumed to knock at the front door.

"Would you tell Caiazzo that Rathe, from Point of Hopes, is here to speak with him?"

"Yes, that is . . . " She paused, and started over. "I'll see if he's in."

"Ah, now, we're not going to play that game, are we? Just tell him—tell him he'll be happier seeing me than not." Rathe let the smile fade from his face.

The clerk hesitated, then stepped back grudgingly to allow Rathe into the tiled hall. "Wait here," she said, and disappeared through a side door. Rathe settled himself to wait.

It was only a few minutes before the clerk was back, emerging onto the gallery at the top of the main staircase. "If you'll come up," she said, "he says he can see you now."

She sounded a little breathless—from surprise, Rathe guessed, which means you know about the second set of books, and the printers at the fair, and maybe a few other things. He filed the thought for future use, and climbed to join her.

Caiazzo's workroom was at the end of the gallery, looking across a side street and his neighbor's garden to the river and the crowding masts of the docks. The trader worked not at a desk but at a kind of attenuated clerk's counter than ran the length of the front wall, broken only by the double windows that reached almost to the ceiling. It was littered with papers, charts and logs and ledgers scattered along its length. Caiazzo flipped over one of the sheets just as the clerk paused in the open door, and said, "Pointsman Rathe, sir."

Caiazzo turned, smiling genially enough, but Rathe had seen the frown fading from his eyes. "Hello, Rathe, come in and stop intimidating my people, will you? All right, Biblis, thanks, I should be safe enough. And it's adjunct point, by the way."

The clerk flushed, but made no comment, and slipped out of the room, closing the door softly behind her.

"Gods, Rathe, what did you say to her?" Caiazzo held up a hand. "Not, of course, that you're ever anything but welcome here."

Rathe shrugged, crossed the room to look at the books in their case, came to rest within easy reach of the narrow counter. "Didn't have to say much, really. I suppose she was in just awe of the system." There was a manifest on the sun-warmed wood beside him, and he tilted his head to look at it. With a faint smile, Caiazzo reached across and turned it facedown.

"Not feeling cooperative this week?" Rathe asked. "That's too bad.

'Cause things are turning nasty out there, Hanse, and there's some even betting on you being involved."

"And here I was hoping you'd come to offer me your services," Caiazzo answered easily. The winter-sun was just rising, and the doubled light leached the color from his skin and dark eyes. "You owe me, Nico. That was a good man you arrested. I still haven't found a replacement for him."

"And I wonder why. Come on, Hanse, it's not that he called himself a duellist, though the laws frown on that, it was his methods," Rathe said, with a boredom he didn't entirely feel. "Crying a fair fight's bad enough, bare murder's something else. I did him a favor. Many more kills like that, and his mind would have gone. It can in duellists, you know."

"For a southriver rat, you know a lot about a very high-class sport," Caiazzo said.

"Blood sports aren't all that high class. If I ever leave the points, you'll be among the first to know." Rathe took his weight off the counter, and reached into his jerkin, left-handed, careful to keep his knife hand in view, and produced the broadsheets Guillot had bought for him. He freed the least offensive one and handed it across. "I want you to have a look at this. Recognize the printer's seal?"

Caiazzo gave him a glance from under lowered eyebrows, but took the proffered paper. "Forged bond mark," he said, turning the page from front to back. "A direct violation of the law, pointsman, I'm shocked you're reading something like this."

Rathe smiled sourly, and gestured for him to continue. Caiazzo lifted an eyebrow, but went on reading. He finished the brief text, and handed it back to Rathe. "Pretty good stuff. Popular, you know. Very dramatic. Why?"

"Lebrune tells me this Agere is printing under your coin," Rathe said.

Caiazzo shook his head sadly. "Some people get so self-righteous when they recover their long-lost status, don't they? They need to cast blame wherever they can, see villainy where there's just . . . free enterprise. I'm told the license fees are fearsome, these days."

"You're denying it."

"Off the books, Nico?"

Rathe hesitated. He'd good information, useful information, from Caiazzo before now, and always off the books, but if Fourie was right, and Caiazzo was involved with the missing children, he couldn't afford to make any deals with him. But it wasn't Caiazzo's style to meddle in something that didn't turn a tidy profit, and neither the children nor the politics was going to bring anything but trouble to a long-distance trader. "All right, Hanse. Off the books." And your word against mine, if I have to, if I find you are involved with these kids, he added silently.

"Yes, I've loaned Franteijn Agere the coin she needs. She's sound, hires decent readers, they cast their own horoscopes and stay strictly away from political matters. Agere prints to the popular interest, and that's it."

"Politics are a popular interest these days, with the starchange," Rathe said. He found the second paper, and handed it across, shaking his head. "Stays strictly away from the political? I bought this off her an hour ago. I'd say you need to do some housecleaning, if you can't keep a printer in line."

Caiazzo's lips tightened as he skimmed the paper. "I appreciate your concern, pointsman, but I assure you it's quite unnecessary."

Rathe sighed. "It would be very bad timing—I would take it personally—if any of Agere's astrologers, or Agere, for that matter, were to disappear just now."

"Don't tell me my business, Rathe." Caiazzo took a deep breath, handed the paper back. "I'm not a fool, how ever many of my people are. So. Why are you really here? Unauthorized printers aren't your line at all, Adjunct Point, especially when there's something more important troubling the city. Unless you've fatally annoyed your superiors at last?" He sounded vaguely hopeful.

Rathe shook his head. "Not so far. But, as you say, there are more important things on my mind than unlicensed printers and politically minded astrologers. And since you—loan money—to more than one of them, I thought I'd warn you, it could go hard if you don't control them better."

"Warning me, Nico? Not your habit at all. You'd love to catch me dead to rights and score a point or two off me."

"Wouldn't I just," Rathe agreed. "But I'm more interested in finding out who's stealing these children, and putting a stop to it. And to tell you something I probably oughtn't, I don't think you're involved in that." He fixed his eyes on Caiazzo's face, watching for any shift, any flicker of expression that might give the trader away. "Of course, if I find you are, it'll just go that much harder for you. Keep your astrologers and printers in line, Hanse. Or they'll go down for a lot more than the usual two months."

"Oh, come on, Rathe. On what charges?"

"Incitement to riot. Petty treason. Possibly great treason, if this one"—he held up Agere's sheet touting the Palatine Marselion's candidacy—"is any example. I could name a few others, if I were pressed, and the judiciary will hear all counts. Just a friendly warning, say."

Caiazzo blinked once, and Rathe knew the warning had been heard. The trader sighed, and turned away from the window. "Why would I be involved with stealing children, Nico? There's no profit in it, not like this."

"I don't know that you are," Rathe answered. "I've no reason to think you are. But you didn't use to dabble in politics, either."

Caiazzo laughed, a short, harsh sound. "I still don't. That"—he nodded to the broadsheet still in Rathe's hand—"will be dealt with. Politics aren't my business, and well you know it. And as for these kids . . . people of mine, their kin anyway, have lost children. There's no sense in it, Nico, and that's not a game I'd play."

Slowly, Rathe nodded. "I know that. So keep an eye on your astrologers and printers, Hanse. I don't want to be dragged off real business to deal with them—and if I do, I'll look a lot closer at your businesses than I necessarily want to."

"I'll bear that in mind," Caiazzo said, after a moment, and this time Rathe believed him.

The clerk let him out—the side door, this time—and Rathe made his way upstream along the Sier, trying to decide what to do next. By rights, he should go back to Point of Hopes, but at the moment that felt unbearably useless, and instead he made his way along the eastern docks, telling himself he was keeping his eyes open for a pair of redheads. There was one other errand he still needed to do—two, he added, if he counted going to the theaters in Point of Dreams, but that could wait until he had a chance to talk to the actors who lived in the attic of his own lodgings. They, and Gavi Jhirassi in particular, knew all the gossip in Point of Dreams; if Foucquet's wayward apprentice had run away to the theaters, one of them would know. He made a face then, heedless of the crowd of laborers busy alongside a battered-looking caravel. That left his errand to the university, and he was hardly eager to ask these particular questions there. But Monteia had told him she wanted horoscopes cast for the children missing from Point of Hopes, and they both knew what the other step should be. The university trained necromancers, as well as every other school of magist, and no pointsman was foolish enough to deny the utility of a necromancer's talent. It was just . . . Rathe allowed himself a sour smile, seeing the double light glinting off the Sier where it curled around the piers that held the Manufactory Bridge. It was just that none of them wanted to ask, for fear that someone would tell them the children were indeed dead. And that was foolishness, superstition, not reason, he told himself fiercely. There wasn't a necromancer in Astreiant who didn't know perfectly well what was going on, who wouldn't come to the points the instant he touched a child's ghost. Even the rawest student knew that much, or at worst would know to go to his teachers, so the absence of reported ghosts could be considered a good sign. At least Istre b'Estorr was a friend as well as a colleague.

He crossed the Sier at the Manufactory Bridge, through the courtyard of Point of Graves that lay astride the approach to the bridge itself. The gallows at the center of the square was empty, and, as always, a few of the Point of Graves runners were sitting on its steps, daring each other to investigate the trap. Rathe passed them without a second glance, aware that the hangman's woman was watching them from the steps of her house, and went on through the massive gatehouse to the bridge.

b'Estorr, like most scholars, lived in University Point, on the grounds of the university itself. He'd come to Chenedolle as a student—necromancy was viewed with deep suspicion in his native Chadron, not least because the kings of Chadron had an unfortunate habit of dying untimely, and rarely by their own hands—and had returned only briefly to serve the old king, who had held a more liberal vision of his talents. Unfortunately, that vision had not extended to his own nobles, and the old Fre had, like so many of his ancestors, been assassinated. b'Estorr had escaped back to Chenedolle, and the sanctuary of the university. He rarely referred to his time at the Chadroni court, but Rathe, surveying the peace of the college yard, broken only by clusters of gargoyles and junior students in full gowns of almost the same slate grey, couldn't help wondering if b'Estorr missed the power he must have had. To be a mere master, his assistance to the points the only break in that routine, must be something of a diminishment.

The Corporation had long ago realized that there was little point in holding students to their normal routine during the week of the Midsummer Fair, and the same truce seemed to hold for the week before. Inquiring at the porter's gate, Rathe was told that b'Estorr was in his rooms, not at class as he'd expected, but he made his way back across the yard without complaint. b'Estorr's rooms, one of the tower lodgings reserved for senior masters, were more congenial than the cold stone classrooms, with their tiers of wooden benches and the master's lectern at the bottom of that slope, like a cross between a bear pit and the public stage. He showed his slate to the crone of a porter who guarded b'Estorr's building, and the woman nodded and unlatched the lower half of her door. Rathe climbed the winding stair to the first floor, knocked hard, knowing b'Estorr's habits.

As he'd expected, it was a few moments before the necromancer opened his door. He was a tall man, unusually fair for a Chadroni, with straw blond hair and dark blue eyes, and at the moment his fair brows were drawn into a faint puzzled frown. That eased into a smile as he saw Rathe, and he pulled the door open wide.

"Nico. Come in."

Rathe stepped into the sunlit space, and, as always, felt a faint prickling at the base of his neck, as though the air were cooler than it should be. Ghosts were b'Estorr's constant companions as well as his strongest tools; even the least sensitive couldn't help but be at least vaguely aware of their drifting presence. And then he saw a trio of small bones lying on a sheet of parchment on the polished wood of the worktable, and drew a quick breath, trying to swallow his panic. b'Estorr saw where he was looking, and refolded the paper over them.

"Not what you're thinking."

"Not my business, then," Rathe said, and knew he sounded edgy.

"Not the business I think you've come to me about," b'Estorr answered. "Unless you're interested in historical murders? These are old, it's been a generation or two at least since they wore flesh."

"When I have the time," Rathe answered. "When children aren't disappearing from Astreiant."

b'Estorr nodded. "I thought that was it. Have you eaten?"

Rathe glanced automatically at the sunstick in the window, saw with some surprise that it was well past noon. "Not since this morning, no." And that had been a bite or two of bread and cheese at the Old Brown Dog.

"Then why don't you join me?" b'Estorr said, and leaned out the door to call for a servant without waiting for the other's answer. When the servant appeared—a girl in a student's gown, Rathe saw without surprise—b'Estorr gave quick orders for a meal, and closed the door again. "There's wine in the jug, help yourself."

Rathe nodded, but made no move. b'Estorr smiled again, and poured himself a glass. It was blown glass, pale blue streaked with an orange pink, not one of the pottery cups Rathe himself used at home, and he wondered if they were university privilege, or like b'Estorr survivors of the court of Chadron. He could not quite, he realized, imagine b'Estorr drinking from pottery.

"So what can I do for you?" b'Estorr asked, and lowered himself into one of the carved chairs, stretching his feet into the patch of sunlight.

Rathe seated himself as well, aware of an eddy of cold air that seemed to shy away from him as he moved. One of b'Estorr's ghosts? he wondered, and shook the thought away. "As you said, the missing children. I don't suppose you've seen—sorry, touched—any of them, or any unusual ghosts at all, these past three weeks?"

b'Estorr shook his head. "I doubt it's much comfort, but no. I haven't, and neither has anyone I know."

"Oh, it's a comfort, I suppose," Rathe said. "It's just not a lot of help." He winced at what he'd said. "I didn't mean that, of course—"

"But it would be easier if you had something to work with," b'Estorr finished. "Don't worry, I won't repeat it."

"Thanks," Rathe said. He ran a hand through his hair. "It's just that these disappearances are so—absolute. People are talking about children being stolen off the streets, but if it were that, gods, we'd have an easier time of it."

b'Estorr tilted his head. "But they are being stolen, surely."

"Apparently, but there's not a woman, or man, who can say they've actually seen a child being stolen. And you can be sure there'd be trouble if they did. We nearly had a riot over in Hopes, in the Street of the Apothecaries, no less, when a journeyman tried to drag home one of his apprentices, and people thought he was stealing the child." Rathe sighed. "No, no one's stealing them, Istre, at least not in the usual way. They just—disappear. They leave good situations, bad situations, no situations at all. They're not runaways, that I'm sure of, not with what some of them—hells, most of them, all of them—leave behind. So, they don't go willingly. But they're not being seized off the streets. And we don't know what is happening to them."

"Some of them are legitimate runaways?" b'Estorr asked.

Rathe nodded. "We've found some of those, but it's harder than ever to tell this year, since of course every parent, guildmaster, or guardian who loses a child would rather think they've been taken than that the child would want to run. So I'm getting less honest answers than usual, I think, from some quarters." Like the surintendant, he added silently. Why he wants me concentrating on Caiazzo when there are plenty of more likely possibilities . . . but there weren't any, that was the problem, and he pushed the thought aside. "But the upshot of it all is, Monteia, and I, are checking even the most outlandish possibilities."

"Which brings you to me?" b'Estorr asked.

The tilt of his eyebrow surprised a grin from Rathe. "Not quite the way that sounded, but yes, sort of. First, is it possible that the children are dead even though no one's reported touching their ghosts? Could somebody be binding them, or could they have been taken far enough away, and killed there?" b'Estorr was shaking his head, and Rathe stopped abruptly.

"It's all possible, but not very likely," the necromancer said. "What do you know about ghosts?"

"What everyone does, I suppose," Rathe answered. He could smell, quite suddenly, baking bread, but the air that brought that scent was unreasonably cold. "They're the spirits of the untimely dead, they can remember everything they knew in life except the day they died, and you can't use their testimony before the judiciary unless two necromancers agree and there's physical evidence to support their word."

b'Estorr grinned. "I doubt everybody knows that last."

Rathe snorted. "They know it by heart in the Court of the Thirty-two Knives. I've had bravos caught red-handed—literally—and tell me that."

This time, b'Estorr laughed aloud. "I can't imagine it would do much good, under those circumstances."

"It depends on how large a fee they can manage," Rathe answered.

"Ah." b'Estorr's smile faded. "The thing that matters, Nico, is the whys of all that. A ghost can't remember the specifics of her or his death because—in effect—the murderer has established a geas over her that prevents her speaking. It's possible, with effort and preparation—true malice aforethought—to extend that geas either to silence the ghost completely, or, more commonly, to bind her to the precise spot where she was killed. If you do it right, the odds that a necromancer, or even a sensitive, would stumble on that spot are vanishingly low. But I doubt that's what's happening. It takes too much time and effort to arrange, and if you're missing, what, fifty children?"

"Eighty-four," Rathe answered. "That's from the entire city."

b'Estorr's eyes widened. "Gods, I didn't realize." He shook his head. "There is one other possibility, though, that you may need to consider. Have you ever given any thought to the meaning of 'untimely' death?"

Rathe looked at him. "I assume it means 'dead before your time,' though I daresay you're going to tell me otherwise."

"It's the question of who defines your time," b'Estorr answered.

Rathe paused. "Your stars?"

"Stars can tell the manner and sometimes the place," b'Estorr answered. "Not the time. No, the person who defines 'untimely' is ultimately the ghost herself. That's why you'll see ghosts of people who've died of plague or sudden illness, they simply weren't willing to acknowledge it was time for them to die. That's also why you don't see many ghosts of the very old, no matter how they die—and why you don't see ghosts of those who die in battle or in duel. In each case, those people had accepted the possibility of their death, and accepted it when it happened. Now some people, a very few, even though their deaths would be reckoned timely by any normal measure, simply won't accept it, and they, too, become ghosts."

"You mean they just say, 'no, I'm not dead yet,' and they're not?" Rathe demanded.

"Not exactly, but close enough. It's a question of how strong a life force they have, and what incentives they have to live, or, more precisely, not to die." b'Estorr's face grew somber, the blue eyes sliding away to fix on something out of sight over Rathe's left shoulder. "The reverse is also true. There are people who simply don't know when they should die, or don't care, and whose deaths, even by bare murder, don't seem to matter. They don't become ghosts because they seem to accept that any death, from whatever cause, is fated."

"Temple priests, and such?" Rathe asked. He couldn't keep from sounding skeptical, and wasn't surprised to see b'Estorr's mouth twist in answer.

"Well, the ones that are contemplative, and there aren't many of them left, these days. But the main group this covers is children."

"Oh." Rathe leaned back in his chair, aware again of the warm breeze drifting in from the yard, carrying with it a strong smell of dust and greenery. b'Estorr's ghosts seemed to have moved off; he could feel the sunlight creeping across the toes of his boots, heating his feet beneath the leather. It made sense, painfully so: children weren't experienced, didn't know what they could and couldn't expect from the world; they might well accept death as their lot, especially the ones born and bred southriver, where life was cheap. . . . He shook his head, rejecting the thought. "Not all of them," he said. "They can't all have, I don't know, given up? And some of them were old enough to know, and to be angry."

b'Estorr nodded. "I agree. It's usually the youngest children, anyway, much younger than apprentice-age, that this applies to. And even then, you occasionally run into someone who's clever enough, strong enough—loved enough, sometimes—to know they shouldn't be dead." For an instant, his voice sounded distinctly fond, and Rathe wondered just what dead child he was remembering. And then the moment was gone, and he was back to business. "And in a group this large of older children—I doubt this is what's happening. But I thought I should at least mention it, even as a remote possibility."

"Thanks," Rathe said.

"Thank me when I do something useful," b'Estorr answered. There was a knock at the door, and he added, "Come in."

The girl student pushed the door open with a hunched shoulder, her hands busy with a covered tray. At b'Estorr's nod, she set it on the worktable, and disappeared again. b'Estorr lifted the covers, releasing a fragrance of onions and oil, and Rathe realized with a start that he was hungry.

"Help yourself," b'Estorr said, and Rathe reached for a spoon and bowl. There was bread as well as the wedge of soft cheese and the bowl of noodles and onions, and he balanced a chunk of each on the edge of his bowl.

"There was one other thing Monteia wanted," he said, around a mouthful of noodles, and b'Estorr lifted an eyebrow.

"I might have known." His smile robbed the words of any offense.

"Yeah, well, she was wanting to have horoscopes cast for our missing kids, for the days of disappearance when we know them, see if anything useful showed up that way," Rathe said. "So I was wondering if you could tell me who would be best for the job."

"I could do it myself, if you'd like," b'Estorr answered. "Or there's Cathala, she's very skilled."

"I'd rather you did it," Rathe answered, "and thanks."

"All I'll need are the nativities, the best you can get me," b'Estorr answered. "You must be hard up for information if you're trying that."

"We've damn all but rumors, and those dangerous ones," Rathe said. "For us, a lot of suspicion is falling on a Leaguer who runs a tavern on the border with Point of Dreams. And, yes, it's a soldiers' haunt, and, yes, a lot of recruiting goes on there. But the people there are adamant that no commander's going to be taking children at this time of year, when he could have his choice from the royal regiments that were just paid off."

"There's a great deal of sense to that," b'Estorr said.

Rathe nodded. "Certainly, but it's not what anyone wants to hear. They just want their kids back."

b'Estorr smiled in agreement. "No theories, then?"

"Oh, everyone has a favorite theory, we've a glut of them." Rathe counted them off on his fingers. "The surintendant favors Hanselin Caiazzo, though the gods alone know what he'd do with eighty-four children. The chief at City Point is looking askance at the manufactories, Temple Point has asked all of us southriver to check the brothels—which we've done, at least once—and in the meantime most of southriver is blaming northriver merchants. Exactly how, they're not sure, but they're positive it's the rich who are doing it to them somehow. Leveller voices are being heard again. Oh, yes, and they're not too sure the points aren't involved, somehow or other."

"I don't quite see that," b'Estorr said.

"At the very least, we've been fee'd to look the other way."

"Oh. Of course." There was a smile behind the necromancer's voice, and Rathe smiled in reply.

"So what are the rumors up here, magist? What theories have the students and masters come up with?"

b'Estorr gave him a bland stare. "Do you think we have time to waste on idle gossip?"

"Yes."

"Well, you're not wrong. There's a lot of talk about the starchange, of course—you've probably heard variations on that theme as well. And when you add politics to the mix, people are in a mood to borrow trouble. Among the juniors there's talk of dark maneuverings by one or more of the potential claimants." b'Estorr frowned slightly, more pensive than annoyed. "Marselion seems to be high on everyone's list—why is that, Nico?"

Rathe grinned. He had seen the Palatine Marselion and her train on her last visit to Astreiant, for the Fall Balance and its associated session of the Great Council. She had carried herself like a queen, and snubbed the city—even the northriver merchants, who had been prepared to welcome her—except for her distributions of alms. "She's been too blatant in her ambition. She thinks it's sewn up, or she acts like it is, and the people don't like that."

"Not that they have much say in the matter." b'Estorr's voice held a faint note of distaste, and Rathe's grin widened fractionally. Chadron was, technically, an elective kingship, which contributed greatly to the death rate among its monarchs.

"Maybe not, but Astreiant is a populist's city, and her majesty has always made it her business to stay in tune with the mood of her people. You don't ignore the rumblings." Rathe paused. "So you lot think it's political?"

"One way or another, that's the concensus," b'Estorr answered. He hesitated. "There's also been talk of freelance astrologers, that they might be involved, but I'm inclined to write that off as professional jealousy."

"Oh?" In spite of himself, Rathe found his attention sharpening. "I've seen one or two of them, or I think I have. What do you know about them?"

b'Estorr shrugged. "That's pretty much all, Nico. I understand the Three Nations complained to the arbiters—the students usually make a good bit of money doing readings at the fair, and this, quite simply, cuts into their profits."

He sounded more amused than anything else, and Rathe nodded. "So your vote is still for politics?"

"I'm not so sure. I think someone's taking advantage of the uncertainty of the starchange—but stealing children? I can't imagine why. Or for what purpose."

Rathe sighed and set the now-empty bowl back on the tray. "No, and that's the problem. It's crazy, stealing children, and even as madness, it doesn't make sense. I have nativities for some of ours, by the way."

"I'll get started on it right away." b'Estorr's face was wry. "Who knows, something may come of it."

"Right," Rathe answered, and knew he sounded even less enthusiastic than the other man. He reached into his purse, found the folded sheet of paper, and slid it across the worktable to the magist. "Those are the nativities we have, and the days they disappeared. We made a guess at the time, but that's all it is."

b'Estorr unfolded it, skimming the careful notation. "At least these kids knew their stars—to the quarter hour, too. That's a help."

"It's the only luck we've had." Rathe glanced at the sunstick again, and pushed himself to his feet. It was more than time he was getting back to Point of Hopes. "Let me know if you hear anything, even if it's just a new rumor, would you? Though it's the last thing I want to hear, I think I need to keep abreast of as much of the popular murmur as possible."

b'Estorr nodded, already engrossed in the first calculations, and Rathe let himself out into the stairwell.

5

The day was hot already, and it still lacked an hour to noon. Eslingen sat in the garden of the Brown Dog, coat hung neatly on a branch of the fruit tree behind him, and wished that the river breeze reached this far inland. The latest batch of broadsheet prophecies lay on the little table beside him, half read; the one on the top of the stack, a nice piece, better printed than most, invoked transits of the moon and predicted that the missing children would be found unharmed. Eslingen had lifted an eyebrow at that. He hoped it was true, hoped that whoever had cast this horoscope had some insight denied the rest of Astreiant, but couldn't quite bring himself to believe it. The rest of the prophecies blamed anyone and everyone, from the denizens of the Court of the Thirty-two Knives to the owners of the manufactories, and a few of them weren't bothering even to keep up the pretense of a prediction. One of those made oblique reference to the queen's childlessness, and suggested that a "northern tree might bear better fruit." Even Eslingen could translate that—the Palatine Marselion, or her supporters, pushing her candidacy—and he shook his head. Chenedolle's monarchy had settled its laws of succession long ago: the crown descended by strict primogeniture in the direct line, but if there were no heirs of the body, the monarch named her heir from among her kin, supposedly on the basis of their stars. Marselion was the queen's cousin, and her closest living relative, but if I were queen, Eslingen thought, I wouldn't look kindly on these little games. Not with the city in the state it is.

"How can you stand to read that trash?"

Eslingen looked up to see Adriana looking down at him. She had been working in the kitchen all morning, and the stove's heat had left her red-faced and sweating; she had unlaced her sleeveless bodice, and pinned up the sleeves of her shift, but it didn't seem to have done much good.

"I like to see what people are thinking," he answered, and shoved the jug of small beer toward her. "Can you join me?"

She shook her head, but lifted the pitcher and drank deeply. "I can't stay, but I had to get out of the kitchen. Sweet Demis, but it's scalding in there."

"Pity you can't serve cold food," Eslingen said.

"Food served cold has to be cooked first," Adriana answered. "But tonight should be easier. Most everything will be served cool, thank the gods—and Mother, of course."

"Not quite the same thing," Eslingen said, straight-faced, and the woman grinned.

"Though you'd never know it to listen to her." She picked up the first broadsheet, scanned it curiously, her brows lifting in amused surprise. "I can't believe this got licensed."

"Look again," Eslingen said, and Adriana swore softly.

"Forged—Tyrseis instead of Sofia."

Eslingen nodded. "Someone has a sense of humor, I think. I didn't notice it until I read it and looked twice."

"Someone's going to spend a few months in the cells for this one," Adriana said. "And they'll have earned it."

"Assuming the points can catch her," Eslingen said. "Or him, I suppose."

"Printing's a mixed craft," Adriana answered. "Oh, they'll call the point on this one easily enough, they're hard on poor printers, and it'll make them look a little better, seeing that they can't catch whoever's stealing the children—or won't."

"You don't believe that," Eslingen said, and was startled by his own vehemence. But it was impossible to imagine Rathe standing idly by while his colleagues helped the child-stealers, even more impossible to imagine him cooperating with them. Of course, he told himself firmly, Rathe wasn't all pointsmen—wasn't even a typical one, by all accounts.

Adriana made a face. "No, I don't, not really. But with everyone pointing the finger at us, it's hard not to blame someone else." She sighed. "Gods, I don't want to get back to work. Let me have another drink of your beer, Philip?"

Eslingen nodded, watched the smooth skin of her neck exposed as she tilted her head to drink. She saw him looking as she lowered the jug, but only smiled, and set it back on the table.

"Thanks. Think of me, slaving away to feed you—"

"Philip!" Devynck's voice cut through whatever else her daughter would have said. "In here, please, now!"

Eslingen shoved himself upright, wondering if she'd finally decided to make known her feelings about any connection with him, and hurried into the inn. He stopped just inside the garden door, his hand going reflexively to the knife he still carried. Devynck was standing by the bar, hands on her hips, the waiters flanking her like soldiers. A lanky woman in a pointswoman's jerkin stood facing her, more pointsmen behind her—at least half a dozen of them—and at her side was a small woman Eslingen thought he should recognize. He frowned, unable to place her, uncertain of his status, or Devynck's, and the innkeeper turned to him.

"Philip. It seems that Chief Point Monteia here has received a formal complaint about the Brown Dog. She feels it her duty to investigate those complaints—" She glanced back at the lanky woman, and added, grudgingly, "not unreasonably, I suppose. She also feels it's necessary to search the building and grounds."

Eslingen nodded once, fixing his eyes on the group. The pointswoman—chief point, he corrected himself, Rathe's superior Monteia—just said, "Mistress Huviet here has lodged a complaint with us, says you're hiding the girl that's missing from the Knives Road. We're obliged to take that seriously."

"And what business is it of Mistress Huviet's?" Devynck asked. "I don't see Bonfais Mailet in here claiming I've got his apprentice."

Monteia gave a thin smile. "Mistress Huviet has kin in the guild, a nephew, I believe, who's a journeyman, and about whom she's worried." The chief point's voice was tinged with irony, and Devynck snorted.

"Not that Paas?" she demanded, and Monteia nodded. "Then she should hope he's taken, it'd save her in the long run."

The little woman drew herself up—rather like a gargoyle, Eslingen thought, or more like a crow, something small, and fierce, and dangerous when roused—and Monteia held up her hand.

"Aagte, that's not funny at the best of times, and times like these, I'm forced to take it seriously. You're not helping yourself with remarks like that."

Devynck made a face, but folded her arms across her breast, visibly refusing to apologize. Monteia's mouth tightened, as though she'd bitten something bitter. "The complaint has been made, and I will search this tavern with or without your cooperation, Devynck."

"And what about the rest of the taverns in Point of Hopes—hells, there are three others off the Knives Road alone. Will you be searching them, Chief Point?"

Monteia shook her head. "I've no cause, no complaints against them."

Devynck snorted. "Go on, then. Philip, go with them, don't let them drink anything they haven't paid for."

Monteia grinned at that, a fleeting expression that lit her horselike face with rueful amusement, but Huviet bristled again.

"He's in it as much as anyone, I told you that. You can't let him lead the search."

"I'm leading the search," Monteia corrected her. "And Aagte—Mistress Devynck—has a right to have one of her people observe."

Huviet compressed her lips, but Monteia's tone brooked no argument. The chief point nodded. "All right. We'll do this orderly, bottom to top, people. And if anything's broken or missing, it comes doubled out of your salary and fees." She eyed the group behind her, and seemed to read agreement, nodded again. "Ganier, watch the front, no one in or out. Leivrith, the same for the back."

Devynck snorted again, and reached for the knot of keys that hung at her belt. "Half your station? I'm flattered." She handed the keys to Eslingen. "They're marked. Let them in wherever they want to go, the only secret here is where I get my good beer."

"Ma'am." Eslingen looked at Monteia, and the chief point sighed. "Right, then. We'll start with the cellars."

Eslingen found that key easily enough—he'd seen it before, a massive thing, passed from hand to hand as needed—and unlocked the trap where the beer barrels were brought in. Monteia lifted an eyebrow at that, and he wondered for an instant if she knew there was a second, easier entrance from the garden. She said nothing, however, just motioned for one of the pointsmen to raise the trap, and swung herself easily down the ladder. Eslingen followed, reached for the lantern that hung ready on the side of the barrel chute. He fumbled in his pocket for flint and steel, but before he could find it, one of the waiters came hurrying with a lit candle, hand cupped around the flame. One of the pointswomen passed it down to him. He lit the lantern and set it back in its place, throwing fitful shadows. Monteia gave him another look, but said nothing, just stepped back to let her people file past, lighting their own candles as they went. The little woman—Huviet—came last of all, bundling her skirts against the cellar dirt.

"Help yourself," Eslingen said, and wished instantly he'd chosen a less ambiguous phrase.

"You should know better," Monteia answered, and nodded to her people. "All right, go to it. Make sure there are no secret rooms—and remember what I said about breakage."

The cellar was large, and essentially undivided, except for the pillars that held the floor above. Monteia's people moved through it with efficient speed, shifting the heavy barrels and the racked wines only enough to be sure that nothing was concealed behind them. Huviet followed close behind, peering over their shoulder as each object was moved. With her skirts still bunched up, and the lack of height that made her hop a little to see past the taller pointsmen, she looked like nothing so much as an indignant gargoyle in the uncertain light, but then Eslingen caught a glimpse of her face, and his amusement died. She was absolutely convinced of Devynck's guilt—of all their guilt, pointsman and Leaguer alike—and she wouldn't be satisfied until a child was found.

"Nothing here, boss," one of the pointsmen announced, and Monteia nodded.

"Upstairs."

Eslingen trailed behind them, the keys jangling in his hand, pausing only to be sure that the lantern was well out. Monteia led her people into the kitchen—Adriana and the cookmaid stood back against the garden wall, arms folded, saying nothing even when one of the pointsmen nearly upset the stew pot—and she herself ran a thin rod into the huge jars of flour. Huviet peered over her shoulder, and into every corner, all the while darting wary glances at Adriana and the scowling maid.

"Nothing here either," a pointsman announced, and Monteia straightened, one hand going to the small of her back.

"Devynck's office," she said. "And then upstairs."

Monteia herself went through Devynck's office, though she disdained to touch the locked strongbox that sat beneath the work table. Huviet looked as though she would protest, seeing that, but Monteia fixed her with a cold stare, and the little woman subsided. At the chief point's gesture, Eslingen led the way into the garden and up the outside stair, then stood back while the pointsmen went into each of the lodgers' rooms.

"I've four people staying with me now," Devynck said, from the top of the stairs, "all known to me, Monteia, except Eslingen, and he came recommended by a woman I'd trust with my life. So that's four rooms out of six, and the others are all empty. But see for yourself."

"We will," Monteia said, without particular emphasis, and Devynck snorted, and climbed down the stairs again, her shoes loud on the wood. The chief point made a face, and nodded to her people. "All right, get on with it—and remember what I said."

Eslingen leaned against the wall, the suns' light hot on his back. At least the other lodgers were away, either at their jobs, or, like Jasanten, at the Temple of Areton, and he made a face at the thought of explaining the searches to some of his more truculent neighbors. Still, he would deal with that later, if anyone noticed. So far, though, the pointsmen had been remarkably tidy in their work. He was just glad Rathe wasn't among the group, and couldn't have said precisely why.

He straightened as Huviet started to follow a pointswoman into one of the rooms, and touched Monteia's shoulder. "Chief Point, I've no objection to her going into the untenanted rooms, but that woman has no status here, and I won't have her in the lodgers' rooms." He left the accusation hanging, delicately, and saw Monteia suppress a grin.

"Mistress Huviet, you will have to stay outside."

Huviet drew herself up. "You keep taking their part, Chief Point. One would think you were on their side."

"I'm here to act for the city's laws," Monteia said. "This search is at your behest, mistress, that's all you have a right to."

Huviet looked as though she was going to say something else, but as visibly swallowed her words. She turned on her heel, and moved down the hall, to stand ostentatiously in the doorway of the next room. "Be sure and check the walls for hidden panels."

Monteia rolled her eyes, then looked at Eslingen. "So you're the new knife. Rathe spoke to you?"

"Yes." Eslingen kept his eyes on the city woman, moving on to the doorway of the next room.

"Good." Monteia nodded. "He speaks well of you, at least on first acquaintance. I hope you'll keep his advice in mind."

"Send to Point of Hopes if we have trouble," he said. Eslingen tilted his head at the pointsmen filling the hallway. "And who do we send to for this, Chief Point?"

Monteia looked at him. "There are a lot of other things I could be doing, Eslingen, things that would close the Brown Dog for good. And that might be simplest right now, seeing that there are plenty of people who'd like to see it closed, just because Devynck's a Leaguer and a soldier when it's a bad time to be either."

Eslingen looked away, acknowledging that she had the right of it. "People are scared," he said, after a moment, not knowing how to apologize.

"I know it," Monteia said, flatly, and then shook her head. "I'd have to be deaf not to hear what's being said, and I've been offered coin to be blind, too, for that matter. To close my eyes and not see, what did she call it, events taking their course."

"Fire?" Eslingen asked, instantly, and as quickly shook his head. "Surely not, not in a neighborhood like this, everything cheek by jowl—"

Monteia gave a twisted smile. "You think like a soldier. I doubt anyone hereabouts would destroy real property, they've had to work too hard to get it. But that's why I'm here, and that's why I'm offending the hells out of an old friend."

Eslingen nodded. It was like war, a little, or more like taking a city. You saved what you could through whatever methods were necessary. You didn't make friends, you usually lost some, but you kept some part of yourself intact. He doubted Monteia would appreciate the analogy, however, said only, "If we get any further trouble, Chief Point, I promise we'll send to you."

"Good."

"We're finished here, ma'am," one of the pointsmen said. "Still nothing."

Monteia nodded briskly. "Right. Downstairs, then."

Eslingen stood aside with an automatic half bow, and the chief point grinned. "Served with Coindarel, did you? He always was one for a pretty man with good manners."

"And I was beginning to like you, Chief Point," Eslingen muttered.

He followed her down into the garden, well aware that Devynck was waiting, hands on hips, beside the fence that marked the edge of the kitchen garden. She fixed him and the chief point with an impartial glare, and said, "Find anyone, Monteia? My keys, Philip."

Eslingen handed her the knot of metal, and she restored it to its place at her belt, still staring at Monteia.

The chief point shook her head. "No. Nor, for the record, did I expect to, and so I told Mistress Huviet when she made her complaint."

"They've just been moved," Huviet said. "She had warning, they took the children away before we could get here."

"Do you have any proof of that?" one of the other pointswomen snapped, and Monteia held up her hand, silencing both of them.

"My people have been in and out of the Old Brown Dog half a dozen times since the children started disappearing—easily half of those since Herisse Robion vanished—and all without warning. There's been no sign of children, or are you calling me a liar, mistress?" Huviet said nothing, and Monteia nodded in satisfaction. "If anything, Devynck's been discouraging the local youth from coming here. I will take it very ill if there's any further disturbance in this neighborhood."

"It won't be us who causes a disturbance, Chief Point," Huviet said, stiffly.

Before Monteia could say anything to that, Loret appeared in the doorway, one hand in the waistband of his breeches where he stashed his cudgel. "Eslingen—"

"Trouble?" Devynck asked, eyes narrowing.

"There's people here, ma'am, they say they know the points are here, and they want to make sure everything's all right."

And I wish I thought that meant they were on our side, Eslingen thought. He said, "I'll deal with it."

"Not alone," Monteia said, and fixed her eyes on Huviet. "If this is your doing, mistress—" She broke off, gestured for Eslingen to precede her into the tavern. To his relief, a pair of pointsmen followed, drawing their truncheons.

The main door was closed and barred, but Eslingen could see blurred shapes moving outside the windows, and could hear the dull buzz of voices. Not angry, not yet, not calling for blood, but the potential was there, clear in the note of the crowd. Monteia's frown deepened, and she looked at Eslingen. "Go ahead and open it. I'll talk to them."

Eslingen's eyebrows rose at that—he lacked the chief point's confidence in her powers of persuasion—but, reluctantly, he slid back the bar. Monteia flung the door open, and stepped out into the sunlit street.

"What's all this, then?"

The pointsmen stepped up to the door, but did not follow her into the street. Looking past them, Eslingen had to admit he admired their restraint. A group of maybe a dozen journeymen, all in butchers' leather aprons, were gathered outside the door, and beyond them the respectable matrons of the neighborhood had gathered, too, along with a couple of master butchers. They looked less certain of the situation, torn between disapproval of the tavern and disapproval of the journeymen's protest, but they made no move to haul their juniors home. Scanning their faces, Eslingen thought he recognized the woman whose son he'd sent home, and wondered whose side she would be on.

"Well?" Monteia demanded, and a familiar figure stepped out from among the journeymen.

"Have you taken the child-thief?" Paas demanded. "Bring her out, let us see her."

"There are no children here," Monteia said, and pitched her voice to carry to the edges of the crowd. She ticked her next words off on her fingers, a grand gesture, calculated to impress. "There are no children, no sign that any children were here, no secret rooms, no suspicious anything. Nothing but a woman trying to go about her business like the rest of us. I have been through this building from cellar to attic, and there's nothing here that shouldn't be. And unless you, Paas Huviet, have more evidence than your mother did, I'll thank you to keep your mouth closed. If you didn't drink too much, you wouldn't be thrown out of taverns."

That shot told, Eslingen saw, and hid a grin. Paas hesitated, obviously not appeased, but unable to think of anything to say. In the silence, a bulky man in a butcher's apron stepped forward. "You give us your word on that, Chief Point? It's my apprentice who's missing."

"Among others," Monteia said, not ungently. "You have my word, Mailet. The girl's not here."

The man nodded, not entirely convinced, but reluctant to challenge her directly. "Very well." He waded into the crowd of journeymen, caught one by the collar. "You, Eysi, who gave you permission to leave your work? Get on home with you, and don't disgrace me further."

The rest of the crowd began to disperse with him, the journeymen in particular looking sheepish and glad to get out from under the chief point's eye, but one woman held her ground, then walked slowly across the dirty street until she was standing face to face with the chief point. It was the boy's mother, Eslingen realized, with a sinking feeling, what was her name, Lucenan.

"So what are you going to do about this place, Monteia?" she asked.

"Do about it?"

"A Leaguer tavern, frequented by soldiers, in and out of work—times like these, we don't need them in our midst."

"Children have disappeared from every point in Astreiant," Monteia said. "Closing one tavern's not going to stop that."

"I've nothing against Leaguers," Lucenan said, "but these people fill children's heads with the most amazing nonsense about a soldier's life. Running after soldiers, who knows what our children might stumble into, even if it's not the soldiers who are stealing them? It's a risk having them here."

Monteia nodded slowly. "I know you, mistress. And your son. He's of an age where he will go off and explore, and if he's soldier-mad, gods know how you'll stop him, without you tie him to your doorpost. And you're frightened, and I wish I could say it was without cause. I'm frightened, too—I've a son his age myself, and a daughter not much younger. But you know as well as I that Devynck doesn't encourage him—she sent him home to you, didn't she, and she'll probably have to do it again." She smiled suddenly. "Admit it, Anfelis, you're mostly annoyed that Devynck's complained against him."

Lucenan blinked, on the verge of affront, and then, slowly, smiled. "I'm not best please about that, Ters, no. But that's not what's behind this. I am worried—I'm more than worried, I'm frankly terrified. I don't want to lose Felis."

"I know," Monteia said. "All I can tell you is, the child-thief isn't here—Felis is probably as safe here as he is at home. Given the complaints between the two of you, the boy will be as well looked after as if he was Aagte's own."

That surprised another rueful smile from Lucenan, but she sobered quickly. "It's the streets in between I'm worried about, as much as anything."

"We're doing what we can," Monteia answered, and the other woman shook her head.

"It's not enough, Chief Point." She turned away before Monteia could answer.

"And don't I know it," Monteia muttered, and stepped back into the tavern. "Well, you heard that, Eslingen. I don't think you'll have a lot to worry about, barring something new. It's mostly the Huviets who are causing the trouble, and they're not well loved here."

"I hope you're right," Eslingen answered.

"And if I'm not—hells, if you have any troubles," Monteia began, and Eslingen finished for her.

"I'll send to Point of Hopes. I assure you, you'll be the first to hear."

* * *

Business was slow that night, and Eslingen, watching the sparse gathering from his usual corner, didn't know whether it was a good or a bad sign. Among the broadsheets he had bought that morning was a plain diviner, listing the planetary positions for the week, with brief comments, the sort of thing senior students at the university cobbled together to raise drinking money, but nevertheless he slipped it out of his cuff and scanned it yet again. It was the night of the new moon—if the astrologer at the fairgrounds had been correct, he was due to change his job soon. He smiled. He suspected that the astrologer's timing was off: he had a new job, related to his work, already. And in any case, it was the general readings he was interested in. The sun and the moon both lay square to the winter-sun; the first was normal, defined the time of year, but the second added to the tension between the mundane and the supernatural. He shook his head, thinking of the missing children—one more indication that there was something dreadfully wrong—and scanned the list of aspects again. The moveable stars lay mostly in squares, particularly Areton, ruler of strife and discord, squaring Argent—and there go the merchants' profits, Eslingen added silently—and the Homestar and Heira. More tension there, for home and society, and with Areton in the Scales and Sickle, there was a real promise of trouble. He made a face, and refolded the paper, tucking it back into the wide cuff of his coat. It was showing signs of wear, and he grimaced again, looked out across the almost-empty room.

Most of the soldiers were gone, either hired on to one of the companies just to get out of the city, or else they'd taken themselves and their drinking to the friendlier taverns along the Horsegate Road, closer to the camp grounds. And who could blame them? Eslingen thought. But it makes for a lonely night. Jasanten was still there, ensconced at his usual table, but he'd already given Devynck his notice, was planning to move to the Green Bell on the Horsegate as soon as possible. It would be easier recruiting there, he said, but they all knew what he really meant.

The rest of the customers were Leaguers, friends of Devynck's—the brewer Marrija Vandeale was still there, her group of five, including a well-grown young man who had to be her son, the largest in the inn. Eslingen shook his head again, and walked over to the bar, more for something to do than because he really wanted another pitcher, even of Vandeale's best. Adriana came to meet him, faced him across the heavy wood with a crooked grin.

"Not a good night," Eslingen said, not knowing what else to say, and the woman's smile widened briefly.

"No. Mother's furious." She nodded to the edge of the paper sticking out above the edge of his cuff. "Any good news there?"

"It depends," Eslingen said, sourly.

"How's business?" Adriana asked, and matched his tone exactly.

"I wouldn't ask."

Adriana glanced over his shoulder at the almost-empty room. "I hardly need to." She reached across the counter for his mug. "What about the children, does it say anything about them?"

Eslingen shrugged, and tucked the diviner deeper into his cuff. "Not a lot—as you'd expect, I suppose. Metenere trines the sun—and the moon, for that matter—which they say is a hopeful sign, but it's inconjunct to the winter-sun and Sofia, which they say means there are still things to be uncovered before the matter is resolved."

"That's safe enough," Adriana said, and set the refilled mug back in front of him. "Gods, you'd think the magists could do better than that."

Eslingen nodded, took a sip of beer he didn't really want. "Or the points. I wonder if they're consulting the astrologers?"

"They generally do. When they're not searching taverns," Adriana answered, and grinned. "Your friend Rathe, he has friends at the university, or so I'm told. Above his station, surely."

"No particular friend of mine," Eslingen said, automatically, and only then thought to wonder at his own response. I wouldn't mind calling him a friend, though.

Adriana's eyebrows rose. "And below yours?" She turned away before he could answer, disappeared through the kitchen door.

Eslingen stared after her for a moment—he hadn't expected her to defend any pointsman—then shrugged, and made his way back to his table. He doubted there would be any call for his services tonight, since the locals seemed to be staying well clear after the abortive search, but he left the beer untouched, and tilted his stool until his back rested against the wall. Monteia had handled the situation well, particularly getting that red-faced butcher on her side, he acknowledged silently. If they got through the evening without trouble, things should be all right.

The clock struck midnight at last, its voice clear in the still air, and Devynck appeared to call time on the last customers. They left in a group, Eslingen was glad to see, Vandeale and her household in the lead, and Devynck herself walked them to the door to wish them safe home. She pulled the heavy door closed behind them, turning the key in the lock, and Loret lifted the bar into its brackets. It looked thick enough to stand at least a small battering ram, Eslingen thought, and wondered if Devynck had foreseen the necessity. He stood then, stretching, and went to help Hulet with the shutters. Each had an iron bar of its own, holding the wood firm against the glass outside; they, too, would stand a siege, and he lifted the last one into place with a distinct feeling of relief. With the tavern secured for the night, all the doors and windows locked and barred, it was unlikely that the butchers' journeymen would find a way to make trouble. Hulet stretched and loosened the ropes that held the central candelabra in place, lowering it so that Adriana could snuff the massive candles.

"Philip." Devynck's voice snapped him out of his reverie. "Go with Loret, make sure the garden gate's barred before we close up for the night."

"Right." Eslingen trailed the yawning waiter out into the sudden dark. The winter-sun had set at midnight, and the air was distinctly chill, pleasant after the heat of the day. Loret fumbled with a candle and lantern, and Eslingen glanced up, looking for the familiar constellations, but a thin drift of cloud veiled all but the brightest stars. Then Loret had gotten his candle lit, and Eslingen followed its glow through the garden and down to the back gate. The bar was already up there, a chain and lock the size of a man's fist holding it firmly in place, but Loret tugged at it anyway before turning back to the inn. Eslingen glanced along the walls, checking for trouble there. They were in good repair, and high, taller than himself by a good yard; he couldn't remember if they were topped with spikes or glass, but would not have been surprised by either. In any case, they would be hard to climb without ladders: it's good enough, he told himself, and followed Loret back to the tavern. Nonetheless, he was careful to lock the door behind him at the top of the stairs, and to bar his own door after him. The banked embers at the bottom of the stove were dead, not even warm to the touch. He considered finding flint and steel, rekindling them, but it was late, and it would be easier in the morning to borrow coals from the kitchen fire. He undressed in the dark, leaving his coat draped neatly over the chair, and crawled into the tall bed.

He woke to the sound of breaking glass, groped under his pillow for his pistol and found only the keys to his chest. He had them in his hand before he was fully awake, and flung back the covers as he heard another window break. The sound was followed by shouts, young, drunken voices, and then he heard another shout from inside the inn: Devynck, waking her people to the trouble. He dragged on his breeches as another window shattered, and stooped to his clothes chest. He hastily unlocked the lid and dragged out his pistol and the bag that held powder and balls. There was no time to load it; he jammed it instead into the waistband of his breeches, the metal cold on his skin, and caught up his knife on the way to the door.

Jasanten was ahead of him in the hall, balanced awkwardly on his crutch, a long knife in his free hand. "What in all hells—?"

"Don't know," Eslingen answered, and unlocked the stairway door. "Stay here, keep an eye on things."

"Like I could go anywhere fast," Jasanten answered, but stopped at the head of the stairs, bracing himself against the frame. Eslingen pushed past him, scanning the garden. It was still dark, and quiet; most of the noise had come from the front of the inn.

"Devynck?" he called, more to give her warning than to find her, and pushed open the tavern door.

A thick pillar candle guttered on the end of the bar, throwing uneven shadows across the wide room and the empty tables. Devynck, ghostly in shift and unbound hair, stood by the main door, a caliver in her hands as she peered cautiously through a newly opened shutter. Slow match smouldered in the lock, a bright point of red. Adriana stood at her mother's back, a half-pike balanced capably in her hands, her legs bare beneath the short hem of her nightshirt.

"They're gone, the little bastards," Devynck said, and turned away from the window. "No thanks to you, Philip."

"No thanks to any of us, Mother," Adriana said, and Devynck made a noise that might have been meant as apology.

"All clear out back," Hulet said, and Eslingen jumped as the two waiters appeared behind him.

"So what happened?" he asked, cautiously.

Devynck disengaged the slow match from the lock, and set the caliver down before answering, holding the still-lit length of match well clear of her loose nightclothes. "Someone—and I daresay we can all guess who—came down the street and broke in our front windows. Areton's spear, what do I have to do to make a living in this city? I'll have the points on them so fast they'll think lightning fell on them."

"We can't prove it was Paas," Adriana said. "Unless you got a better look at them than I did."

"Who else could it have been?" Devynck demanded, but she sounded less certain.

"Do you want me to go to the station?" Eslingen asked. "Rathe—

and Monteia—said we should tell them if there was trouble."

Devynck shook her head. "No one of mine is going out on the streets tonight. I doubt we'll have any more trouble, anyway, they got what they wanted."

"Whatever that was," Hulet said, and shook his head. Behind him, Loret nodded, stuffing his shirt into the waistband of his trousers.

"I could go to Point of Hopes," he offered, and Devynck glared at him.

"I said no one, and I meant it. It's, what, it lacks an hour to dawn, that's time enough, once the sun's up and there are sensible people on the streets, to send to the points." She fixed her eyes on Eslingen's waist. "Is that a lock, Philip—and if it is, I trust you've got permission to carry it in the city?"

Eslingen felt himself flush, and was grateful for the candlelight. In the heat of the moment, he had forgotten Astreiant's laws. "Well—"

"I'll take that as a no," Devynck said, sourly. "Well, my lad, you can come with me to Point of Hopes, then, and I'll see if I can't get Monteia to grant you a writ for it. After tonight, I think she'll be willing enough."

"How bad is the damage?" Eslingen asked.

"All our front windows smashed," Devynck answered, "and a nice profit the glaziers'll make off of me for it. I haven't taken the shutters down to see how many panes were actually broken—time enough for that in the morning." She looked around the dimly lit room. "Hulet, you and Loret stay up, keep an eye on things. If they come back, give me a shout, and you, Loret, run to Point of Hopes. But I don't think they will."

Eslingen shivered, suddenly aware of how cool the air was on his bare chest and back. Adriana gave him a sympathetic glance, hugging herself, the half-pike still tucked in the crook of her arm.

"Right," Devynck said, briskly. "Back to bed, all of you. Philip, I'll leave for Point of Hopes at eight, and I want you with me."

"Yes, ma'am," Eslingen answered, and took himself out the garden door. It wasn't as bad as it could have been, he thought, hearing the tower clock strike the half hour. At least he could get another few hours sleep before he had to face the pointsmen.

Jasanten was still waiting at the top of the stairs, the knife—longer than the city regulations, Eslingen was willing to swear—still poised in his hand. He relaxed slightly, seeing the younger man, and said, "So the alarm's past?"

"For tonight, or so Devynck says." Eslingen sighed, and eased the pistol from his waistband. "Some of the local youth, she thinks, broke in the front windows."

"Not good times," Jasanten said, and stood out of the doorway, balancing himself awkwardly on his crutch. "Not good times at all."

And likely to get worse before they get better, Eslingen thought, remembering the diviner. "Get some sleep, Flor," he said, and went back into his own room, locking the door behind him. He hesitated for an instant, looking at the unloaded pistol, but in the end decided not to load it. Devynck knew her neighbors, or so he would trust; still, he set it on the table in easy reach before he undressed and climbed back into bed.

He woke to the noise of someone knocking on the door, and groped blearily for the pistol before he realized that the sun was well up. He swore under his breath—he was already late, if the sun was that bright—and Adriana's voice came from beyond the door.

"Philip? Mother says you should hurry. I brought shaving water and something for breakfast."

"All the gods bless you," Eslingen said, scrambling into shirt and breeches, and unlocked the door. Adriana looked remarkably awake and cheerful, considering the night, and he couldn't repress a grimace.

She grinned, and set a bowl and plate down on the table, lifting the plate away to reveal the hot water. Eslingen took it gratefully, washed face and hands and carried it across to the circle of polished brass that he used as a mirror. In full light, and with care, he could shave, and it was cheaper than the barber's—not to mention, he added silently, running the razor over the stone, safer, given current sentiment. "Do you think there's any chance of my getting a dispensation, or have I lost a good pistol?" he said, and began cautiously to shave.

In the mirror, he saw Adriana shrug. "Mother's had one for years, for the same reason she'll give for you, to protect her property against people who don't like Leaguers. Monteia—no, it wasn't Monteia, it was Wetterli, he was chief point before Monteia—he gave it to her when she first came here. It wasn't long after the League wars, people weren't always friendly."

"Whatever possessed her to settle here, and not in University Point?" Eslingen wiped his face, studying the sketchy job, and decided not to press his luck.

"You mean over by the Horsegate? Too much competition there." Adriana grinned again. "As you may have noticed, Mother doesn't like to share."

Eslingen lifted an eyebrow at her, but decided not to pursue the comment. He reached instead into his clothes chest and pulled out his best shirt. He had managed to get it laundered, but that had done the already thinning fabric little good; he could see seams starting to give way at shoulder and cuff. There was nothing he could do about it now, however, and he was not about to make an appearance at the points station with an illegal lock in his second-best. He stripped off the shirt he'd pulled on before, pulled on the better one more carefully, wincing as he heard stitches give somewhere. He decided to ignore it, and reached for the thick slice of bread that Adriana had brought him. It smelled of sugar and spices, the sort of heavy cakebread that was common in the League. He finished it in three bites, grateful for the sharp, sweet flavor of it, and shrugged himself into his best coat. It, too, was looking more than a little the worse for wear—not surprising, after a winter campaign and then most of a summer—but he managed to make himself look more or less presentable. Adriana nodded her approval, and collected the bowl and plate.

"Better hurry, Mother's waiting."

Eslingen made a face, but rewrapped the pistol in the rag that had protected it, and tucked the unwieldy package under his arm. "Let's go."

Devynck was waiting in the inn's main room, the caliver slung over her shoulder. The lock was conspicuously empty of match, the barrel was sheathed in a canvas sleeve, and a badge with the royal seal swung from it, but even so Eslingen blinked, trying to imagine the locals' response to seeing Devynck stalking the streets with that in hand.

She saw his look and scowled. "Well, I'm not going to risk drawing the ball, am I? I'll get Monteia to let me fire it off instead."

If she'll let you, Eslingen added, but thought better of saying it. It was safer, of course, and he couldn't blame Devynck for not wanting to fire it in her own back garden. He could only begin to imagine the neighbors' response to shots, or even a single shot, coming from the Old Brown Dog.

"Are you ready?" the innkeeper demanded, and Eslingen shook himself back to reality.

"Ready enough." He held up the wrapped pistol. "I suppose I bring this with me?"

"Of course." Devynck's glare softened for an instant. "You won't lose it, Philip—and if you do, I'll stand the cost of its replacement."

"I appreciate that," Eslingen answered. It would be a poor second best, and they both knew it: pistols were idiosyncratic; even the ones made by the best gunsmiths had their peculiar habits, and it was never easy to replace a lock that worked well. Still, under the circumstances and given the cost of a pistol, it was a generous offer.

Devynck nodded. "Right then. Let's go." She shoved open the main door, letting in the morning light and the faint scent of hay and the butchers' halls. The doorstep and the ground beyond it glittered faintly, scattered with glass from the broken windows. There were shards of lead as well, and Eslingen grimaced, thinking of the cost. He followed Devynck out the door, and looked back to see the half-emptied frames, the leads twisted out of true, the glass strewn across the dirt of the yard. With the shutters still barred behind them, they looked vaguely like eyes, and he was reminded, suddenly and vividly, of a dead man he'd stumbled over at the siege of Hirn. He had looked like a shopkeeper, the spectacles shattered over his closed eyes. He shook the thought away, and Loret appeared in the doorway with a broom, heading out to sweep up the debris.

To his relief, the streets were relatively quiet, and the few people who were out gave them a wide berth. They reached the Point of Hopes station without remark, and Devynck marched through the open gate without a backward glance. Eslingen followed more slowly, unable to resist the chance to look around him. He had never been inside a points station before—and had hoped never to be, he added silently—but had to admit that it wasn't quite what he'd expected. The courtyard walls were as high and solid as any city fort's, the gatehouse and portcullis sturdy and defensible, but the guard's niches were drifted with dust and a few stray wisps of straw. The stable looked as though it had been unused for years; a thin girl, maybe thirteen or fourteen, sat on the edge of the dry trough outside it, putting neat stitches in a cap. She looked up at their approach, alert and curious, but didn't move. An apprentice? Eslingen wondered. Or a runner? She looked too calm to be there on any business of her own.

Devynck pushed open the main door, and Eslingen winced at the smell of cold cabbage and cheap scent that rushed out past her. Despite the pair of windows, the shutters of both open wide to let in as much light as possible, the room was dark, and the candle on the duty pointsman's desk was still lit. He looked up at their entrance, eyes going wide, and quickly closed the daybook.

"Mistress Devynck?"

He had been one of the ones who'd searched the tavern, Eslingen remembered, but couldn't place the man's name.

"Where's Monteia?" Devynck said.

"Not in yet, mistress—"

"Then you'd better send for her," Devynck said, grimly, and one of the doors in the back wall opened.

"I'm here, if that helps, Aagte." Rathe stepped out into the main room, the bird's-wing eyebrows drawing down into sharper angles as he looked from Devynck and her wrapped caliver to Eslingen. "I take it there's been trouble."

Devynck nodded. "No offense, Nico, but Monteia needs to hear it, too."

"None taken," Rathe said, equably enough, and stepped past them to the door. "Asheri! Run to the chief point's house, tell her she's needed here. Tell her Aagte Devynck's come to us with a complaint." He turned back into the main room, a scarecrow silhouette in his shapeless coat. "Come on into her workroom—but leave the artillery outside, please."

Devynck hesitated, but, grudgingly, set the caliver into a corner. "It's loaded," she said. "No match, of course, but one of the things I've come for is to fire it off."

"If things were bad enough to bring out the guns," Rathe said, "why didn't you send to us last night?"

"They were here and gone before I had the time," Devynck answered. "And then there seemed no point in one of my people risking the streets before daylight."

Rathe's eyebrows flicked up at that, but he said nothing, just motioned for the others to precede him into the narrow room. It, too, was dark, and Eslingen stumbled against something, bruising his shin, before Rathe could open the shutters. This window looked onto a garden of sorts, and laundry hung from a line strung between the corner of the station and a straggling tree. Eslingen felt his eyebrows rise at that, and realized that Rathe was looking at him.

"All the comforts of home?"

Rathe shrugged, seemingly unembarrassed. "Has to get done sometime, and some of the people here can't afford their own laundresses. So Monteia makes sure one comes in once a week."

Before Eslingen could answer, Devynck slammed her palm down on the table, making the inkstand rattle. "Areton's balls, what do I have to do to get the points to protect my interests? Or would the two of you rather sit here and gossip about laundry?"

"I thought you wanted to wait for Monteia," Rathe answered.

"Which I do." Devynck glared, but Rathe went on calmly.

"And, to get to what business I can, what were you doing with that gun of yours, Aagte?"

"How could I know they would just break my windows and run—"

Rathe shook his head. "It takes time to load one of those, Aagte, I know that. If they just broke your windows and ran, you wouldn't've had time to load it. So what else did they do, and why didn't you send to us? Or were you expecting trouble, had it ready just in case?"

Eslingen kept his expression steady with an effort. He hadn't expected the pointsman to know that much about guns, enough to have caught Devynck in the weakest part of her story. Most city folk didn't, didn't encounter them much in the course of their lives, or if they did, they knew the newer flintlocks, not old-fashioned ones like Devynck's matchlock. Flints didn't take as long to load—were generally less temperamental than a matchlock—but he was surprised that Rathe, who didn't seem to like soldiers much, would have bothered to find that out. Or did the points still act as militia? he wondered suddenly.

Devynck fixed Rathe with a glare, and the pointsman returned the look blandly. "As it happened," she said, after a moment, "I'd loaded before bed, just to be on the safe side. After your lot searched us yesterday, pointsman, it seemed wise to expect a certain amount of—awkwardness."

Rathe nodded again, apparently appeased. "Yeah, I heard about that. Huviet's getting above herself, wants guild office, or so I hear."

"Not through my misfortunes," Devynck retorted.

"I agree. But, bond or no bond, Aagte, you shoot someone, and it's manslaughter in the law's eyes."

"Or self-defense."

"If you can prove it," Rathe said. "And with the way tempers are these days, it wouldn't be easy." He held up his hand, forestalling Devynck's automatic outburst. "I'm not begging fees, Aagte, or telling you not to protect your property. But I wish you'd sent to us as soon as it happened, that's all. I'd've welcomed an excuse to put Paas Huviet in cells for a night or two, think of it that way. I'm assuming he was the ringleader?"

Devynck sighed. "I think so. I didn't get a good look at him, but I'd know the voice."

Eslingen eyed Rathe with new respect. Not only was what he said solid common sense, it had appeased Devynck—not the easiest thing at the best of times, and this was hardly that.

Rathe looked at Eslingen. "Did you see him?"

The soldier shook his head. "I'm afraid not. I heard the shouting, but I couldn't swear to the voice."

Devynck made a sour face. "No, you hardly could." She looked back at Rathe. "Does this mean you can't do anything?"

Before he could answer, the workroom door opened, and Monteia said, "I hear there was trouble, Aagte?"

Eslingen edged back against the shelves where the station's books were kept, and the chief point eased past him, her skirts brushing his legs, to settle herself behind the worktable. Rathe moved gracefully out of her way, leaned against the wall by the window.

"Trouble enough," Devynck answered, and Monteia made a face.

"Sit down, for the gods' sake, there's a stool behind you. I'd hoped we'd nipped that in the bud."

"I told you it wouldn't help matters," Devynck said, not without relish, and dragged the tall stool out from its corner. She perched on it, arms folded across her breasts, and Monteia grimaced again.

"Tell me about it."

"We had a very slow night last night, not a single Chenedolliste from the neighborhood, and damn few of the Leaguers," Devynck answered. "And after we'd closed up—and locked up, we're not taking any chances these days—and were all in bed, a band of the local youth comes by and smashes in my front windows. It's going to cost me more than a few seillings to get them repaired, that's for certain."

"What time was it that it happened?" Monteia asked. Rathe, Eslingen saw, without surprise, had pulled out a set of tablets and was scratching notes in the wax plates.

Devynck shrugged. "The winter-sun was well down, and I heard the clock strike four a while after. Sometime after three, I think."

"And you didn't send to us."

"As I told Nico here, I didn't want to send my people into the streets, not when I was pretty sure they were gone." Devynck sighed. "They were drunken journeymen, Tersennes. They weren't going to do much more damage to my property, or so I thought, after we'd scared them off, but that sort's more than capable of beating one of my waiters if they caught him unaware. It may have been a mistake, I admit it, but I've my people to think of, as well as the house."

Monteia nodded. "I gather you didn't recognize anyone."

"I'm morally certain Paas Huviet was the ringleader," Devynck answered, "but, no, I can't swear to it."

Monteia nodded again. She took Devynck through her story in detail, calling on Eslingen now and then for confirmation—a confirmation he was only able to provide in the negative, much to his chagrin—and finally leaned back in her chair. "I'm sorry it's come to this, Aagte. I'd hoped we'd put a stop to the rumors. I'll send some of my people around to ask questions—"

"I'll take charge of that, Chief," Rathe said, and there was a note in his voice that boded ill for the local journeymen.

"Good. And we'll do what else we can. I'll make sure our watchmen take in the Knives Road regularly."

Rathe stirred at that, but said nothing. Even so, Monteia gave him a minatory look, and Eslingen wondered what wasn't being said. He knew that the points were only an occasional presence on the streets and in the markets, mostly when there was trouble expected; this didn't seem to be anything out of the ordinary. But then, he added silently, nothing was ordinary right now, not with the children missing.

Devynck said, "Thanks, Tersennes, I appreciate what you're doing for us. There is one other thing, though—two, really."

Monteia spread her hands in silent invitation, and Devynck plunged ahead. "First, my caliver out there. It's loaded, and I don't want to ruin the barrel trying to draw it, not to mention the other hazards. So can I fire it off in your yard?"

"Gods," Monteia said, but nodded. "What's the other?"

Devynck jerked her head toward Eslingen. "Philip here—being a stranger to Astreiant and obviously not fully aware of its laws—"

"Of course," Rathe murmured, with a grin, but softly enough that the Leaguer woman could ignore him.

"—has a pistol of his own in my house. Under the circumstances, rather than give it up, I'd like to post bond for him."

Monteia shook her head, sighing. "And I can't say that's unreasonable, either. It won't come cheap, though, Aagte, not with that monster you already keep."

"I'm prepared to pay." Devynck reached through the slit in her outer skirt, produced a pocket that made a dull clank when she set it on the worktable. "There's two pillars there, in silver."

Monteia made a face, but nodded. "I'll have the bond drawn up—Nico, fetch the scrivener, will you? And in the meantime, you can fire off that gun of yours."

The preparations for firing the caliver were almost more elaborate than for writing the bond. Eslingen lounged against the doorpost of the station, trying unsuccessfully to hide his grin as a pointswoman brought out a red and black pennant and hung it from the staff above the gatehouse. The duty pointsman recorded the event in the station's daybook, and Monteia and Rathe countersigned the entry, as did Devynck. Rathe looked up then.

"Eslingen? We need another witness."

"What am I witnessing to?" Eslingen asked, but went back into the station.

"That you know Devynck, that you know the gun's loaded, that we've posted the flag—the usual." Rathe grinned. "Not like Coindarel's Dragons, I daresay."

"We had more of this than you'd think," Eslingen answered, and scrawled his name below Devynck's. It did remind him of his time in the royal regiments, actually; there had been the same insistence on signatures and countersignatures for everything from drawing powder to receiving pay. It had made it harder for the officers to cheat their men, but not impossible, and he suspected that the same was true in civilian life.

"Right, then," Monteia said. "Let's get on with it."

Eslingen followed her and the others out into the yard, and saw with some amusement that the thin girl and half a dozen other children had gathered at the stable doors. Most of those would be the station's runners—a couple even looked old enough to be genuinely apprentices—but he could see more children peering in through the gatehouse. Monteia smiled, seeing them, but nodded to the pointswoman.

"Fetch a candle."

The woman did as she was told, and Devynck carefully lit the length of slow match she had carried under her hat. She fitted it deftly into the serpentine, tightened the screw, primed the pan, and then looked around. "I'm ready here."

"Go ahead," Monteia answered, and behind her Eslingen saw several of the runners cover their ears.

Devynck lifted the caliver to her shoulder, aimed directly into the sky, and pulled the trigger. There was a puff of smoke as the priming powder flashed and then, a moment later, the caliver fired, belching a cloud of smoke. One of the children outside the gatehouse shrieked, and most of the runners jumped; Devynck ignored them, lowered the caliver, and freed the match from the lock. She ground out the coal under her shoe, and only then looked at Monteia.

"That's cleared it."

"One would hope," Rathe murmured, and Monteia frowned at him.

"Right. Is the bond ready?"

"I'll see." Rathe disappeared into the points station, to reappear a moment later in the doorway holding a sheet of paper, which he waved gently in the air to dry the ink. "Done. Just needs your signature and seal."

Monteia nodded, and went back inside. Eslingen looked at Devynck, who was methodically checking over her weapon. Behind her, the neighborhood children were dispersing, only a few still gawking from the shelter of the gatehouse. The runners, too, had vanished back into the shelter of the stables, and he could hear voices raised in shrill debate, apparently about the power and provenance of the gun.

"Here you are," Rathe said, from behind him. "Careful, the wax is still soft."

Eslingen took the paper, scanning the scrivener's tidy, impersonal hand, and Monteia's spiky scrawl at the base. Rathe hadn't signed it, and he was momentarily disappointed; he shook the feeling away, and folded the sheet cautiously, written side out. The seal carried the same tower and monogram that topped the pointsmen's truncheons. "Thanks."

"And for Astree's sake, the next time there's trouble, send to us."

"Have you ever tried to go against her?" Eslingen asked, and tilted his head toward Devynck, just sliding her caliver back into its sleeve.

Rathe smiled, the expression crooked. "I understand. I'll probably be in this afternoon, to see the damage—just so you don't worry when you see me coming."

"I'll try not to," Eslingen answered, and turned away.

They made their way back to the Old Brown Dog as uneventfully as they'd left, but as they turned down the side street that led to the inn's door, Devynck swore under her breath. Eslingen glanced around quickly, saw nothing on the street behind them, and only then recognized that the young man sitting on the bench outside the door was wearing a butcher's badge in his flat cap. He met Devynck's stare defiantly, but said nothing. Devynck swore again, and stalked past him into the inn.

Inside, Adriana was beside the bar, Loret and Hulet to either side. She whirled as the door opened, scowling, relaxed slightly as she saw who it was.

"Mother! I thought it was that Yvor."

"What in Areton's name is going on?" Devynck asked, and unslung her caliver with a movement that suggested she would prefer it to be unsheathed and loaded.

"You saw Yvor outside," Adriana answered. "He and, oh, three or four of his friends came here, said they wanted to drink. I told them we weren't open yet, and he said he'd wait." She shook her head, looking suddenly miserable. "I thought he was a friend, at least."

"Areton's balls," Devynck said. She looked at the two waiters, then at Eslingen. "Did they say anything else?"

"They just said they wanted beer," Adriana said. She seemed suddenly to droop, her stiff shoulders collapsing. "Maybe I'm overreacting, but after last night . . . "

Devynck sucked air through her teeth, frowning. "The gods know, I don't want to give them an excuse to cause us more trouble, but I can't think they want to drink here for good purpose."

"You should tell Monteia," Eslingen said.

Devynck stared at him. "Tell her what, my neighbors want to buy my beer?"

"They made Adriana nervous," Eslingen answered. "She's not stupid or a coward, and none of us think they're here just to drink." Hulet nodded at that, but said nothing.

Devynck hesitated for a moment longer, then sighed. "All right. Loret, run to Point of Hopes—go out the back—and tell the chief point or Rathe exactly what's happened. Tell her I'm concerned, after last night, and I don't want there to be any misunderstandings."

"Yes, ma'am." Loret nodded, and headed out the garden door.

"You, Philip," Devynck went on, "can tell young Yvor that we won't open until second sunrise today, thanks to the damage. If he and his friends want to drink then, well, their coin is good to me. But I won't tolerate any trouble, any more than I usually do."

Eslingen nodded, and stepped back out into the dusty street. The young man Yvor was still sitting on the bench, but he looked up warily as the door opened.

"What's the matter, aren't we good enough to drink here?"

"Mistress Devynck says we won't be open until the second sunrise," Eslingen repeated, deliberately. "It's the damage to the windows, you understand."

The young man had the grace to look fleetingly abashed at that, but his wide mouth firmed almost at once into a stern pout. "And then?"

Eslingen eyed him without favor. "Then your money's as good as any, I suppose. I take it this is your half-day, then?"

Yvor's hand started toward the badge in his cap, but he stopped himself almost instantly. "And if it is?"

"I was wondering how you had the leisure to drink so early," Eslingen answered.

"That's hardly your business, Leaguer."

"Nothing about you is my business," Eslingen agreed. "Until you make it so." He went back into the inn without waiting for the younger man to answer.

Devynck opened her taps a little after noon, as she had promised, and, equally as promised, the butchers' journeymen appeared. The first group—Yvor and a pair of younger friends—bought a pitcher of beer and drank it as slowly as they could; when they left, another trio appeared, and then a third. A pointswoman arrived as well, dusty in her leather jerkin. She bought a drink herself, watching them, but admitted there was nothing she could do as long as they didn't make trouble.

"They're watching me, damn them," Devynck said, fiercely, and gestured for Eslingen to close the door of her counting room behind him. "They're watching me, and I know it, and there's damn all I can do about it."

"Kick them out," Eslingen said.

"Don't be stupid," Devynck snapped. "They're just waiting for me to try it. No, I can't be rid of them unless I close completely, not without provoking the trouble I want to prevent."

"So maybe you should close," Eslingen said. He held up his hand to forestall Devynck's angry curse. "You haven't been doing much business the last few nights, it might be safer—smarter—to close for a few days and see if it doesn't blow over."

Devynck shook her head. "I will see them in hell and me with them before I let them bully me."

And that, Eslingen thought, is that. He lifted both hands in surrender. "You're the boss," he said, and went back out into the main room. The journeymen—five of them, this time, and a different group—were still there, and he smiled brightly at them as he settled himself at his usual table. He reached for the stack of broadsheets, but couldn't seem to concentrate on the printed letters. He could hear snatches of the young men's conversations, animadversions against Leaguers and soldiers and child-thieves, suspected he was meant to hear, and met their glares with the same blank smile. They finished their first pitcher, and, after a muttered consultation and much searching of pockets, the youngest of the group got up and went to the bar with the empty jug. Hulet refilled it, narrow-eyed and sullen; the journeyman—he was little more than a boy, really—glared back, but had the sense to say nothing. As he returned to the table, a voice rose above the rest.

"—points searched the place, didn't find them."

Eslingen's attention sharpened at that, though he didn't move. Was someone going to make the commonsense argument at last? he wondered, and sighed almost inaudibly as a big man, fair as a Leaguer, shook his blond head.

"They were well fee'd not to find them, that's all. They're in it as deep as anyone—and that's what comes of giving ordinary folk that kind of power."

The oldest of the group leaned forward and said something, and the voices quieted again. Eslingen let himself relax, picked up another broadsheet at random, but it was no more successful than any of the others. He made himself read through it, however, all fifteen lines of obscure verse—the poet-astrologer was obviously a Demean in her sentiments—but couldn't tell whether the oblique intention was to blame foreigners or the city's regents. Not that it mattered, anyway, he added silently, and set the sheet aside. What mattered was what the butchers on the Knives Road believed, and they'd made that all too clear already.

The main door opened then, letting in a wedge of the doubled afternoon sunlight, and Rathe made his way into the bar. He was barely recognizable as a pointsman, his jerkin scarred and worn, the truncheon almost out of sight under its skirts, and one of the journeyman started to smile at him before he recognized what he was. The smile vanished then, and he turned his back ostentatiously. Rathe's eyebrows rose, but he said nothing directly, and came across the room to lean on Eslingen's table.

"I'll want to talk with you after I'm done with Devynck," he said, and Eslingen nodded, wondering what was going on. "There's been a nasty bit of damage here, and to real property," the pointsman went on, lifting his voice to carry to the young men at the other table. "That'll be an expensive point, when we catch who did it."

Eslingen hid a smile at that, but said nothing. The pointsman's mouth twitched in an answering almost-smile, and he turned away to disappear behind the bar. Eslingen leaned back in his chair again, watching the journeymen at their table, and wasn't surprised to see them leaning heads together. Their hands were moving, too, suppressed, choppy gestures, and then the oldest-looking stood up, shaking his head. He said something, but kept his voice low enough that Eslingen only caught two words, "hotheads" and then "Huviet." Another young man stood with the other, and then a third; the oldest looked down at the others, his head tilted to one side in obvious inquiry. They looked away, and the first three turned and pushed their way out of the main door. A quarrel over tactics? Eslingen wondered. Damaging property seemed to be a cardinal evil in Astreiant.

The kitchen door opened again, and Rathe came out. His gaze swept over the now-diminished table, and Eslingen almost would have sworn he smiled, but then the pointsman pointed toward the garden door. Eslingen sighed, and followed the other man out into the summer air. The garden was empty, the stools stacked on top of the tables, and he squinted toward the gate that led out into Point of Dreams, wondering if it was still locked and barred. He couldn't see for certain, not at this distance, but would have been surprised to find it open: Devynck was not one to take unnecessary chances. Rathe leaned his hip against the nearest table, as easy and comfortable as if he were drinking in his own neighborhood, and Eslingen gave him a sour look.

Rathe met it blandly. "I take it you haven't had any trouble with that lot in there?"

"Not yet," Eslingen answered, and knew he sounded bitter.

Rathe nodded. "I told Aagte she should close for a day or two, let this blow over."

"Do you really think this would go away in a day or two?" Eslingen demanded.

"No, not really. But they might find someone more likely to blame."

"They might," Eslingen said. "Anyway, when I suggested it, she said no."

Rathe nodded again. "She told me no, too." He sighed. "So how are they behaving themselves, these junior butchers?"

Eslingen made a face. "Well enough, at least today. Though I still think Aagte's right, it was them who broke our windows. But today, they're just sitting here. They pay for their beer politely enough, and they keep their voices down, haven't given me an excuse to be rid of them—or the pointswoman who was here earlier."

"That was Amerel Ghiraldy," Rathe said. "She's good."

Eslingen grunted. "Aagte thinks they're watching us, and I agree. I don't know whether they think you didn't find the missing children yesterday because you were bribed or because we were clever, or just because the kids weren't here, but they—the journeymen, anyway—are convinced that we're involved in all this, and they're going to keep an eye on us until they find something to blame us for. And if you hadn't given Huviet that much credence, searching our place, we might not be in this state."

For a minute, he thought he'd gone too far, and then the corners of Rathe's mouth turned up in a sour smile. "Monteia searched the place because she thought it'd make a difference. For you, not against you, I might add. Huviet is not universally loved, it seemed a good bet to call her bluff." The smile widened. "But I'll grant you it hasn't worked the way she planned."

"No." Eslingen leaned against another table, looked across the kitchen garden with its patches of herbs and vegetables. He smelled basil suddenly, and saw a gargoyle run a paw across the fragrant leaves. It reached beyond them, then, into the vegetables, and he stooped quickly, found a pebble, and slung it in the creature's direction. It lifted instantly, scolding, and he looked back at Rathe. "Instead of solving the problem of them thinking Leaguers are stealing their apprentices, they're now thinking the points are conspiring with us."

Rathe swore under his breath. "You're sure—no, sorry, that was stupid."

"It's what I've overheard," Eslingen answered.

Rathe muttered something else. The gargoyle circled the garden plot again, spiraling lower, heedless of the scarecrow, and he glanced down at the dirt beneath his feet. He found a heavier stone, and flung it with a violence that was startling. The gargoyle sheered away, barely able to dodge, and Rathe looked abashed. "Sorry. I should've expected it, I suppose."

"It seems to me—" Eslingen chose his words with care. "It seems to me that you might have done, yes. Given what I've paid in fees, and what I know Aagte and all the others here pay in fees—" He stopped at the look on Rathe's face, spread his hands in instant apology.

Rathe took a deep breath. "We don't all take fees for everything," he said, his voice ragged with temper, "and not for something like this. Gods, put the worst face on it, it'd be bad for business, making everyone hate us like this. Rather puts paid to our chance of getting more fees, don't you think?"

"I don't think," Eslingen said, and let the ambiguity stand. "I don't believe it, no. But it's how people are thinking now."

Rathe sighed again, visibly making himself relax. "No, I know it." He shrugged, managed a sudden, almost genuine grin. "People are getting used to us, to the points, but it's a slow process because it's not precisely what most people call a natural situation. People like me—a southriver rat, I know what they say, and half of them are serious—enforcing the laws on people like them, property owners, burghers, even guild-masters? It's not quite comfortable."

And from the sound of it, Eslingen thought, that's the part you like best about being a pointsman. He knew better than to say it aloud, however, after his previous gaffe, contented himself with saying, "So they're quick to think the worst."

Rathe nodded, the brief lightness going out of his face. "As I said, I should've expected it."

Eslingen hesitated, a new thought rising in his mind. If the points were under suspicion, what better way to defuse that than to find a scapegoat, and what better scapegoat would they find, at least in Point of Hopes, than Devynck and the people at the Old Brown Dog. He opened his mouth to voice that fear, took another look at Rathe, and closed it again. Neither Rathe nor Monteia would be party to that; all he would have to worry about was the journeymen's anger. "Is there any chance of a pointsman keeping watch here tonight? I daresay Aagte could find the extra fees, if it came to that."

Rathe's mouth twisted again. "She already asked. I said I'd try, but we're stretched pretty thin, with the fair beginning tomorrow and the nightwatch already overworked. They'll come by regularly, I'll see to that, but I can't promise to post anyone. I'll speak to the masters, too, see if that helps at all."

Eslingen sighed, but nodded. "I appreciate it, Rathe. As I'm sure Aagte does."

Rathe smiled wryly. "Oh, I still don't take fees, Eslingen, not even at times like these. As I said, I want to enjoy my points." He pushed himself away from the table, stretching slightly, eyes fixed on nothing in particular. In that instant, Eslingen was aware of dark shadows under the other man's eyes, lines that had not seemed as deeply carved bracketing his mouth. Obviously, he cared deeply about this business. And then Rathe shook himself, and the moment vanished. He lifted a hand in abstracted farewell, and went back through the inn. Eslingen followed, more slowly, hoping that the pointsman's plan would work.

The rest of the afternoon passed uneventfully enough, and as the first sundown approached, Eslingen began to hope that maybe the trouble would defuse itself. The knot of journeymen remained, but as the afternoon turned to evening and the sunlight faded to the silvery light of the winter-sun, they, too, seemed to mellow, seemed more relaxed at their table. A pointsman's clapper sounded from the street, the slow, steady beat of the wooden knot that marked the nightwatch, and he listened carefully as it moved close and then retreated. Rathe was keeping his promise there, at any rate. Jasanten appeared on his crutch, and no one said anything, or made his way more difficult than need be. Seeing that, Eslingen allowed himself a sigh of relief, and addressed his dinner—another of Devynck's stews, vegetables, and meat in a broth thickened with beer and bread—with something like a normal appetite. The brewer didn't make an appearance, but her son and a pair of his lemen, big, broad-shouldered men like himself came in for a quick pint. They kept a scrupulous distance between themselves and the journeymen, but the one exchange of words was polite enough. Eslingen drew a slow breath as they moved apart again, and saw Adriana's eyes on them as she brought him another pitcher of small beer.

"So far, so good," he said softly, and immediately wished he hadn't spoken. There was no point in tempting the gods.

She made a face, and Eslingen knew she was thinking the same thing. She set the pitcher in front of him, and then displayed her hands, fingers crossed in propitiation. "Only two more hours to second sunset. Sweet Tyrseis, I'll be glad when we close."

Eslingen nodded, and she turned away to answer a call from the kitchen. He poured himself another cup, but didn't bother to taste it, his attention instead on the others in the empty room. The brewer's son and his friends finished their drinks and the plate of bread and cheese and left, still quiet; the journeymen remained, were joined by another man who looked a little older than the rest. He, too, wore a butcher's badge at his collar, and even from a distance Eslingen could tell that it was made of silver, not the pewter the others wore. Someone of real rank within the guild, then, he thought, and wondered if it were a good or a bad sign. The group of journeymen seemed more relaxed, at any rate; he could see more smiles among them, and once heard laughter, but he wasn't sorry to hear the nightwatch's clapper in the street outside.

The light was fading steadily, paling toward true night. He went out to the garden privy, glad of the cooler air—the inn held the day's heat in its walls and floor, a benefit in winter, but uncomfortable at the height of the year—and on his way back looked west to see the diamond point of the winter-sun almost down between the housetops, poised between two chimney pots. Even this low, it was still too bright to look at directly, and he blinked, and went back into the main room, a point of green haze dancing in the center of his vision.

Loret emerged from the kitchen in almost the same moment, began closing the shutters on the garden wall. He had to stretch to fasten the upper bolts, and in the same moment, one of the journeymen called, "Hey, what are you doing?"

"Last call," Adriana said, from behind the bar. "It's almost closing, so if you want another round, this is your chance."

Eslingen moved closer to the bar, keeping an eye on the group at the table. They were the only customers, except for Jasanten, drowsing at his corner table, and there were only four of them; not bad odds, Eslingen thought, but I hope it doesn't come to that. The journeymen exchanged glances, and then the oldest one, the one with the silver badge, stood, stretching.

"Not for us, I think. Come on, let's pay and be gone."

The others copied him, reaching into purses and pockets to come up with a handful of copper coins. There was only the last pitcher to pay for; they counted out the coins, and the leader, shrugging, added a last demming to bring it up to the mark. Eslingen heard Adriana release a held breath, and nodded to Loret, who came to take the coins, touching his forehead in perfunctory salute. The journeymen ignored him, as they'd been ignoring him all night, and turned in a body for the door. Eslingen pulled himself away from the bar and followed, intending to bar the door as soon as they'd gone.

Before he could reach it, however, there was a shout from outside. He stepped hastily into the doorway, blocking it completely, and looked back over his shoulder for Loret. "Go to Point of Hopes, now."

The waiter's eyes widened, and he darted out the garden door.

"Trouble?" Adriana called, and banged on the kitchen door, a deliberate, prearranged pattern.

Eslingen nodded, not taking his eyes from the street. A new group was moving toward him from the Knives Road, a dozen people, maybe more. The leaders, at least, carried torches, and behind them their followers' shapes blended, in the new dark, into a single mass. The torchlight glinted from more badges at hat and coat, and Eslingen realized with a sinking feeling that at least some of these were masters, not mere journeymen. The group who had been drinking in the Old Brown Dog had stopped in the dooryard, and Eslingen could have sworn he saw confusion in the leader's face.

"You, soldier!"

The voice was unfamiliar, sounded older than the run of journeymen, and Eslingen couldn't suppress a grimace. If the masters were leading, this time, it would be a hell of a lot harder to get them to back down.

"Stand aside," the voice went on, and Eslingen shook his head.

"I'm sorry, sir, we're closed."

"What in all hells do they want?" Devynck demanded, but softly.

Eslingen didn't dare look back at her, but he could feel her presence at his elbow. "I don't know yet," he answered, and kept his voice equally low, "but I sent Loret to Point of Hopes."

"Good man." Devynck pressed something into the palm of his hand, and with a shock Eslingen recognized the butt of his own pistol. He took it, keeping it hidden behind the skirts of his coat, looked out into the street.

"Stand aside, soldier," the voice came again, and Devynck swore under her breath.

"That's Nigaud, I thought he was a friend."

"We know you've got the children here," a lighter voice chimed in, "and we're not going away until we've found them."

"Huviet," Eslingen said, and didn't bother to hide his disgust. He lifted his voice to carry to the group's leader. "His mother made the same complaint yesterday, brought the pointsmen here and searched, and found nothing. I don't see why we're still suspected. There are no children here."

"Then stand aside and let us see for ourselves," Nigaud answered.

"Over my dead body," Devynck muttered. "Adriana. Fetch my sword, and Philip's."

Eslingen didn't move, though he heard the rustle of cloth as Adriana did as she was told. "We've been searched already, by those with the right to do it. If I let you in, when you find nothing, what'll you do, break the rest of our windows?"

"If you don't have anything to hide, why don't you let us in?" Paas Huviet shouted, and there was a little murmur of agreement from the crowd.

"I won't let you in because you don't have a right to be here," Eslingen called, "and you don't offer me any promises that you won't loot the place while you're here. Gods, man, there were people from your guild drinking here all day, ask them if they saw any sign of the children."

There was a little pause, and the leader of the last group stepped into the circle of torchlight. "I didn't see anything, I admit. But they could be somewhere else in the building."

"See?" Huviet shouted.

"They're going to come in," Eslingen said, under his breath, and heard Devynck's grunt of agreement.

"Loret's gone for the points, see if we can at least get them to agree to that."

Eslingen nodded. "Masters," he called, "we understand your concerns for the children—we're worried, too, we all know someone who's lost a child." That was an exaggeration, but he hoped it would pass in the dark and the excitement. "But I've a responsibility to this house and to Mistress Devynck. Send someone to the points, Point of Hopes or Point of Dreams, it doesn't matter, but send to them. Let one of them come with you, keep everything on the right side of the law, and I'll gladly let you pass."

There was a murmur at that, half approving, half uncertain, and Paas's voice rose over the general noise. "They fee'd the points not to find them, why should we trust them?"

"Be quiet," Nigaud snapped.

At his side, Eslingen felt Adriana's sudden presence, glanced down to see her holding his sword at the ready. Behind her, Jasanten perched on a table, Devynck's caliver and another pistol in his lap, busy loading them with powder and ball. Hulet stood in the garden door, half-pike in hand.

"Even if the points are fee'd in this," Nigaud went on, "which I'm not convinced of, Paas, for all your talk, they still can't stop us from searching where we please. I'm prepared to send for a pointsman, soldier—unless you've already done so?"

"Go ahead," Eslingen answered, and Nigaud nodded to one of the younger journeymen.

"Go on, then, go to Point of Hopes."

Eslingen held his breath, not moving from the inn's doorway. The longer they could postpone this, the more time the butchers had to think about what they were doing and about what they might do. The masters, at least, were property owners; the more time they had to think about the precedent they were setting, the better for Devynck. The more time they waited, without hostilities, without provocation, the more time there was for the blood to cool, and it was a rare man who, untrained, could order an attack in cold blood. The group's leaders, Nigaud and another man in a full-skirted coat, a master's badge in his hat, were talking again, their voices too low to be heard more than a few feet away. After a moment, the leader of the last group of journeymen moved to join them, and Eslingen saw him spread his hands in an expressive shrug.

Then he heard the sound of the nightwatch's wooden clapper again, faster now, as though its holder was running, coming from the western end of the Knives Road. About half the gathered journeymen turned to look, and one of the torchbearers turned with them, lifting her torch to send its light further down the dark street. A pointsman appeared at the end of the street, his lantern swinging with the beat of the clapper; the young journeyman trailed breathlessly at his heels.

"What's all this, then?" the pointsman asked, and put his free hand on his truncheon. Eslingen swore under his breath, and heard Devynck curse.

"What do that stars have against me, that it should be Ranazy?" she muttered. "We're in trouble now, Philip."

"This is an illegal gathering," the pointsman went on, lifting his voice to carry over the angry murmur that answered his first words. "I'll have to tell you to disperse, or face the point."

"Like hell we will," someone shouted, and Nigaud waved his arms for silence.

"Pointsman, we have cause to think that the missing children—our missing children, anyway—are being held at the Old Brown Dog. I, and Master Estienes, and Master Follet, are all willing to swear the complaint, and anything else you like, but we won't leave here until that place has been searched from top to bottom."

Ranazy stopped in the middle of the street, seemed for the first time to become aware of the crowd's temper. "Master—Nigaud, isn't it?"

Nigaud nodded. Obviously, Eslingen thought, the man was well known, a man of real importance in Point of Hopes—and not the person we want standing against us.

"Master, this house was searched yesterday, and we found nothing. The children aren't here." Ranazy spread his hands, the lantern and the clapper jangling.

"Ranazy!" The shout came from the end of the street. Rathe's voice, Eslingen realized, with real relief, and in the same instant saw a tight knot of pointsmen, maybe ten in all, turn the corner. They, too, carried lanterns, and in their light Eslingen could see the dull gleam of armor under the leather jerkins. They carried calivers as well, new-fashioned flintlocks, as well as half-pikes and halberds: Rathe and his people had come prepared for serious trouble.

"I searched it myself," Ranazy went on, and Paas Huviet's voice rose above the angry murmuring.

"You see? I told you they were fee'd to let them go. Search the inn ourselves, we won't get the kids back any other way."

"Hold it," Rathe shouted again, but his voice was drowned in the roar of agreement.

"Break in the door," another voice shouted. "Save the children."

The journeymen surged toward the inn's door. Eslingen took a deep breath, and brought the pistol out from behind his coat. "Stop there," he called, and leveled the barrel at the knot of young men. At this distance he could hardly miss hitting one of them, but he doubted they were cool enough to realize it. Adriana pressed the hilt of his sword into his left hand, and he took it, already bracing himself for the rush that would follow the first shot.

"We're willing to let the points in," he tried again, and Paas's voice rose in answer.

"Because you paid them. Get him!"

"I'll fire," Eslingen warned, and promised Areton an incense cake if the lock did not misfire. The pointsmen were hurrying toward him, half-pikes held across their bodies, but the bulk of the journeymen were between them and the inn, and showed no sign of giving way.

"Cowards!" Paas shouted. "Get the Leaguer bastard!" He lunged for the door, drawing his knife, and there were half a dozen men behind him. Eslingen swore again, and pulled the trigger. The lock fired, the flash and bang of the powder momentarily blinding everyone, and then he'd slung the pistol behind him onto the inn's floor and drew his sword right-handed. Paas staggered back, clutching his chest—the shot was mortal, Eslingen knew instantly, and didn't know whether he was glad or sorry—and collapsed in the arms of the journeymen behind him.

"Hold it!" Rathe shouted again, and he and his troop shoved their way through the crowd that seemed abruptly chastened by the violence. "Nigaud, get your boys in hand, or I'll call points on the lot of you."

"He shot Paas," one of the journeymen called, and his voice broke painfully.

"I saw it," Rathe answered, "and I saw Paas charge the door, too." He glanced over his shoulder. "Where's the nearest physician, Clock Street?" He seemed to get an answer from one of the pointsmen, and nodded. "Fetch her, quick, then, see what can be done for the boy. Now, Nigaud, what in Astree's name is going on here?"

"They're hiding the children," Nigaud said, and Eslingen let himself relax at last. Somehow, exactly how he didn't know, Rathe had gotten control of the situation again. Astreiant's common folk might not like giving one of their own authority, but in a crisis, it seemed it was better than nothing.

Rathe said, "The chief point herself searched this house yesterday, and nothing was found. You've seen something that makes you think they're here now? I know you had people watching this house, I saw them here this afternoon."

Nigaud's gaze faltered, but he rallied quickly enough. "The chief point may have been here, but none of us were, and the rest of the points were people like him." He pointed to Ranazy. "We know how much his fees are, we all pay them. The Leaguer has money enough to buy his silence."

Eslingen jumped as Devynck touched his shoulder.

"Let me out," she said, and he stepped sideways to let her edge past him. "Rathe! I'm willing to let the masters search my house this time, if only you'll supervise them, and I told them that all along."

Rathe nodded, looked at Nigaud. "That's more than you have a right to, Master Nigaud, but I'm willing to go with you, and the other masters here."

Nigaud nodded back, but the well-dressed master—Follet, Eslingen thought—said, "And what about Paas? He was a hothead, but he was my journeyman."

The physician had arrived from Clock Street, an apprentice, barefoot and tousled, lugging her case of instruments. She knelt beside the injured man, her movements brisk and certain, but she looked up at that, and shook her head. "I've done what I can. It's in Demis's hands now."

In translation, Eslingen thought, he's a dead man. Why in Areton's name didn't I aim for something less mortal? The damned astrologer got it all wrong. He shook the thought away—he'd had no choice, if he'd missed Paas he would almost certainly have hit one of the others in as deadly a spot—and looked at Rathe, wondering what would happen now. Rathe looked back at him, his face expressionless in the uncertain light of the lanterns and the dying torches.

"It's manslaughter at the least, though there's an argument for self-defense. Eslingen, I'm calling a point on you. Hand over your weapons and go quietly."

Eslingen drew breath to protest, but swallowed the words unspoken. The situation was still delicate, even he could see that much, and surely Rathe was right when he hinted that he could claim self-defense. "Very well," he said shortly, and extended his sword, hilt first, toward the pointsman.

Rathe took it, unsurprised by the weight and balance, rested its point cautiously on the top of his boot. "And the pistol?"

Eslingen jerked his head toward the inn door. "Inside, on the floor somewhere."

"Adriana!" Rathe called, and a moment later the woman appeared warily in the doorway. "Bring me Eslingen's pistol, please."

For an instant, Eslingen thought she was going to refuse, but she only tossed her head, and vanished back into the shadows. She reappeared a moment later carrying the pistol, and crossed the dooryard without looking at the butchers. Rathe took the gun, slipping it into his belt beside his truncheon; Adriana turned on her heel, and went to join her mother. The pointsman looked back at Eslingen, who braced himself to hear the sentence.

"Benech and Savine will take you to Point of Sighs." He lifted his voice to carry to the crowd. "The cells there are more secure than at Point of Hopes." Eslingen thought he saw a fugitive smile cross Rathe's face. "And a bit more comfortable than a stall, which is what ours are. Do you give me your word you'll go quietly, lieutenant?"

Eslingen hesitated, wondering if he shouldn't run—he could take the two pointsmen, of that he felt certain, and he had killed the journeyman, not to mention being a Leaguer in the wrong place at the wrong time—but then put the thought away. He hadn't stolen the children, and neither had Devynck; and if he ran, he would only put her further in the wrong. "You have my word on it," he said, stiffly, and Rathe nodded.

"Right, then. See that he gets there safely."

"Thank you for that," Eslingen said, not entirely sarcastically, and turned to face the two pointsmen. "Lead on."

6

It took the better part of the next two hours to lead Nigaud and a handful of his journeymen through the Old Brown Dog. Rathe was careful to stand aside and let them do most of the work, intervening only when Devynck's stores seemed threatened, and at the end of it Nigaud faced him with visible embarrassment.

"There's no one here," he said, at last, and Rathe barely stopped himself from nodding.

"No," he said, instead, and kept his tone and face impassive. "Will you say as much to your people, Master Nigaud, you and Master Follet?"

"We will," Nigaud said shortly, and Follet cleared his throat.

"And how much of a difference does this make in terms of a point?"

Rathe cocked his head to one side. "What do you mean?"

Follet took a deep breath. "People of mine are liable for riot, I can see that, just as that knife of Devynck's is liable for manslaughter. So where do we stand with that, Adjunct Point?"

Rathe studied him for a long moment, torn between anger and a grudging respect for the man. Follet's journeymen—and Nigaud's and probably a few others'—could indeed be taken up for provoking trouble and assault, especially after they'd all been warned the day before; at least he was acknowledging it, even if he was also angling for a fee. "Given the circumstances, Master Follet—I've been working on the business of Mailet's missing apprentice myself, along with a dozen others, I know how frantic we all are. Given the circumstances, I'm prepared to overlook the formal point on your journeymen. Paas Huviet's hurt, maybe dying, that's enough for me. However, we will require two things from you, masters. First, I want you to post a bond for good behavior for the ringleaders among the journeymen—you know who they are as well as I do, and I'll give you the names in the morning." He held up his hand to forestall the automatic protest. "This is a bond, not a fee, you'll get it back when they make their appearance at the fall assizes as long as there's no more trouble from them. I don't want fees from you, or from anyone right now. I want to be free to chase these child-thieves where or whoever they are. Is that clear?"

He could hear himself on the verge of anger, was not surprised to see Follet's matching frown, but Nigaud lifted both hands in surrender. "The guild will pay the bonds, Adjunct Point."

Follet nodded. "You said two things?"

"That's right." Rathe did his best to moderate his tone. "Devynck's knife, Eslingen—I don't expect you to press the point. It was self-defense and defense of property, and that's where it will stand."

Nigaud looked at Follet. "He was your journeyman."

Follet made a face, as though he'd bitten into something sour. "And he was at fault, I admit it. All right. I won't press the point."

"Good." Rathe sighed, suddenly aware of how late it was, and in the same moment heard the tower clock strike three. "Then let's get your people home."

He made it back to his own lodgings in time to snatch a few hours' sleep, but dragged himself out of bed as the local clock sounded eight. Someone from the Butchers' Guild would be coming to pay the journeymen's bond, and he wanted to be there personally to oversee the process. Still, he was later than usual as he entered the gate at Point of Hopes, and glanced around to see if the guild's representative had somehow gotten there ahead of him. There was no sign of him or her, and he allowed himself a sigh of relief.

"We're sent for," Monteia said.

Rathe paused in the station doorway, coat already halfway off his shoulders. He looked at her, seeing the unexpected tidiness of her clothes—her best skirt, unmistakably, and probably her best bodice beneath the polished leather of her jerkin—and the truncheon slung neatly at her waist. "The sur?" he asked, and Monteia gave a grim smile.

"The city." She nodded to the table where the duty recorder sat, trying very hard to pretend she wasn't all ears. A half sheet of good paper lay among the clutter of slates and reused broadsheets, the city seal at its foot visible from across the room.

Rathe's eyebrows rose at that, and he shrugged himself back into his coat, crossed to the table to pick up the summons. It was from the Council of Regents, all right, signed by the grande bourgeoise herself, and her seal lay just above the more massive slab of wax that was the city's.

"The sur will be there, of course," Monteia went on, "but it's for us—me, primarily. Madame Gausaron dislikes disorder."

Rathe nodded absently, skimming through the neat lines of secretarial hand. "All right," he said, "but I don't know what she thinks we should have done."

"Nor I." Monteia studied him thoughtfully. "Houssaye! I won't have you, Nico, appearing before the regents like that. It won't help us any if you look hungry."

"Chief Point—"

"Ma'am?" That was Houssaye, the station's junior pointsman, coming in from the garden belting his trousers. He finished that and reached for the buttons of his coat, but Monteia shook her head at him.

"Don't bother. You're loaning that to Nico—we've business with the regents."

Houssaye blinked, but slipped obediently out of the coat. "Yes, Chief."

"I have clothes of my own," Rathe said.

"And no time to fetch them," Monteia answered. "This is important, Nico."

Rathe started to bridle, but she was right, of course, it mattered how one looked, prosperous but sober, particularly when one was dealing with the women of the Council of Regents, but he had dressed for the work he expected, not for a council visit. Not that his best clothes were anything out of the ordinary—he was hard on clothes, and knew it, had learned to buy good plain materials that stood the wear—but it stung to be dressed like a child in someone else's best. Still, Houssaye was his size and build and coloring; as he pulled the light wool over his shoulders, he had to admit that it wasn't too far from something he might have bought himself. He fastened the waist buttons—loose; Houssaye had an inch or three on him there—and hastily rewound the stock that fastened the neck of his shirt. "We've got people from the Butchers' Guild coming to post bond, and I wanted to be there," he muttered, a last protest, and reached for his jerkin and the truncheon that hung beneath it.

"Oh, you can still have that one," Monteia answered, and looked at Houssaye. "You're in charge until Salineis gets in or we get back—I told her she could sleep in, after last night. The release order is in my office, get a fair copy made and send it off to Point of Sighs as soon as you can. Use the station seal. When the guildmasters show up, tell them they'll have to wait—and you can tell them why."

"Yes, Chief."

"What's going to happen to Eslingen?" Rathe said. "It wasn't exactly fair, calling the point on him, no matter how necessary it was." He still felt obscurely guilty for calling a point on the Leaguer, couldn't quite work up much indignation for Paas Huviet, even if he had been shot. His eye fell on the daybook, and the most recent entry: Paas Huviet had died close to first sunrise, according to the physician who'd tended him. He considered it, but even the death didn't make much difference. Huviet had been a troublemaker, Eslingen had been doing his job, and that, he hoped, would be an end to it.

"It's technically manslaughter," Monteia said, and jammed her hat onto her piled hair. Rathe looked at her, and she sighed. "But I've ordered his release, you heard me do it, and I won't be pressing charges unless and until someone's stupid enough to force me to it. Does that meet with your approval, Adjunct Point?"

Rathe nodded. "He did the best he could—better than I'd've expected, frankly, it was a nasty situation. And it wasn't him who started it."

"I know," Monteia said. "And you know why you had to do it. Now, come on." She swept through the door without waiting for an answer.

Rathe followed, aware of the unfamiliar weight of the coat's skirts around his legs. They hampered his knife hand, got in the way of his reach either for purse or tablets, but he had to admit that the beer brown wool looked good against his skin, and against the decent linen of his shirts. It might be nice to have a coat like this, for best—he put the thought firmly aside. The coat might look well enough now, but after a month of his wearing, it would be as shapeless as any other he owned. Monteia had a nice eye for clothes on a man—but then, she had a son just reaching apprenticeship, and the vanities that went with it.

They crossed the Hopes-point Bridge, squinting in the morning light that glinted from the river. The sun was still low in the sky, the shadows long, the winter-sun not yet risen, and there was dew on the grass as they crossed the gardens of the Maternite. It would be hot later, Rathe thought, and made a face at the irrelevance of the concern.

The only heat he needed to worry about would come from the council.

The regents met at All-Guilds at the heart of the Mercandry. The massive building dominated the little square, four stories high, new halls built against the walls of the original until the walls rose like stair-steps to the point of the roof. The old-style carvings above the arch of the main entrance showed Heira presiding over a banquet of the various craft deities. Rathe recognized Didonae and Hesion and a few of the deities invoked by the lesser guilds, but there were a good half dozen he couldn't place at once. Which wasn't that surprising, he added silently: each craft was its own mystery, and had its own rites and special patrons. No one could know them all, not even the university specialists. Only Bonfortune was missing: the god of the long-distance traders had no place in this gathering of Merchants Resident.

One of the four doors was open, and Monteia led the way into the sudden shadow. Inside, the hall was startlingly cool, the heavy stones still holding a faint chill from the winter's cold. The people hurrying past—young women, mostly, the long blue robes of guild affiliation thrown casually over brighter skirts and bodices, clutching ledgers and tablets—barely seemed to notice their existence, or no more than was necessary to avoid running into them. Rathe made a face, but knew enough to keep his mouth shut, and followed Monteia to the foot of the main staircase. There was a guard there, a greying man in council livery and polished back-and-breast, half-pike in hand: more symbolic than anything, Rathe thought, but it wasn't a symbol he much liked.

"Chief Point Monteia, Point of Hopes," Monteia said. "And Adjunct Point Rathe."

The soldier nodded gravely. "Down the hall to your left, Chief Point. Madame Gausaron is waiting."

Monteia nodded back, and turned away. Sunlight striped the stones of the hall, falling through windows cut into the wall above the roof of the building's latest addition, and Rathe was grateful for its intermittent warmth. Another young woman in the blue guilds'-coat was waiting by a carved door; as they got closer, he could see the council's badge, a stylized version of Heira's Banquet, embroidered above her left breast. She bowed her head slightly at their approach, and said, "Chief Point Monteia?"

"Yes." Only the twitch of Monteia's lips betrayed any emotion at all. "And Adjunct Point Rathe. For the grande bourgeoise."

The woman nodded again, and swung the door open for them. "Chief Point Monteia and Adjunct Point Rathe."

The room was very bright, startlingly so after the shadows of the entrance and the intermittent sunlight of the hallway. Two of the four walls were fretted stone, a pattern of flowers filled in with orbs of colored glass, so that they looked out into the garden behind All-Guilds through another garden made of light and shade. Rathe blinked, dazzled, and brought himself to attention at Monteia's side. He had never been this far into All-Guilds—never been this close to any of the guild mistresses who controlled the city's day-to-day government—but he refused to show his ignorance.

"So. What the devil is going on southriver, Surintendant, that your people can't keep control of a tavern fight?" The speaker was a tall woman in the expensive respectable black of a merchant whose family had kept shop on the Mercandry for a hundred years. There was fine lace at her collar and cuffs, and on her cap, forming a incongruously delicate frame for her long, heavy-fleshed face. She looked, Rathe thought, with sudden, inward delight, rather like Monteia would, if the chief point were fattened for a season or three.

"Madame, the situation is hardly normal," the surintendant began, and Gausaron waved a hand that glinted with gold leaf.

"No, Surintendant, it's all too normal. The points do nothing—for what reason I don't know, and make no judgment, yet—until the situation is past bearing. And then a man, an honest journeyman-butcher, is shot dead in the street."

"This is not a question of fees—" Monteia began, and the surintendant cut in hastily.

"Madame, the people who attacked the tavern were and are concerned for their missing children, but they were still outside the law."

"We're all concerned about the missing children." The voice came from the shadows behind the grande bourgeoise's desk, a cool, pleasant voice that somehow suggested a smile. The speaker—she had been sitting in the shadows all the while, Rathe realized—rose slowly and came around the edge of the desk, skirts rustling with the unmistakable sound of silk. The metropolitan of Astreiant, the queen's half-niece and one of the stronger candidates for the throne, leaned back against the desk, and smiled benevolently over the gathering. "And I know some of the actions the points have already taken, thanks to you, Surintendant. But I'd like to hear from you, Chief Point, what happened last night. And from the beginning, if you please."

"Your Grace." Monteia took a deep breath, and launched into an account of the trouble, beginning with the Old Brown Dog and its history, through the complaints that Devynck was hiding the missing children and her own search of the premises, to the violence of the night before. Her voice was remote, almost stilted, faltering only slightly when she came to Paas's death. Rathe, who had heard her speak a hundred times before, watched Astreiant instead. She looked no older than himself, tall and strongly built, with the body of someone who faced active sports and the table with equal pleasure. She wore her hair loose, the thick tarnished-brass curls caught back under a brimless cap. The style flattered her handsome features—lucky for her that's the latest fashion, Rathe thought, and only then thought to wonder if she'd started it.

"And you're certain this Devynck has nothing to do with these missing children," Astreiant said, and Rathe recalled himself to the business at hand.

"Absolutely certain, Your Grace," Monteia answered.

The grande bourgeoise made a soft noise through her teeth, and Astreiant darted an amused glance in her direction. "I think what Madame is too polite to say is that you've taken Devynck's fees."

"I have," Monteia answered. "And I've taken fees from every other shopkeeper and guildmistress and tavern-keeper in Point of Hopes, too. It'd be more to the point, Madame, Your Grace, to say I'm Aagte Devynck's friend, because I am, and I make no secret of it. But it's because I know her, because I'm her friend and I know what she will and won't sell, that I can tell you she would never be involved in something like this. I'm as sure of that as I'm sure of my own stars."

Astreiant nodded gravely. "Will the rest of Point of Hopes believe it, though? I'm as concerned as Madame Gausaron with keeping the peace southriver."

Monteia looked away, looked toward the surintendant as though for reassurance, then back at Astreiant. "Your Grace, I think so. It's morning, they're chastened by what they did." She darted a glance at the grande bourgeoise. "As Madame said, there was a death to no purpose. I think it's sobered them all down."

"Yes, the journeyman-butcher," Astreiant said. She looked at Gausaron. "I must say, Madame, I think he got what he deserved. Threatening a woman's property—the knife, what's-his-name, seems to have been within his right."

"What's being done with the knife?" Gausaron asked.

"Madame, he was taken to the cells at Point of Sighs," Monteia answered.

"He'll be released today," Rathe said, and heard the challenge in his voice too late. "The point's bound to be disallowed—it was self-defense, not just defense of property."

Astreiant fixed her gaze on him for the first time. Her eyes were very pale, a color between blue and grey, and tilted slightly downward at the outer corners. "It seems a reasonable interpretation," she said, after a moment, and Rathe wondered what she had been going to say. She looked at Gausaron. "Madame, it's a dangerous time, and you're right to be concerned, but I have to say, I think the chief point handled this as well as anyone could have."

The grand bourgeoise nodded, rather grudgingly. "Though there'd be less to worry about if they'd find out who's stealing our children."

"Madame, we are trying," the surintendant said, through clenched teeth.

"And I would appreciate your keeping me informed of your progress," Astreiant said, and pushed herself away from Gausaron's desk. "And in the meantime, I know we've taken enough of your time."

It was unmistakably a dismissal. Rathe bowed, not as reluctantly as sometimes, and followed the other pointsmen from the room. As the door closed behind them, the surintendant touched his shoulder.

"That was well handled, Monteia. I want to borrow Rathe, if you don't mind."

"I'm glad Astreiant was there," Monteia said, and only then seemed to hear the rest of the surintendant's words. "I'll need him back, sir, and soon."

"Only for a moment," the surintendant answered, and Monteia shook her head, lips tightening.

"Very well, sir. Rathe, I'll want to talk to you when you get back." She turned, skirts swirling, walked away down the hall, her low heels ringing on the stones.

"Yes, Chief," Rathe said, to her departing back, and wondered what was going to happen now. He knew Monteia distrusted Fourie—he shared the feeling himself at times—and found himself, not for the first time, reviewing the list of his most recent behavior.

Fourie's thin lips were twisted into an ironic smile, as though he'd read the thought. "I may have just made more trouble for you, Rathe. Sorry."

And if you are, that's the first time, Rathe thought, but couldn't muster real resentment. This was the way the surintendant worked; he could accept it or not, but live with it he had to. "What was it you wanted, sir?"

Fourie shook his head, looking around the busy hall. "This is no place to talk. Come with me."

Rathe followed him through the Clockmakers' Square and then

along the arcaded walk that ran along the southern edge of the Temple Fair, feeling if anything rather like a dog of somewhat dubious breed. Fourie made no comment, never even looked back, until at last he stopped by one of the tall casements that looked out across the dust-drifted paving. The ballad-sellers and the printers seemed to be doing their usual brisk business, but there were fewer children than usual among the crowd. Rathe looked again, but saw no sign of black robes or grey, freelance astrologers or students.

"They're only interested because it's bad for business," Fourie said. His tone was conversational, but Rathe wasn't fooled. The surintendant was angrier than he had let on in the grande bourgeoise's presence—in Astreiant's presence—angry that two of his people had been questioned by the regents's representative, angry that none of them had done anything to find the missing children, angriest of all that he didn't have any more likely course of action than he had the day the first child had disappeared. And don't we all feel that way, Rathe thought, but I wish I were elsewhere just now.

"If it weren't for the fair," Fourie went on, "they wouldn't be quite so concerned. Of course, if it were just southriver brats going missing, they wouldn't even have noticed. Makes me sick. Do your jobs, but expect us to interfere every chance we got, and don't, whatever you do, let doing your jobs disturb us."

"Astreiant seems a bit more—reasonable," Rathe ventured, wondering where this was leading.

The surintendant seemed on the verge of a snort, then shook his head. "No, you're right about that. Astreiant seems to have a finer understanding of what's involved in the enforcement of the queen's law. Gods only know where she got it. It doesn't seem to run in the nobility."

"Or the haut bourgeoisie," Rathe said, unable to stop himself, and Fourie responded with another thin smile.

"Oh, they're worse. And I daresay you and I could go on like this all day with our grievances, but that would get nothing done. So, Rathe. What have you done about Caiazzo?"

Not precisely the haut bourgeoisie, no long-distance trader is, but close enough, Rathe thought. I might have known where this was leading. "I wasn't aware, sir, that you precisely wanted me to do anything. I thought my writ was to keep an eye on him, for any possible involvement in these disappearances, and that I've done. I've spoken with him, mostly on the matter of his printers. And that knife of his I made the point on at the end of the Dog Moon." He shook his head. "But—

I'm sorry, sir—I just don't see that this is anything Caiazzo would get himself involved in. Where's the reason behind it, sir? And, more to the point, where's the profit? Oh, I know what you said about political profit, but that's never been his style, it's too—too far down the road. Caiazzo always wants results he can see now as well as make use of later. Sure, he could make use of a political profit later, but where's the immediate profit?"

Fourie shrugged, a faint frown creasing the space between his eyebrows, and Rathe realized he'd let himself get carried away by his own argument. "Have your investigations turned up something more likely, Adjunct Point?"

"I'll agree it's likely the starchange is involved," Rathe said, stung, and remembered b'Estorr's account of the rumors circulating at the university. "As a matter of fact, I've been wondering about these hedge-astrologers the Three Nations were complaining about." He hadn't meant it, had just been looking for an alternative, but as his own words sank in, he pursued the thought. "Think of it—where have they come from? They don't claim association with any of the altars, or with the university—and they've pissed off the students as a body, which sensible people don't do—and ostensibly claim no political affiliation. And if you're not buying that bill of goods for Caiazzo, sir, you can't buy it from these."

The surintendant studied him with a jaundiced gaze. "Then I trust the arbiters of the fair, or Fairs' Point, or University Point, are looking into it, as well as you. But at the same time, I don't want you ignoring the possibility of Caiazzo's involvement in favor of your own theories—I very carefully don't say because you like him. This is too important, Nico. Whatever you think of my feelings toward him, I wouldn't order you do to something like this if I didn't think—feel—there was good reason. But I want it done."

Rathe took a deep breath, held it until his own temper subsided. Fourie had spent more time in the company—the presence—of the grande bourgeoise. If Gausaron had left Monteia, and Rathe himself, a little short-tempered, it was astonishing that the surintendant had kept his notoriously short temper in check for so long. "I'll keep an eye on him, sir, though I won't pretend it'll be easy."

Fourie smiled, a bloodless expression, without humor. "If it were easy, Nico, I wouldn't have insisted on your doing it."

And that, Rathe thought, was as close to a commendation as anyone got from the sur, short of a eulogy.

When he got back to the station, the hour-stick was just showing midday, and he made a face at it: it had already been a long day, and didn't look to get any shorter. He found Houssaye, returned his coat to him, and shrugged gratefully back into his own, welcoming its familiarity. He had just settled in at his worktable when Salineis poked her head in the door.

"Lieutenant Eslingen to see you, Nico."

Rathe bit back a groan—he doubted the Leaguer was there to thank him for anything—but nodded. "All right, send him in."

Eslingen had clearly found—or taken—the time to tidy himself up from the depredations of a night spent in one of Sighs' cells. His hair was caught neatly back, though the ribbon no longer matched the color of his coat, his hat was brushed, its plume uncrushed, and his linen was bright. Rathe wished for a moment that he hadn't been in such a hurry to return Houssaye's coat, then put the thought aside with impatience. The Eslingens of this world would always seek to gain advantage through appearance, and the Rathes could never hope to match them. What did surprise Rathe was the lack of resentment he felt toward the soldier.

"Adjunct Point." Eslingen's voice was icy, and Rathe's heart sank. Clearly, Eslingen felt rather differently about the whole thing.

"Eslingen, look, I'm sorry about what happened, but I didn't have a choice."

"It wasn't me who started this—Seidos's Horse, you ought to thank me for ridding you of a troublemaker."

"We don't generally shoot them dead," Rathe shot back, and, hearing his voice rise, got up to close the door of the narrow anteroom. He shook his head. "Forget it, it's not worth arguing about."

"I'm inclined to disagree with you, Adjunct Point, seeing as it's lost me my job."

Rathe turned to stare at Eslingen. "You're joking. No, no—sorry, forget I said that. She let you go?"

"Can you blame her? In times like these, does she want a Leaguer who, even in self-defense, and—what was it the magistrate said the release said—defense of property, was seen to kill a member of one of the most influential guilds in the city? I'd say that would be bad for business in a bad time, wouldn't you, Adjunct Point? So now I'm in your city without employment or a roof over my head. All because I did what you told me to, Rathe, and that's send for the points if there was any trouble. I did, and look what happened." He gestured widely, and for the first time Rathe noticed the heavy saddlebags on the floor at the other man's feet. "Hells, I thought we Leaguers were looked on with disfavor, I didn't realize the extent of the loathing people have for your lot."

"That was Ranazy," Rathe said, and didn't add, *and you know it.* "He's a bully and not a cheap one. And he makes us all look bad. You know how Devynck feels about Monteia—for that matter, you know how Devynck feels about me. So you can tar us all with the same brush, fine, everyone else does, or you can see that it's the truth. We're all blamed for the actions of a few. Sound familiar?"

Eslingen stared at the pointsman for a long minute, the anger fading as he recognized the justice of what Rathe had said, and done. "It sounds familiar," he said. "Can I sit?" He nodded to the chair along the wall.

Rathe rubbed his eyes. "Of course. Sorry. Not a good morning for you, and the night won't have been much better, for all they're a decent lot at Sighs." He sat back down behind his table, leaning his elbows on its well-worn surface. "What can I do?"

Confronted by it, Eslingen found himself at a loss. He had been bolstering himself with his anger, thoughts of the demands he would make on the pointsman, but now he could only shake his head. "Gods know, Rathe. I need a place to live, I need a job." He grinned suddenly. "But don't think I'm applying for a job with the points. I don't think we'd suit, so you?"

"I've seen odder," Rathe answered, but tipped his chair back to stare thoughtfully at the ceiling. "There ought to be plenty of work available just now—" He heard Eslingen draw breath to protest, and hurried on. "—but I can understand a lot of it's not really what you're looking for." He tipped his head in a shrug. "It's never easy for gentlemen to find appropriate work, and that's what your commission would make you, isn't it? So hiring on as a fairground knife would be right out."

"Putting that aside, since I will get hungry eventually, would anyone hire a Leaguer right now?" Eslingen asked.

"Some would," Rathe answered, absently, but then the thought struck him. There was one job that he knew of, was almost sure the place hadn't been filled, and it would get him personally out of a good deal of trouble. . . . "Some might." Oh, gods, he added silently, am I really going to do this? He leaned forward, intent now. "Look, Eslingen, you've got every right to be angry—my having no choice doesn't help you losing your place—but maybe, just maybe, I can make it up to you. That was what you came here for, wasn't it?"

Eslingen nodded, the faintest of smiles on his handsome face. "That, and the thought of wringing your neck."

"Which would have put you back in cells," Rathe pointed out, "and here rather than Sighs."

"I've slept in stables before." The smile might have widened a fraction, but Rathe couldn't be sure.

"All right then. But I want to be plain with you about this. I think the job would suit you. The man I'm thinking of lives like a gentleman, and is highly respected throughout Astreiant."

"I'm sensing a 'but,' " Eslingen said.

"A couple of them, actually. His name's Hanselin Caiazzo, and if you were still working at Devynck's, I'd tell you to ask her about him, you'd get an honest answer. He's a long-distance trader—merchant-venturer," he added, and Eslingen nodded again. "A large part of his business is perfectly legal and above board, but there's a sizeable percentage of it that isn't." Rathe cocked his head at the other man. "I don't know how much time you've spent in Astreiant, all in, or what you know about a place called the Court of the Thirty-two Knives."

Eslingen sat back in his chair, one dark eyebrow winging upwards. "I've heard of it," he said. "Devynck told all her soldier friends to stay away from it. That was enough for me."

Rathe nodded. "Good. There's nothing they like better in the Court for a bunch of roistering, on-leave soldiers to come in thinking they're tough enough to handle it, because they're not. But Caiazzo has contacts and businesses within the Court. He can walk in and out, pretty much at will—but then, he is southriver born."

"And you?" Eslingen asked, when it seemed clear that Rathe had finished. The pointsman looked startled.

"Me? Yeah, I'm southriver born, too."

"Can you walk in and out of this Court with impunity?"

"I've done it."

"But not like Caiazzo does it," Eslingen finished, and Rathe grinned. There's a lot you're not telling me, Adjunct Point, Eslingen thought, and decided not to pursue the matter. Rathe had said enough to get his message across. "So what's so special about this Caiazzo, then? I assume there are reasons none of your lot have scored a point on him yet."

"Oh, there are, chief among them being he's good at covering his tracks, most of his success comes from his legal businesses, and people are loyal to him. And he has canny associates, as well as a deft hand with a fee." Rathe paused. "But the thing is, he had this bodyguard—"

"Oh, no, I'm sorry, I don't step into a dead man's shoes. Not like this. Thank you kindly, Rathe, but—"

"Will you shut up for a moment?" Rathe said, equably. "His last bravo's alive and well and sitting in a Customs Point cell." Eslingen looked at him, and Rathe met the stare with a bland smile. "Duelling."

"So who are you doing the favor?" Eslingen demanded. "This Caiazzo or me? For that matter, it seems extraordinary that you have to make amends to two different people for matters of point scoring. I'm beginning to be just the slightest bit afraid of you, pointsman. You're not safe."

"It's not as elaborate as all that. Caiazzo's tough deserved what he got, and better for him this way." Rathe shook his head. "Look, he called himself a duellist, but he didn't call his duels formally. He just sort of took it upon himself to, well, execute them. Caiazzo was having fits trying to figure out how to be rid of him anyway. Not that I did it to oblige him, but when I was able to make the point, fair and square, on a charge of murder, I did it and Caiazzo didn't make more than a token complaint. And if he'd—Douvregn, I mean—if he'd gone on like that much longer, he'd've gone mad. Duellists can, you know, especially if they don't cry fair and public."

"You know a lot about duelling. I presume that's just in pursuit of the law," Eslingen said, eyeing the blade that lay along Rathe's leg.

"Not really," Rathe answered, and Eslingen looked dubious.

"Oh?"

Rathe shrugged. "A friend of mine's a duellist. Course, he's also a necromancer, so he has an outlet. Of sorts."

Both Eslingen's eyebrows rose. "What an interesting life you lead, pointsman." He took a breath. "I want to know about Caiazzo. You said there were a couple of 'buts' involved."

"It's about these children." Rathe looked unhappy. "The surintendant—the surintendant of points, my ultimate boss—thinks Caiazzo might be involved. I don't. I've been after Caiazzo for almost five years now, I know the kind of mud puddles he likes to play in, and children aren't it. I'm certain in my heart he's not involved, but the sur wants me to keep an eye on him. Took me aside this morning to tell me that, though how I'm supposed to do that when I have all these disappearances in my book, and have to check up on illegal printers . . . " He paused and took a breath, darting a rueful glance at Eslingen. "Sorry. But if the sur wants Caiazzo watched, then I have to take care of it. Hanse—Caiazzo needs a new bravo. You need a job and a place to live, and I can promise you, his house is a lot grander than the Brown Dog."

"It would have to be," Eslingen murmured, but there was no denying the sudden surge within him. He had to husband his coin if it was to last to the next campaign season, and if he could live in a gentleman's comfort till then, all the better. "How's he treat the hired help, then?"

"Better than they deserve, I imagine," Rathe said. "Douvregn was always very well turned out."

"Not livery?"

"I told you, he's not a gentleman, Eslingen, he's a merchant, a southriver merchant, and proud of it. He's not the sort to ape the nobility, so set your heart at rest. You'll be able to afford to dress as well as ever, without the spectre of livery."

"But with the very real spectre, I imagine, of finding myself dead in the Sier if he should find out I'm spying on him," Eslingen said.

Rathe shook his head. "Caiazzo's not like that—not quite like that. He's no idiot. I'm trusting you to find out that he's not involved in these disappearances. I expect you to find out he's not involved."

"And if I find out he is?"

Rathe grimaced. "Then get out, fast, and let me know."

"Why am I even considering this?" Eslingen demanded.

"Because it's a long summer until anyone good is hiring again, you told me so yourself, especially soldiers of your rank. Because you saw what happened at the Old Brown Dog. Leaguers aren't well loved at the best of times, and right now—"

"Right now, we're right up there with pointsmen in popularity, aren't we?" Eslingen said, with a return of his earlier anger. Rathe ignored it.

"Because these are children who are disappearing. Southriver, northriver, from all over the city. Gone without a trace, and I tell you, Eslingen, usually only a runaway can manage that." He frowned into the distance, eyes fixed on something only he could see. "I've seen that happen enough times. The serious runaways, the ones with real, hard reasons to run. They'll do it, and we can turn over every stone, and not find them. Because they know when and how fast to run. But this number of kids, from so wide a range of backgrounds . . . they're not running, Eslingen. Someone's taking them. And I don't think it's Caiazzo, but I can't make that decision, I can't take that risk. You need a job, a place to live. I need to be able to keep an eye on Caiazzo without having to give up the other jobs at hand, which I refuse to do." He broke off, glaring at Eslingen, but the look wasn't really directed at him, the Leaguer realized. He was angry with whoever had suggested he write off the children already gone. And Rathe never would.

"I was a runaway," he said quietly. "And you're right. I knew when and how far and fast to run. But I was reasonably lucky. It might not have ended up this well. All right. I may be out of my mind, Rathe, but if this Caiazzo will have me, I'll keep an eye on things for you."

Rathe smiled, and the easing of lines from his face made Eslingen wonder just how many hours a day the adjunct point was working on this business. "You want to meet him now?"

"Are you off duty already?"

Rathe made a face. "Oh, calling on Caiazzo is part of being on duty, it seems." He stood, stretched, and came around the desk. "So, if you're interested . . . "

"Oh, I am," Eslingen assured him, and immediately wondered if he was doing the right thing. The astrologer had said his status could change at the new moon, but he couldn't think this was quite what he had had in mind. Before he could say anything more, however, the door opened, and Monteia appeared.

"Good, Rathe, you're back. Oh. Lieutenant Eslingen." Monteia shut the door behind her. "How are you?"

"Well, thank you, Chief Point."

Rathe gave him a wary glance, not quite trusting the demure tone, but the Leaguer didn't meet his eyes.

"Good," Monteia went on. "It shouldn't have happened, none of it, but once it did we had no choice but to bring you in. I want to thank you for your understanding."

"Not at all, Chief Point." This time, it was Eslingen who looked at Rathe, and the adjunct point who wouldn't meet his eyes. Apparently, Eslingen thought, he wasn't intending to inform the chief point of the plan to use a deputy to spy on Caiazzo. Probably as well.

"What did the sur want, Nico?" Monteia asked.

"Mostly to ask me if I'd found anything against Caiazzo, anything that would show he was involved." Rathe grinned. "And to complain about the grande bourgeoise."

"He won't get any argument from me on that, but this business with Caiazzo . . . " Monteia shook her head. "It's beginning to sound unhealthily like an obsession."

Rathe sighed, almost inaudibly. It seemed, Eslingen thought, to be a standing problem between them. "I don't think so, Chief, with respect. I think the sur is getting some information we're not privy to, maybe from court, maybe from gods know where, but political. Because that's the connection he keeps pushing—the succession."

Monteia looked askance. "Not very likely, is it, Nico?"

Rathe sighed again, louder this time. "No, it's not, but what am I supposed to do, tell the surintendant of points, no, sir, you're wrong, and I won't do it? I've tried to tell him, gods know. But he won't let me off."

"It's a waste of time," Monteia said. "Aside from anything else, the last thing we need is for the families to think we've forgotten about them. So if you can do what the sur wants without its cutting into your real work, Nico, that would be lovely."

"Yes, Chief," Rathe said. He glanced involuntarily at Eslingen, wondering if he should mention his plan to Monteia, but decided against it. It wasn't as though he was authorizing any fees for Eslingen against the station's expenses—that would be Caiazzo's responsibility. Not that Monteia wouldn't appreciate the irony, but the fewer people who knew, the better for Eslingen.

Monteia nodded. "So be off with you, then, Nico. The council wasted enough of our time this morning. Oh, and Nico?"

Rathe turned in the doorway.

"I don't expect to see you back here tonight, understand?"

Rathe smiled and nodded. "Yes, Chief. And thanks."

She waved a hand. "Go on, get out. Good luck to you, Lieutenant."

Eslingen nodded, recognizing dismissal when he heard it, and followed the adjunct point out into the main room. Rathe said something, low-voiced, to the woman at the duty desk, and then slung his jerkin over the shabby coat.

"Shall we go?"

"Why not?" Eslingen murmured, and trailed behind him through the station's yard into the busy street. They took the river roads, along the upper levels of the Factor's Walk, and as he threaded his way through the busy crowd, Eslingen had to admit some misgivings. After all, was a job with a southriver-rat-made-good really what he was looking for? The man might be wealthy—was wealthy, according to Rathe, who would know—but not all of that wealth was honestly come by. That Rathe seemed to think well of him, or at least to praise him with faint damns, was something of a reassurance, but, all in all, Eslingen thought, I might have been better off staying Devynck's knife. The towers of Point of Sighs—Point Assize, its true name was, a typical Astreianter sour joke—rose among the wharf-side buildings, and he looked away, swearing under his breath. Wiser it might be to stay a tavern knife, but Devynck wanted no part of him after last night, and there weren't that many tavern-keepers who would hire a Leaguer and a soldier. Which left Rathe's merchant, this Caiazzo. He could almost picture the man, the sort of gross merchant one found on the broadsheet prophecies, usually at the head of predictions involving Bonfortune and Tyrseis. He would be large and loud, his clothes rich and tasteless, canny, cunning, shrewd, but without the tact that redeemed those qualities—a bully, Eslingen thought, a man of weight who wouldn't hesitate to use it.

They had reached the eastern docks by then, and Rathe paused, scanning the pennants that drooped from the crowding masts. Eslingen copied him automatically, though he recognized only one of the house-signs, the blue and white stripes of Gauquier Daughters. It would be granddaughters now, or great-granddaughters, he thought, and wondered if he should change his mind now, before Rathe had gone to the trouble of an introduction. But then Rathe's hand was on his arm.

"See? One of Hanse's ships was reported in this morning, so I knew we'd find him here. I wanted you to get an idea of the man, better than what I've given you."

"Marvelous," Eslingen said, and knew he sounded less than gracious. "Thank you." He followed Rathe through a tangle of untended handcarts, and out onto the wharf itself. It was almost as wide as a city street, but only a single ship, a tidy caravel, the sort that Eslingen had seen in every port along the southern coasts, was tied up at the dock. The pennant at its single mast was a long streamer of scarlet, a gold shape like an inverted heart at the broad end: Caiazzo's house-sign, it had to be, Eslingen thought, and scanned the caravel's crowded deck for the man of his imaginings. There was no one among the dozen sailors and bare-backed laborers who matched that description, and the knot of factors gathered by the hoist looked equally unlikely. A woman in a neat skirt and bodice, a blue coat with split sleeves open over it, was standing to one side, and Rathe moved toward her. Eslingen followed, and saw a magist's bar vivid on one shoulder. He hesitated, but Rathe didn't seem to notice.

"Aicelin, where's Hanse?"

The magist lifted an eyebrow that was as grey as the feathers of the gargoyles that fought the seagulls for the dockside scraps. "Business, pointsman?"

Rathe cocked his head. "Of a sort. He still looking for a bravo?"

"He's not had a lot of time to interview candidates. Why? I know you're not offering your services, much to both our disappointment." She glanced at Eslingen, both eyebrows rising now in silent question.

"Lieutenant Eslingen here recently mustered out of the Dragons," Rathe said, "and is in need of a position."

"Until last night, he was working at the Old Brown Dog in Point of Hopes," a new voice said. One of the factors—not a factor, Eslingen corrected himself instantly, the fabric and the cut of the plain coat were far too good to be a mere factor's, not a factor at all, but the merchant-venturer himself—detached himself from the group by the steadily growing stack of cargo, and came to join the magist. "Devynck's new knife. Now, as I see it, good knives prevent trouble."

He smiled, showing teeth, but the expression didn't reach his black eyes. He was a wiry man, built a little like Rathe himself, but his face was narrower, the bones of cheek and jaw stark under the olive skin. Up close, his clothes looked even more expensive, his shirt of fine linen, freshly washed and pressed, fastened at the neck with a lace-edged stock, the coat plain grey silk with only the jet buttons for decoration, but cut to flatter the slim build. He was young to be as rich as Rathe had hinted, Eslingen thought, maybe forty, but then, it took a young man to outface the law.

"You're remarkably well informed, Hanse," Rathe said, sounding bored. "If you know that, you also know it can hardly be laid at Eslingen's door, now, can it?"

"I'd be more inclined to lay it at yours." Caiazzo showed teeth again, but this time the lines at the corners of his eyes deepened in real amusement. "Not yours personally, Nico, but the points? Yes, I'd say they have something to answer to Devynck for."

Rathe looked sour. "You can leave that to Monteia and Devynck to settle between them, I think." He shrugged. "But I thought I could at least introduce Eslingen to you."

Caiazzo laughed softly, and turned to Eslingen. "Known our Nico long, have you, lieutenant?" His voice was pleasant enough, still touched with the sharp southriver vowels, but Eslingen's scalp prickled.

"Only a week. Long enough to lose my job, though."

"Only a week? Gods, Nico, even for you that's quick."

"The times are like that," Rathe answered. "You've heard the story, I thought I owed Eslingen something for it, the situation not being his fault. You need a new bravo, Eslingen needs a new place. . . . It seemed to make sense."

"It does," Caiazzo agreed, and sounded almost rueful. He looked at Eslingen again, the glance frankly assessing. "Duellist?"

It wasn't hard to guess the required answer, not after what Rathe had told him. Eslingen shook his head. "Soldiers are rarely duellists, sir. It's not our skill, and only fools try to do two things that well. If you want a duellist, you'll have to hire someone else."

"I had a bodyguard who *thought* he was a duellist," Caiazzo said. "What I want is a knife with brains, not pretensions." He glanced at the magist, and Eslingen thought he saw her head tip forward slightly. Caiazzo nodded himself, decisively. "All right, Eslingen, let's try it. Nico, I'm obliged—I think, and to a point."

"A little in-good-standing?" Rathe asked, demurely.

Caiazzo's head lifted slightly, the gesture of an angry horse, but then he had himself under control again. "I'll think of it that way." He looked back at Eslingen. "I'll pay you a snake for a week, Eslingen, keep you or not, and we'll talk wages at the end of that time. What do you say?"

"I'm in," Eslingen answered, and wondered if he was doing the right thing. Caiazzo wasn't what he'd imagined, but there was something a good deal more dangerous about the trader than he'd expected.

Caiazzo beckoned to the magist. "Aicelin Denizard, my left hand. We'll try him for a week, Aice, see how it works?

"Despite the doubtful provenance, I think it's worth it," the magist answered. Face and voice were sober, but there was laughter in her eyes, and Eslingen caught himself smiling in answer. Denizard held out a painted hand—black and silver on pale skin, intricate and unsmudged—and Eslingen took it carefully. "A pleasure, lieutenant."

"Mine, surely, magist," Eslingen replied, and bent his head to her.

"Where's your gear, Eslingen?" Caiazzo asked.

Eslingen nudged the saddlebags he'd set down when Rathe had spoken to the magist. "This is it."

"Not your weapons, surely."

Eslingen shook his head. "They're at the Aretoneia."

Caiazzo looked over his shoulder at the caravel, and then at the group of factors. Something he saw there made his mouth tighten, but he said nothing, and looked back at the soldier. "Right, then. Aice, go with him, pay whatever bond they want—I'm sure the points will want their share—and bring him back to the house. Take the boat, I'll be here a while."

And I don't envy his factors, Eslingen thought. He glanced at Rathe, and saw the same thought reflected in the pointsman's half smile. He held out a hand, and Rathe's smile widened. "Thanks."

Rathe lifted a shoulder, but looked faintly pleased. "Like I said, I owed you this much, after last night. I wish you good luck with it." He looked up at the sky, gauging the position of the winter-sun. "Hanse, I'll be seeing you."

"Like my shadow," Caiazzo agreed, and Rathe turned away.

"This way," Denizard said. "What's your first name?"

"Philip." Eslingen slung the bags over his shoulder again, and followed her down to the end of the wharf where a private barge was moored. It was small, only four oarsmen and a steersman for crew, but Eslingen couldn't help being impressed. It took money to keep a boat in Astreiant, almost as much as it took to keep horse and grooms—but then, if Caiazzo's business took him along the wharves, then it was probably as much necessity as luxury. The steersman held out his hand to help Denizard down into the cushioned seats, and Eslingen glanced back to catch a last glimpse of Rathe as he turned away down the river road. It was just as well he'd gone quickly; Caiazzo had good reason to be wary of anything brought him by any pointsman, and Eslingen was quite sure that at least one reason he had been sent with Denizard was to give the magist a chance to gather her impressions of him, arcane as well as mundane. The thought of her ghostly investigation was enough to make him shiver a little as he stepped into the boat beside her, and he thought he saw her smile. She gestured for him to seat himself, and he did so, schooling himself to impassivity as the boatmen began to cast off. The astrologer had warned him against water—but there was no avoiding this. He was determined to give them no cause for suspicion: whatever Rathe's motives had been, placing him here, this had the chance of becoming a decent position, and he wasn't well off enough to risk losing it, at least not yet. If the trader was involved with the missing children, well, that would change everything, but even Rathe didn't seem to believe that. The boat lurched against the current before the oarsmen could find their stroke, and he smiled blandly at the magist, trying to ignore his sudden unease.

Denizard smiled back, and fished a small silver medallion from under her bodice, cupped it in both hands. Eslingen eyed her warily, recognizing a truth-stone, and the magist's smile widened. "Now, lieutenant—Philip, if I may. Tell me about your service. From the beginning, please."

Rathe made his way west again along the river, skirting the Rivermarket and the warrens of the Factors' Walk, ignoring the small twist of conscience within him. He had, after all, told Eslingen exactly why he was recommending him for the job, and what he was—and wasn't—

looking for. Nor was it entirely self-serving; Eslingen did need a job and a place to live, and Caiazzo's service was a good deal richer than Devynck's. And it was unlikely that Caiazzo would put him into a position that would bring him into danger, at least not yet, not until Caiazzo had decided that he could trust his new man, and by then Eslingen would have seen enough to make the decision for himself. . . . Still, the soldier was virtually a stranger here, with little knowledge of the city and its more notorious citizens; Rathe couldn't stop himself from feeling slightly guilty for what he'd done.

And that, he told himself firmly, was foolish. He'd done the best he could for Eslingen, and for himself; he had other work to do before he could take Monteia's offer and declare himself off duty. He reached into his pocket, checked his tablets. The last set of nativities—one for a girl who'd vanished from the family inn two days before Herisse Robion, the other for a boy just under apprentice-age, son of a weaver—should be ready; he could at least collect those and bring them to b'Estorr along with the rest. He glanced at the sun again, and smiled, slowly. Better still, he would send a runner to University Point and ask b'Estorr to meet him at Wicked's. At least that way he could be sure of getting one decent meal.

The sun was low in the sky as he finally reached the tavern, the papers with the nativities folded securely in his pocket. The building itself, long and low and old, wooden walls on a solid stone foundation, had once been a temple, though that had been generations ago, before the Pantheon had been built. On the clearest of days, with all the windows open to daylight, you could see some of the old carvings, high on the walls just below the ceilings, but those were the only lingering traces of its former life. Nor did anyone—these days, at least—consider its current use an especial blasphemy, not least because no one could remember what god it had served. There was an offering tablet, one of the blank stones that stood for all-the-gods, and a candle beside it to appease the prudish, but that was all. The name was more of a joke than anything, a typical southriver joke. Astreiant was, Rathe thought, usually a city that could laugh at itself. Only these days, people weren't finding much to laugh at, and neither did he. But there was always Wicked's, to put aside immediate worries.

The crowd was still thin, though some of it spilled into the tiny front yard, shopkeeper's girls enjoying a chance at the soft weather after a day spent within doors. Rathe went inside: the dim, cool light was more welcoming after a day spent crisscrossing the city. Though it was still early, Wicked herself sat at one end of the massive stone bar, surveying her customers dispassionately. The current Wicked—there had been at least three predecessors, Rathe knew from neighborhood gossip, though no one knew for sure if they had been kin—had run the tavern for as long as Rathe had been a regular. She had been there when he'd signed his apprenticeship papers, and she was still there, not looking much different than before, though she had to be fifty if she was a day. She raised an eyebrow as she saw Rathe, and lifted a hand to beckon him over.

"You'd better not be visiting Devynck's troubles on me, boy," she said by way of greeting, but the tone took away most of the sting from her words.

Rathe shook his head, and held out empty hands. "You see before you an off-duty pointsman, hungry, very thirsty, and in extreme need of good company. So where else would I go? Beer makes people mad, Wicked, wine makes them wise."

"Donis help us when pointsmen turn philosopher."

"It's that or run mad these days." Rathe dropped into a chair at the table nearest to her, glanced around the room. There was no sign of b'Estorr yet, and at the moment, he found he didn't particularly care. Wicked detached herself from the bar, and came to stand looming above him, hands on ample hips.

"You look like something that washed up after a particularly nasty flood tide," she said, and shrugged. "But then, it could be the coat."

Rathe lifted his head, then decided it wasn't worth arguing with her, especially when he'd reached the same conclusion just that morning. "Thank you," he said. "Might I have some wine, please, mistress?"

Wicked snorted, but smiled, and stalked back to the bar, disappearing through the door behind it that led to the kitchens and her private stockroom. When she came out, she was carrying a tall stone bottle and two heavy glasses—real glasses, not the usual pottery cups. She set it all down on the table, and sat down opposite him.

"Because you don't like my coat?" Rathe asked.

Wicked leaned forward across the table. "Because, first, I think you need it. Second, Istre sent your runner back by here to say he would be here after first sunset, and to bespeak a very nice bottle of wine that one, knows his stuff for all he's Chadroni. And, third, even if he did and you didn't, I wouldn't bother. I don't waste this on people who'd waste it. I figure you're probably here for a while, pointsman, and better for you it is, too, than moping at home or at the station."

"I had reached that decision myself," Rathe said, with dignity. "I suppose I'd better get some dinner if I'm not to insult one of your—what, Silklands vintages?"

Wicked shook her head. "Believe it or not, Chadroni. Istre tells me their beer is vile. Maybe there's hope for the regicidal bastards." She tugged the cork free with a grunt of effort, set bottle and cork in front of him with a flourish.

Rathe spread his hands. "If you say so, Wicked, I have to believe it. And I'll have whatever's going from the kitchen tonight."

"You'll have what I give you," Wicked answered, and pushed herself up from the table. "I've lasanon with cheese and herbs that'll be better with that than a custard pie."

"Thank you," Rathe said, knowing better than to argue, and the innkeeper turned away. Rathe leaned back in his chair, and reached for the papers folded into his pocket. He pulled them out, eight sheets, each with their neatly inked circles and the symbols of the planets set in their places, looking for some connection, however tenuous, between the eight. Approximate age was all they had in common, certainly not background, and that was what had the city in an uproar. And he didn't see anything in these papers to change that.

He made a face, and turned them facedown on the scarred table, wishing b'Estorr would arrive. The door was still open to the evening breeze, a southern breeze, warm, but without the river's damp. He could hear the sounds of the businesses around Wicked's closing up for the day, tables and carts pulled in, shutters down or across, the clank of iron as locks and chains were snugged home. First sunset was definitely past; over in Point of Dreams, the day-shows would be well over, and the playhouses sweeping up, getting ready for the night-show. It had been weeks—a moon-month, he realized, guiltily—since he had seen a play, even a night-show farce. The actors who shared the garret above his own lodgings had seemed cold lately; he would have to make amends, when he had the time. And he would need to make time, he realized. They if anyone could help him with Foucquet's missing apprentice, especially if the boy wasn't missing at all . . .

"So how do you like the wine?"

Rathe looked up, and pushed the papers aside. "Don't know. Haven't dared try it yet. I thought, being Chadroni, it might come ready mixed with its own poison."

b'Estorr looked thoughtful. "I don't think it's from the royal cellars."

"How'd you know I'd need it?"

"Poison or a drink?" b'Estorr asked, and seated himself opposite the other man.

Rathe gave him a sour look, but conceded the point. "The drink."

"These days, don't we all," b'Estorr answered, and filled both glasses. Rathe took one, lifted it in silent toast, and sipped curiously at the amber liquid. It was good, very good, but not astonishing. He had been in the mood for something astonishing, and he set the glass down again with a vague sense of disappointment. b'Estorr went on, as if he hadn't noticed, "I heard about the trouble at Devynck's—I had cause to go to All-Guilds today, the clerks were talking about nothing else."

"And blaming the points, I daresay," Rathe muttered.

"Among others," b'Estorr answered.

Rathe looked at him. "Strange to say, though, you people are the only ones I haven't heard suspected."

"Well, who'd dare?" b'Estorr returned. "I take it you mean magists, and not Chadroni."

Rathe smiled in spite of himself. "I think that people feel if Chadroni were involved, it wouldn't be this . . . disguised. Good straightforward people, the Chadroni, if a little bloodthirsty."

b'Estorr twirled the stem of his wine glass between his fingers. "That's true enough." He smiled, not pleasantly. "The only reason they didn't latch onto me as the guilty party when the old Fre was murdered was that they'd've been insulted at the thought of any but their own class murdering the king. In Chenedolle, in any of the League cities—in the Silklands, for Astree's sake—I'd've been dragged off to execution without a second thought. But in Chadron, murder is the province of the high nobility."

"Fun place to set up a points station," Rathe said, and b'Estorr nearly choked on his wine. Rathe grinned—that had evened the score for the remark about poison—but sobered quickly. Something he'd said himself hadn't quite rung true. . . . "But I'm wrong, aren't I, there's one group of magists people do suspect."

b'Estorr lifted an eyebrow.

"Those hedge-astrologers, the freelances, the ones the Three Nations have been complaining about."

"Magists are generally astrologers," b'Estorr said, with dignity, "but few astrologers are magists."

"I'm not sure most people make that distinction." Rathe frowned suddenly, impatient with the game. "Seriously, Istre, have you heard anything more about them?"

b'Estorr shrugged. "Not much more than before, I'm afraid.

They're still around—and they don't charge nearly enough for what they're doing. The students are pissed, of course, and the arbiters have promised to do what they can, but every time they get close to one of them, they seem to fade away."

"Well, joy of it to me, we need to keep an eye on them, too," Rathe said.

"I'd have thought that was the arbiters' business," b'Estorr said.

"And also ours." Rathe glanced toward the open door, hearing sudden loud voices, and then relaxed slightly, recognizing the tone if not the speakers. They sounded light, for a change, almost happy, and Rathe realized for the first time just how tense he had become. Then a knot of people—actors all, Rathe knew, and his upstairs neighbor Gavi Jhirassi at their center—burst through the open door.

"They can threaten to close us down, but they know right now there'd be riots if they tried it. And that's just what Astreiant wants to avoid, so they won't. And meanwhile, it's marvelous business for us."

"Still, it's a risky piece, Gavi, and Aconin should mind his pen." That was a rangy woman in a plumed cap, her eyes still smudged with the paint she wore on stage.

Jhirassi made a moue, and his eyes lighted on Rathe. "Nico! Have they actually let you out? We were beginning to think you were working all hours."

b'Estorr glanced at Rathe, eyes amused. Rathe shook his head. "Gavi's my upstairs neighbor. And an actor, though I probably don't need to tell you that. Quite a good one, really."

"You're too kind," Jhirassi said, and leaned on the back of the empty chair.

Rathe sighed. "Gavi Jhirassi, Istre b'Estorr, Istre's at the university."

"Not a student," Jhirassi said. "A master, then?"

"Join us, why don't you, Gavi?" Rathe said, and the actor spun the chair dexterously away from the table. "I wanted to talk to you anyway, and this saves me a trip to the theaters, since we're never home the same hours these days."

Jhirassi nodded. "It has been a while since we've seen you, Nico. Not that I can blame you, with what's been on recently, I mean, really, *The Seven Seekers*? It's not particularly subtle, and this staging isn't particularly inventive. At least Aconin doesn't write me ingenue parts—" He broke off, looking at Rathe. "What did you want to talk to me about?"

Rathe allowed himself a wry smile, and quickly retold Foucquet's story of her missing clerk-apprentice. Jhirassi's face grew more intent as he listened, and for once he didn't interrupt. When Rathe had finished, he said, "And you're afraid he's become one of the missing, obviously, for all you're saying everything else. Well, we've not had any new brats—sorry, children—" The correction was patently insincere. "—hanging about, but you said he might have gone to Savatier's." He tipped his head to one side, considering, then shrugged. "It's possible. I'll ask there tomorrow, if you'd like."

"Please," Rathe said.

"And if I find him?"

"Let me know, and I'll let Foucquet know. She can handle it from there, sort it out with the boy's mother."

"If Savatier has him," Jhirassi said, "if she's taken him on, he's likely to be good, Nico. It could be a shame to force him back into the judiciary."

"I know," Rathe answered. "But his mother has a right to know if he hasn't gone missing. Who knows, she might be so delighted to hear he's with Savatier, and not disappeared, she might let him stay on." He didn't sound terribly convincing, and knew it, and so, from the look on the actor's face, did Jhirassi. The judiciary was a good career, and a rich one, ideal for those who had the proper stars, and that range was broadly defined. Clerkships like the one Albe Cytel had held were as jealously guarded as any guild apprenticeship, and for the same reasons: their holders had an advantage over the hundreds of others who tried to make their living in the trade, and that advantage could be passed from mother to child. Cytel's mother would be reluctant to lose that, no matter what the boy's stars said, and there would be ambition and expectation involved as well. Sometimes it was hard to make the parent's desires give way to sidereal sense. He himself had been lucky, Rathe thought. He might have been an apothecary, or an herbalist, given his parents' occupations, but it had been clear from his stars that Metenere's service was not for him, and they had made no protest. He looked again at the sheaf of papers with their scribbled nativities. There had been nothing in common among those children's stars, or at least nothing that he could see, not even a common like or dislike of their present circumstances.

"I'll ask at Savatier's," Jhirassi said again. "But I can't promise anything."

"I appreciate it," Rathe answered.

Jhirassi nodded, mischief glinting in his eyes, but then common sense reasserted itself. He rose gracefully from the table, smiled at b'Estorr, and crossed to the corner table where the rest of the actors were sitting. Rathe watched him go, but his mind wasn't on the slim figure.

"That sounds—interesting," b'Estorr said, and Rathe rolled his eyes.

"In other circumstances, yes. It might almost be amusing, but not just at the moment, thank you. Not with people—respectable guildfolk, mind you—trying to do our jobs for us."

"Is it true someone was killed last night?" b'Estorr asked.

Rathe nodded. "A journeyman butcher, name of Paas Huviet. He was threatening to attack the inn, and when he wouldn't heed the warnings, Eslingen—he was Devynck's knife—shot him dead." He managed a crooked smile. "Which I don't think comes under your purview, Istre."

"I would think not," the magist agreed. "So what happened to him, the knife, I mean?"

Rathe grimaced. "Oh, gods, that was a mess. We had to call the point on him, if only to keep the rest of the crowd quiet, but of course it was disallowed. It had to be, really, he'd only fired in self-defense and in defense of real property. But Devynck let him go, since she didn't want there to be more trouble because of him. So I . . . I got him a position in Caiazzo's household."

b'Estorr stared at Rathe, then laughed. "What possessed you to lodge him with Caiazzo, of all people? I take it you don't much like this knife—Eslingen, was it?"

Rathe looked faintly embarrassed. "Yeah, that's his name. And, no, in actual fact, I like him, he's a good sort, clever—"

"So why, in the Good Counsellor's name, stick him with Caiazzo?" b'Estorr paused. "Or do I have it turned around?"

Rathe hesitated, but there were few men he trusted more than the Chadroni. And besides, he added silently, I wouldn't mind having someone tell me I'd done the right thing. "I need someone in Caiazzo's household," he said, lowering his voice. "The sur thinks he might be involved with the missing children somehow, but I've got my hands too full investigating the disappearances themselves to waste time on something I don't think is very likely. It seemed a natural conjunction."

b'Estorr shook his head. "Gods, Nico, remind me never to call in any favors from you, you have the most backhanded way of returning them. He agreed?"

"He agreed. I didn't exactly hold a knife to his throat, either, Istre," Rathe said.

"It's not a bad idea, though," b'Estorr said, thoughtfully. "As long as Caiazzo doesn't find out, that is."

That was something Rathe did not particularly want to think about. He reached for the pieces of paper instead, slid them across the table toward b'Estorr. "Here. These are for you. We've managed to gather some more information on the children missing from Hopes—I think you have all the nativities now. I don't know, maybe if you look at them in line with Herisse's, or something, maybe the days of their disappearance, you'll find something we've missed."

b'Estorr set down his glass and spread the papers out on the table, studying each in turn. Rathe watched him, absurdly fearful that he would see some dire pattern just glancing at them, something the points could and should have seen. And that's just being ridiculous, he told himself firmly, hearing more than an echo of his mother in his mind. But the papers looked pathetic, lives in limbo, reduced to so many numbers and calculations. He wasn't an astrologer, at least no more so than most people in Astreiant, possessing a rudimentary knowledge of the mathegistry that defined their lives. b'Estorr could read the figures Rathe had given him as easily as Rathe could read the broadsheets, and Rathe wondered what picture the nativities conjured up for the magist. Could he see these children, get a sense for who they were—are, he corrected firmly—what their dreams, hopes, futures might be? He shook his head, at himself this time, and took another swallow of his wine, never taking his eyes from b'Estorr. Finally, the magist rolled up the papers and placed them carefully in his leather pocket case. He smiled a little sheepishly at Rathe.

"Sorry. There's little enough I can do right now, but I get caught up. It's interesting, but I'm not seeing any obvious patterns off the top of it. No common positions, bar the gross solar position of the winter-sun and its satellites for most of them. And of course the Starsmith."

Rathe nodded. The winter-sun and its three kindred stars stayed in each of the solar signs for about fourteen years; everyone born within that period shared those signs. The Starsmith took even longer to move through its unique zodiac. "That hardly counts, though, right?"

"Right. And not all of them were born with the winter-sun in the Anvil, either, some of them are young enough that it was in the first degrees of the Sea-bull." b'Estorr shook his head again. "For that matter, they weren't even all of them born in Astreiant."

"That we had noticed," Rathe said. "It's almost as though there's less of a pattern than there should be, and where you expect to find one, no matter how meaningless—I expected, we reasonably could have expected, all the kids to have been born here—it's not there. It's the kind of negative pattern you couldn't create if you tried, you'd be bound to slip up somewhere."

"That's an interesting thought," b'Estorr said, and this time it was Rathe who shook his head.

"It could just be frustration speaking. Damn it, there has to be some pattern there, somewhere."

b'Estorr nodded. "And the absence of pattern would be meaningful, too. Don't give up hope yet, Nico."

Rathe smiled ruefully, leaned back in his chair as a waiter appeared with his dinner—the promised lasanon, he saw without surprise, smelling strongly of the garlic and summer herbs layered with the cheese and the strips of noodle dough. Wicked was right, the wine would complement that, or vice versa, and for the first time that evening, felt his mood begin to lift. "I'm not. It's just—"

"Eat," b'Estorr said, firmly.

"You sound like my mother," Rathe complained, but did as he was told. A string of cheese clung to his chin, and he wiped it away, enjoying the rich taste.

"I sound like my mother," b'Estorr answered, "and they were both right."

Rathe smiled again, genuine affection this time, and turned his attention to his plate. b'Estorr was right, they were doing all they could, and it was still too early to give up hope.

They pushed the missing children from their minds for the rest of dinner, talking idly of other things. Rathe found himself relaxing at last, though he couldn't be sure how much of that was the excellent wine. He drained the last swallow left in his glass, and set it carefully back on the table.

"Time I was getting home," he said aloud, and the chime of a clock merged with his last word. He frowned slightly at that—he hadn't thought it was that late—and saw the same confusion on b'Estorr's face.

"That's odd," the necromancer began, and a second clock struck, not the quarter hour, as the first had done, but repeatedly, a steady chiming. In the distance, Rathe could hear another clock join in, and then a third and a fourth.

"What in the name of all the gods?" he began, but he was already pushing himself up out of his seat. All across the long room, people were standing, faces pale in the lamplight, and Wicked herself appeared in the kitchen doorway, broad face drawn into a scowl. It sounded like the earthquake, though the ground had never moved, the way all the bells and chimes had sounded, shaken into voice by the tremor, and he shoved his way to the door, and out into the narrow yard.

The chimes were still sounding, and Rathe had lost count of the number, knew only that it was more than twelve, more than there ever should be. The shopgirls were on their feet, too, one with her hand on her belt knife as though she faced a physical threat, another pair shoulder to shoulder, steadying each other against an earthquake that hadn't happened. The nearest clock was at the end of the Hopes-point Bridge, and he turned toward it, searching the darkening sky for its white-painted face and the massive bronze hands. It was hard to see in the winter-sun's twilight, but for an instant he thought he saw the hands spinning aimlessly against the pale disk. Then the chimes stopped, as abruptly as they had begun, and the hands settled, frozen, proclaiming the hour to be six. And that was impossible, that time had passed a good six hours ago, or wouldn't come for another six. Rathe's mouth thinned, and he looked back toward the tavern to see b'Estorr there, Wicked framed in the door behind him. As though the silence had released some spell, voices rose in the tavern, high, excited, and afraid.

"What in Tyrseis's name was that?" Rathe asked, and b'Estorr shook his head, his fine-boned face troubled.

"I don't know. Something—a serious disturbance in the stars, but what . . . " His voice trailed off, and he shook his head again. "I don't know."

"Damn," Rathe said. He could hear more voices in the streets now, loud with the same note of excited fear, and lifted his voice to carry to the people behind Wicked. "All right, then, it's over. Nothing to panic about."

"But—" one of the shopgirls began, and stopped, her hand flying to her mouth.

Her fellow, braver than the rest, or maybe just less in awe of the points, put her hands on her hips. "The clock's out of true, pointsman, what are we going to do about that?"

"The university will have the correct time, and the regents will see that the clocks are reset," Rathe answered, and tried to project a confidence he didn't feel. It wasn't as simple as that, and they all knew it—when the clocks had been unstrung by the earthquake, it had taken days for everything to be sorted out.

b'Estorr said, his voice pitched to carry, "The Great Clock, at the university—it's made to keep time through any upheaval. It should be all right. And it's a good clear night. There'll be no problem checking the time against the stars."

Rathe nodded his thanks, and Wicked heaved herself out of the doorway, came to join them in the center of the yard. "So what in Demis's name would cause such a turmoil?" she demanded. "I've seen a lightning storm do something like it, but that was one clock—"

"And this is a fine clear night," Rathe finished for her. "I don't know, Wicked."

"No more do I," b'Estorr said again, "though I intend to find out."

"Would it have anything to do with the children?" Rathe asked, his voice softer now, and b'Estorr spread his hands.

"I don't know," he said again. "I don't see how, what the connection would be, but I don't trust coincidence." Rathe sighed, nodding agreement, and the necromancer looked toward river. "I should be heading back, they'll want every scholar working on it."

"Go," Rathe said, and b'Estorr hurried past him, stride lengthening as he headed for the bridge. He could smell smoke, and with it the pungent scent of herbs, and guessed that people were already beginning to light balefires in the squares and crossroads, offering the sweet smoke of Demis leaf and lowstar to appease the gods. That was all to the good, as long as they didn't go burning anything else, and he looked at Wicked. "I'd better go, too. They'll be wanting me at Point of Hopes."

She nodded, her face grim. "I daresay. But I doubt there'll be trouble, Nico. This is too—strange, too big for a riot."

"I hope you're right," Rathe answered, and headed for the station. The streets were crowded, as they'd been after the earthquake, and there were smoky fires in every open space. They were well tended, he saw without surprise, and didn't know if he was glad or worried to see so many sober, rich-robed guild folk feeding the flames. The neighborhood temples were jammed, and there was a steady stream of people heading for the bridge—heading to the Pantheon and the other temples in the old city, Rathe guessed, and could only be grateful that their fear had taken them that way, rather than in anger.

The portcullis was down at Point of Hopes, though the postern gate was still open, and two pointsmen in back-and-breast stood outside. They carried calivers, too, Rathe saw: clearly Monteia was taking this seriously. He nodded a greeting, received a sober nod in return, and went on into the station's yard.

Monteia was standing in the doorway, talking to a young man whose wine-colored coat bore the badge of the city regents, but she broke off, seeing him, and beckoned him over. "Good, Nico. You'd better hear this, too."

The messenger said, "The city and the university will be confirming the correct time tonight in a public ceremony, to start at once. The regents would like all the points stations to proclaim and post the notice."

"Does that mean the university clock is all right?" Rathe asked, and the messenger looked at him.

"So far as I know—well, so far as they can tell. That's why they're checking, of course."

Rathe nodded, remembering b'Estorr's assurance, and Monteia said briskly, "I've already started getting the word out, Nico, but I'd take it as a favor if you'd attend the ceremony. People tend to trust you, and I don't want the ones who don't get there to say that we neglected our duty."

"All right," Rathe said. He wasn't sorry to have the excuse, after all; it would be a sight worth seeing, but, more than that, he was as eager as anyone to see with his own eyes that the time had been put right. He turned away, but Monteia's voice stopped him.

"Nico."

"Yes, Chief?" He turned back, to see her holding a wooden case. It had brass feet and a brass-bound door, and only then did he recognize it as the station's case-clock.

"See that this gets set right," Monteia said, and handed it to him.

Rathe took the box gingerly, appalled at the thought of the fragile gears and delicate springs of the workings, but shook the fear away. The case-clock had been designed for travel; more than that, it had survived at least ten years in the station's main room. It would easily survive a simple trip to University Point and back. "I'll take care of it," he said aloud, and headed back out into the street.

It seemed as though the news of the ceremony had already reached the neighborhood. The streets, and then the bridge itself, were jammed with bodies, all flowing toward the university precinct. Rathe let himself be carried with the crowd, but at the university gates displayed his truncheon, and was admitted grudgingly into the main courtyard. All the lights had been quenched there, even the mage-fires that usually burned blue above the dormitories' doorways, and in the darkened center of the yard a group of magists—all high-ranking, senior officials and scholars, by the cut and colors of their robes and hoods—clustered around a long table covered with the tools of their trade. Even at this distance, and in the dark, he could recognize the concentric spheres of the university's pride and joy, the great orrery, the largest and most exact ever made. He had been in dame school the day it had been unveiled, and all the city's students had been taken to view it, and then given a week's holiday, to impress on their memory that they had seen something special. In spite of himself, he took a step forward, and nearly collided with a student in a gargoyle grey gown.

"Sorry, sir, but no one's allowed any closer."

"I'm sorry," Rathe said. "Tell me, I was sent with a clock, to reset it, where should I go?"

The student rolled her eyes. "So was everyone, sir. Anywhere will be all right, they'll call the time once they know it."

"Thanks," Rathe said, and moved away. It was true enough, he saw. A number of the crowd, maybe one in ten, clutched case-clocks or traveling dials, waiting patiently for the scholars to restore the time. Some were servants from the nobles' houses along the Western Reach, but an equal number were from the city, guildfolk and respectable traders, and Rathe shivered, thinking again of the clocks chiming out of tune, out of order. Astreiant needed its clocks, not just for telling the time of day, but for matching one's actions to the stars, and there were more and more trades in which that was not just a useful addition, but a necessity. To be without clocks was almost as bad as being without the stars themselves.

At the center of the yard, the robed scholars were moving through their stately choreography, lifting astrolabes and sighting staffs and other instruments Rathe didn't recognize. He could hear their voices, too, but couldn't make out the words, just the sonorous roll of the phrases, punctuated by the occasional sweet tone of a bell. Then at last a pair of scholars—senior magists, resplendent in heavy gowns and gold chains and the heavy hoods that marked ten years of study—lifted the great orrery, and another senior magist solemnly adjusted first one set of rings, and then the next. It seemed to take forever, but then at last she stepped away, and the bell sounded again.

"Quarter past one," a voice cried, and the words were taken up and repeated across the courtyard. Rathe allowed himself a sigh of relief, and flipped open the clock case to turn the hands himself. He closed it again, ready to head back to Point of Hopes, and heard a familiar voice from among the scholars.

"Nico!"

He turned, to see b'Estorr pushing through the crowd toward him. He was wearing his full academic regalia, a blue hood clasped with the Starsmith's star-and-anvil thrown over his shoulders, but loosened the robe as he approached, revealing a plain shirt and patched breeches.

"Istre. That settles it, does it?"

"Everything except why," b'Estorr answered.

Rathe sighed, but nodded. "Does anyone have any ideas?"

"Not really, at least not yet. It may have something to do with the starchange—there are a lot of odd phenomena associated with it, and the Starsmith is closer this passage than last time." b'Estorr shook his head again. "But there's one thing you should know, even if it's not public knowledge."

"Oh?" Rathe could feel the night air chill on his face.

"Our clock, the university clock. It struck then, too."

"What?" Rathe frowned. "I thought you said it was built to withstand upheavals."

"It's built to stand natural phenomena," b'Estorr answered. "It's carefully crafted, well warded—half the gears are cast with aurichalcum, for Dis's sake—which worries me."

"I should think that was an understatement," Rathe muttered, and, to his surprise, b'Estorr grinned. The mage-lights were returning, casting odd blue highlights in the necromancer's fair hair.

"Yes, well, I agree. The masters and scholars are looking into it, of course, but I thought at least one pointsman ought to know."

"Thanks." Rathe shook his head. "I can't help thinking about the children. I'm not fond of coincidences, Istre."

"Neither am I," b'Estorr answered. "I just don't see how." He sighed and worked his shoulders, wincing. "Gods, I'm tired. But at least the clocks can be reset now."

"That's something," Rathe said, and knew he sounded uncertain. "You'll let me know if there is a connection?"

"Of course. If we find anything, I'll let you know."

"Thanks," Rathe said again, and touched the other man's shoulder, then started back toward Point of Hopes. At the gate to the precinct, he looked back, to see b'Estorr still standing in the mage-light, the gown hanging loose from his shoulders. The necromancer looked tired, and unhappy; Rathe shook his head, hoping it wasn't an omen, and kept walking.

7

Eslingen set his diptych, Areton and Phoebe, on the altar table, and placed the Hearthmistress's candle in front of it, then turned to survey the room. It was half again as large as his room at the Old Brown Dog, and the furniture was better than anything he'd seen since the glorious three days he and his troop had occupied an abandoned manor house. That hadn't lasted—they had been driven back again on the fourth day, with casualties—and he shook the thought away as ill-omened, touching first Areton and then Phoebe in propitiation. It had been a good day so far, better than he'd had any right to expect; there was no point in tempting the gods, or the less pleasant fates. The magist, Denizard, had seemed pleased enough by his answers to her questions—and he had been careful to tell the truth in everything, though he'd shaded it a bit when it came to Rathe. But it was absolutely true that he'd known the pointsman for less than two weeks, and that Rathe had been partly responsible for his losing his place at Devynck's; the fact that, despite everything, he rather liked the man hadn't entered the conversation, and most certainly he hadn't mentioned Rathe's request. The truthstone hadn't recognized his equivocation—and how could it? he asked silently. Denizard hadn't known enough to ask the question that would uncover that link, and he had been very careful in his answers. Besides, he was bound to tell Rathe only if the missing children were involved, and Rathe himself didn't seem to think that was likely. Fooling Caiazzo might be a different matter, even if the man was no magist, but so far the long-distance trader hadn't returned to the house.

He glanced around the room again, his own meager belongings looking small and rather shabby by contrast, and hoped he was doing the right thing. At worst, it would be for a week, and at the end of it he'd have two heirats—not much, he thought, but not nothing, either. And, at best, it would be work he could do, and decent pay, and conditions a good deal better than the Old Brown Dog had offered.

There was a knock at the door, and a woman came in without waiting for his word. She was thin and stern-faced, and carried a tray piled high with covered dishes. "Magist Denizard said you hadn't eaten," she said, by way of greeting. "You can set the tray outside when you're done."

"Thank you," Eslingen said, and gave her his best smile, but she set the tray on the table and disappeared without responding. He raised an eyebrow at the closing door—nothing could have made his status more clear, on trial, not yet of the household—but lifted the covers from the dishes. The food smelled good, onions and wine and the ubiquitous Astreianter noodles, these long and thin and drenched in a sauce of oil and a melange of herbs, and he realized suddenly that he was hungry. He ate eagerly—Caiazzo's cook was a woman of real talent—but when he'd finished, found himself at something of a loss. For a single bleak moment, he would have given most of his savings to be back at Devynck's arguing with Adriana over the latest broadsheet, but made himself put that thought firmly aside. That option had been closed to him since he'd shot Paas Huviet—since the moment Devynck had put the pistol into his hand, really, and there was no turning back. He carried the tray to the door, and set it carefully outside, close to the wall.

As he straightened, he heard a clock strike, and frowned, startled that it was so late. An instant later, a second clock sounded, this one within the house, its two-note chime oddly syncopated against the rhythm of the distant tower clock. Other clocks were striking now, too, and kept sounding, past what was reasonable. He counted eleven, twelve, then thirteen and fourteen, and heard a voice shrill from the end of the hall.

"What in the name of all the gods—?"

A second voice—Denizard's, he thought—answered, "Be quiet, and keep the others quiet, too." The chiming stopped then, on a last sour note as though a bell had cracked under the steady blows, and the magist went on, "It's over. Get back to the kitchen and keep everybody calm, there's no need to panic yet."

Eslingen saw the first woman drop a shaky curtsey, and Denizard looked at him. "Good. Come on, Eslingen, Hanse will be wanting us."

Eslingen reached behind him for his coat, and the long knife on its narrow belt, and followed the magist down the long hall, shrugging into his clothes as he went. Caiazzo himself was standing at the top of the main stairway, scowling up at the house clock that stood against the wall behind him. The hands, Eslingen saw, declared it to be half past six, and he shivered in spite of himself.

"What in all hells was that?" the trader demanded, and Denizard spread her hands. She had flung her gown over chemise and skirts, and Eslingen could see the hard line of her stays as the gown swung open. Her grey-streaked hair hung loose over her shoulders, and she shook it back impatiently.

"I don't know," she answered, glancing over her shoulder, and lowered her voice. "Not an earthquake, or lightning—"

"That's obvious," Caiazzo snapped.

"—which means some other sort of natural disturbance," the magist went on, as though he hadn't spoken. "The starchange means things are unsettled, but I've never heard of anything like this."

"Wonderful," Caiazzo said, and looked up at the clock. "So what do we do now, magist?"

Denizard sighed, drawing her gown closed around her. "Reassure your people first, I think. Then send someone to the university, the Great Clock there is unlikely to have gone out of tune, and even if it has, they'll be able to reset it from the stars. And then—I don't know, Hanse. Try to find out what happened, I suppose."

"And what do you think happened?" Caiazzo asked. His voice was calmer now, and Denizard sighed again.

"I'm only guessing, mind, my speciality isn't astrology. But the starchange means that the Starsmith is coming closer and closer to the normal stars, and that means it has more and more influence on them. It's possible that its approach could upset the clocks—they're set to the ordinary stars, not the Starsmith."

"But if that's what happened," Caiazzo said, "why haven't I heard of anything like this before? The last starchange was in living memory, surely something like this would've started stories."

"I don't know," Denizard said again. "The Starsmith will be moving into the Charioteer, that's a shared sign, one of the moon's signs, and it hasn't done that for, oh, six hundred years. I don't think even the university has good records for that long ago."

Caiazzo muttered something under his breath. Eslingen smelled smoke suddenly, strong and close at hand, and turned instantly to the main door. Before he could reach it, however, it opened, and the stocky man who'd been introduced as the household steward came into the hall.

"Sir. The neighbors are lighting balefires, and with your permission, I'd like to have our people do the same. And there's a crier saying that the university is checking the proper time."

Caiazzo's eyes flicked to Denizard, who shrugged, and then back to the steward. "Go ahead. It'll give them something to do besides worry."

"Sir," the steward said again, and started toward the kitchen.

Caiazzo looked back at the magist. "As for you, Aice, take Eslingen here and get over to the university. Take my travel clock, and make sure we get the right time."

Denizard nodded. "You'll want a clocksmith in for the big one, though."

"Another damned expense," Caiazzo muttered, and turned on his heel and stalked away.

Denizard looked at Eslingen, the corners of her mouth turning up in a wry smile. "Well. You heard our orders. Let me dress, and we'll be on our way."

The streets were crowded, every crossroads filled with a smouldering balefire, and the Manufactory Bridge was filled with people heading northriver. Toward the university, Eslingen guessed, and wasn't surprised to see a bigger crowd gathered outside the university gate. A number of them, he saw, carried clocks of one kind or another: not surprising, he thought, and did his best to help Denizard elbow her way to the gate. Most people gave way before her magist's gown, but the guard on duty at the gate shook his head apologetically.

"I'm sorry, magist, but you've come too late. The ceremony's started—almost finished, by the sound of it."

Even as he spoke, a bell sounded from inside the compound, a high, sweet sound, and a voice called something. There was a noise like a great sigh of relief, and another voice repeated the words.

"Quarter past one!"

"Quarter past one," Denizard said, and nodded to the guard. She turned away, shielding Caiazzo's clock against her body, and adjusted the mechanism. "Well, that finishes that."

"Does it?" Eslingen asked, involuntarily, and the magist gave him a wry smile.

"Probably not. But that's all we can do about it now."

"I suppose."

"You have a better idea?" Denizard asked, but her smile cut the hardness of her words.

Eslingen smiled back, and shook his head. "No, I admit. But—I just can't say it feels right."

"No," Denizard agreed. "We—you and I in particular, Eslingen—will need to keep a careful eye on things for the next few days, I'd say. This can't be a good omen."

Eslingen nodded back, wondering again if he should ever have accepted Rathe's advice, and fell into step beside her, heading back to Customs Point and Caiazzo's house.

Another servant, rounder-faced and more cheerful than the woman who'd served him the night before, woke him with breakfast and shaving water the next morning, and the news that Caiazzo would want to see him sometime before noon. "He'll send for you, though," she added, "so be ready."

"Do you know when—?" Eslingen asked, and left a suggestive pause, hoping she'd fill in her name.

The woman shook her head, as much to refuse the unspoken question as in answer. "I've no idea, sir."

"Crushed again," Eslingen murmured, just loud enough to be heard, and thought her smile widened briefly. But then she was gone, and he turned his attention to the business at hand. He was still on sufferance, obviously, and would be for some time, especially after the events of the night before; the household would be closing ranks against outsiders. All he could do was tolerate the snubs, and look for some way of proving his usefulness.

One of the junior servants—a boy who could have been from either the counting house or the kitchen; there was nothing to betray his rank in the neat breeches and dull jerkin—came for him as the house clock was striking ten. Eslingen, who had been listening to the distant, musical notes, dragged himself away from that further evidence of Caiazzo's status, and gave his stock a last quick tug before he followed the boy from the room. He was aware of more signs of Caiazzo's wealth as they moved from the servants' quarters into the main house—panelling with spare, geometric carvings, glass and silver on the sideboards in the main hall, wax candles in every room—but schooled himself to impassivity. He would lose nothing by seeming familiar with the trappings of wealth, and gain nothing by sneering. Not, he added silently, that there was much to sneer at. Caiazzo's taste, at least in the public rooms, was impeccable, even a little severe for a man who'd been born a southriver bookbinder's son.

The boy led him up the front staircase, past a knot of clerks with ledgers and a neatly dressed matron who looked torn between anger and nervousness. The edges of her fingernails were rimmed in black; the remains of paint, he thought at first, and then realized it was ink. One of the printers Rathe had mentioned? he wondered, but knew better than even to think of asking. Caiazzo's workroom was at the end of the gallery, overlooking the side alley and the next-door garden, and as the boy tapped on the door and announced him, Eslingen took that chance to make a brief survey of the room. It was large, and well lit—only to be expected, for a man who made a sizeable part of his living on paper—and the clerk's counter that ran the length of one wall was drifted with papers. There was a worktable as well, neater, and a thin woman in a shade of red that didn't flatter her sallow complexion was flicking the last coins into the hollows of a tallyboard. A status of Bonfortune stood in a niche in the wall behind her, fresh flowers at its feet—propitiation, Eslingen wondered, or just common caution? The magist Denizard leaned against the opposite end of that table, her robe open over a sharply cut skirt and bodice, and Caiazzo himself stood by the tall windows, staring toward the masts that soared above the housetops. He turned at the boy's appearance, and nodded to the woman in red.

"All right, Vianey, that's all for now. Bring me the full accounting as soon as you have it."

"Of course," the woman answered, sounding vaguely affronted, but covered the board and swept out with it clutched to her breast.

"So, Lieutenant Eslingen," Caiazzo said, and took his place in the carved chair behind the worktable. Eslingen, with a sudden rush of insight, guessed that the trader rarely used it for work, but often for interviews. "Devynck speaks well of you."

Decent, under the circumstances, Eslingen thought, but said nothing, managed a half bow instead.

"But you didn't tell me you know one of my people," Caiazzo went on. "Dausset Cijntien works for one of my caravan-masters."

"Does he?" For a moment, Eslingen's mind was as blank as his face. "I knew he worked for a caravan, but not whose."

Caiazzo fixed black eyes on him for a moment longer, as though wondering what else he would say, but Eslingen met his stare squarely. He thought he saw the hint of a smile, of approval, flicker across the trader's face, but then it was gone. "Aice says the other names you gave me speak well of you, too. I'm prepared, despite the otherwise questionable provenance—"Caiazzo lifted a hand, forestalling a comment Eslingen had not been about to make. "—a recommendation from the points, and especially Adjunct Point Rathe, isn't always the best thing for a member of my household—to put you on my books." He smiled again, this time more openly. "As I told you yesterday, I do need a knife, and one who looks like a gentleman can only be an improvement over one who thought he was."

"Thank you," Eslingen said, though he wasn't at all sure it was a compliment.

Caiazzo's smile widened slightly, as though he'd guessed the thought and rather enjoyed it. "Right, then—"

He broke off as the door opened, and a harrassed-looking clerk came in. "I'm very sorry to disturb you, sir, but Rouvalles is here, and he insists on seeing you."

Caiazzo gave the statue of Bonfortune a reproachful glance, but sighed. "Eslingen, you'll stay. Show him in, Pradon."

The clerk bowed, and hurried away, closing the door again behind her.

"I'm not armed," Eslingen said hastily, "bar my knife—"

Caiazzo waved a dismissive hand. "It won't come to that." He looked at Denizard, who straightened, hauling herself off the end of the table. Eslingen hesitated, then took his place at Caiazzo's right. The long-distance trader didn't say anything, but Eslingen saw the flicker of eyes that acknowledged his presence.

The door opened again, and the clerk stood aside to let a tall, neatly dressed man into the room. He was young, Eslingen realized with some surprise, or at least young to be running Caiazzo's Silklands caravan, didn't look any older than Eslingen himself. And he was handsome, too, in a genial, good-fellow sort of way, an open face and an easy smile beneath a ragged mane of wavy hair that was just the color of bronze, but there was something in his pale eyes than belied the easy manner. He checked slightly, seeing Caiazzo in his chair, and Eslingen saw the blue eyes flick left and right, taking in first Denizard and then himself.

"Standing on ceremony, Hanse? You don't need your knife against me."

"I was in the process of hiring a new one," Caiazzo answered, "and I figured he might as well start now." He nodded toward the soldier. "This is Eslingen, served with Coindarel, and now of my household. I understand one of your own men speaks highly of him."

The caravan-master—Rouvalles, the clerk had called him, Eslingen remembered—blinked. "One of them may, for all I know. Who?"

"Dausset Cijntien," Denizard said.

"Then you can ask him yourself, he's below."

Caiazzo nodded thoughtfully. "So what was it you wanted, Rouvalles?"

The caravan-master took a deep breath. "Look, I wouldn't have come myself, except it's getting late. We need to leave within the week to make this season work, and I still have goods and supplies to buy. I need coin, Hanse, and soon."

His voice had just the hint of a Chadroni accent, Eslingen realized. He glanced at Caiazzo, but the long-distance trader's expression was little more than a mask.

"You'll have to wait," he said, without inflection.

Rouvalles's eyes narrowed, and Eslingen caught a glimpse of the cold steel beneath the good humor. Not surprising, he thought, and I'd bet it serves him well both trading and on the road, but he's not a man I'd like to cross.

"How long?" The caravan-master matched Caiazzo's tone.

"Two days."

Eslingen thought he heard a hint of relief beneath the projected boredom, and glanced again at Caiazzo. Rathe had hinted that not all of the long-distance trader's businesses were legitimate, but the caravan was public enough that it surely had to be—unless it was the source of the coin that was problematic? There had been talk in the kitchen the night before about a ship that had just come in. . . . He shook himself away from that line of thought, and concentrated on the conversation at hand.

Rouvalles hesitated for a moment, but then nodded, showing his easy grin. "Right, we can wait that long, but we're cutting it very close this year, Hanse."

"I know it," Caiazzo answered. "There've been some—unexpected events."

"Like last night?"

"Not like that."

"What I might call problems, then?" Rouvalles asked, almost cheerfully, but his eyes didn't match his tone.

Caiazzo nodded once. "You probably would. But it's nothing that'll affect you."

"No more than it already has," Rouvalles answered.

"Not seriously," Caiazzo corrected. It looked for a moment as though Rouvalles might protest, but Caiazzo fixed him with a stare, and the younger man spread his hands in silent acceptance.

"There's one other thing," Caiazzo went on. "Your troop-master, Cijntien, you said he was here?"

Rouvalles nodded, looking wary.

"You said I could ask him myself," Caiazzo said. "About Eslingen here. Well, I want to."

"I'll send him up," Rouvalles answered, but Caiazzo shook his head.

"Aice can go."

The magist showed no sign of annoyance at being asked to do a servant's job, but slipped almost silently out the door. She returned a few minutes later, Cijntien in tow. The troop-master looked uneasy at being brought upstairs, Eslingen thought, with some sympathy, but kept his own face expressionless.

Caiazzo leaned back in his chair. "I understand you know someone I've taken into my household."

Cijntien glanced toward Eslingen. "Philip?" he asked, and then looked as though he wanted to recall the word. He looked instead at Rouvalles, who nodded.

"I guess you do, then. Go ahead."

The troop-master relaxed slightly. "I know Eslingen, yes, sir. I served with him, oh, seven, eight years. He was a corporal, then a sergeant under me." He glanced again at Eslingen, then back at Caiazzo. "He's a good man."

"Reliable, or clever?" Caiazzo asked. He enjoyed the awkwardness of the situation, Eslingen realized suddenly, not quite out of malice, but more out of temper. Rouvalles had made him uncomfortable; he was perfectly happy to visit the same discomfort on everyone else in reach.

"Both." This time, Cijntien refused to look at his former subordinate. "Clever enough to lead raiding parties—hells, he was the man I'd pick first for that, over anyone else—but I'd trust him at my side. Or my back."

"And that's where it really counts," Caiazzo murmured, and looked at Rouvalles.

"If Cijntien speaks well of him, you're safe enough." Rouvalles smiled again, suddenly, with more than a hint of mischief in his eyes. "After all, I've been trusting him with your business for two years now."

And that, Eslingen thought, is a score for the Chadroni.

"Right, then," Caiazzo said. "Thank you, Cijntien. Rouvalles, I'll send word as soon as the coin is ready."

"I'll expect to hear from you," Rouvalles answered, with a nod, and turned away before Caiazzo could dismiss him more explicitly. The door closed again behind him and Cijntien, and Caiazzo looked at Eslingen.

"As you will have gathered, things are—complicated—for me at the moment. I can't afford not to investigate all the possibilities, especially where my knife's concerned."

It was, Eslingen realized with some surprise, a sort of apology. He gave another half bow, and said, in his most neutral voice, "Of course, sir."

Caiazzo studied him for a moment longer, as though wondering what lay behind those words, then looked at Denizard. "Aice, get him settled—find him decent rooms, some better clothes, make sure he knows what's expected of him. And send Vianey back in."

"Right," Denizard answered, and gestured for Eslingen to precede her from the room. He obeyed, wondering again just what Rathe had landed him in.

Over the next few days, he began to find a place for himself in the household. No one mentioned the night of the clocks, not even in whispers, and he didn't know whether to be relieved or nervous. The university published an official explanation—the approach of the Starsmith, it said, had caused the clocks, more attuned to the ordinary stars, to slip momentarily out of gear—but few of Caiazzo's people seemed convinced. Nor, for that matter, were most Astreianters, if the broadsheets were anything to go by, Eslingen thought. They blamed evil magists—foreign, of course—and the changes in society since the old queen's day, and in general anything else they could think of. One or two blamed whoever it was who was stealing the children, or at least called it a punishment or a warning to find the missing ones before worse happened. That was something Eslingen could agree with wholeheartedly, but he had little time for such matters. Caiazzo required his presence at most meetings, including a second encounter with the Chadroni caravan-master. There was no money for him this time, either, and Eslingen was beginning to be certain there was something very wrong. Clearly, Caiazzo had expected to have cash in hand by now—even had the trader been inclined to take that kind of advantage of his business partners, Rouvalles was not the sort to put up with these delays for more than one season—and Eslingen found himself wondering if Rathe had been wrong after all, if the trader was involved with the child-thief. But he could see no connection between a lack of funds and vanishing children: if Caiazzo was involved, he decided finally, he would be more likely to have coin in hand, not to be short of money. Still, he found himself listening carefully to the dinner gossip—he was eating with the rest of the middle servants now, the cook and the steward and the chief clerk Vianey, though not Denizard—and equally carefully to the sessions in Caiazzo's counting room.

On the fifth day of his employment, he was leaning against the casement while Vianey droned through a list of expenses—mostly relating to the upkeep of the house and boat—when a knock came at the door. Caiazzo stopped pacing to glare in the direction of the sound, and Denizard said, "Come in."

"I'm sorry, sir." That was one of the male servants, a tall man Eslingen knew only by sight. "But he insisted on seeing you."

He had a boy by the collar of a thoroughly disreputable jacket, Eslingen realized, and the boy himself was even less prepossessing than the clothes, a thin creature with a missing eye-tooth and the first scattering of what promised to be a bumper crop of adolescent pimples. Caiazzo eyed him with disfavor, but, to Eslingen's surprise, didn't explode immediately.

"I've a message for you, sir," the boy said, and held out a much-folded sheet of paper.

Caiazzo crossed to him in a single stride, took the paper from him and scanned it quickly, his frown deepening as he read. "Right. Take him down to the kitchen, see if he wants anything to eat. Aice, Eslingen, come with me."

The servant bowed—he had never loosed his hold on the boy—and backed away, dragging the boy with him. Denizard frowned too, looking more worried than Eslingen had ever seen, and reached for the coat she had left over the back of a chair.

"Where are we going?" Eslingen asked, and Caiazzo swung to face him.

"Does it matter?"

"Yes." Eslingen spread empty hands. "Your safety's my business; if you want me to do my job, I need to know where we're going. You're not happy, but that could mean anything—we could be going to your factor, or anywhere."

Reluctantly, Caiazzo smiled. "We're not going to my factor, no. I—have business, in the Court."

Eslingen blinked, but then managed the translation. Even in the few weeks he'd spent in Astreiant, and especially these last few days in Caiazzo's house, he'd learned the difference between business at court, business in the courts, and business in the Court. And if it was the last . . . no wonder Caiazzo wanted his bodyguard along, if he was visiting the Court of the Thirty-two Knives. He had wheedled the story behind the name out of one of the maids—it had been the base of a band of knives who had controlled most of the southriver neighborhoods a century ago, and it had taken three regiments of Royal Dragons to bring them down—and if even half the stories about their descendants were true, Rathe's and Devynck's warnings had been restrained. "I'll fetch my pistol, then," he said aloud, and Caiazzo nodded.

"Do that."

Denizard looked up sharply. "She won't like that."

"Then she can come here, next time," Caiazzo answered. "Get your pistol, Eslingen, and hurry."

They went by river, for all it was a short journey, just to the public landing north of Point of Graves. The city gallows stood there, Eslingen knew, and wondered if it was for the pointsmen's convenience. He followed Caiazzo and Denizard through the narrowing streets, aware of the curious and covetous looks, aware, too, of the way women and men melted out of sight into doorways and alley mouths. Warning someone? he wondered. Or themselves warned off by Caiazzo's presence? Caiazzo didn't seem to see, but when Eslingen looked closer, he could see a small line like a scar twitching to the left of the trader's mouth. He was still angry, and Eslingen wondered again just what he was getting into.

The streets narrowed further, walls springing up between the buildings themselves, and Eslingen realized with a small shock that they were in the Court proper. Once, generations ago, it might have been some noble's country house, back when the landames kept their country houses on the south bank of the river, but it had long since been broken up, first into merchants' houses, and then into tenements, until the shells of the once-elegant building had acquired odd accretions, and rickety lean-tos propped up the tottering stones of the walls. It would have been a bad place to attack, Eslingen though, thinking of the other Royal Dragons, would still be a bad place to attack, or to be attacked. He could feel the weight of the pistol in the pocket of his coat, balanced by the familiar drag of his sword, and was not fully reassured. They were being watched, more closely than before, and he risked another glance at Caiazzo. The trader's mouth was set, but the scar was no longer twitching, and Eslingen hoped that was a good sign.

Caiazzo stopped at last in front of a low shopfront, low enough that he had to bend his head to pass under the broad lintel. Denizard followed without a backward glance, and Eslingen went in after her, the skin between his shoulder blades prickling. If they were attacked inside, the low doorway would make it very hard to escape. To his surprise, however, the only visible occupant of the shop was an old woman, neat in a black skirt and bodice, an embroidered cap covering her grey hair. She sat on a high stool in front of a writing board, ledger open in front of her, her feet not quite touching the ground, fixed Caiazzo with an unblinking stare. There were no goods on the counter, Eslingen realized, no indication of what—if anything—this shop sold.

"How's business, dame?" Caiazzo asked, and tipped his head in what was almost a bow.

The old woman shook her head, closing the ledger, and hopped down off her stool. Standing, her head barely reached to the trader's armpit, but Eslingen was not deceived. There would be a bravo, probably more than one, within easy call, and the gods only knew what other protection.

"Well enough," she said. "My business. But what about yours, Hanselin? That's less well, by all accounts. You bring not only your left hand, you bring a new dagger with you, whom I've never seen before. Do you feel the need of a dagger?"

Caiazzo shrugged, the movement elegant beneath his dark coat. "Times are uncertain."

The old woman looked far from convinced, but she nodded. "Inside." She turned without waiting for an answer, and pushed through a door that had been almost invisible in the paneling. Caiazzo made a face, but moved to follow. Eslingen put a hand on his arm, all his nerves tingling now.

"Permit me," he said, and stepped in front of the trader to go through the door behind the old woman. There was no shot, no hiss of drawn steel, and he glanced around the narrow room, allowing himself a small sigh of relief as he realized it was empty except for a table and chairs.

The old woman took her place at the head of the table, fixed Eslingen with a dark stare. "Not what you expected, eh, knife? Thought it would be more dangerous?"

Eslingen blinked once, decided to risk an answer. "I see enough danger right here, ma'am. I've been a soldier, I know what old women can do."

Caiazzo shot him a warning glance, but the woman laughed. "I dare say you do, soldier. I knew you were one, from your boots."

Caiazzo said, "No hurry, dame, but you said it was important."

The old woman looked at him. "That's rude, Hanselin, and not like you. Business must be bad."

"Business, in general, is well enough," Caiazzo said, through clenched teeth, "except for the one small thing that you know about. Somewhere between here and the Ile'nord something's breaking down. If it's here, dame, you've got problems."

The woman's stare didn't waver. "We both have the same problem, Hanselin. Nothing has come in from the Ile'nord. Nothing. Not coin, not goods, not word."

Caiazzo flung himself into the chair opposite her, swallowing an oath. "It's your business, too, dame. What're you doing about it?"

She raised an eyebrow, clearly getting close to the end of her patience, and Eslingen saw Denizard tense fractionally. The old woman merely folded her hands on the table top, and said, "The same as you. I sent men north, a few weeks back, when you first mentioned the problem to me. Yours or mine, one of them will find out what's keeping her, Hanselin. She owes us—forgive me, owes you too much to be playing us foul like this. I expect one or both of mine back within the next few days."

"Mine should be in soon, too," Caiazzo said. "But the fair is well underway. I have two seasons of trade to underwrite. Without that gold, it could be a very cold winter, and I won't be the only one feeling the chill."

The old woman leaned forward, her hands flattening, palms down, on the smooth wood. "Your knife is new, untested, and you trust him with knowledge like this?"

Eslingen felt his shoulder blades twitch again, wondering if Caiazzo had blundered, and if he, Eslingen, was going to be the one to answer for it. The trader barely glanced his way.

"Oh, and am I so poor a judge of character? A fool who's useful for channeling the gold—forgive me, goods—we both need, but not to be trusted in matters of my own business, my own household?" With a single fluid movement, Caiazzo pulled a short, wide-bladed knife from beneath his coat, and drove it into the table between him and the old woman. She didn't move, her eyes going first to the knife and the new cut, the first, it made in the polished wood, and then back to Caiazzo. "I know you, dame," Caiazzo went on. "You've still got the arm for it. If you can't trust me, or worse, think I'm too fatally stupid to be your associate in this, then do something about it. Otherwise—"

He let the word hang, and the old woman looked back at him, cold eyes unchanging. Gods, the man's mad, Eslingen thought, and if it's on his challenge, there's damn all I can do. He slipped his hand into the pocket of his coat, wrapping his fingers cautiously around the butt of his pistol, and, out of the corner of his eye, he saw Denizard's hand close on the back of Caiazzo's chair, the knuckles white beneath the skin.

The old woman reached out, jerked the knife free with an expert's hand, her expression still the same, and Eslingen thought, gods, if she goes for his heart, I'll go for hers, and we can sort it out later. He tilted the pistol, still in his pocket, hoping the flint would work in the confined space. It would be more likely to set his coat on fire, if it fired at all, but there wasn't room to draw his sword, and his knife was no good at this range.

"I'd forgotten," she said at last, "that your mother was a binder." She laid the knife down flat on the table, and pushed it back across to Caiazzo. "You've kept it well. She'd be pleased." She looked at Eslingen, and he let the pistol ease back into its place. "My apologies if I touched your honor." She leaned forward as Caiazzo reached for his knife, placed her hand on his. "I do trust you, Hanselin, as I would my own child. This business with the Ile'nord . . . " She shook her head. "If I didn't trust you, if I didn't trust your judgment and acumen—well, as you say, we wouldn't be doing business together. I'll send word to you as soon as I hear anything."

It was clearly a dismissal, and Eslingen glanced curiously at Caiazzo. The trader rose, nodding. "And I'll do the same. But you know that's of use only if they bring the gold."

"If they bring word only, Hanselin, your autumn ventures are still safe. Your reputation is still more than sound. One way or another, the money will be there for you."

"Yes, but . . ." Caiazzo gave a grim smile. "Then where will my reputation be? I appreciate it, dame. I don't want to take you up on your offer."

"Nevertheless, it stands." The old woman smiled back, widely this time, and Eslingen shivered. The implication was clear enough even to him: if Caiazzo failed, she would provide the capital, but at a price.

Caiazzo bowed again, his temper barely in check, and stalked from the room. Eslingen followed hastily, and heard Denizard shut the door again behind them. Caiazzo said nothing until they were well clear of the Court of the Thirty-two Knives, and had turned onto the street that sloped down to the landing.

"I bet it stands," he said at last. "Nothing she'd like better than to get that far inside my business. Well, it's not going to happen—" He broke off, head going back like a startled horse, black eyes fixing on something beyond the landing. Eslingen reached automatically for his pistol, and Caiazzo laughed aloud, looked up to the sky. "Gods, Bonfortune, it's about time the stars turned my way."

Eslingen looked again, and saw another caravel, larger than the one he'd seen before, making its way cautiously up the river. Caiazzo's red and gold pennant flew from its mast, and the deck was piled high with cargo.

"Aurien, by the Good Counsellor," Denizard said, sounding as startled as the trader, and Caiazzo laughed again.

"A half month early, thank Bonfortune, and heavy laden. We'll meet him, Aice, see what he's brought me. You, Eslingen—" He turned to face his knife, his whole expression suddenly alive and excited. "Go to my counting house—do you know where it is? Tailors' Row, by the Red Style—tell Siramy and Noan to meet me at the wharf. Then—" he grinned, gestured expansively, "take the afternoon off."

"Yes, sir," Eslingen said, and the trader hurried toward the waiting boat.

Eslingen watched him go, suddenly aware that he had been left on his own at the edges of the Court of the Thirty-two Knives, and then, impatient, shook the thought away. The Tailors' Row was well clear of the Court, back toward Point of Sighs; he lifted a hand to the boat, saw Denizard wave in return, and then turned west toward the Tailors' Row.

It wasn't a long walk to the counting house, a narrow, three-story building tucked between two much larger warehouses. He delivered his message to a clerk and then to Siramy herself, watching her expression change from uncertainty to a delight that hid—relief? He couldn't be sure, and hid his own misgivings behind an impassive face. Caiazzo was definitely short of coin, that much was obvious, but why and what it meant was anybody's guess—except that it probably meant that the long-distance trader was not involved with the missing children. Rathe had been right about one thing: Caiazzo didn't get involved with anything that didn't promise a hefty profit, and this venture with the old woman, whatever it was, had certainly been intended to provide decent funds. Except, of course, that it had clearly gone wrong. Eslingen sighed, wondering if he should use his unexpected freedom to find Rathe and let the pointsman know what had happened. There would be less risk now than any other time, but he found himself suddenly reluctant to betray Caiazzo's interests. The man was having enough troubles; the last thing Eslingen wanted to do was to add to them. The two factors—and a harassed-looking clerk, arms filled with tablets and a bound ledger—hurried past him toward the river, and Eslingen turned toward the Rivermarket. Whatever else he did, whether he contacted Rathe or not, he did have to buy some new shirts. He could make his decision after he'd searched the market for something decent.

The Rivermarket was less crowded than it had been the other times he'd ventured into its confines. Probably most people were shopping at the Midsummer Fair, he thought, and hoped that would mean he would be able to strike a few bargains with the secondhand clothes dealers. There was a woman who claimed contacts at the queen's court, who swore that she had the pickings of the landames' cast-offs, and he threaded his way through the confusion until he found her stall. The clothes, some good, some much-mended or threadbare, good only for a seamstress to take a pattern from it, were piled every which way on a crude trestle table, watched by the woman and a beetle-browed man whose knife was easily at the legal limit. He was dividing his attention between the stock and a thin girl a little younger than apprentice-age, and Eslingen wondered just which one he'd been hired to watch. The man saw him looking, and frowned; Eslingen met the stare with a bland smile, and began sorting through the piled clothes, pulling out shirts. Most were too worn to be of use, though one still had a modest band of lace at the collar and cuffs, and he set that one aside to examine more closely later. The lace was good quality; maybe, he thought, he could pick it loose and find a seamstress to attach it to a different garment. He dug deeper into the pile, found another shirt that looked almost new, and spread it out to check for damage. The linen was barely worn, the only sign of its provenance a ripped hem—and that, he thought, holding it up to gauge the size, he could even mend himself. It would be large, but not unwearable, and he bundled it with the other, bracing himself to haggle.

"Eslingen!"

It was Rathe's voice, and Eslingen turned, not knowing whether he was glad or sorry that the decision was taken out of his hands. The pointsman had abandoned his jerkin and truncheon, was wearing a plain half-coat open over shirt and trousers, and he carried a basket loaded with what looked like the makings of a decent dinner. Eslingen blinked at that—he had somehow assumed that Rathe would have someone to do his housekeeping—and nodded a greeting. "Rathe."

"I hope you're doing well in your new employment," Rathe went on, the grey green eyes sweeping over the other man's clothes and the shirts he held in his hands.

"Well enough," Eslingen answered, and took a deep breath as the stall-keeper moved toward them. "I need to talk to you, if you've got the time."

Rathe nodded, without surprise. "Always. Can I buy you a drink?"

"I'm not sure that would be fully politic," Eslingen said, grimly, and Rathe grinned.

"Maybe not, at that. New clothes?"

Eslingen nodded, and the stall-keeper said, "Those are from Her Majesty's own court, good clothes that'll stand a second owner. And they don't come cheap."

Eslingen took a breath, irritated by the assumption, and Rathe said, "From Her Majesty's court, maybe, but by way of the other Court." He looked at Eslingen. "You wouldn't credit the trouble we have with laundry thieves."

Eslingen grinned, and the woman said, "That's not true, or fair, I get my goods legitimately and you know it."

"And charge court prices for clothes you bought from northriver merchants," Rathe answered.

It seemed to be a standing argument. Eslingen said hastily, "How much?"

The woman darted a look at Rathe, then resolutely turned her shoulder to him. "A snake and two seillings—and the lace alone is worth that much."

It probably was, Eslingen admitted, but pretended to study the shirts a second time.

The woman crossed her arms. "That's my only price, Leaguer. Take it or leave it."

"I'll take it," Eslingen said, and fumbled in his pocket for the necessary coins. The woman took them, and Eslingen folded the shirts into a relatively discreet package. "Shall we?"

Rathe nodded. "Where are you bound?"

"I hadn't decided. I was told to take the afternoon off."

"You should see the fair, then," Rathe answered.

"Actually, I had some business at Temple Fair," Eslingen said. "I'd like to see what the latest word is on the clocks."

"Bad, that."

"And what do the points say it was?" Eslingen asked.

"The same as the university," Rathe answered. "I'll walk you to the Hopes-point Bridge."

"Good enough," Eslingen said, accepting the rebuff.

They made their way through the market and climbed the gentle slope to the Factors' Walk in a surprisingly companionable silence. At the base of the bridge, the Factors' Walk ended in a paved square where the low-flyers gathered between fares. In the summer heat, the air smelled richly of manure and the sour tang of old feed, but the fountain and trough at the center of the space was surprisingly clean. Eslingen paused to scoop up a drink in his cupped hands, disdaining the cup chained above the spigot, and Rathe said, "So. You wanted to talk to me, you said."

Eslingen stopped himself from glancing around—there would have been nothing more suspicious—and shook the water from his palms. "Yes. I suppose so, anyway."

He stopped there, not knowing where to begin, and Rathe said, "Anything on the children?"

"No. And I doubt there will be." Eslingen hesitated, resettling the shirts under his arm. "Caiazzo's having troubles, yes, but I don't think it has anything to do with the children—the opposite, in fact." Quickly, he went through the events of the past few days, from the caravan-master's visit to the meeting with the old woman to Caiazzo's relief at the arrival of the ship. "It seems to me," he finished, "that if Caiazzo was involved in all this, he'd have money in hand, not be seeking it."

Rathe tipped his head to one side, eyes fixed on something in the middle distance. "Unless the business, whatever it was, had gone wrong somehow." He broke off, shaking his head.

Eslingen said, "If he's acting for someone else, which I think he'd have to be, from what I've heard, well, that someone would have to be a fool, to keep Caiazzo short of coin. If nothing else, it draws suspicion—as witness our conversation, pointsman."

Rathe grinned at that. "No, I daresay you're right, Eslingen. I wish to Sofia I knew what he was up to, though."

Eslingen shook his head in turn. "Oh, no, that's not part of the bargain. The children only, thank you, Rathe." He smiled then. "I'm starting to enjoy my work."

"I was afraid you would," Rathe answered. "But, thanks, Eslingen. I appreciate this much."

Eslingen shrugged, unaccountably embarrassed. "It matters," he said. "These kids—" He broke off, shaking his head. "It matters," he said again, and turned away before the pointsman could say anything more. He could feel Rathe's gaze on him as he climbed the steps to the bridge, but refused to look back. He had done as much as he'd agreed to do; Rathe was repaid for his favor, and that was an end to it.

Rathe watched him go, the blue coat soon lost among the brightly dressed crowd on the bridge. He hoped the soldier was right—and logically, he should be; if Caiazzo were involved, he should have coin to spare, not be scrambling to outfit his caravans, or forced into dealings with mysterious old women. Rathe had a shrewd idea of who she was—Catarin Isart was a blood descendant of the Chief of the Thirty-two Knives, and had long been rumored to have dealings with Caiazzo—and he didn't envy the long-distance trader if ever she did get a finger into his business. But Isart would deal in children if the price was right, and that meant, he acknowledged silently, that a trip of his own to the court was in order. He had contacts there, people he couldn't quite call friends, but on whom he could rely, at least up to a point. And for once the job in hand would work to his advantage: no one, not even the sharpest of knives, would dare, or want, to protect the child-thief. But first, he decided, he would go back by Point of Hopes, and tell Monteia where he was going. There was no point in taking chances with the court and its denizens.

It was late in the afternoon by the time he reached the court, crossing the rickety bridge that spanned one of the nastier gutters running down to the Sier. He let his blade show under his open half-coat, knowing he was being watched, and knowing, too, that the watchers would assume a second, hidden weapon, or maybe more than one. He followed the main path through the warrens, counting intersections, turned at the fifth, beneath a sign that had once been a purple fish, but was now fading to an unlovely puce. The building he was looking for stood three doors further on, its door sagging from rusting hinges. It had been part of the original mansion, but the stones were beginning to sag, the mortar crumbling from between them, the frames of the windows and the wooden sill starting to rot. He grimaced, thinking of the floor beams, and stepped back to glance up to the second story windows. A lantern stood in the center of the three, unlit but very visible, and he smiled, and pushed open the main door. The stairs looked as rotten as the window frames, though he knew at least some of the dilapidation was designed to trap the unwary, and he stepped carefully, testing each step before committing his weight to it. Several of the boards creaked alarmingly, and one cracked sharply, but he reached the second floor without mishap, and stepped onto a landing that looked a good deal sturdier than anything else in the building. There was only one door, but before he could raise his hand to know, it was pulled open. A woman stood there, leather bodice laced over a sleeveless shift, skirts kilted to her knees. She was holding a knife several inches longer than the one Rathe carried, and he lifted his hands away from his side.

"That's not legal, that is," he said. "How's business, Mariell?"

"You don't want to know, pointsman, trust me."

"That good," Rathe said, and knew he sounded bitter. "Is Mikael in?"

"Why?" Mariell's eyes narrowed. "He's not been working, you know. Or have you come on a hire?"

"I try to do my own dirty work," Rathe said, mildly. "And I know he hasn't been working, but even if he had been, that's not what I'm here about."

"It's all right, Mariell, let him in."

The speaker was a dark giant of a man, his face unexpectedly ruddy under a thatch of coarse black hair, only his beard showing a sprinkling of grey. Mariell stepped back, still frowning lightly, and Rathe edged past her. The door was narrow, had had slats added to it to make it narrower, and he couldn't help wondering how Mikael himself got in and out of it.

Mikael smiled, genial, looking for all the world like a guild-master well satisfied with life—as well he might, Rathe thought. Mikael was at the top of his profession, and Rathe was irresistibly reminded of Mailet. The butcher was clearly a man of choleric nature who was good with a knife, whose stars had steered him to a peaceable profession. Mikael was a good-natured man who also happened to be very good with a knife, whose stars had led him to a less peaceful life, sometimes as bodyguard or bravo, sometimes as a killer.

"So, Nico. What brings you this far in? Business?" Mikael seated himself in a barrel chair by the open window, gestured for Rathe to take the stool opposite. The air was a little fresher up here, and there were herbs scattered along the floor and hanging from the rafters. Rathe recognized one of the hanging bunches as woundwort, and for a moment was dizzied by the thought of Mikael as physician as well as executioner. Well, he thought, why not. In the Court, it made as much sense as anything.

"Business of a sort," he answered.

"Blaming us for the clock-night, probably," Mariell said.

Mikael ignored her and held up a sweating stone pitcher in silent offer. Rathe nodded. Mariell made a disgusted noise, and disappeared into an inner room, slamming the door behind her.

Mikael shook his head, but said nothing, picked up a mug and filled it, handing it to Rathe.

Rathe decided not to pursue the issue. "Who's good these days?" he asked, and nodded toward the wine jug.

Mikael made a face. "Piss poor most of it is, I tell you, but Harin has gotten in a couple hogsheads that I'm not embarrassed to drink, and she's not embarrassed to sell. It's all been piss poor even since old Grien died."

"Did Grien die?" Rathe asked, all innocence. "All I'd heard was that she'd disappeared, and young Grien took off for parts unknown. Good thing Harin stepped into the breach."

"Yes, wasn't it?" Mikael replied, equally bland. "So, what sort of business?"

Which meant Mikael had had enough of that topic. Rathe leaned back, balancing awkwardly on the stool, not particularly reassured by the weight of the knife at his side. "The city's strange these days, Mikael. You must have felt it. You been working more or less than usual?"

"What kind of question is that for a working man, Nico?" Mikael demanded, and Rathe spread his hands.

"Off the books, Mikael, I'm just trying to figure out what's going on these days. Kids disappearing . . . "

"And you only take notice because they're merchants' spawn, don't you?" The tone was less angry than the words, almost a token protest.

Rathe sighed. "That's not fair, Mikael. You have to admit, this is something outside the ordinary. The Quentiers were telling me they'd lost a—prentice, I guess you'd call him."

Mikael's lips twisted beneath the beard. "Bet they didn't go to the points, did they?"

"Well, they told me, and I've added it to my books." Rathe matched the other man's half smile. "Unofficially, of course, Estel wouldn't thank me if I made it official. But that's not all of it. Caiazzo is more than commonly edgy these days. I mean, we all know he's not the most serene individual, but he's close to the edge. And that's bad for business, Mikael."

Mikael's eyes narrowed, and Rathe knew the other man had taken his oblique meaning. "You've been trying to close Caiazzo down for, what, five years now, Nico?" the knife said at last, and Rathe shrugged.

"Sure. But the fact of the matter is, his business keeps the peace along much of the southriver and in the outer Court."

"His and Dame Isart's," Mikael corrected automatically. Rathe met his stare, and it was the big man who looked away first.

"What is it you really want to know, Nico?"

"Just what I said, really," Rathe answered. "What's going on with Hanse? Things aren't right with him, and he's letting it show. Have you done any work for him this summer?"

Mikael shook his head. "All right, Nico, and this I'll give you for free. No, I haven't worked for him this summer, and that's not usual, not through the fair. He usually hires me on to keep an eye on things for a couple of his merchants who come in for the fair. And there's a banker you might know, Dezir Chevassu, changes a lot of Hanse's money as it comes in and out. Usually that's good for two weeks solid hire, and not too much heavy work, there never is with bankers, not really. This year . . . " He gestured, showing empty palms. "Nothing. Not a damned thing. He hasn't even told me he won't be needing my services, and you know Hanse, polite to the last, or if you've offended him, you don't know it until it's too late."

"Yes, but who could he hire to finish you, Mikael?" Rathe asked. "How many takers do you think there'd be for a job like that?"

Mikael favored the younger man with a smile that was almost indulgent. "And how many young hotheads do you have in the points, Nico? Idiots who should know that a job is suicide, but see it as their way of proving themselves? No, there are plenty of people who'd try to hit Mikael, if Caiazzo wanted to hire someone, I can give you the names of half a dozen. But he hasn't. And he hasn't given me the brush. Just—nothing. And that's not normal." He paused then, the animation draining from his face, and Rathe guessed he was thinking of the children, making the same unwelcome connections that Rathe himself had been making. "Go see Chevassu," Mikael said at last. "She might have some answers for you. Truth be told, I think Hanse took more than a little business away from her. She used to have some interests as a merchant-venturer."

"So is she now a resident?" Rathe asked, and Mikael shook his head.

"Chevassu favors the money side of things. She's solely banking and exchange these days."

Rathe set his empty cup on the table—ruddywood inlaid with white stone, a pretty piece of work, and probably good to have at hand in a brawl. He wondered if Mikael had liberated it from one of the locals. "I'll do that," he said, and stood slowly. Mikael didn't favor sudden movements. "I assume this Chevassu isn't located in the Court."

Mikael snorted. "Not likely. Chevassu lives well north of the river—further north than most of her clients. And that argues a lack of diplomacy, to my mind. You'll find her in the Chancery district, on the Temple Road. Or at the Heironeia, during business hours. And, Nico." He fixed the younger man with a sudden, baleful stare. "If Hanse is involved in the child-stealing, I expect you'll let me know. He's a good employer, but this—this is bad, bad business, bad for business. I don't like it."

Rathe met the stare squarely. "If he is involved—and I don't have any real reason to think he is, Mikael, I'm clutching straws here—then he's mine. This is a points matter."

"Unless I get there first," Mikael answered.

Rathe nodded slowly, acknowledging what he couldn't prevent. "But I'll do my best to stop you. I want this one very badly, Mikael. Just so you know."

"I'll bear that in mind," Mikael said, and opened the narrow door.

Rathe made his way back toward Point of Hopes, his mood hovering vaguely between satisfaction and guilt. Mikael had spoken honestly, for once, and that was good, but Rathe wished it hadn't been at the price of spreading suspicion against Caiazzo. He sighed then. Worse than that was the nagging fear that the surintendant might be right after all.

Chevassu lived in Manufactory Point—well northriver, as Mikael had said, but not as undiplomatic a choice as the knife had implied. It was a good neighborhood, but not old; for a woman who'd almost certainly been born southriver, it was a wise choice. The adjunct point at Manufactory was a woman named Talairan, small, with a deceptively lazy air. Rathe had seen her crack skulls once, during an ugly guild fight, and was not deceived. She grinned up at him as he came into the station, and jerked her head toward a side room. Rathe nodded, relieved—he wasn't particularly fond of Huyser, Manufactory's chief point—and followed her into the narrow workroom. She closed the door firmly behind him, and perched on the end of the bare table.

"What in all hells is going on southriver, anyway, Rathe? One riot, one near riot, and a man shot dead in the street? And before the clocks, so there's no excuse."

"That was self-defense," Rathe said, automatically, and Talairan shook her head.

"Sounds like you're having a rare old time down there."

"Nothing we'd like more than to share it with you," Rathe said dryly. "You telling me it's all peace and tranquility here?"

Talairan's mouth twitched. "Hardly. Not only are these missing kids not in the manufactories, no matter what they think southriver, we've lost some of the ones that are supposed to be working there. Now, some of them are just runaways—and I can't fully blame them, not from most of those places, it's not like they're learning a trade. My feeling is, the older ones are thinking, well, if I get caught, I can always blame it on the child-thieves."

Rathe nodded, not surprised. The manufactories weren't the worst places to work in the city, but they weren't the best, and they lacked the community of the guild system, and room for advancement. A chairmaker there would make chairs all her life; an apprentice carpenter had at least some faint chance of becoming a master, though that, too, was changing. "I've a question for you," he said, and saw Talairan's gaze sharpen.

"About the children?"

"I don't know yet. I don't think so. But the sur thinks possibly."

Talairan lifted an eyebrow. "You're flying high these days, my son. All right, try it on."

Rathe nodded, and took a breath, wondering precisely how to phrase his questions. "There's a banker lives hereabout, name of Chevassu. Know her?"

Talairan laughed. "Sure I know her. I keep my beady eye on her, seeing as I'm sure she shaves the rate of exchange the way her lessers shave coins. Last I heard, though, bankers were hardly the most likely suspects."

"Tell me about her," Rathe said.

Talairan blew air from puffed cheeks. "Where to begin? She's a respected woman hereabouts, the question is how she got that respectable—seeing as she came from southriver." Rathe nodded, unsurprised, and Talairan went on, "Rumor has it she has partial interest in a couple of the better class houses over in Hearts, which is where her own coin comes from, and, of course, they say she banks for folk in the Court—not the queen's—and the 'Serry and the Old Crossing. Why?"

Rathe ignored the question. "Is she a fence?"

"No. Or not anymore. Like I said, my main concern is how she juggles her books and with whom." She fixed him with a sudden glare. "I would take it very badly, Rathe, if you were going after her on my ground."

Rathe shook his head. "No—my word on it, Tal. It's just . . . well, you mentioned court connections. I hear they're with Caiazzo, probably legal enough, and I've some questions for her. That's all."

Talairan nodded, appeased. "I've been hearing some very odd talk about him, trickling up from Fairs' Point. Business problems, I heard. Is there a connection with the children?"

"I don't know—I didn't think so, still don't, really. But there's no denying there's something wrong there."

"He's never dealt in human flesh," Talairan said, doubtfully, "and especially not children."

Rathe nodded, ran a hand through already disheveled hair. "Tell me about it. But I don't like the coincidence, what pointsman does?"

"A lazy one," Talairan answered, and jerked her head toward the wall she shared with Huyser's office.

Rathe smiled, but wryly. "So I need to look into it."

"Caiazzo's rightfully Customs Point's concern."

"Customs Point," Rathe said, enunciating each syllable with acid precision, "thinks Hanselin Caiazzo is an honest businessman and a boon to the district."

Talairan stared at him. "They said that?"

"They've said it," Rathe said grimly.

She whistled softly. "His fees must be powerful."

"So they tell me. Thanks for your help, Tal."

"You're welcome, for what it was worth. I'll ask for the return of the favor some day."

"I don't doubt you will," Rathe answered, and let himself out.

Despite what Mikael had said, Chevassu was not at the Heironeia. Swearing under his breath, Rathe retraced his steps, threaded his way through Manufactory's crowded streets to the banker's house. It was an expensive-looking place, but at second glance he could see that the glass in the upper windows was of distinctly lesser quality, and the stone of the facade was not matched on the sides. Monetary difficulties? he wondered, as he tugged the heavy chain of the bell, or just southriver practicality? The door opened after only a moderate wait, and a tall, greying man in footman's livery looked down at him. The discrepancies between facade and sides were just practicality, Rathe decided, looking at the quality of the linen and the metal braid that guarded every seam of the man's narrow coat. If she could afford to dress her servants like that, she could afford good glass if she wanted it.

The footman opened his mouth—to direct him to the trades door, Rathe was sure—and Rathe cut him off with a smile that showed teeth. "Adjunct Point Rathe from Point of Hopes. They told me at the Heironeia that Madame Chevassu's here."

"Point of Hopes?" The man was visibly startled, but recovered himself quickly. "We're in Manufactory Point—"

Rathe shook his head, and the man stopped.

"May I ask your business?"

"You may not," Rathe answered, pleasantly. "Just tell Chevassu that I'd like to speak to her, please. I don't think she'd refuse." He let the words hang.

For a moment, it looked as though the footman would protest further, but then southriver habits took over, and he stepped back from the doorway. Rathe followed him in, as always a little annoyed by his own methods. It was bad enough to use a woman's past against her, worse when it was the same as his own—and worst of all when it made him into a bully.

"Wait here," the footman said, and disappeared up the main staircase. He was back a moment later, and paused disdainfully at the top of the stairs.

"Madame will see you now."

Rathe nodded, and climbed to join him, the wood of the railing warm under his hand. The house smelled expensive, herbs and wax; the furnishings were good, obviously chosen by someone with an eye for quality, and he revised his opinion of Chevassu's fortunes once again. If she needed funds, all she would have to do was sell one or two of the tapestries that adorned her upper hall—so what, he wondered silently, is Caiazzo up to, that he doesn't just borrow from her?

"Pointsman Rathe, madame," the footman said, flinging open a painted door. "Point of Hopes." He stressed the last word, and Rathe couldn't repress a grin of his own.

"Adjunct Point, actually, madame," he said, and stepped past the man into Chevassu's workroom. It was a cluttered place, full of good furniture and better paintings, and the fittings on table and sideboard were all of silver. "I appreciate your seeing me."

Chevassu was easily sixty, maybe older, her hair a grey somewhere between iron and silver. Her skin was the color of very old ivory, and her eyes were the palest blue Rathe had even seen, barely darker than the ice blue silk of her gown. She didn't rise from behind her table, but gestured for Rathe to take one of the fragile chairs instead. It was a nice balance of courtesy and status, Rathe reflected, and perched carefully on the carved and gilded seat. It creaked under his weight, but he thought it was stronger than it looked.

"I'll be blunt, I'm curious what Point of Hopes wants with me," Chevassu answered. She wore no paint, either on hands or face, and her skin was crisscrossed with a web of fine lines, like soft and crumpled paper. "I've done no business there these past, sweet Heira, seven years. Do you tell me my past has come back to haunt me?"

"I'm more interested in your present, madame, and I'll say straight out it's nothing to do with Point of Hopes," Rathe answered. He watched her closely as he spoke, but saw no change in her calm expression. "I understand you handle the exchange for Hanselin Caiazzo."

"I have done," she answered, and Rathe tilted his head to one side.

"But not this year?"

"I fail to see why I should tell you—" Chevassu began, sounding almost indulgent, and Rathe lifted a hand.

"Bear with me a moment, madame. You know what's been happening in Astreiant this summer, you know why we in the points are looking sideways at anything out of the ordinary. And you also know that Caiazzo's dealings, business and otherwise, have not been exactly ordinary. I understand, you do business with him, you wouldn't want to jeopardize that, and I wouldn't ask you to—in the normal way of things. But things are not normal."

"Are you accusing Caiazzo of being behind these child-thefts?" Chevassu demanded. She sounded, Rathe thought, almost more outraged by that than by anything else he'd said.

"I don't know," he answered, bluntly. "But there are people who do think so, and I'm duty bound to make sure he's not."

Chevassu tipped her head back, bringing him into the far-sighted focus of the old. "Off the books, pointsman?"

"As far as I'm able."

She studied him for a moment longer, expression thoughtful, then nodded. "I'll take the chance. Hanselin Caiazzo's not one to deal in these goods. Let me tell you a little bit about him." It was the tone a grandmother used to begin a story on a winter-eve, and Rathe smiled back at her, not the least deceived.

"Hanselin is one of the canniest and most intelligent businessmen I've worked with, not excepting his mother, who was as canny as they come. The two don't always go together, but Hanselin—ah, he has both, in roughly equal portion, and what I wouldn't give to see a copy of his nativity."

So would I, Rathe thought. He knew almost nothing of the trader's stars, he realized, with some surprise, not even the major signs of his birth.

"It's not the usual nativity of a long-distance trader, I would wager," Chevassu went on, "and it's equally not your usual southriver knife's, however much he likes walking that line. How many questionable businesses do you think he fees, either the whole or in part, here in Astreiant?"

She seemed to expect an answer, and Rathe shrugged. "I've lost count, but then, I have a suspicious mind."

She gave him an approving nod, as though he'd passed some test. "You probably do, it's a hazard of your profession, and I'm not surprised you've lost count, because it changes year to year. He keeps the money moving in and out and that keeps his—associates—on their toes, and that keeps them all the safer. But there's always been one thing that puzzles all of us. For all he's a shrewd judge of the chance, and a hard man for a bargain, he's had more coin than he ought for the past several years. Oh, the Silklands caravan is well managed, extremely well managed indeed, and that pays well and in coin, but he's always had more to hand than he reasonably should have, coin that's not tied up in goods until he chooses to spend it. Now, here it is, time for him to be changing monies, setting his Silklands caravan on the road, outfitting his ships . . . and things have been very quiet from Customs Point this year. Aurien's caravel coming in, that was luck, but it hasn't helped. So, Caiazzo's problem is a money problem, pointsman, and one that has roots years back. Whatever's wrong can't have anything to do with the children, but it could get him into serious trouble, in and out of the court. Which I would surely hate to see." She smiled. "And now you're wondering why I'd tell you this much."

Rathe blinked. "Frankly, yes."

Her smile widened. "Hanselin has a nice hand in his business, a subtle hand. There are people who would like to take his place whom I would very much dislike dealing with. Which is why this old woman has been rambling on at you, pointsman, and you're very kind to listen to her."

Rathe blinked again, a kind of awe filling him. She had told him everything he could have thought to ask, and never once had directly implicated herself or anyone. "Not at all, madame, it's been my pleasure to listen to you ramble."

"Because that's all it is, of course, pointsman."

Rathe's eyes met hers, his expression as ingenuous as her own. He'd agreed to keep it off the books; she could and would deny ever having said any of this, if he were foolish enough to try to make a points matter of it. But he did believe her—if nothing else, it fit in too well with what Eslingen had said. Caiazzo was having problems, and with something that had worked well in the past. And that argued that he didn't have anything to do with the missing children: the two events just didn't fit. In other times, the sources of his coin might be Rathe's concern, but at the moment, he could leave that to Customs Point, and concentrate on the children. "Of course, madame. And I thank you for letting me take up so much of your time. You must be very busy."

She sighed, and lifted an enameled bell that stood beside the silver inkwell. "I could be busier, and hope to be so soon. My man will see you out."

The door opened, and the footman loomed in the doorway. Rathe nodded politely to Chevassu—almost a bow—and followed the servant out.

Caiazzo's temper had improved markedly since the arrival of Aurien's caravel, and for the first time, Eslingen began to understand why the long-distance trader's household was so fiercely loyal to their employer. With the immediate problems somewhat relieved, Caiazzo relaxed, showing a deft awareness of his people that surprised and, unexpectedly, charmed the soldier. The household relaxed, too, as the night of the clocks receded without further consequence, and Eslingen found himself made cautiously welcome.

"You've done well, settling in," Denizard said, as they climbed together toward Caiazzo's workroom.

Eslingen shrugged. "I'm not ungrateful, but I'm also not unaware that at least some of them think I'm good luck. And that's a chancy reputation."

Denizard grinned. "Oh, don't worry about Azemar, she'd follow every broadsheet astrologer in the city if she could just figure out how to do it all at once. No, seriously, you've done well. I think Hanse will want to keep you on, if you're willing."

Eslingen hesitated. Now that it had come to an offer, he found himself surprisingly reluctant, but then he shook the thought away, impatient with himself. This was the best place he'd had, not excepting his post with Coindarel, and he'd be a fool to turn it down, particularly when he couldn't have put a name to the reluctance. "Thanks," he said. "I—it's a good place, I'd be glad to stay."

"Good—" Denizard broke off as the door to the counting room snapped open, and Caiazzo himself stood framed in the doorway.

"Oh, there you are. Good. Eslingen, I want you to go to the fair, to the caravan-masters, and tell Rouvalles he can send for his coin tomorrow—any time after second sunrise, tell him. And you can make reasonable apologies for me, but don't give him any explanations."

"Sir," Eslingen said.

"After that—" He rolled his eyes at Denizard. "After that, meet me at the public landing at the northriver end of the Manufactory—the Point of Graves—Bridge. You're in for a treat, Eslingen, we're going to see my merchant resident."

"Sir?" Eslingen said again, and immediately wished he'd left the question unasked.

Caiazzo's grin widened. "Oh, you'll like Madame Allyns, Eslingen, and, more to the point, she'll certainly like you." He glanced over his shoulder at the standing clock. "Be there by noon, that should give you enough time with Rouvalles."

The dismissal was obvious. "Sir," Eslingen said, for the third time, and took himself off.

The fair was in full swing at last, and Eslingen wasn't sorry to have an excuse to explore its byways. The older members of the household grumbled that this fair was a shadow of its usual self, that the commons of Astreiant were too busy looking over their shoulders and keeping a hand firmly on their children to loose their purse strings, but for Eslingen the rows of stalls—some of them easily as big as an ordinary shopfront, and as well stocked—were an almost magical experience. He had been to the various fairs of Esling as a boy, and once to the Crossroads Fair held at the autumn balance outside Galhac, south of the Chadroni Gap, but none of them compared with this display of goods. He took a roundabout road to the corrals on the eastern edge of the fairground, dizzying himself with the scent of spices from the Silklands and the strange, musky ambers and crystal flowers from the petty kingdoms north and west of Chadron. They lay in baskets and shallow dishes on every counter, and the suns' light sent the pungent odors skyward. Between the drapers and the dyers, he nearly walked into a black-robed astrologer, orrery out as he spoke to a girl in an apprentice's blue coat. Eslingen murmured an apology, but the astrologer had already turned away, pocketing his orrery, and faded into the crowd.

"Hey," the girl called, but he was already almost out of sight. She swore and started after him. Eslingen blinked, startled—what had the man been promising her, to run so fast—but shrugged the thought away. The leathersellers' alley was too crowded to pass—Astreiant was noted for its leatherwork, but bought most of its hides from the League—and he skirted the mob of masters, each with her train of apprentices and journeymen. Handcarts trundled between the stalls and the river, hides in various stages of preparation stacked so high that the sweating laborers could barely see the path in front of them. Eslingen kept a wary eye out, and wasn't sorry to reach the end of that section.

The caravan-masters, by a commonsense tradition, had the two rows of stalls on the eastern edge of the fairground, by the corrals where they and their people lived for the duration of the fair. Someone had set up an altar to Bonfortune at the southern end of the makeshift street, and the smiling statue was draped with flower wreaths and printed offering-slips. The ground at its feet was dark, sticky with spilled wine and shreds of rice and noodles: the caravaners were impartial in their allegiances, and in their methods of worship.

Caiazzo's booth—another small shop, really, with a bright blue canvas roof over half-height wooden walls—lay closer to the western end of the street, marked by the pennants with his house-sign hanging from the tent poles. Eslingen waited until the factor had finished with her customer, a stocky woman in plain brown who clutched a letter, credit or introduction, in one painted hand, before he stepped up to the counter. It was padded with leather to protect the bolts of silk brocade and silk velvet from the rough wood. There was silk gauze as well, a length embroidered and re-embroidered with gold and pearls; he reached out to touch it, in spite of knowing better, and winced as his fingers caught on the delicate fabric. A bolt of this was worth a common man's salary for years, and the nobles who bought it paid in gold; he was not surprised to see a solid-looking man watching him from the shadows inside the stall.

"Can I help you, sir?" the factor said, and blinked. "You're Hanse's new knife, aren't you? Trouble?"

Eslingen shook his head. "No trouble, and yes, I'm Eslingen. I have a message for Rouvalles, if he's here."

"He's back at the corrals," the factor answered. "Do you know the way?"

"No, but I can probably find it," Eslingen answered.

The factor grinned. "You can't miss his camp, it's got the house pennants all over it. We use the fourth corral—it's almost directly behind where we are now—and Rouvalles has the stable beyond that."

"It sounds simple enough," Eslingen said, dubious, and the factor's smile widened.

"Look for the house pennants," she advised, and turned to greet a tall woman in a beautifully cut bodice and skirt.

Eslingen sighed, but knew better than to come between her and a potential customer, especially one as well dressed as this woman. He found a path between two of the stalls that seemed to be in general use, and emerged into the confusion of the corrals. There were five of the wood and stone enclosures, each one filled with horses; the low buildings beyond, clearly built as stables, seemed to be being shared impartially by people and animals. The air was hazed with dust, and a thicker plume of it rose over the furthest pen, where a trio stripped to shirts and breeches were attempting to cut a single animal out of the herd. The horses, each one marked by a ribbon braided into its mane, snorted and swirled, unwilling to be caught; Eslingen snorted himself—he would never had let his troopers handle their mounts that badly—and made his way toward Caiazzo's pennant hanging above a stable door.

The stalls in that section seemed to be occupied exclusively by horses, and Eslingen nodded his approval even as he glanced around for someone who could direct him. Rouvalles was wise to keep his horses out of the common herd; you never knew how well anyone else kept their animals, and the last thing you needed was to have your best mounts down sick when you were ready to move out. A skinny man was mucking out the furthest stall, and Eslingen moved toward him, inhaling the familiar scent of hay and dung.

"I'm looking for Rouvalles," he said, raising his voice a little to be heard over the noise outside.

The skinny man straightened, showing a wall eye that made him look rather like the horse he was tending, and jerked his thumb over his shoulder. "Above."

Looking more closely, Eslingen could see the stones of a steep stairway set into the wall at the end of the building. "Thanks," he said, and climbed to the floor above. The space had obviously once been intended for hay storage, and indeed the broad boards were still scattered with bits of straw, but at the moment it had been turned into an indoor campsite. Bedding was piled in neat rows along each wall, beneath windows propped open to the fitful breeze, and carpets hung from a web of ropes at the far end of the space, creating a makeshift room. A group of four or five men, mostly Chenedolliste, by their looks, were sitting around an unlit brazier, tossing dice on its flat cover. The nearest stood easily, seeing Eslingen, and stepped into his path.

"Can I help you?" he asked, around a stick of the sugar-candy the Astreianters sold ten-for-a-demming, and Eslingen lifted the badge he wore on a ribbon around his neck.

"I'm here to see Rouvalles," Eslingen said, patiently. "From Caiazzo."

The man scowled around his candy, and Eslingen wondered just how much bad feeling the delay had engendered. "I'll see if he's free," he said, and ducked under the carpets without waiting for an answer. He reappeared a moment later, scowling even more deeply, and Rouvalles himself held aside the carpet that served as a door.

"Come on in—Eslingen, isn't it?"

Eslingen nodded, and ducked under the heavy fabric. It smelled of horses and smoke and sweat and leather, all the scents of a campaign, and he took a deep breath, savoring even the heat of the enclosed space. Rouvalles gave him a wry smile.

"Regretting your change of employment already?"

The smile, Eslingen saw, didn't touch his eyes. "Not so far," he answered. "But this does bring back memories.

Rouvalles gave a short laugh, easing some of the tension and anger in his face, and gestured to one of the stools. "I bet it does. So, tell me, what does Hanse want?"

Eslingen seated himself, taking his time with the skirts of his coat. All the furniture around him was portable, he saw, from the stools to the narrow table and the narrow bedstead; all would break down into easily-carried pieces. The entire room, carpets, bedding, furniture, even the strongbox that lay half-hidden under a worn square of blanket, would fit easily on a single pack animal.

"Cijntien told me he'd made you an offer," Rouvalles said, and shrugged. "I suppose it still holds, though Hanse wouldn't thank you—and I'm not sure how much I care about that, just now."

Eslingen brought himself back to the matter at hand. "No, so far I'm quite comfortable with my employment, thanks. Caiazzo sent me to tell you that the money will be ready tomorrow. You can send a couple of men to collect it any time after second sunrise."

Rouvalles paused in the act of pouring two glasses of wine: anger at the delay notwithstanding, customs of hospitality, bred on the caravan routes, died hard. He turned to Eslingen, one eyebrow lifted, then Eslingen thought he saw the other man's shoulders relax slightly.

"Well, that's good news at least," the Chadroni said, after a moment. He made a face, as though he had forgotten he was holding the cups, and handed one to Eslingen. "I rather thought you'd come to put me off again."

Eslingen took a careful swallow of what proved to be a heavy, aromatic wine. He said, "Not this time. And I can't say I blame you for wanting to leave the city as soon as possible."

Rouvalles frowned slightly, as though puzzled, then his face cleared. "Oh, the children. I thought you meant the clock-night. No, neither one's made my life any easier, let me tell you."

"Nor anyone's," Eslingen said, and remembered what Jasanten had said—had it only been a week ago? Children born under Seidos might well find employment with the caravans, though why a caravan-master would steal children was beyond him—unless, he thought suddenly, there was someone foreign, someone in the Silklands, say, who wanted them? It didn't seem likely, but he owed Rathe at least that much of an effort. "Have the broadsheets been blaming you lot, then?"

Rouvalles scowled, the pale eyes narrowing. "Along with everybody else, yes, they've mentioned the caravans, and we've had a few worried mothers wandering through, peering in corners when they think we're not looking." He shook his head as though amazed at the thought, then looked sharply at Eslingen. "And you can tell Hanse I don't hire kids, and never have done, he should know that."

So much for being subtle, Eslingen thought. At least he assumed I was asking on Caiazzo's behalf. He said, "I'll pass that on. But—and this is me asking, not Caiazzo, I'm just curious—does that mean you don't take apprentices?"

"Did you see any apprentices in the hall?" he asked, but his tone was milder than his words. "Oh, we take apprentices, all right, or I do, but what we get . . . it's always the ones who've already failed at something else. Nobody in Astreiant—nobody anywhere—sets out to become a caravaner."

"Did you?" Eslingen asked. "I mean, if you're going to be good at something, it doesn't seem as though you'd go into it by default. And from what Caiazzo says, you're probably the best."

Rouvalles tilted his head, stared into space for a few moments, then said, "I didn't set out to become a caravaner, no. Never thought it was—open—to me. But once I did, I discovered I liked it, and had a knack for it. Rather like you and soldiering, I would imagine?" he asked, making it not quite a question, and the blue eyes were pale, cool.

"A lot like soldiering," Eslingen agreed. He finished the rest of his wine, stood up. "Thanks for the drink, it's a thirsty day."

"Are you sure you won't come along?" Rouvalles asked. "This is no time to be a Leaguer, either, in Astreiant."

"I'm trusting Caiazzo can protect me," Eslingen answered, with more confidence than he entirely felt. "If you'll send to him tomorrow, after second sunrise, he'll have the money for you."

"We'll be there," Rouvalles said, and Eslingen thought there was the hint of a threat in his tone. He lifted an eyebrow in question, and the Chadroni spread his hands. "No ill meant, Eslingen, but I'm a week later than I should be, and I still have supplies and goods to buy, so it'll be another two weeks before I'm on the road. Hanse—but Caiazzo knows all this."

Eslingen nodded in restrained sympathy. "I'll tell him, but, as you say, he knows."

"If he knows," Rouvalles said, and the good-humored face was suddenly grim, "if he knows, why in all the hells hasn't he sent the money I need?"

Eslingen shrugged, regretting his casual remark. "You'll have to ask him yourself."

"Don't think I haven't," Rouvalles answered.

Eslingen didn't answer, but ducked through the improvised door into the hall. The group was still gathered around the brazier, he saw without surprise, making a very bad pretense of interest in the dice game. The carpets would absorb some sound, but not all of it; it was no wonder they had listened. He smiled cheerfully at them, and went down the staircase to the stables.

He was early at the landing, and sat in the sun nibbling half a dozen ripe strawberries purchased on the edge of the market while he watched Caiazzo's boatmen bring the barge expertly across the current and alongside the landing. The long-distance trader sprang out almost before the ropes were snugged home, Denizard following more decorously, and stalked up the gentle slope toward the street. "Come on, then," he said, as he drew level with the soldier, "we don't want to keep madame waiting.

Eslingen fell into step half a pace behind him, wondering why not, but the look of mischief in Caiazzo's eyes was enough to keep him from asking aloud. He risked a glance at Denizard, but the magist looked, if anything, a little bored. Eslingen sighed, and resigned himself to whatever would happen. Caiazzo led them through the Manufactory district, skirting half a dozen brick-walled compounds that smelled of wood and glue and other, less-identifiable substances, and up the queen's-road into a neighborhood where sober-looking shops alternating with small, well-built houses. He turned into the courtyard of one of the larger of the latter, and the door opened before he could knock. A servant in sober livery bowed them into a reception hall, murmuring something Eslingen couldn't quite hear, and vanished through a narrow door.

As the door closed behind him, Eslingen glanced surreptitiously around the hall, impressed in spite of himself by the carved panels and the interlaced tiles that faced the hearth. There was real silver on the sideboard—put out for show as well as use, surely—and the livery had been of good linen, generously cut. The candles—unlit, at this hour, when the sun poured through the unshuttered windows, filling the room with light—were wax pillars as thick as a man's wrist. Surprisingly good taste from a woman who was partner to a southriver rat, he thought, but his heart wasn't in the sneer, not confronted by this restrained wealth, the dark wood that showed highlights as cool as the polished silver, the quiet service. Oh, the house itself might be on the wrong side—the Manufactory side—of the queen's-road, but the interior was as rich as any petty-noble's palace, or richer.

Caiazzo saw him looking then, and smiled. It was an expression Eslingen had already learned to distrust; he glanced sideways at Denizard, and saw her grave and unsmiling as ever, her painted hands folded into the sleeves of her master's robe. That was reassuring—if there were real trouble, Denizard would be tensed for it—and Eslingen sighed as unobtrusively as possible. So it really was just one of Caiazzo's jokes, something he thought would startle or shock his new knife, and Eslingen braced himself to meet the surprise as calmly as possible.

The door to the rest of the house opened then, and a liveried servant stepped through. "Madame Allyns," he said, and Eslingen caught his breath.

The woman who swept through the doorway was enormous and beautiful, skin like rich cream from the top of her breasts to the roots of her golden hair, eyes blue as summer skies, lips—slightly pouting—the pink of the inside of a shell. A strand of pearls a half-shade lighter than her skin wound twice around her neck, and vanished into the shadowed valley of her cleavage. A brooch the size of a man's hand—Oriane and the Sea-bull, Eslingen thought, not quite incredulous, in full congress—clasped her bodice, drawing the eye irrevocably to the divide between her massive breasts. She was as large as any two women, and four times as lovely.

"Hanse," she said, and swept forward, hands outstretched in greeting.

Caiazzo caught them, brought each in turn to his lips, bowing slightly. "Iniz. How pleasant to see you again."

"I trust so," Allyns answered, and turned, smiling, to the others. "Mistress Denizard I know—and I'm delighted to see you again, my dear—but this gentleman—" The smile was back, full of heavy-lidded speculation. "I haven't had the pleasure."

Eslingen swallowed hard, willing his arousal to subside. Caiazzo said, "May I present Philip Eslingen, late of Coindarel's Dragons? My new knife."

"A soldier," Allyns said. "How charming." She held out her hand, and Eslingen bowed over it. She smelled of roses, heavy-scented, late season flowers, a fragrance men could drown in. . . . And then she had twitched her hand deftly out of his grasp, and turned back to Caiazzo, one delicate brow lifting. "And I hear you have need of a knife these days, Hanse. I'm—concerned."

"There's no cause for worry," Caiazzo answered, and Allyns smiled again, too sweetly.

"But there is for concern, is there not? Our partnership has been a profitable one. I'd hate to have to find another long-distance trader, especially this late in the season. But I'd hate it even more if my investments failed to materialize."

"I doubt very much it will come to that," Caiazzo answered. "Even considering your legendary prudence, Iniz. Shall we go in?"

Allyns regarded him for a moment longer, and then nodded. She turned away, the rich silks of her skirts hissing against the stone floor, against each other. Caiazzo, suddenly, startlingly drab against her opulence, followed, and the servant shut the door behind them. Eslingen glanced at Denizard, wondering if he should follow, but the magist shook her head fractionally. She seemed to be listening for something, and Eslingen tilted his head to one side, too, not sure what he was waiting for. The house was very quiet; in the distance, he heard a door close, and then, from the street, the rattle of wheels and the sound of a horse's hooves.

At last Denizard relaxed, looked at him with a rather wry expression. Eslingen said, "It's all right, then?"

The magist nodded. "Oh, yes. Or, if it's not, it's far too late to worry about it." She saw Eslingen stiffen, and added, "They've been partners for fifteen years, Philip. We're as safe here as in our own house."

Eslingen nodded back, reluctantly. He knew that most long-distance traders—Merchants-Venturer, as the guild called itself—formed partnerships with Astreiant's Merchants Resident: each needed what the other could supply, goods exchanged for capital, and markets for each other's products, but that didn't explain the particulars of the situation. "She didn't sound happy," he said, and Denizard looked away.

"There have been some—difficulties this year," she said, after a moment. "As you've probably gathered."

Eslingen nodded. "Is it something I should know about? To do my job?"

Denizard sighed. "Hanse said I should use my discretion, telling you. And since you've said you'll stay on . . . about five years ago, when Seidos was in the Gargoyle, Hanse and Madame Allyns bought a seigneurial holding in the Ile'nord—in the Ajanes, west of the Gap."

"I thought," Eslingen said, and chose his words carefully, "I thought only nobles—nobles of four quarterings—could own those holdings."

Denizard nodded. "That's right. But there was a woman, a woman of I think eight quarters, who owed Madame quite a bit of money. So they made a bargain: d'Or—this woman would take the title, paid for with Madame's money, and Hanse's, and send a share of the estate's takings to them as payment."

Eslingen took a slow breath, let it out soundlessly. Caiazzo played dangerous games, and not just the ones southriver. Under the law, a commoner who presumed to purchase a noble title would lose her investment if she were found out, might, if the offense were particularly egregious or open, be sentenced to a fine—but that wasn't the real deterrent. The nobles of the Ajanes were jealous of their privileges, jealous to the point of having forced the queen's grandmother to agree to attach the rule of four quarters to the sale of all estates in their domain. And they were old-fashioned enough to try to wipe out such an insult in the commoner's blood. Eslingen could feel the hairs stirring on the nape of his neck at the thought of trying to protect Caiazzo from Ajanine nobles and their servants. He had served under an Ajanine captain once, for eight months when he was sixteen; it had been the first time he had deserted, and that had been the only thing that had saved his life. Three days after he had run, the Ajanine had thrown his company into a mad assault on a well-garrisoned Chadroni fort, and had lost them all in the space of an hour. Eslingen, and the ten men sent to track him down, had been the only survivors; they had enlisted together under a sober League captain less than a moon-month after that battle. He shook that memory away, said, still cautiously, "But what's to stop this woman from refusing to pay, now she's got the estate?"

Denizard gave him a grim look. "Madame Iniz still holds notes of her hand, for one thing, worth more than that estate."

"Notes can be repudiated," Eslingen said.

Denizard nodded. "Not easily, but, yes, they can be. But Hanse trades through there, too. And I wouldn't want to annoy Master Caiazzo, would you?"

"No," Eslingen agreed. *But I'm not an eight-quarter noble from the Ajanes.* The words hung between them, unspoken, and Denizard made a face.

"It seemed worth the risk. There's a gold mine on the estate, and merchants are always short of gold."

Eslingen started to whistle, cut the sound off in a hiss of breath. Gold made all the difference, made the risks worth taking, both the risk of buying the property and of threatening the true noble who held it for them. Merchants are always short of gold, indeed; it's gold that builds the manufactories and pays the caravan masters and the Silklands merchants when there's nothing else to trade. I see why they did it, why it's worth it, but, Seidos's Horse, it's a risk.

"And," Denizard went on, "the stars were favorable."

They would have to be. Eslingen squinted slightly. Seidos had been in the Gargoyle, she had said, which made sense. The Gargoyle was Argent's sign, and Argent-Bonfortune was the god of the merchants: the planet of the nobility in the sign of the merchant, a reasonable omen. But if Seidos was in the Gargoyle in the Demean reckoning, that meant it was—somewhere else—in the Phoeban zodiac. "If Seidos was in the Gargoyle," he said aloud, "it was also in, what, Cock-and-Hens?"

Denizard looked away. "We're common, it's Demis who rules our lives."

But that's noble land. Eslingen killed that response—he was no magist, and his astrological education came from the broadsheets he read assiduously; there was no reason to think he was right, when Denizard said otherwise. But the estate in question was noble, and fell under Phoebe's rule, under the signs of her solar zodiac. And by that reckoning, Seidos was in the sign of the Cock-and-Hens, the wintersun's sign, sign of changing seasons, of change and suffering and impending, inevitable death. You could interpret the purchase as a change, and a kind of death, but still . . . it's not a chance I'd want to take.

8

Rathe leaned over Salineis's shoulder as she made the last of the nightwatch's entries in the station's daybook—a call to locate a strayed maidservant, who'd turned out to be standing at the well chatting with her leman, barely a quarter hour overdue, the sort of thing they were all seeing entirely too much of these days—and then added his initials to the entry. It was his day to supervise the station, something of a welcome break in what had begun to seem like months of walking from point to point in search of clues to the missing children. It also meant that Monteia would not be there, and, since Rathe had had little chance to pursue the question of the unlicensed printers, he was just as glad not to have to explain that to her.

"Not a bad night, on the whole," Salineis said, and Rathe dragged his attention back to her.

"How're things by the Old Brown Dog?"

The woman shrugged, and unclasped her heavy jerkin. The bodice beneath it was sweat-dark at her underarms, and another damp patch showed between her shoulder blades as she turned to hang it on the wall. "Not too bad, actually. The Huviet boy's master, what's his name, Follet, he's let it be known he blames Paas, and that's shut up most of them. Of course, Follet's never liked Mistress Huviet—who does?—but at least it seems to be keeping the peace."

Rathe nodded. "And Aagte?"

"Devynck," Salineis said, with some precision, "is keeping her mouth shut and herself out of sight, for which I thank her stars and all my gods." She shook her head, set a dashing cap on top of her piled hair. "And it seems to be working. They're doing a decent business again, and Timo says he saw some of the locals drinking there when he checked in last night. If they blame anyone, it's that knife of hers."

"That's good news," Rathe said, and meant it. Eslingen was well clear of Point of Hopes; he could afford to take the blame for a little longer, at least until it had been forgotten.

"Well, we've needed some, after clock-night," Salineis answered, and turned away.

Rathe seated himself in front of the daybook, paged idly through the events of the last three days. The clock-night had frightened and sobered the city, it seemed; since then things had been relatively quiet, except for the false alarms, and, best of all, no children had gone missing in that period. Half a dozen had been reported, but all of those had been found within a few hours. And that reminds me, he thought, I still have to get myself over to Point of Dreams and see if the Cytel boy is really with Savatier's company. The memory brought with it a twinge of real dread: surely, he thought, if Albe was there, and safe, Gavi would have told me. . . . But Jhirassi had been working; their waking hours had not overlapped. Still, he decided, I'll make it my business to walk by there on my way home tonight.

The front door opened then, and he looked up, expecting one of the duty points or someone come to report another missing child. To his surprise, Monteia swept in, bringing with her the distinct scent of manure. She scowled at him, scraping her shoes on the iron blade set in the floor by the sill, and Rathe said, cautiously, "I didn't expect you in today, Chief."

"No more did I." Monteia inspected her soles, swore under her breath, and scraped again. "I dined with the other chiefs last night, Nico, and there's some business that won't wait." She looked at her shoes again, nodded, satisfied, and leaned back out the door. "Vatan! Send one of the runners to sweep the gate and clean up here, and then get in here yourself. I need to talk to Nico."

Rathe rose, already dreading her news, and followed her into the workroom. Monteia kicked her shoes into a corner, padded in stocking feet to her chair and sat down, planting both elbows solidly on the cluttered surface.

"Sit, man," she said. "It's not you I'm annoyed with, not personally."

There was no good answer to that, and Rathe perched warily on the nearest stool.

"I take it the night was quiet?" Monteia went on.

"According to Sal, yeah. Nothing but false alarms, though by the look of the book that kept them on the run."

Monteia grunted. "That's what I'm hearing from all the points, and it's one piece of good news, I suppose. There hasn't been a child stolen in the last ten days—oh, plenty of reports, but those kids have all been found."

"So what's the bad news?" Rathe asked, after a moment. "Aside from the fact we haven't found the first eighty-five."

Monteia gave him a sour look. "The bad news is what I'm hearing from our own markets. Not only are all of us too busy to do more than shake our fists at the illegal printers, the printers are blaming us for the kids—and I want to see that stopped. Claes tells me you were inquiring after one called Agere?"

Rathe nodded. "She's printed some of the worst that I've seen sold here. I told Claes we'd split the point if we made it, since Agere works out of Fairs' Point. I handed the sheets I got over to the judiciary."

"Fair enough." Monteia's scowl deepened again. "But I want her."

Rathe hid a sigh. Tracking down illegal printers seemed less than vital, given the missing children, but he knew Monteia was right. They couldn't abandon everything else, no matter how much they might want to concentrate on the children. "I'll do what I can, Chief."

"I know." Monteia shook her head. "Sorry, Nico, it was a long night."

"More bad news?" Even as he asked, Rathe knew that wasn't it, or not precisely so, and wasn't surprised when Monteia shook her head again.

"Not exactly—it might even turn out to be good news. Have you heard there's a new species of astrologer working the fair?"

"I've heard something. I've spoken with a few people about them. Not affiliated with the university or the temples, and the Three Nations are all upset because they're undercutting the student prices."

"That about covers it," Monteia said. "Fairs' Point say they think there are six or eight of them, but they're very shy of the points."

"Probably don't want to pay the fees," Rathe said.

Monteia gave him a thin smile. "Only Claes says he thinks they're paying entirely too much attention to children."

"Did he question them on it?" Rathe demanded.

"Of course he did, do you think he's an apprentice?" Monteia reined in her temper with a visible effort. "They say—and I'll be damned if I can contradict them—that of course they are, since children are most in need of protection and advice these days."

"But still—" Rathe leaned forward, unable to keep still. "No one knows who these people are, or where they've come from, right? So we should find out, and fast, before anyone else goes missing."

"They could be a visitation from the gods," Monteia said, and snorted. "After clock-night, I'd believe it. Some people would rather blame anybody else before they'd question an astrologer." She held up her hand, forestalling Rathe's instant response. "But I agree with you, Nico. Claes is having them watched, but I want you to start on it from our end. See what you can find out, see if there's any connection between them and our missing, and do it fast, before this lull ends, and we start losing children again."

Rathe pushed himself up from the stool, his mind already racing. He would visit Mailet's workshop first, he decided; the rest of the children came from families or work places that were less settled than the butcher's, would be harder to find. "I'll talk to Istre, too," he said aloud. "The university has a stake in dealing with these hedge-astrologers."

Monteia nodded. "We've been working them pretty hard, even your friend. We're not the only people who had the clever notion of sending nativities to the magists. Between the twelve of us, I think we've sent nearly eighty birth-stars over there, and none of us have gotten anything back yet."

That was sobering, but Rathe shoved aside the uncertainty. "I'll ask Istre when I speak to him," he said. "Gods, this could be the chance we've been waiting for."

He made his way quickly through the streets, barely aware of the uncertain glances, truculent and oddly embarrassed all at once, as he reached the Knives Road. Mailet's hall was busy—busy enough, Rathe saw, that Mailet himself was working the front of the shop, flanked by sweating journeymen. The air smelled of animals and blood, and Rathe was glad they were working in the street and not in the close confines of the building. Mailet glanced up at Rathe's approach, brows drawing together in a scowl, but he mastered himself instantly, and finished his business with his customer before turning on the pointsman.

"And what do you want here this time, Rathe?"

"I want to speak to Trijntje Ollre," Rathe said, and curbed his own excitement before it could turn into irritation.

"Why—?" Mailet broke off, his eyes focussing on something over Rathe's right shoulder. "Not before time, Liron. Now, get these stones sluiced down."

Rathe glanced back, to see an older apprentice hurrying toward them, water buckets hanging from a carrying yoke balanced on his shoulders. He turned his attention back to Mailet, and said, "I need to talk to her because we have some new information." He grimaced at the sudden hope in Mailet's face. "It's nothing solid, not yet, but—it would help if I could talk to Trijntje."

Mailet took a deep breath, but jerked his head toward the main door. "You know your way by now. She's in the hall with the others."

"Thanks," Rathe said, and ducked past him into the shop.

As promised, the apprentices were at work at their long tables, knives flashing in the sunlight that poured in through the high windows. They seemed in less of a rush this time—Rathe didn't see a magist to keep track of favorable stars—but the piles of vegetables at each broad table were still visibly diminishing. He could smell the peppery, pungent odor of all-save, and saw a young apprentice moving from table to table distributing the shabby bunches. The journeyman Grosejl saw him then, and moved quickly to intercept him, her face drawing into a wary frown.

"Any news?"

Rathe shook his head. "Not directly, no. But there are some questions I need to ask Trijntje—we have some new information that may help." He saw the hope flare in her eyes, and added, guiltily, "I don't know for certain—I can't promise anything."

"Something's better than nothing," Grosejl answered, and waved toward the line of tables. "Trijntje! Come here a moment."

The girl put down her knife obediently, and came toward them, wiping her hands on her apron. "Is—" She broke off, unable to finish the question, and Rathe shook his head.

"We haven't found anything, either way, but there are some questions I need to ask."

"I don't know what else I can tell you." She wound her hands in her apron, then frowned at herself, and stopped.

Rathe said, "Have you—did you and Herisse consult any astrologers recently? Or did any of the other girls?"

Ollre looked up at him, her frown deepening, but more perplexed, he thought, than angry. He caught himself holding his breath, not wanting to say more, for fear of telling her what he wanted to hear.

"At the First Fair, we did," she said at last, and shrugged. "It's supposed to be auspicious for butchers, and then Metenere was trine the sun, and all. So we had our stars read."

Rathe nodded. "You and Herisse together?"

"Yes."

He held his breath again. "What stall did you visit, do you remember? Or did you go to one of the students?"

Ollre shook her head. "We didn't have to go to one of the booths or the Three Nations, which was a good thing, too, at their prices. There were some astrologers walking around, I don't know their affiliation—I thought they were students, at first, but their robes were black, not grey. So we went to one of them." She seemed to see something in Rathe's expression, and her head lifted. "Well, neither one of us had coin to waste, and he was cheap enough, and honest-sounding. Not at all forbidding, or obnoxious, like the Three Nations."

"What sort of a reading did he give you?" Rathe asked. He heard the sharp intake of breath, saw the startled look on her face: it was not good manners to inquire into someone's stars, but he was past caring, swept on before she could protest. "Did he give you anything—a written horoscope, a broadsheet, anything?"

Ollre blinked at him, visibly uncertain, and Grosejl said, "I don't see what the details have to do with anything, pointsman."

"I need to know what kind of service he provided," Rathe said. He looked at Ollre. "You don't have to tell me the details, but I do need to know how he read you, what he did for you."

Ollre looked suddenly embarrassed. "Well, he didn't actually do much for me, my nativity's not that good, just to the hour. So he just said general things, and said he couldn't help me much—except for this." She reached under her apron, into the pocket she wore beneath the skirt, and brought out a small disk. "He said it was for luck, that the stars were going to be unsettled for a while, and that I'd need it." She made a face. "He was right there, wasn't he?"

Rathe stared for a moment at the dark round of wax, then said, "May I?"

Ollre shrugged and held it out, and he took it from her hand. It was a crude thing, stamped with planetary signs around a central figure of Areton with his shield. He recognized most of them, but couldn't begin to guess what the sequence meant. But b'Estorr would know, he thought, and turned it over. The reverse was blank. "Did Herisse get one of these?"

"Oh, yes, and she talked to him for a lot longer—of course, she knows her stars to the minute." Ollre's fond smile vanished suddenly. "Here, you don't think that has anything to do with her vanishing, do you?"

"I don't know," Rathe said. "It's possible, yeah, but we don't know for sure. Can I keep this?"

"If it had anything to do with—" Ollre shuddered. "I don't ever want to see it again."

"And if it didn't," Rathe said gently, "I'll see it gets back to you. Can you tell me what this astrologer looked like?"

The girl shrugged, looked embarrassed again. He'd been of middle years, not grey, not young; of middle height and middle color and spoke without an accent, beyond the normal tang of Astreianter speech. It wasn't much, but Rathe hadn't been expecting much, and nodded politely. "Thanks, Trijntje, this has been a help."

The girl nodded, looking as though she wanted to ask something more, but Grosejl touched her arm. "All right, Trijntje, get back to work." She looked at Rathe as the apprentice moved slowly back toward her table. "What'll you do with it, anyway?"

Rathe looked down at the little charm, then, very carefully, slipped it into his purse, knotting the strings securely over it. "Take it to a magist I know at the university."

Grosejl nodded. "Gods, I hope you find her—all of them. It's the not hearing, you see. It's the—the blindness of it all. No word, no knowing what might have happened." Her lips twisted. "Death isn't all bad, pointsman. At least it's an end."

You don't have a friend who's a necromancer, Rathe thought. He could feel the excitement rising in him at the first real evidence he'd found, and thrust it sternly down before the journeyman could see and misunderstand. He made his excuses quickly, and headed back out to the street. He would visit the other shops and families, at least the ones he could find, and then he'd head to the fair, let Claes know about this new connection. And then . . . he fought back the sense of certainty. Then he would go to the university, and see what b'Estorr had to say about the charm.

It took him the better part of three hours to contact the relatives and employers of the children on his book, and the results were less than conclusive. The brewers' apprentices had certainly gone to the First Fair, and had had their stars read, though the remaining apprentices couldn't say whether it had been by the Three Nations or the black-robed strangers. The price would have mattered, they admitted, but they simply didn't know. One of the shop boys had been star-mad, had his stars read at every possible opportunity, and he had definitely spoken to one of the hedge-astrologers—but, the counterwoman had warned, he'd also spoken to a student of the Three Nations, and had at least gone into a booth run by the Temple of Sofia. As for the rest, no one could remember whether or not they'd spoken to any astrologers, but at least, Rathe thought, they couldn't say they hadn't either. He knew the dangers of overconfidence, of building too much on too little fact, but couldn't seem to stop himself from hoping. It was the first decent piece of luck they'd had—Astree, send it's the right piece, he thought, and paused at one of the shrines outside the Pantheon to buy and light a stick of incense.

The fair was as busy as ever, and Rathe knew from experience that he was more likely to find Claes at the point station than in the fairground itself. Even so, he couldn't resist the chance to pass through the teeming market, keeping an eye out for black-robed astrologers. It was too much to hope he'd catch them at something—if they were involved, they'd been far too careful to arouse suspicion—but still, it would be good to get a look at them.

He reached the printers' row without seeing any sign of them, however, and the sight of Agere's faded sign took the edge off his pleasure. He turned toward it, falling in behind a well-dressed matron whose broad body and full skirts helped screen his approach, and then reached around her to slip a sheet from the top of its pile. Agere turned toward him, her smile faltering as she recognized the jerkin and the truncheon at his belt.

"You're not with Fairs' Point," she said, confidently enough. "You've no jurisdiction here, pointsman."

"Unfair, Agere, I might just want to buy a sheet." Rathe skimmed through the smudged printing, feeling his face stiffen with anger. "Not this one, though." It was the worst he'd seen yet, openly blaming the points for failing to protect the missing children, and hinting that they—and perhaps the metropolitan and the city government—were somehow behind the disappearances. He set the page back on its pile, and gave Agere his least pleasant smile. "So now we're conspiring with Astreiant herself? You flatter us, usually it's the Leaguers, or the manufactories, or the soldiers—of whatever nation—or anyone else you think you can attack and get away with. And I don't see a bond-mark here."

"I don't print those," Agere said, without inflection. "I'm selling them for someone else."

That was the usual excuse, and Rathe's lips thinned. "Oh, Agere, couldn't you say something I hadn't heard a hundred times already?"

"I didn't print it," Agere snapped. "Is it a fee you're after? Then have the decency to say so."

Rathe regarded her a moment longer. She had been right about one thing, he had no jurisdiction here. To make the point stand, he would have to fetch someone from Fairs' Point to make the arrest, and by the time he'd done that, Agere would simply have disposed of the offending broadsheet. He said, "No fee for a warning, Agere. Caiazzo's not fond of politics—yeah, I know you print under his coin—and there's not a fee high enough to buy me off when I can watch Caiazzo drop you. And then we will score you without that counterfeit license to protect you. Have a good fair, printer."

He walked away, aware of the printer's eyes burning into him, her anger only just leashed. He turned the next corner, blindly, found himself in the leathersellers's quarter, and stopped, surprised that his hands were shaking. It was one thing to listen to the rumors, the insults, to have it told to him, but to see it in print, in the broadsheets that were the lifeblood of Astreiant . . . the plain black-and-white of the type was somehow more threatening that any spoken accusation. Words disappeared as soon as they were spoken, but the letters on paper stayed to haunt a man.

He found Claes at the Fairs' Point station, as he'd expected, presiding over the ordinary chaos of the main room with a tankard in one hand and his truncheon in the other. Rathe sidestepped a drunken carter, bloody-nosed and furious, and lifted his hand to get Claes's attention.

"Can it wait?" the chief point called back. "We've a pack of fools here who started their drinking with the first sunrise."

"It's important," Rathe said, and waited.

Claes swore. "It had better be. You, Gasquet, take over here, sort them down into the cells—and I'll take it very ill if you let them kill each other before they've had a chance to sober up." He gestured for Rathe to precede him into the station's counting room, and shut the heavy door behind them. Rathe blinked in the sudden quiet, and Claes said, "So. What in Tyrseis's name is so important?"

"Monteia said you were worried about these hedge-astrologers," Rathe said. "The freelances. I've talked to the kin of our missing children. One of them, the butcher's girl, she got a charm from them a few days before she disappeared, and at least three of the others probably consulted them. The others may or may not have talked to them, but I can't prove they didn't."

Claes was silent for a long moment. "That's thin, Rathe. Very thin."

"It's more than we've had before," Rathe answered, and the chief point sighed.

"True. But that was nothing at all."

Rathe swallowed hard, banking down his irritation. "Look, I know it's not much. But four of our kids who probably talked to them—one definitely, and she got a charm from him, which I'm taking to the university to see what the magists make of it—gods, Claes, we can't afford to ignore it."

"And I don't intend to ignore it," Claes answered. "I don't trust them, I don't know what they're doing here, and they don't charge nearly enough not to want something besides their fees. But I can't act on just this, and you know it."

Rathe nodded. "I know. But I did think, the sooner you knew about it, the sooner you—and all of us—could start checking on the other kids, see how many of them talked to these astrologers before they disappeared."

Claes grinned. "And you're right, certainly—and, yes, this was important, I'll give you that. But I'd like more to go on, Rathe, that's all." He waved a hand in dismissal, and Rathe opened the workroom door.

"I'm working on it," he said, and made his way back out into the streets of the fair.

Claes was right, of course. It wasn't much to go on, and Rathe felt his mood plummet as rapidly as it had improved. And that, he knew, was as unreasonable as his earlier optimism. The connection with the astrologers was still the most solid—the only—link they had between the child-thefts; he couldn't afford to ignore it, or to build too much on it, at least not yet.

He made his way back through the fair by a different route, avoiding the printers and the crowds that always filled the leathersellers' district, and found himself among the smaller booths, where the smaller merchants venturer sold their mix of goods directly. It was crowded here, too—most of the stalls carried less expensive items, trinkets, small packets of spices, silk thread, Chadroni ribbons, beads, the coarse southern glassware, that even an apprentice could afford—but this year there were few enough of them in evidence. There were few children in general—occasionally a northriver child, escorted not just by the usual nurse, but also by an armed man or woman of the household; more often a plain-dressed girl or boy hurrying on some errand, unable to give more than a wistful glance at the gaudy displays—and Rathe was suddenly angry again. This was no way for a child to see the fair, and, especially for the older ones, the ones who worked for their keep, their mistresses' fears were depriving them of one of the few long holidays in the working year. Not that anyone could afford to let their apprentices and the like have the full three weeks of the fair completely free, of course, but most employers tolerated a certain relaxation of standards over the course of the fair. He himself, when he had been a runner, could remember getting two or three days off—days to explore and spend one's carefully hoarded demmings on strange foods and goods from the kingdoms beyond Chenedolle—and vying for errands that would send him near the fairgrounds. But this year, it looked as though the average apprentice was getting none of that.

Without consciously meaning to, his roundabout course had brought into the center of the fairground, where the cookstalls were set up. The air was heavy with the smell of Silklands spices, almost drowning the heavy scent of mutton stew and the constant tang of hot, much-used oil. He threaded his way past a gang of Leaguers, carters by their clothes, who were monopolizing the stall of a cheerful-looking brewer, and dodged another stall where a woman in a Silklands headscarf twirled skewers of vegetables over a long brazier. Half a dozen children, the first large group he'd seen, were clustered around a woman selling fried noodles, and another pair was standing gravely in front of a candyseller, choosing from among figures shaped like zodiacal beasts. He checked for a moment, torn between admiration and fear, and then made himself walk on. Heat radiated from the open fires and he was glad to reach the edge of the cooking areas. So, by the look of things, were most people: the spaces between the stalls were wider here, and people stood in groups of twos and threes, talking and eating. Rathe glanced around instinctively, looking for any sign of the astrologers, and to his surprise recognized a slim, dark-haired woman who stood in the shade of one of the awnings, nibbling on a fried pastry. Cassia LaSier usually preferred to work later in the day, when the pickings were richer—and at the moment she seemed to be concentrating on her meal, one hand cupped to catch anything that fell from the fragile shell—but she might also enjoy the challenge of the noon-time crowd. Rathe turned toward her, and she looked up sharply, her mouth curving into a wry smile.

"Working the fairground, Rathe? I wouldn't've thought it was your patch."

Rathe shook his head. "It's not. I had some errands here."

"Well, that's a relief for honest working people," LaSier answered, and swallowed the last of her pastry.

"Oh, are you working?"

"Not if you are," she retorted, and Rathe allowed himself a grin. "Not the fair, anyway."

"The children?" LaSier's eyes were suddenly alert. "No luck, then, still?"

"Maybe," Rathe answered, and shook his head at the sudden eagerness in the woman's face. "But we're still having horoscopes done for the missing kids, which should tell you how 'maybe' it is."

"Damn." LaSier licked grease from her fingers, wiped them discreetly on the hem of her skirt. "Are all the stations doing it?"

"From what Monteia says, yes. Why?"

"We didn't make a formal complaint to Sighs, of course, so I suppose I can't complain. Still, it'd be nice if Gavaret had the same chance of being found as the others."

It would, and it would be more than nice, Rathe thought, it would be the only fair thing to do. The Cordiere child might grow into a serious nuisance to the points, but he certainly had the right to live that long. He said, "He's as entitled as anyone, but he'd have to know his stars pretty closely for it to be much help."

"But he did," LaSier said, and corrected herself. "He does. And they were good for our line of work, let me tell you—who'd want an apprentice who was born to be hanged, right?" She shook her head in regret. "No, Gavaret knows his nativity, and he revels in it."

"Do you know it?" Rathe asked.

LaSier gave him a sidelong glance. "Thought you said you weren't working."

"Thought I said yes, on the children." Rathe sighed. "I can take it for you, off the books, though why I'd want your apprentice found is beyond me."

"And a damn dull world it would be without us," LaSier answered. "He was born on Midsummer Eve fourteen years ago, in Dhenin. He crowned at midnight, his mother told him, and was born at the half-hour stroke."

Rathe made the note in his tablets. Midsummer was a major day; any half-competent astrologer—anyone who owned an ephemeris, for that matter—could calculate the full nativity from what LaSier had told him. "Born under Tyrseis," he said aloud, "and the Gargoyle. How appropriate."

LaSier grinned. "And not born to hang."

"We don't hang pickpockets, Cassia," Rathe said.

"I know." She looked down, brushed a few crumbs from her bodice. "Well, good luck, Nico. You'll need it."

"Thanks. I'll let you know if we find anything."

"Oh, yes. Good luck with that, too," she answered, and turned away. Rathe watched her go, the slim figure with its waterfall of black hair soon lost in the crowd. It was rare enough for one of the 'Serry's inhabitants to wish any pointsman well, and he was grateful for the gesture. He glanced again at the notation in his tablets—one more reason to visit b'Estorr—and replaced them in his pocket. Gavaret Cordiere was a child like thousands other southriver, and like so many of them, he would find his livelihood in the 'Serry or the Court, maybe lodge with the points more than once, maybe live to old age, or more likely die at the hand of a rival or the wrong victim. Except that Gavaret Cordiere knew his nativity, and those stars marked him as appropriate for an apprenticeship with the Quentiers, a step up in the world, by the 'Serry's reckoning, at any rate. Rathe had never quite realized before just how similar their family business was to the more conventional guilds. He shrugged to himself. It made sense, in any business: why take on anyone born to fail at this line of work? Though, of course, a person's desire didn't always run in tandem with their stars, and the stars didn't guarantee, they merely indicated. . . . Those were the phrases one learned in dame school, and he shook them away.

A flutter of black caught his eye, and he looked sideways to see a figure in dark robes moving slowly across the central space, occasionally nodding to a passerby. Rathe tensed, ready to call for assistance, then hesitated. The robes might be black, might mark one of the astrologers, but they might also be dark grey, and the man just another university student adding to a limited income. He started after the man, but a whistle sounded, shrill and imperious, and he stopped abruptly as a trash wagon rumbled past, cutting off his view of the stranger and bathing him in its sour stench. He dodged around it, nose wrinkling, but the man was nowhere to be seen. He swore under his breath, scanning the crowd a final time, then turned toward the bright blue pennants that marked the tents where the Temple of Astree was acting as arbiter of the fair. *Maybe the arbiters will listen,* he thought, *even if Claes can't act. At the very least, they should be warned.*

The other temples had set up their booths around Astree's tents, some under Areton's shield for changing money, some offering horoscopes, a few, like the Demeans, offering certification of foreign goods. This part of the fair was the busiest yet, and Rathe had to work his way through a solid crowd before he could reach the arbiters' tents. Their flaps were drawn closed, though muffled voices leaked through the heavy cloth, and a tall woman whose coat bore the wheel-and-web badge of Astree was shaking her head at a pair of women who carried a basket. The two women stalked away, obviously angry, and the first woman looked at Rathe. "Can I help you, pointsman? As you can see, we're—occupied—at the moment. . . ."

"It's not business," Rathe said, "or not that kind of business. But I'd like to speak to a senior arbiter, if one's free."

The woman touched her badge. "I'm free enough at the moment. Gui Vauquelin."

"Nicolas Rathe. I'm the Adjunct Point at Point of Hopes."

"You're a ways from home," Vauquelin observed, but her tone was neutral.

"I know." Rathe took a breath. "These astrologers, the new ones—what do you know about them?"

"Aside from the fact that they're a pain in the ass?" Vauquelin sighed. "Which I shouldn't say, but they've been more headache than they're worth. Don't tell me the points are interested."

"Maybe," Rathe said again, and her gaze sharpened.

"The children?"

"We don't know. There may be a connection." Quickly, Rathe outlined what he'd found, scrupulous to point out that Claes, whose point this rightfully would be, didn't think there was anything they could do yet. When he'd finished, Vauquelin shook her head.

"We've had trouble with them from the day they arrived. Oh—" She held up a hand. "That's not fully fair, either. We haven't had any trouble from them, they seem ordinary enough, except that they're ostentatious about not owing allegiance to any particular temple. We've had our juniors talk to them, officially, and unofficially, we had one of our girls get her stars done, and they seem sound enough. It's basic, but not outright wrong, so there's no basis for complaint there. But the Three Nations are up in arms—and I offer thanks daily that that's not literally true—because they're taking the students' business."

"Couldn't you do anything on those grounds?"

"The student monopoly is customary, not legal," Vauquelin answered, and shrugged. "Besides, there are plenty of people here—northriver, I mean—who'd like to see the students taken down a few pegs. I've had a woman tell me to my face that these new astrologers have to be better just because they aren't students."

Rathe swore again under his breath. He had forgotten, more precisely, he rarely encountered, the old rivalry that pitted the students' Three Nations against the ordinary folk who had the misfortune to share their neighborhoods. It had been almost five years since the last riots, and he'd hoped that tensions had eased since.

Vauquelin smiled, ruefully. "Which makes it difficult to question these people without seeming to favor the students, and that I will not, cannot, do."

"But if they are involved—" Rathe broke off, gesturing an apology.

"We are watching them," Vauquelin said firmly. "And I know your people are doing the same. Yes, they talk to children, but we've never seen a child fail to return from talking to them. And it could be coincidence. Children are most at risk, these days, no wonder they want to offer any guidance they can."

"I suppose," Rathe said. It was the same thing the astrologers had told Claes's people, and it was true enough, but still, he wished he could share her detachment. Vauquelin was Astree's arbiter, had to be scrupulously balanced in her judgment—but it was hard to be blamed oneself, and see a more likely suspect embraced by at least the northriver populace.

Vauquelin looked at him as though she'd read the thought. "Don't mistake me, Adjunct Point. If we see anything to make us at all suspicious, we'll let you and yours know."

Rathe nodded, embarrassed that she'd read him so accurately. "I know. And I appreciate it, really." He turned away, his stride lengthening as he headed across the fair toward University Point.

b'Estorr was not at the university. Rathe stood for a moment at the foot of the stairway, staring at the doorkeeper, then shook himself hard. "When will he be back?" he asked, and the old woman shrugged.

"By first sunset, I expect, pointsman."

She started to close the upper half of her door, but Rathe caught it, forced a smile. "Will you tell him—no, can I leave a note?"

The old woman's eyebrows rose, but after a moment's search she found a slate and half a broken chalk pencil. Rathe scrawled a quick note, the crude point squeaking over the stone—NEED TO TALK TO YOU, WILL BE BACK TONIGHT, NICO—and handed it across. "It's important that he get this," he said, without much hope, and the old woman sniffed, and shut the door without comment. Rathe sighed, and headed back across the Hopes-point Bridge.

It was almost the end of his shift, but he stopped by the station anyway, read over the daybook before he hung up jerkin and truncheon and headed back to his lodgings. It lacked an hour to the first sunset; the sensible thing to do, he told himself, was to eat a decent dinner and put his thoughts in order before he went back to the university.

He rented three rooms—almost half the floor—on the second floor of what had once been a rich merchant's or petty noble's house, and shared what had been the courtyard gardens with the half a dozen other households that lived in the warren of rooms. The gardens were, usually, a luxury at this time of year, but now he winced as he passed his plot, straggling and unwatered, and hoped that the goats that the weaver kept in the former stable would eat the worst of the weeds before he was utterly disgraced. The air in the stairwell was close, and he winced again as he opened the door of his room. He had left the shutters closed and latched; the air was hot and still, tasting of dust and something gone rotten in the vegetable basket. He swore, loudly this time, and flung open the shutters, then stirred the stove until he found the last embers under the banked ash and lit a stick of incense. He set that in the holder in the center of the Hearthmistress's circular altar, and then glared at the stove. No amount of banking would keep those few embers going overnight, but he didn't relish the idea of building up the fire in this heat. Nor did he particularly enjoy the thought of fumbling with flint and tinder once he'd gotten back from the university, but that was his only alternative. And I cannot, he decided, face a fire just now. He set his tinderbox and a candle in a good, wide-saucered stand on the table by the door, and then caught up the end of a loaf of bread and went back down to the garden.

The well at its center was still good, still supplied the entire structure with water, and he hauled up the bucket, the cup attached to its handle clattering musically against the wooden sides. He drank, then poured the rest of the bucket into the standing trough, for the gods, and went back to where a stone bench stood against the wall beside the base of the stairs. It was still warm, but he could feel the first touch of the evening breeze, and the winter-sun was almost directly overhead. He sighed, then began methodically to eat the bread, thinking about the missing children. The Cordiere boy was, by all accounts, no different from the rest, except in his profession. He'd disappeared without warning, without a word, and his nativity contained nothing immediately remarkable. Being born on the stroke of midnight was a little unusual, but not completely out of the ordinary. He stopped then, considering. Cordiere knew his stars to the minute, assuming the town clocks in Dhenin were accurate—and town clocks were, the city regents paid good money to be sure of it, just because people took their nativities from them. That was why the clock-night had been so bad, had shaken the city into something like good behavior for the last week. And Herisse Robion knew hers to the quarter hour, as did the missing brewers—as did every single child who'd been reported missing to Point of Hopes. They all knew their birth stars to the quarter hour or better.

Rathe sat up straight, his dinner forgotten. One or two, and especially the children of guildfolk, he would have expected that, but all of them? Most southriver women worked too hard for birth to be much more than an interruption in the business of existence; they noted the times as best they could, but when you had only the person helping with the birth—and her not a trained midwife, more often than not, just a sister or a neighbor—small wonder times were inexact. There were the exceptions, notable days like the earthquake, and there were enough clocktowers so that with care a woman could note the time, but still, for so many—for all of them—to know their nativities so precisely . . . it had to mean something, was too strange to be mere coincidence.

He looked again at the sky, guessing the time to first sunset, and a voice said from the side gate, "Unbelievable. First at Wicked's, and now here? I don't know if I can stand the shock."

Rathe smiled, almost in spite of himself, and Jhirassi closed the gate behind him, came across the beaten dirt to join him. "I have some news for you—good news," Jhirassi added hastily. "I was going to tease you with it, but I don't think that would be playing fair. The clerk's child you asked me about, he's with Savatier. Frightened witless when he realized his mother thought he'd gone the way of the others, but there. He's not bad, for a boy. And Savatier thinks he could make something of himself." He sighed. "Just what we all need, more competition."

"Keeps you young," Rathe said, automatically, a slight frown forming between his brows. There had been something odd about Albe Cytel's nativity—there wasn't one, he remembered suddenly. For some reason, premature labor, or just ordinary carelessness. Cytel's mother had not managed to note the time of her son's birth, and that was the child who was not truly missing.

"What's wrong?" Jhirassi asked, and Rathe shook his head.

"Nothing, I don't think. Gavi, I want to talk to him—Albe. Can you take me to him?"

"I just got home," Jhirassi protested, but sighed, seeing Rathe's intent expression. "Oh, very well. I don't suppose you can afford to buy me dinner in return?"

"No."

"I didn't think so," Jhirassi said, sadly. "All right, I'll take you to Savatier. Maybe I'll buy dinner."

Rathe followed him through the knotted streets where Point of Hopes joined Point of Dreams, and then out into the broader squares where the better theaters stood. Savatier's was a good house, fully roofed, but at the moment the front doors were closed and locked. Jhirassi ignored that, and led the way to a side door that gave onto a narrow hall. It ended in a tangle of ropes that controlled the stage machinery, and Rathe followed gingerly as Jhirassi wove his way through them. There was a narrow staircase beyond that, and Jhirassi went up it, to tap on a red painted door.

"The counting-house," he said, succinctly, and the door opened. A stocky woman—Savatier, Rathe assumed—stood looking out at them, barefoot, a sweating metal cup in one hand.

"Gavi? What can I do for you?"

"I'm sorry to bother you, but this is Nicolas Rathe—he's adjunct point at Point of Hopes, and a friend of mine, too. He wants to talk to Albe."

Savatier leaned heavily against the door frame. "We're not stealing children, Adjunct Point, the boy came here of his own free will, theater-mad, and not without talent." Her eyes narrowed. "And what business is it of Point of Hopes, anyway?"

"You're Dreams' business, Savatier," Rathe agreed, "and I don't think you're stealing children. But I do need to talk to the boy. He may have some information."

"About these disappearances?" Savatier asked.

"Yes."

She looked at him a moment longer, then sighed deeply. "All right. Gavi, he's down in the yard with the rest." She looked back at Rathe. "A new script we're rehearsing, and it's not coming together. And if bes'Hallen can't make it work . . . " She shook her head, as much at herself as at them. "Go on then," she said, and closed the door firmly in their faces.

Rathe looked at Jhirassi, who smiled, and started back down the stairs. "And if it's the piece I think it is, it's not going to get any better. We passed on it."

He led the way back through the backstage and then a narrow door into a small courtyard. There were perhaps a dozen actors there, women and men about evenly mixed, some leaning against the high walls, a group of three huddled over a tattered-looking sheaf of paper.

There were a few apprentices as well, and Rathe guessed that the youngest, a fair-haired, ruddy-skinned boy, was the missing Albe Cytel. As the door opened, one of the women detached herself from the group, and lifted a hand to Jhirassi. She was a striking woman, hair worn loose under a Silklander scarf, and Rathe recognized her as Anjesine bes'Hallen. He had seen her several times before on stage, usually as tragic queens, and he wondered if she would be able to make this impossible play work. She looked determined enough for it, anyway.

"Gavi, joy, I thought you were settled with Mattie," she said, and Jhirassi sighed.

"Anj, this is Adjunct Point Nicolas Rathe, from Point of Hopes. He's also my downstairs neighbor, so I'll vouch for him. He'd like to talk to Albe."

The boy moved closer to the actress, and bes'Hallen put a hand on his shoulder. Rathe remembered the gesture from one of last year's successful plays, only, since the playwright had been Chresta Aconin, better known as Aconite, he had to think the original intent had been ironic.

"His mother will just have to send someone from Dreams if she wants him back," bes'Hallen said. "We're not letting him go with just anyone, pointsman, not under the circumstances—no offense, Gav, but you know what they're saying about the points."

"Oh, for the dogs' sake," Gavi snapped, "that only plays well on a really large stage."

Rathe blinked—that was not the tack he'd expected Jhirassi to take—but after a heartbeat, bes'Hallen grinned, and let her hand fall from Cytel's shoulder. "Oh, it plays better in the small spaces than you might think, dear, if you weren't afraid of a little honest emotion. But, really, we can't—"

"Nico just wants to talk to him—I don't even know if he's told Dreams or not—"

"I haven't," Rathe said. "I will, but I haven't had the time."

"I'll chaperone," Jhirassi finished. "If that will make you happier."

bes'Hallen lifted an eyebrow at that—another practiced gesture—but nudged the boy forward. "All right. Go with Gavi, dear, and don't worry. You're welcome here. Savatier has said so, and so have I."

"Let's go in," Jhirassi said. "It's more private."

Rathe stood aside to let the boy follow Jhirassi, and then went with them into the crowded backstage. Savatier's troupe clearly spent a decent sum on stage settings: there were at least a dozen rolled canvases stacked against the wall, and there was real furniture scattered about the space. Jhirassi chose one of the chairs, shook it to make sure it would hold his weight, and sat with grace.

"Sit down, Albe—find a stool, for Oriane's sake." He looked at Rathe. "You'd think you were going to eat him for dinner."

Rathe sighed. "Albe, I'm not here to bring you back to your mother—you heard bes'Hallen, I'm from Point of Hopes, and this is Point of Dreams' affair. But I do need to ask you some questions." He paused, looking at the boy's wary face. "It may help find the other children, or I wouldn't be bothering."

The boy nodded slowly. "All right."

"First," Rathe said, "do you know your nativity?"

Cytel scowled. "Yes, well, sort of. Within the hour anyway." He seemed to see Jhirassi's surprise, and burst out, "It's not my fault, I was born early, the midwife wasn't very good. But, no, I don't have a real good nativity."

Rathe allowed himself a sigh of relief. So far, the pattern was holding true, at least in the cases he'd dealt with. "Now, did you go to the fair, or the First Fair, before you—came—to Savatier's?"

Cytel blinked, but nodded. "Yes."

"By yourself, or with other people?"

Cytel shrugged one shoulder. "Maseigne Foucquet gave a dozen of us an early afternoon so we could go. Palissy—she's the senior clerk-journeyman—she went with us."

Rathe nodded. "And once there, I'm assuming you did the usual things. Did you get your stars read?"

The boy looked embarrassed again, and Rathe willed him not to become mulish. "I was thinking about it, yes, because I don't want to go to the judiciary, and I do want to be an actor, and I wanted to see what my stars said about that." He scowled. "Even my mother admits they're not right for the law."

Rathe held his breath. A negative answer wouldn't disprove any of his theories, but if the boy had spoken to one of the hedge-astrologers . . . "But you didn't?" he asked, when Cytel seemed unwilling to continue. "Get them read, I mean?"

"Is it important?"

"Yes," Rathe said, and only just controlled the intensity in his voice. "It's important."

Cytel shrugged again. "Well, I did, only not at the temples. They're expensive, and I didn't have much money with me. There was an astrologer, one of the new ones, who offered to read them for me. He said I looked like I had a career ahead of me." His lips curled slightly.

"Which is pretty safe to say, I suppose. But when I told him my stars, he told me it'd be hard to give me a proper reading because I didn't have the details—like I didn't know that—but he only charged me half a demming so I can't complain."

"So he didn't do a reading," Rathe said.

"I told you, he did sort of a one, but it wasn't very detailed. About what you'd expect, I guess."

"Did he give you any kind of charm, say anything about trouble coming?" Rathe asked.

"Oh." Cytel looked startled, reached into his pockets. "Yes, he said times were going to be hard for people in my sign, and I should take care—he gave me a sigil, just a piece of wax, but I think I've lost it."

"That's all right," Rathe said. "But if you should find it—send it to me, or to any pointsman. Don't keep it."

Cytel's eyes widened. "You don't think—"

"I don't know that it's anything," Rathe said, firmly, "but this is not the time to take chances."

"I won't," Cytel answered.

"Good. Thanks for your help." Rathe sighed, thinking of Foucquet and his responsibilities there. It seemed a shame to send the boy back when he was obviously happy here, but he shoved the thought away. "I'll have to tell Maseigne Foucquet where you are. And she will tell your mother. But it looks as though Savatier wants you here."

"She's never met my mother," Cytel said.

"I'll put in a word with Maseigne," Rathe said, "but I can't promise anything. But I will talk to her."

"Thank you," the boy said, with doubting courtesy. He pushed himself to his feet, and, at Rathe's nod, hurried back toward the courtyard.

"Did you get what you want?" Jhirassi asked, and stood, stretching.

Rathe spread his hands, trying to contain his excitement. "I don't know. I don't even know for sure what I'm looking for. But—yes, I think so. It's what I hoped he'd say."

Jhirassi lifted his eyebrows, but visibly decided not to pursue the question. "Well, then. Shall we get dinner? I'm starving, myself."

"You go ahead," Rathe answered. "I have business at the university."

"Your friend from Wicked's?" Jhirassi asked.

"Yes."

"Do say hello to him for me, would you? And if he doesn't remember who I am, I don't want to hear about it, Nico. Lie."

"Oh, he'll remember. Istre doesn't forget people—" Rathe saw the other draw himself up in mock anger, and added hastily. "And I doubt anyone who's ever met you has forgotten you."

"Better," Jhirassi said. "All right, then, go on, and here I was going to buy you dinner from Wicked's. You won't get better at the university, you know."

"I know," Rathe agreed, and let himself out the side door.

By the time he reached the university precinct, the sun was well down, and the winter-sun's cool light threw pale shadows across the grassy yard. A gang of students, all male, and mostly Ile'norders by their accents, were arguing loudly on the steps of one of the dormitories; from an upper window, the delicate notes of a cittern floated down, sour now where the player missed her fingering, and a trio of gargoyles tumbled quarreling across the path in front of him. It was all appallingly ordinary, all signs of the clock-night erased, as though the troubles that had hit the rest of Astreiant had bypassed the university completely, and for an instant he could understand northriver folk's anger at the students. But then he passed one of the outside gates, and saw the bright tassels of protective charms dangling from the posts. There was a guard, too, a big man, leather-jerkined, sitting unobtrusively in the shadow of the nearest building, and Rathe shook his head. The university knew, and was taking precautions.

b'Estorr had left word he was expected, and the old woman swung open her door before he could even ask. Rathe climbed the long flight of stairs, lit by hanging oil lamps against the winter-sun's twilight, and found b'Estorr's door ajar. He caught his breath, and in the same instant dismissed his fear. No one would rob a magist, especially not on his own home ground. He tapped on the frame, and pushed open the door. The room was dim, only a single lamp lit on the worktable. b'Estorr himself was sitting in one of the window seats, a tablet tilted to the pale light, looked up with a smile at Rathe's appearance.

"Good, you're here."

Rathe closed the door behind him, and flicked the latch into place. "Is it because your stuff is hard to fence that you leave the door wide open?" As he spoke, there was a familiar eddy of cold air, like the trailing of fingertips across the nape of his neck. They were the real reasons for b'Estorr's confidence, of course; the palpable presence of the ghosts would discourage all but the most hardened thieves, and those would know better than to give a ghost the chance to reveal their identities.

b'Estorr grinned. "Oh, I daresay there are shops around here that would buy a used orrery or an astrolabe, and no questions asked." He folded his tablets, and crossed to the table to light the candles that stood in a six-armed candelabrum. The warm light spread, filling the center of the room, but Rathe could still feel the cool presence of the ghosts. It was stronger at night, when the shadows seemed to give visible shape to the odd breezes, and he had to make an effort not to peer into corners.

"Have you eaten?" b'Estorr asked, and gestured to the remains of a pie that stood on the table. There was a dish of strawberries as well, and cone-sugar and a grater, and Rathe felt his mouth water.

"No, I haven't, but you don't have to keep feeding me."

"You might as well eat when you can," b'Estorr answered, and poured a glass of wine without being asked. Rathe took it, glad of its delicate tang, and accepted a wedge of the pie as well. He had eaten at the fair, a fried pie snatched in haste, and there had been the bread at his own lodgings, but this, cold cheese and onions, was far better than anything he'd had in days.

"Anything more on the clocks?" Rathe asked, his mouth full, and b'Estorr's eyebrows twitched.

"Not really. There are no records of anything similar happening at starchange, though of course, the records aren't great for the last time the Starsmith was in a shared sign—for one thing, clocks were very rare then."

"That was, what, six hundred years ago?" Rathe asked. Before Chenedolle had become one kingdom, before Astreiant itself was more than a minor fief of a petty not-yet-palatine.

"About that," b'Estorr answered. "You should know, though, that there's a minority view that holds that it was someone playing with powers they shouldn't."

"Gods above," Rathe said, involuntarily, and b'Estorr gave him a sour smile.

"I doubt it's that—the sheer scale of the power is just too great—but the masters and scholars are looking sidelong at each other, and at all the tricksters among the students. It's a mess, Nico."

"Better yours than mine," Rathe answered.

"Thank you. Is there any news of the children?" the necromancer went on, and Rathe nodded, swallowing hastily.

"Maybe, but it's more than we've had yet. There are two things, really, and I need your help with both of them." He reached into his pocket, brought out his purse and carefully unknotted the strings. He poured its contents onto the tabletop, the wax disk he'd gotten from

Ollre dark among the mix of coins and tokens and a pair of flawed dice. He handed the disk to b'Estorr and swept the rest of it back into the purse, saying, "Trinjtje Ollre—she's Herisse Robion's leman, they're both apprentice butchers—she tells me they had their stars read by one of these hedge-astrologers, and he gave her this."

b'Estorr picked it up curiously, held it in the sphere of brightest light from the candles. "A pretty poor piece of work it is, too. It's supposed to be sort of a generic 'from-harm'—you know, the sort of things mothers give their babies before they go off to dame school—but it's not very well made. All the signs are generic, and it wouldn't be much more effective than throwing coins in a wishing bowl." He shook his head, and handed it back. "You say it's from one of those new astrologers? I can't say I'm surprised. They can't be that well trained."

"So it's not harmful," Rathe said.

b'Estorr shook his head again. "Not likely. It's not helpful, either, and if the girl paid money for it, well . . . "

Rathe waved that away. "What would you say if I told you I'd found another child—obviously not one of the missing—who'd gotten a charm from another one of these astrologers?"

"I'd be—intrigued," b'Estorr said. "Can I see it?"

Rathe shook his head regretfully. "The boy didn't have it, said he'd lost it, but from the sound of it, it was pretty much the same as this one. What makes it really interesting, though, is that half the kids who've gone missing from Point of Hopes had their stars read before they vanished, and probably by one of the hedge-astrologers."

"You're right," b'Estorr said. "That's very interesting." He lifted the charm again, holding it to the light. "Mind you," he went on, reluctantly, "it could just be coincidence—these aren't very effective, and maybe they just didn't work."

"It has to mean something," Rathe said. "We don't have anything else to go on." He took a deep breath. "There's one other thing."

"Oh?" b'Estorr gave him an odd look, and set the charm down again. "I wonder if it's the same thing we've been noticing, with these nativities."

Rathe bared teeth in an angry smile. "It could be. And there's one in particular that clinches it for me. When I was at the fair this afternoon, I ran into a woman I know, a pickpocket, part of a dynasty, really, working out of the old Caravansary. They'd lost one of their apprentices, told me about it a couple weeks back."

"I thought the 'Serry was in Point of Sighs," b'Estorr said.

"It is." Rathe shrugged. "What were they going to do, go to Sighs and say, please help us, one of our apprentice pickpockets is missing?"

"But you've asked around," b'Estorr said, and Rathe nodded.

"And when I ran into Cassia, I mentioned the horoscopes, and she said it was a shame Gavaret—that's the boy—wasn't getting the same chance as the rest of the kids. I didn't think there'd be a chance of getting a nativity on him, and I said so, but she had it. And it's very detailed, Istre, close to the minute." He reached into his pocket, pulled out his tablet and read from the dark wax. "Born on Midsummer Eve fourteen years ago in Dhenin. The mother said he crowned as the town clock struck midnight and was born at the half hour. You don't get much better than that, not even in nobles' houses. And all of our missing kids, every last one of them, have nativities just as precisely noted. It's not natural, and it's got to mean something."

b'Estorr was nodding even before he'd finished. "It's not just your kids, Nico. We—those of us here who've been doing the horoscopes for the stations—we've all noticed it. All of the children, eighty-four of them, for Dis's sake, know their births to better than a quarter hour. Your pickpocket—he's just one more." He leaned back. "Of course, we haven't found anything else in common, but we are looking."

"There's another oddity here, too," Rathe said quietly. "The boy who'd lost his charm, he's northriver born—son of a judiciary clerk, in fact. But he doesn't know his birth stars, only to the hour. And he's not missing, even though he did talk to one of these astrologers, though I haven't got a shred of real evidence that they're involved."

"Can't you do something?" b'Estorr asked. "Ban them from the fair—hells, can't you arrest them on suspicion? I'd think the city would be delighted to see that happen."

Rathe shook his head. "The arbiters control the fair, and they say they can't ban them because people think of them as a good thing, and a good alternative to the Three Nations, for that matter."

"Ah." b'Estorr sat back in his chair, frowning.

"And as for arresting them, gods, I'd like nothing better," Rathe went on. "We don't have the authority."

"If you don't, who does?" b'Estorr snapped, and Rathe held up his hand.

"Bear with me, will you? It's complicated. The points are relatively new here, we started out with the writ to keep the peace, and the rest, everything else we do, has developed from that."

"Including tracking down lost property—and children?" b'Estorr asked.

"It's all a matter of the queen's peace, isn't it?" Rathe answered. "The theory being that if a woman's household and her property aren't safe, then she's more likely to break the peace trying to preserve them—which I'll admit is a good argument. But that's where our authority comes from, not anything else. Right now, yeah, we spend most of our time trying to figure out who's done what to whom, and even why, but we don't really have the queen's warrant for that. And if we tried to arrest the hedge-astrologers, well, you've seen the broadsheets. People would cry we were blaming them to save ourselves, and the judiciary would probably uphold them as a matter of the queen's peace."

"So where does that leave you?" b'Estorr asked, after a moment.

Rathe sighed. "Confused. Why would astrologers be stealing children, anyway?"

"Stealing children who know their nativities to better than a quarter hour," b'Estorr corrected, frowning again. "We've been trying to see what these nativities have in common, but maybe we're going at it backwards." He looked up sharply, the blue eyes suddenly vivid. "Maybe the astrologers already know the link, and they're picking out the children accordingly."

"Which would explain why only the ones who know their stars closely are missing," Rathe agreed, "but it doesn't tell us why they're wanted."

"No." b'Estorr lifted one shoulder. "Finding that's just a matter of time and effort, though, sorting through books. Look, thousands of magistical procedures require the worker to have a specific horoscope—it's like any job, only more so, and we all trade off, depending on when we were born, do a favor here, get a favor there." He broke off, shaking his head at his own distraction. "But there aren't that many for which you'd want children—for most of them, in fact, children would be all wrong. And the sheer number involved is unusual. That's got to help narrow it down."

"If you say so," Rathe said, dubiously. He looked down at the charm again, thinking of what Monteia would say when he told her about this, and then remembered something else she had told him that morning. "There may be another problem, Istre. There haven't been any real disappearances over the past few days, not since the twentieth of the Gargoyle. We were thinking it was good news, but now I'm not so sure."

"You're thinking they—whoever they are—have gotten everyone

they need," b'Estorr said. He shook his head. "You'd think someone would have noticed someone trying to hide eighty children somewhere."

"Unless they were taken out of the city," Rathe answered. "And they must've been, someone would've seen them. The city's been looking too hard not to."

"Well, then, you'd think someone would notice anyone trying to herd eighty-four, no, eighty-five with your pickpocket, eighty-five children anywhere, it has to be harder than trying to hide them," b'Estorr muttered.

"They must have been moved in small groups," Rathe said, and stopped. Even so, the only people who could hope to hide, or travel with, large numbers of children would be people who were expected to travel, and that meant another trip to the fair. He had friends among the caravaners, could ask them what they'd heard. He sighed then, thinking of the one hedge-astrologer he'd seen. "The astrologers are still around, though who knows for how long." He stopped then, staring at the books that filled one tall case and overflowed onto the table beside it. The candlelight trembled on the rubbed gilt of the bindings, drew smudged highlights from the heavy leather. If this were an ordinary crime, he thought, something southriver, stolen goods, say, or pimping, we'd send someone to buy from them, see what happened. Could I do that here? I'd have to send a runner, none of the points at Hopes could pass for apprentice-age, and that's bad enough—unless Istre could provide some sort of protection? He said, slowly, "Istre, is there anyway you, or someone here, could protect a child from being stolen?"

"If we could," b'Estorr said, sourly, "don't you think we'd've done it?"

"I mean, knowing they're looking for something—"

"Without knowing what," b'Estorr said, "there's damn all I can do." He looked at the pointsman. "Why?"

Rathe made a face. "I told you, we'd have to catch them actually doing something before we can claim the point on them. I was thinking about offering them some bait. If any of our runners know their stars well enough, or even if they don't, maybe we could fake a nativity for them, we could send them to the fair, see what the astrologers do about them." He saw b'Estorr's startled look, and looked disgusted with himself. "Yeah, I know, it'd be dangerous. I'd take everyone I could from Point of Hopes—hells, I'll borrow from Fairs, if Claes'll let me—and make damn sure the kids never get out of our sight. But it's something to do, before they all disappear back to wherever they took the kids."

b'Estorr was silent for a long moment, then slowly nodded. "It might work—but don't try faking nativities, to do it right takes time, and unless you do it very carefully, they'll know something's off. It's a risk, of course, but what are the odds they'll have the right conjunction?" He leaned back in his chair again, stretching to reach a sheaf of scribbled papers. "Right now, I'd say don't use anyone who has Areton in the Anvil—that's the one thing I've seen more of than I'd expect. Of course, that means about as much as saying most of them have sun or moon in a mutable sign, anything or nothing."

Rathe nodded, and scratched the prohibition into his tablet. "Is there anything else I should know about?"

b'Estorr shook his head, his pale hair gleaming in the candlelight. "I wish there were, but, as I told you, there isn't a pattern. Just—have them be very careful. Anyway, you say you'll be watching them?"

"Oh, yes," Rathe said, grimly. And if none of our kids know their stars well enough, someone from Dreams or Sighs will, he added silently. And I'll make very sure they come home safe again. He stood and stretched, hearing the muscles crack along his spine. "Thanks for dinner, Istre, but I'd better go now, if I want to get home before second sunset."

"I'll let you know if I—we—figure out anything," b'Estorr said, and smiled. "Whatever the hour."

"Thanks," Rathe said again, and let himself out into the dimly lit stairway. It wasn't much, he thought, but it was more than he'd had before. Monteia wouldn't like it—hells, he thought, I'm not sure I like it—but it stands a chance of working. He lengthened his stride, heading through the shadowed streets toward the Hopes-point Bridge. And I'm very much afraid it's a chance we'll have to take.

9

The winter-sun had passed the zenith, was declining toward the housetops across the wide road. Eslingen eyed it cautiously, wishing there were more clocks in Point of Hearts, guessed that he and Denizard had been waiting for more than an hour. Not that it wasn't a perfectly nice tavern, the service deft and discreet—Point of Hearts was living up to its reputation as the neighborhood for assignations—and the wine excellent, but still, he thought, whoever it is we're waiting for should have been here by now.

A shadow fell across the table, and he looked up to see Denizard returning from the open doorway. She was frowning, her fingers tapping against the bowl of her wine glass, and one of the waiters hurried to her side.

"Is everything all right, madame?"

Denizard forced a smile, nodded. "Fine, thanks." She glanced at the table, littered now with emptied plates. "You can bring us another serving of the cakes, however."

"At once, madame." The waiter bowed, and hurried away.

Denizard made a face, and reseated herself, settling her skirts neatly around her.

"No sign of—?" Eslingen asked, and left the sentence delicately unfinished.

The magist sighed. "No. And if he's not here by now, I doubt he's coming."

Eslingen waited, but no more information seemed to be forthcoming. "Do you want to tell me what's going on? Can you tell me, I mean? I'm generally more useful when I have some idea of the circumstances I'm dealing with."

Despite his best efforts, the words came out more sharply than he'd intended, and Denizard gave him a hard glance. "You're not indispensable, however, Eslingen."

Eslingen held up his hands. "Agreed. But, until you dispense with me . . . " He gave her his best smile, and, to his surprise, the magist smiled back reluctantly.

"True. And Hanse said I should use my discretion." She glanced around again, and Eslingen looked with her. The tavern was hardly crowded, most of the drinkers clustered at the far side of the wide room by the unlit fireplace. A man and a woman, the woman in a wide-brimmed hat and hood that effectively hid her face, sat at a corner table, leaning close, their plates forgotten. Conspirators or clandestine lovers, Eslingen guessed, and not much interested in anything except each other.

"It's the Ajanine property," Denizard said. She kept her voice low, but didn't whisper. "Hanse—and Madame Allyns, but mostly Hanse; he takes the risk for her—has owned this land for four years now, and we've never had any trouble, but this year . . . " She shook her head again. "This year, we haven't seen our gold, or had word from the so-called landame. The mine is seigneurial, the landame has full control of the takings. So she pays her debt in gold, and we—Hanse has the funds he needs to finance his caravans and caravels. But this year, Maseigne de Mailhac hasn't done her part."

Which explained a great deal, Eslingen thought. It explained Rouvalles's impatience, and Caiazzo's temper, and probably even the old woman in the Court. He said aloud, "You can't mean we're waiting for the gold. Not just the two of us."

"I thought you were good, soldier," Denizard answered.

"No one's that good."

Denizard grinned. "At least you're honest. We're waiting for one of Hanse's men, he sent him north a good month ago, and he should have been back some days since." She shook her head, the smile fading. "There's something very wrong at Mailhac, Eslingen, that's for sure. And I'm very much afraid Hanse is going to have to send one of us to deal with the situation."

Eslingen nodded, but said nothing. Denizard sighed again, and pushed herself away from the table, went to the door again to peer out into the soft twilight. Eslingen watched her go, turning the stem of his wine glass in his hand, and wondered what he should do with this knowledge. He had promised Rathe word of anything strange about Caiazzo's business, and part ownership of an Ajanine gold mine—an Ajanine gold mine located of necessity on noble land—was certainly out of the ordinary. Except, he added, with an inward grin, maybe for Hanselin Caiazzo. He had known from Rathe's own words that Caiazzo's dealings weren't all legal, but he was only just beginning to understand the scope of the long-distance trader's operations, legitimate as well as not. Perhaps an Ajanine manor wasn't so far out of Caiazzo's usual range as he'd thought.

He leaned back as the waiter returned with the dish of cakes, replacing the previous dishes with quick deference. He liked Caiazzo's service, liked the sober elegance of the house and his own place in it, suspected he would be aping the cut of Caiazzo's coat for years to come. He didn't want to give it up—and why should he, especially for Rathe, whom he'd known less than a solar month?—and he'd be lucky if the job was all he lost if he betrayed Caiazzo to the points. He remembered the old woman in her empty shop at the heart of the Court of the Thirty-two Knives, and shivered, trying to blame it on the evening air. If she found out he'd betrayed Caiazzo, he'd be fighting off her bravos for the rest of the year, and think himself lucky to escape to the border fighting. Besides, illegal Caiazzo's dealings might be—were, he corrected himself, unmistakably outside Chenedolle's laws—but they had nothing whatsoever to do with the missing children. That was all he'd promised Rathe; unless and until he found any indication Caiazzo was dabbling in that, he would keep Caiazzo's business strictly to himself.

As Rathe had expected, Monteia didn't like the idea of using the runners to force the hedge-astrologers into the open. She shook her head when he had finished, and leaned back against the window frame, her long face very sober.

"It's a long shot, Nico, a very long shot," she said at last. "I think you're right, this has to be the reason these kids are being taken, but to risk our runners . . . " She shook her head, her voice trailing off into silence.

"Can you think of a better way of stopping them?" Rathe asked, and Monteia shook her head again.

"Not offhand, no. But I want to try. I owe them that much, Nico." She drew herself up, planted her elbows on the table. "I'm going to draft a letter to all the points, and to Claes in particular—that might get his attention better than just sending you to talk to him."

Rathe made a face, but admitted that Monteia was probably right. Claes was ready to be annoyed with Hopes over his presence in the fair the day before; better to follow protocol than to risk angering him just when they would need him most.

"On the other hand," Monteia went on, "there's one thing you said that we can follow up on, and we haven't yet. If the kids aren't in the city, then where are they?"

"They have to have been taken away," Rathe said. "We'd've found them otherwise."

Monteia nodded. "I agree. And I know you've got friends in the caravans."

"In a manner of speaking," Rathe said. "I did Monferriol a favor once."

"Then he can do you one," Monteia said. "Give a shout for Andry and Houssaye, will you?"

Rathe did as he was told, and a moment later the pointsmen appeared in the doorway, looking puzzled.

"Come on in," Monteia said, "and close the door. I've got work for you."

The two filed in, wedging themselves into the space between Rathe's chair and the wall, and Houssaye shut the door carefully behind him.

Monteia nodded. "All right. Nico, you'll take the caravans at the fair, since you know Monferriol. Andry, I want you and Houssaye to take the river, Exemption Docks to the Chain. We're looking for any way that these child-thieves could have taken the kids out of the city—anything out of the ordinary, someone leaving too soon or too late, hiding his cargo, anything at all."

The pointsmen exchanged glances, and then Andry said, cautiously, "We've done a lot of that already, Chief. And so far, nobody's noticed anything."

"Well, do it again," Monteia answered. She hesitated, then said, almost reluctantly, "We may have something to go on. Nico and his necromancer friend have found something all the kids have in common, though the gods alone know why it matters. All of them knew their stars to better than the quarter hour. You can pass that on as you see fit—it may calm some people down—but be careful with it."

Andry nodded, his face thoughtful, and Houssaye said, slowly, "I don't think the river-folk are involved, Chief. I've spoken to friends of mine in Hearts and Dreams, and they say they've been keeping a close watch on the Chain. Nobody's gone upriver without being searched."

That was not good news, Rathe thought. The Sier was a major highway for trade, but if the upriver traffic was being searched, then that left only the downriver, and that led to the sea and the Silklands. He shivered in spite of himself at the thought of the missing children being taken out of Chenedolle entirely, and saw from Andry's expression that the same thought was in his mind as well.

"Look anyway," Monteia said. "Gods, if they were taken to sea—" She broke off again, not wanting to articulate the thought, but the three men nodded. She didn't need to articulate it: they had no authority outside Astreiant, but at least anywhere in Chenedolle they could appeal to the royal authority. If the children were outside the kingdom, the gods only knew whether the local rulers would listen to them. And, worst of all, least to be spoken, there was the chance that the children had simply been taken to sea and abandoned to the waves. In ancient times, Oriane's worship had demanded those sacrifices; Rathe crossed his fingers, praying that no one had decided to revive those customs.

"Our best chance is probably the caravans or the horsemarket at the Little Fair," Monteia said briskly, and Rathe shook away his fears. "Nico, I'm sorry to be asking you to handle it alone, but it's more discreet that way. I don't want to antagonize Fairs if I can avoid it."

Rathe nodded. "I'll be careful," he said and Monteia nodded.

"Right. Be off with you, then."

Rathe made his way to the fair by the Manufactory Bridge, skirting the fairgrounds proper until he reached the quarter where the caravaners camped. It was busy, as usual; he had to wait while an incoming train, a good two dozen packhorses, all heavily laden, plus attendants, made their way up the main street and were turned into a waiting corral. He followed them toward the stables, walking carefully, and felt a sudden pang of uncertainty. The arriving caravan was obviously one of the ones working the shorter routes—to Cazaril in the south, say, or across to the Chadroni gap. They came in almost daily throughout the fair, and most of them would stay a few days beyond the official closing, to ensure they sold all their goods. The ones working the longer routes, however, would almost certainly leave earlier, well before the end of the fair, especially if they had to take a northern route. And Monferriol was a northern traveller. Bonfortune send I haven't missed him, Rathe thought, and in the same instant saw a familiar blue and yellow pennant flying over one of the tents set up outside the stables. Monferriol worked for a consortium of small traders, had a knack for taking his principals' goods safely through the Chadroni Gap, across Chadron itself, and into the Vestara beyond, keeping just ahead of the worst weather until he reached Al'manon-of-the-Snows. He wintered there, and returning to Astreiant with the first thaws, bringing the first shipments of the northern goods, wools, uncured leathers, wine, and all the rest. Of necessity, his timing was precise, and his awareness of his surroundings exquisitely tuned: he would know if anyone had left ahead of him, and where they were going, and why.

He turned toward the stables, stopped the first hostler he saw who carried Monferriol's yellow and blue ribbons. "Is Monferriol about?"

The woman looked up at him, took in the jerkin and truncheon, and sighed. "Oh, gods, did he forget to pay his damned bond again? I wish he'd stop playing these games with you lot, the rest of us have work to do."

Rathe shook his head. "I'm not from Fairs' Point, I'm from Point of Hopes—and I'm a friend of Jevis's, just wanted to say hello."

The hostler pushed her hair back from her face, leaving a streak of dust along one cheekbone. "I think you'll find him in the factors' tent, pointsman."

"If he's busy—"

She looked at him, her mouth twisting into a gap-toothed grin. "Do you know a single factor who's up at this hour, or at least here? I don't, and I don't think I'd want to. No, he's just gloating over the route again, the bastard. You know where it is? Right, the fancy one." She turned back to the corral even as she spoke, and Rathe turned toward the factors' tent.

It was elaborate, he thought, but then, the consortium probably had to make more of a display than established traders like Caiazzo or older consortia like the Talhafers. And it was bright, crimson canvas—not much faded, yet—flying a bright yellow pennant with Monferriol's blue ferret rampant in a circle. He could hear a toneless, rumbling humming through the walls, and pulled the flap aside.

"Jevis? Planning new tortures for your people?"

"Gods above, boy, don't scare me like that, I thought you were the competition," Monferriol bellowed, and Rathe saw that, indeed, he did have a knife in his hand. Rathe's expert eye gauged it as just within the city's legal limits. It might be a little longer, but not enough to make it worth a pointsman's while to question it.

"Is business getting that cutthroat?" he asked, and Monferriol dropped back onto his high stool, snorting. He was a huge man, tall and heavy-set, hair and beard an untidy hedge.

"Isn't it always? That bastard Caiazzo's got the eastern route sewed up, and a damned good caravan-master he has too, but he can't touch me in the north, for all he keeps trying."

"That's something to be satisfied with, surely," Rathe said, mildly. He knew perfectly well that Monferriol and his consortium had been trying to make inroads into the eastern route for the last few years.

"It's something to keep me awake nights," Monferriol answered, and looked back at the maps spread out on the table beside him. "Though why I should lie awake when none of my principals do, I bloody well don't know."

"It's their money and they trust you?" Rathe guessed, and Monferriol made a face.

"More to the point, it's my blood and my reputation on the line, every time we cross the blighted Gap. Godless people, the Chadroni." He looked down at the maps, shaking his head. "It figures Caiazzo would have one for his master."

"Then why do it?" Rathe asked. He should get to his own business, he knew, but the sheer scale of Monferriol's affairs—and ego—always fascinated him.

"Why? Gods, boy, because I can. Because I'm the best there is at managing a caravan through the Gap and Chadron and the Vestara. Why in all hells are you a pointsman? Because you're good at it, and if you didn't do it, someone else would, and get all the glory—or else muck it up and leave you fuming at them for a pack of incompetents."

And that was true enough, Rathe reflected, and not what he'd expected to hear. He saw an almanac open beside the map, and nodded to it. "What are the temples forecasting for this winter?"

Monferriol stuck out his lower lip as he looked down at the little book. "Heavy snows in the Gap, they're saying, the worst in memory. Of course, last year they predicted a mild winter, and we all know how accurate that was."

Rathe grinned. The previous winter had been unusually bad, with snow before Midwinter in Astreiant itself.

"So," Monferriol said, and swung around so that his back was to the table. "What can I do for you, Nico?"

"I need your—advice, your expert knowledge," Rathe said. "It's about the children."

"Oh, that. That's a bad business. What are you lot doing about it?"

"What we can," Rathe answered. "What I want to know from you is whether you've noticed anything odd among the caravans this fair."

"We're an odd lot," Monferriol answered, but Rathe thought he looked wary. "What did you have in mind?"

"Has anyone changed their usual plans, left earlier than expected, not come in till late, anything?"

Monferriol's face screwed up in thought. He was acting, Rathe thought suddenly, and bit back his sudden anger. Before either man could speak, however, the flap was pulled back again. "Gods above," Monferriol roared, and Rathe thought there was as much relief as anger in his tone. "What is this, a waystation? Oh, it's you, Rouvalles. What do you want."

The newcomer lifted an eyebrow, but said, equably enough, "I've come about those extra horses you wanted. I can spare you two, but you'll pay."

"I always do when I deal with the godless Chadroni," Monferriol muttered.

The other man—Rouvalles—lifted a shoulder in a shrug. He was almost as tall as Monferriol, his long hair drawn back with a strip of braided leather that had probably come from a broken harness. "They're good horses and you know it."

"Better than those last screws you sold me?"

"Those screws are pure Vestaran blood, Jevis, but if you don't want them you don't, and there's no point in my forcing them on you." Rouvalles glanced at Rathe, nodded politely. "Sorry to interrupt."

"How in the name of all the gods, and poor Bonfortune above all, does Caiazzo ever turn a profit with you?" Monferriol demanded, rolling his eyes to the tent's peak. "You won't bargain, you won't even allow the possibility of haggling—"

"I don't have time to haggle," Rouvalles said, cutting through the tirade with what sounded like the ease of long practice. "I'm already two weeks late, as you damn well know. You can have the horses or not, it makes no difference to me."

"Money came through finally, did it?" Monferriol asked, and Rouvalles shrugged.

"As you also know."

"So you're Caiazzo's caravan-master," Rathe interjected. He hoped he sounded casual, but doubted it.

Rouvalles glanced at him, the smile ready enough, but the pale eyes cool and assessing. "You know Hanselin, then—oh, I see. Pointsman." He grinned suddenly, and the humor looked genuine. "Then I guess you would know him. Yes, I'm his caravan-master, and no, I'm not spiriting any children out of Astreiant. You can check my camp if you like, but you wouldn't find any children there in any case, they're useless on a long route like mine."

"Fairs' Point already spoke to you, then," Rathe said, apologetically, and was surprised when Rouvalles shook his head, one dirty gold curl escaping from the tied leather.

"No. Hanse's new knife, in actual fact, which should count in Hanse's favor. Have you been looking in his direction, pointsman? It wouldn't be like him, you know."

"I do know," Rathe agreed. "You said you're late leaving the city. You haven't noticed anyone who's left early, or in a hurry, or just been acting odd?"

Rouvalles shook his head again. "Not that I've noticed." He looked at Monferriol. "So, Jevis, you want the horses?"

"I want the damn horses, yes."

"All right, then, I'll have them brought round once you send the money. How many children are you missing, pointsman?"

Monferriol slid off his stood. "Oh, very funny, Rouvalles, indeed. Would you get out?"

"No, I'm curious." Rouvalles lifted a hand, and Monferriol subsided, muttering. Gesture and response seemed automatic: the Chadroni was almost aristocratic, for a caravaner, Rathe thought, and stilled his own instinctive rebellion. "How many?"

"Throughout the city, eighty-five. Why?" He fixed his eyes on Rouvalles, and the Chadroni looked away.

"You should probably ask Jevis why he's buying horses so late in the season."

"You bastard," Monferriol flared, and Rouvalles glared at him.

"I've heard the same story from half a dozen people, and if you lot won't go to the points you brag of in every other city in the world—well, by all the gods, I will."

"Jevis?" Rathe looked at Monferriol, and the big man threw up his hands.

"There's no law against selling horses, for Bonfortune's sake. And there's no reason to think this had anything to do with the children."

"Except," Rouvalles said, "that this pointsman is asking about anything out of the ordinary. And by Tyrseis, this is just that."

Rathe looked from one to the other. "One of you can start from the beginning and explain. Jevis?"

Monferriol looked distinctly abashed. "It's nothing, really—almost certainly. But, oh, a week or two ago, maybe seven, eight days, a man came to me and wanted to buy a pair of draft horses. Suitable for pulling a baggage wagon—hells, I thought he was a damn mercenary, there are enough of them around these days. But he offered me half again what the beasts were worth, and when I hesitated—I thought I'd heard him wrong—he upped the price again. So I sold them, and even at his prices—" He jerked his head at Rouvalles. "—I'll still make a profit." He stopped then, glaring first at Rouvalles and then at the pointsman.

Rathe shook his head. "Interesting, but I don't see—"

Rouvalles stirred, and Monferriol said hastily, "The thing is, the same thing's happened to a dozen of us, a man coming and wanting to buy draft horses. And offering too good a price to turn him down. It hasn't been the same man, always, but still, well, it got some of us wondering. They're not traders, that's for sure, but beyond that, who knows? We didn't know if we should go to the points or not. Nico, it might have been something ordinary."

Rathe nodded, absently, his mind racing. A dozen traders, selling one or two horses each—that would easily be enough to transport eighty-five children. The only question was, where had they been taken? He said, "I don't suppose you have any idea who this person was?"

Monferriol shook his head. "I told you, I thought he was a mercenary, the successful kind. He dressed like an upper servant, mind you, nice coat, nice manners."

"What did he look like?" Rathe asked, without much hope, and wasn't surprised when the big man shrugged.

"Ordinary. I'm sorry, boy, he was—well, middling everything. You know the sort, sort of wood-colored."

Rathe grinned in spite of himself, in spite of the situation. He knew exactly the sort of man Monferriol was describing, brown-haired, brown-skinned, brown-eyed, utterly unremarkable features—the points took dozens of them for thieving every year, and released half of them for lack of a victim to swear to them. "What about you?" he said to Rouvalles, and the Chadroni shook his head.

"All I know is what I've heard from Jevis and some others. I don't use draft horses, you can't take carts over the land-bridge."

Rathe sighed—that would have been too much good luck—and looked back at Monferriol. "Jevis, I'm going to tell you this once, and I want you to do it for me. Consider it the favor you owe me."

"We'll see," Monferriol said, but nodded.

"Go to Fairs' Point with this," Rathe said. "Get together everybody who's sold to these people, and go to Guillot Claes, he's the chief at Fairs', and tell him what you've told me. They've probably left the city, but it's worth trying to find them, and this is Fairs' business, not mine."

"You couldn't keep us company," Monferriol said, without real hope, and Rathe shook his head.

"It would look better if it was just you."

"Right." Monferriol made a face. "Bonfortune help me, but I'll do it."

"Thanks," Rathe said, and included Rouvalles in his nod.

The Chadroni smiled, the expression a little melancholy. "It's a bad business, this," he said. "Not to mention bad *for* business. I hope you find them." He looked back at Monferriol. "Send the money, and I'll send the horses. And sooner would be better than later, I'm going to be busy the next few days."

"You'll get your money," Monferriol growled. Rouvalles waved a hand, acknowledgement and farewell, and ducked back out the tent flap. Monferriol looked at Rathe. "I would've gone to the points sooner, Nico, but—hells, I didn't realize, none of us did, just how many horses were being bought this way."

"Go now," Rathe said, gently. "Claes will be grateful, I'm sure of that. It's one of the first solid things we've had."

"I hope you catch the bastards," Monferriol answered. "Hanging's too good for them."

"We're doing what we can," Rathe answered, and followed Rouvalles out of the tent. And that was more than he'd thought they'd be able to do yesterday, he thought, as he made his way back toward Point of Hopes, but still not enough.

Monteia was waiting in the station's main room, fingers tapping impatiently on the edge of the worktable. She rose as he came in, saying, "Well?"

"More news, Chief," he answered. "Monferriol says that some people—not traders, not anything he recognized—have been buying draft horses from various of the caravaners. A lot of horses, Chief, enough to pull enough wagons to carry eighty-five children."

Monteia went very still. "Any idea of who, or where they went?"

Rathe shook his head. "I told Jevis—Monferriol—to take himself and the others over to Fairs' Point, let them work on it. But I think we know how they're being moved now."

"And damn all good it does us," Monteia muttered. "We know two hows, how they're choosing the kids and some of how they're moving them, but that doesn't get us anything useful."

"Not yet," Rathe answered, and hoped it was true.

Monteia sighed. "I've been thinking about what you said this morning. I still don't like it, but I can't think of anything better. Let's get the runners in here, and see if any of them are willing to be bait."

Rathe flinched—put that baldly, the idea seemed to have even less merit—but went to the door and looked out. The youngest of the runners, a child from the Brewers' Court who looked even younger than his ten years, was sitting on the edge of the empty horse trough, and Rathe beckoned to him. "Laci! Find the rest of the runners, will you, and ask them to come in here, please."

"Are we in trouble?" The boy looked warily at him, and Rathe felt his smile turn sickly.

"No." Not unless we make some bad mistakes, he added silently, and Astree send we don't. "The chief has a job for some of you, that's all."

"All right." The boy turned away, and Rathe called after him.

"As soon as possible, please."

Laci lifted a hand in answer, and darted away. Rathe stood for a moment, looking at the now-empty yard, and then went back into the station. To his surprise, however, Laci was back in less than a quarter of an hour, and half a dozen of the other runners were with him.

"This was all I could find, Nico," Laci announced. "Is that all right?"

"That's fine," Rathe answered. He stood back, letting the little group file past him into the station, and saw Monteia shake her head.

"In the workroom, please," she said aloud, and the runners edged in, whispering and murmuring among themselves. Rathe followed them in, and closed the door behind them. He knew all of them, of course: Laci; raw-boned Jacme, who'd been kicked out of his own house and slept behind the bar at the Cazaril Grey; willowy Biatris, who would get her apprenticeship next year if the station itself had to pay her fees; Surgi, dark and stocky, born in the Rivermarket docks; Fasquelle de Galhac, who had a brain despite the pretensions of her name; stolid Lennar with his crooked nose; and finally Asheri, his favorite of this year's group. She was standing a little apart from the rest, her thin face very grave, and he wondered if something was wrong. Then Monteia had seated herself behind the table, gestured for the runners to make themselves comfortable.

"As you may or may not have heard, we've found something all the missing kids have in common," she began bluntly. "They all knew their stars to a quarter hour or better, and a lot of them, maybe all of them, had their stars read by one of these new astrologers we've been hearing about. Which gives us an obvious option."

Biatris was already nodding, her thumbs hooked into the belt she wore beneath her sleeveless bodice. Asheri tipped her head to one side but made no other move, while Surgi and Lennar exchanged nervous glances. Monteia gave them all a jaundiced look.

"I'll say from the start that I'm not particularly happy with this idea, but it could work, and it's vital that we catch these bastards." She took a deep breath. "What we need is someone of the right age—your ages—who knows her stars close enough to go and get a reading done. We'll be watching you, of course, myself and Nico and Houssaye and Salineis, but there's a chance something could go wrong. So think about that before you answer."

Surgi and Lennar exchanged looks again, and Lennar said, "I'd do it—"

"—in a minute," Surgi agreed.

"—but I don't know my stars that well," Lennar finished. "And neither does Surgi. Couldn't we pretend?"

"I asked about that at the university," Rathe said. "Istre—a friend of mine who's a necromancer—said that they'd be able to tell."

"Oh." Surgi's shoulders sagged visibly, but then he brightened. "We could go with everybody, help make sure the astrologers don't steal them."

"We'll see," Monteia said. "All right. Do any of you know your stars to the quarter hour?"

There was a little silence then, and Asheri said, "I do. Better than that, actually, I was born on the hour."

Biatris nodded. "I know mine to just about the quarter."

Monteia nodded again. "And would you be willing to do this—knowing it could be dangerous?"

There was another silence, longer this time, and then Biatris shrugged. "If it might help, yeah, sure."

Asheri looked at her shoes, and Rathe felt unreasonably guilty. She didn't want to be a pointswoman, he knew that well enough—her real love was needlework, and one of the reasons she worked as a runner was to save the fees she needed to join the Embroiderers' Guild. He tilted his head, trying to see her face, and was relieved to see it merely thoughtful, neither afraid nor angry. She looked up then, and nodded. "All right. I'm willing."

"I think we should all go," Lennar said, and Jacme nodded. He was the oldest of the group, seemed older, Rathe knew, because he'd been on his own so long.

"I agree." He grinned, showing the gap at the side of his mouth where a tooth had been knocked out. "Even with Nico and everybody keeping an eye on us, they'll have to stay back to keep from upsetting these astrologers, and hells, it'd have to be harder to steal just one from among a group."

"It's been done," Rathe said, but looked at Monteia, and nodded. "I think he's right, Chief."

"I agree." Monteia reached under the worktable, pulled out the station's strongbox, and fished under her bodice for the key. She unlocked the heavy chest, and took out a bag of coins. "What did you say they charged, Nico?"

"Half a demming, or so most of the kids who didn't get taken said," Rathe answered, and Monteia grunted.

"Better give you a few more than that," she said, and counted out three demmings for each of the runners. "If you don't spend it, keep it. And there'll be a seilling apiece when we all get back."

A seilling was decent money, and Rathe saw several of the runners exchange glances, suddenly sobered. If Monteia was willing to pay that much, they were obviously thinking, then it must be serious. Good, he thought, and said aloud, "One thing more. These astrologers are also offering charms against the current troubles. If he offers you one, take it, but give it to one of us as soon as you can, all right? We can take it to the university."

Biatris and Asheri nodded.

"All right," Monteia said. "Stay together as much as you can without looking suspicious—Biatris, you and Asheri stay tight, that'll make it easier to watch you. Everyone understand?" The runners nodded. "Right, then. Let's go to the fair."

It didn't take long to collect the rest of the duty pointsmen and women, and to abandon the semiuniform of jerkin and truncheon. Rathe trailed behind the little knot of children as they passed the edge of the fair precinct, aware of Houssaye strolling a little behind him, parasol balanced on his shoulder. At the midafternoon, things were a little less busy than usual; a number of the stalls had fewer workers in evidence, and Rathe could see merchants snatching a hurried meal in the back of others. At least it would be easier to watch the kids than it would have been in the full crowds, he thought, as long as the astrologers do their part.

They made their way across the full width of the fairground without result, though Laci stopped to spend some of his coins on stick candy and a cup of thick, sweet Silklands tea. At the northern edge, where the linen-sellers had their booths, the group of runners paused, and Rathe stepped back into the shade of an awning, pretending to examine the bolts of coarse cloth.

"That's good for shirts, sir," the woman behind the counter said. "Wears like iron, and only an aster a yard. You won't get a better shirt for two seillings."

Rathe nodded, not really listening. Out of the corner of his eye, he could see the runners arguing about something, Biatris and Asheri pointing back toward the center of the fair, Lennar pointing toward the distant corrals. Rathe frowned—what were they thinking of, to split the group?—and then he saw the way that Laci was fidgeting. Even as he realized what was happening, Jacme caught the younger boy by the hand and started off at speed toward the corrals and the latrines beyond. Rathe swore under his breath, and turned away from the stall, looking around for one of the other pointsmen. Before he could do anything, however, he saw Salineis, conspicuous in a broad-brimmed hat, take off after them. He allowed himself a sigh of relief—at least someone would be watching them, even if they weren't in the most likely group—and turned to follow the others.

They had gotten a little ahead of him, were just turning into the row of stalls that sold needles and fine thread. Asheri's doing, Rathe thought, and did his best not to hurry after them. She took her time making her way along the rows of stalls, obviously drawn in by the displays: silk and linen and even cotton thread in every thickness and every color of the rainbow; packets of pins wrapped in bright dyed paper; polishing glasses, dark and light; needles and needle-cases and shears in every size from the length of a finger to heavy iron things nearly as long as a woman's forearm. Biatris stayed close to her side, though from the glazed look on her face, she would rather have been somewhere else, but the rest of the runners had drawn ahead of them, and at last Fasquelle stopped, turned back to stare at them.

"Come on, will you?" Her clear voice floated above the noise of the fair, audible along the length of the row.

Biatris lifted a hand, and then touched Asheri's shoulder. The younger girl sighed, and moved reluctantly away from the array of threads. Rathe grinned, sympathizing with both sides, and the expression froze on his face as he saw a man in a black robe turn into the row of stalls. He seemed ordinary enough, the shabby scholar's robe half open over a plain dark suit, his round face a little pink from the heat, but Rathe felt his spine tingle. The man spoke to the first group of runners, and Rathe saw Surgi shake his head. The astrologer shrugged, smiling, and moved on. Asheri had seen him, too, and as he drew abreast, she stepped into his path. She said something—asking for a reading, Rathe knew, and didn't know if he was impressed or appalled by her bravery—and jerked her head toward Biatris, who moved up to join her. The astrologer looked from one to the other, nodding, and then motioned for them to follow him. He led them back the way they'd come, and Rathe looked away, pretended to be examining a length of embroidered ribbon, as they passed him. He counted to twenty, then shook his head at the stall-keeper, and trailed after the black-robed figure. Out of the corner of his eye, he saw Houssaye's parasol, and then Monteia's oxblood skirt and bodice suit. If the astrologer tried anything, they would be ready.

The astrologer paused then, and gestured for the girls to precede him down an alley that ran between two of the larger stalls. Asheri hesitated for a fraction of a second, but Biatris stepped firmly on, and the younger girl followed, the astrologer in his black robe trailing after them both. Rathe swore under his breath, and looked around wildly. Monteia was already moving to put herself at the far end of the alley, and Houssaye and Andry were in place as well. The sight was steadying, and Rathe made himself walk casually past the alley-mouth. He could do nothing more than glance in, not without rousing suspicion, but in that instant he caught a glimpse of the two girls standing fascinated, eyes on the orrery held by the astrologer. He was adjusting one of the rings that gave the planetary positions, and seemed to be explaining something at the same time. And then Rathe was past, and made himself stop at the nearest stall, trying to pretend to study the display of needles.

"Andry's gone round the other end with the chief," Houssaye said, softly, and leaned over the other man's shoulder. His parasol was neatly folded now, Rathe saw, ready for action.

"Good," Rathe answered. "Is there any way of getting closer?"

Houssaye shook his head, his face reflecting the same frustration Rathe was feeling. "Not without being seen. Gods—" He broke off then, shaking his head, and Rathe laid a hand on his shoulder.

"There's no other way in or out," he said, with more confidence than he felt. "So we wait."

It seemed an interminable time before the girls reappeared, walking solemnly on either side of the astrologer. Both looked thoughtful, and Rathe found himself holding his breath. If the astrologer has already placed some geas on them—but that was supposed to be impossible, or at best extremely difficult without the proper tools and carefully chosen stars, he reminded himself. The astrologer said something to the girls, and then turned away, heading toward the center of the fair.

Rathe nudged Houssaye. "Follow him," he said, and himself moved up to join the runners. The rest of the runners hurried over, too, and Rathe gathered them into a tight group.

"Are you all right?" he said, to Asheri and Biatris, and both girls nodded.

"It wasn't anything, really," Biatris said, and Rathe held up his hand.

"We'll talk when we get back to the station. Where's Jacme and Laci?"

"Laci had to piss," Fasquelle answered, and Salineis loomed over her shoulder.

"They're with me, Nico. The chief says we should get back to the station. She'll meet us there."

Rathe nodded. "We'll take a boat," he said, and added silently, and I'll pay for it myself if the station won't.

It took a few minutes to find a boat that would take the entire group upstream, but eventually they found a small barge and Rathe herded everyone aboard. Despite the current, it didn't take long to reach the landing at the Rivermarket, and Rathe led them quickly back through the streets to the station house. To his surprise, Monteia was there ahead of them, sitting scowling at the main desk. Her frown eased a little as she saw them, and she gestured for the runners to find seats in the clutter of the main room.

"Sal, shut the door. Nico, where's Houssaye?"

"I told him to follow the astrologer," Rathe answered, and Monteia nodded.

"Good luck to him, then. All right, what happened?"

Biatris and Asheri exchanged glances, and the older girl said, "Not a whole lot, really. Asheri asked if he read stars, and what he'd charge to read ours. And he said it'd be a demming for both of us, and asked what our stars were. I told him mine, and he said that, since I knew mine so well, he could give me a proper reading, with his orrery. So we went between a couple of stalls where it was quiet, and he did. He didn't say much, though, not much more than I could've gotten from a broadsheet."

"I told him mine, too," Asheri said, "and he gave me a hard time about them, kept on about was I sure that was right." She made a face. "I think he could tell I was southriver born, and wanted to make sure I wasn't lying. But I asked him if he thought I would ever be able to join the Embroiderers' Guild, and he did a reding for that. He had a really fancy orrery, though."

"I thought it looked pretty battered," Biatris objected, and Asheri nodded.

"It was, but it was—well, more complicated than a lot of ones I've seen. It had a lot more rings to it." She shrugged. "Anyway, then he warned us to be very careful, that the trouble was almost over, but that we couldn't relax yet. And that was the end of it."

"Did he give you anything?" Rathe asked.

"Oh, gods." Biatris reached into the pocket under her skirt. "He said it was a charm against the current troubles." She produced a disk of dark wax, marked with the same sort of symbols Rathe had seen on the other charms. He took it from her, turning it over in his hand, and looked at Asheri.

"Did you get one, too?"

She was nodding already, held out a second wax disk. "It's funny, I thought it looked a little different—" She broke off, eyes widening, and Rathe held the two disks in the light from the window.

"They are different," Monteia said, and came to look over Rathe's shoulder.

He nodded, turning the disks in the light. Asheri's was a different color, more green than black, though still very dark, and the symbols embossed on its surface seemed to be arranged in a different order. "I think Istre should see these right away," he said, and heard the shadow of fear in his own voice.

Monteia nodded. "I agree." She looked at the runners. "And I think you should stay here, the lot of you, at least until we know what's happening."

Rathe pocketed the charms. "I'll be as quick as I can," he said, and hurried out into the afternoon heat.

b'Estorr was not in his rooms, but a grey-gowned student volunteered that she thought the necromancer was at the library. Rathe thanked her, and made his way back across the wide yard to the massive building that housed the university's library. It looked as formidable as many fortresses, thick walls and narrow windows, and the narrow lobby was cold even in the summer heat, the stones hoarding the chill. Statues of Sofia and Donis and Oriane and the Starsmith stood in orderly ranks above the barred doors that led to the library proper, staring past the mere mortals who walked below them. The proctor on duty, tall and painfully thin, shook her head when Rathe asked to be admitted.

"I'm sorry, we can't let just anyone in—"

"It's an emergency," Rathe said. And one partly of my making. He killed that thought, and fixed the woman with a stare. "Can you send for him?"

She hesitated, then nodded, and reached under her table for a bell. She rang it, and a few minutes later one of the heavy doors creaked open, admitting a student as round as the proctor was thin.

"Would you fetch Magist b'Estorr, please?" the proctor asked. "This—"

"Tell him Nicolas Rathe."

The proctor nodded. "Tell him Master Rathe is here, and that it's an emergency."

The student's eyes widened, but she faded back through the door without a murmur. Rathe fought the instinct to pace, made himself stand still, counting the signs carved across the tops of the doorways, until at last the central door flew open again.

"Nico! What's happened?" b'Estorr hurried toward him, his dark grey gown flying loose from his shoulders.

"I sent the runners to the fair," Rathe said. "And Asheri came back with a charm that's different."

b'Estorr drew breath sharply. "Let me see."

Rathe held the disks out wordlessly, and the necromancer took them from him, held them side by side in the dim light.

"It's active," he said at last. Rathe flinched, and b'Estorr shook his head. "No need to panic, not yet, but I'd like to take a closer look at them. My place?"

"Fine," Rathe said, and retraced his path through the yard. If I've put Asheri in danger, he thought, gods, what will I do? I thought—you thought the danger would come from the astrologers, he told himself, and you were wrong. Now you have to make it right.

In b'Estorr's rooms, the necromancer flung the shutters wide, letting the doubled afternoon sunlight into the room. He set the disks on the table, side by side in the sunlight, and Rathe caught his breath again. In the strong light, the difference in color was very clear, Asheri's more green than black, and the different pattern of the symbols was starkly obvious. b'Estorr barely glanced at them, however, but went to the case of books and pulled out a battered volume. He flipped through it, glancing occasionally at the disks, and finally set it aside, shaking his head.

"I don't recognize the markings, except generally, and they're not in Autixier. The closest thing—" He reached for the book again, opened it to a drawing of a square charm. Rathe looked at it, and shook his head.

"I'm sorry, Istre. . . ."

The necromancer went on as though he hadn't spoken. "The closest one listed is that, and that's kind of, well, archaic. It's meant to bind one's possessions—"

"It's to track her," Rathe said with sudden conviction. "Gods, Istre, I've practically handed her to them."

b'Estorr nodded slowly, still staring at the charms. "You could be—I think you are right," he said. "It could act as a marker, help someone find her later."

And that would make sense, Rathe thought. The astrologers to identify the children, someone else to steal them away, later, when they thought they were safe, could be taken unawares. He shook the fear away. "I took it from her within an hour of the reading—she gave it to me. Can they track her without the charm?"

"I don't know," b'Estorr answered. "This is very powerful—more powerful than I would have expected. She should change her clothes, at the very least not wear them again until this is resolved. It might be better to burn them."

"Sweet Tyrseis," Rathe said. Asheri would be hard put to afford a second set of clothes; he and Monteia between them might be able to provide something, but it would be expensive. If Houssaye could follow the astrologer, of course, track him back to his lair, that might do something, but there was no guarantee that the pointsman would succeed. Rathe shook his head. "Istre, I thought the real danger would be from the astrologers themselves, not something like this. How in all the hells can we protect her?"

b'Estorr lifted the charm again, studying the markings. "That she gave it to you, and you gave it to me—that should help. And then, as I said, get rid of the clothes she was wearing. Burning would be best, but I know what clothing costs."

Rathe nodded. "I'll tell her that, certainly."

"And she should be very careful." b'Estorr looked up, shaking his head. "Which she and you know already, I know. I wish there were more I could do, Nico."

"You've done a lot," Rathe answered. He forced a smile. "Now we know a little more of how they're being stolen, and how they're being chosen—though, as Monteia says, the hows don't get us anywhere right now."

"Whoever's doing this," b'Estorr said, "must be very powerful."

"Magistically or politically?" Rathe asked.

"Either." b'Estorr gave him an apologetic look. "Not that you didn't know that, too, but this charm is a pretty piece of work—not at all like the others—and it must cost money to field this many astrologers."

Rathe nodded. "I just wish that narrowed the possibilities."

He took a low-flyer back to Point of Hopes, wincing at the fee but desperately afraid that Asheri or the others might have left before he could reach them with his warning. As he paid off the driver at the main gate, he could see the knot of runners still gathered in the stable doorway. The younger ones, Laci and Surgi and Lennar, were playing at jacks, while Fasquelle jeered at them from the edge of the trough. Asheri was there, too, setting stitches in a square of linen. It was a practice piece, Rathe knew, against the day she could afford a place in the embroiderers', and he could taste the fear again at the back of his mouth.

"Asheri," he said, and she looked up, automatically folding the cloth over her work. "I need to talk to you."

"All right," she said, sounding doubtful, and followed him into the station.

Monteia looked up as they arrived, and Rathe saw, with a sinking sensation in the pit of his stomach, that Houssaye was with her.

"No luck?" he asked, and the other pointsman shook his head.

"He went back toward the caravans, but I lost him there. They seem to have a gift for vanishing. I'm sorry, Nico."

Rathe drew breath, and Monteia said firmly, "You did the best you could. What did you find out from the university, Nico?"

"Bad news, I'm afraid," Rathe answered. He looked at Asheri. "Asheri, I'm sorry I ever got you into this. The charm he gave you, it's some kind of a marker. I think you're in serious danger."

"A marker?" Monteia echoed, and Rathe looked back at her.

"That's what Istre said. Something to help someone find a child they want to steal."

"Gods," the chief point murmured, and Rathe saw her hand move in a propitiating gesture. "What do we do?"

"I gave you the marker," Asheri said, her voice suddenly high and thin. "I don't have it anymore, surely that makes it all right."

"It helps," Rathe answered. "But Istre said you should also change your clothes. He said you ought to burn these, or at least put them away, don't wear them until we've caught these people."

"I can't burn them," Asheri said. "I don't have anything else half this good, not that fits me anymore."

Monteia said, "We may be able to do something about that, Ash, since you're losing the use of them on station business. But if b'Estorr says you shouldn't wear them, I'd do what he says." She looked at Rathe. "In the meantime, I'm sending to Fairs with what we have. That's enough to make Claes arrest these bastards, and if we can catch one, maybe we can get more information out of them."

Rathe nodded, some of the fear easing. Monteia was right about that, and Claes would act quickly enough, given this evidence. And if the hedge-astrologers were dodging pointsmen, surely they'd be too busy to steal another child. "I'll walk you home, Asheri," he said aloud. "You can change there."

The girl made a face, but nodded. "All right. But I'm not burning them. I made this shirt myself. And the cap."

"Then put them away," Monteia said. "And I want to see you here tomorrow morning, eight o'clock. Agreed?"

"Agreed," Asheri said, and Rathe touched her shoulder, turning her toward the door.

"We should be able to stop them, now that we know what's happening," he said, and hoped it was true.

10

Eslingen squatted beside the chest that held his weapons, considering the pair of pistols Caiazzo had redeemed from the Aretoneia. He distrusted midnight meetings, liked them even less when the messenger had failed to appear twice already, and a pistol might provide some measure of surprise, if there was trouble. He glanced at the half-open window. On the other hand, it was a damp night, and they were going by river, which increased the chance of misfire; besides, he added, with an inward smile as he shut the chest, a pistol shot inevitably attracted attention, and he'd had entirely too much of that lately. Caiazzo probably wouldn't thank him, either, for inviting interference in his business. He stood, and belted sword and dagger at his waist, adjusting the open seam of the coat's skirt so that it left the sword hilt free, and glanced in the long mirror that hung beside the clothes press. The full skirts hid most of the weapon, only the hilt visible at his hip, and it was dark metal and leather, unobtrusive against the dark blue fabric.

"Are you ready, Eslingen?"

He turned, to see Denizard standing in the open door. She had put aside her scholar's gown for a black riding suit, shorter skirt, and a longer, almost mannish coat that buttoned high on the throat, hiding her linen. She carried a broad-brimmed hat as well, also black, and a longish knife—probably right at the legal limit—on one hip.

She saw where he was looking and smiled, gestured to his own blade. "I assume the bond's paid on that?"

"Caiazzo paid it," Eslingen answered, and she nodded.

"Be sure you bring the seal."

Eslingen touched his pocket, feeling the paper crackle under his hand. "I have it, believe me."

"Well, with a pointsman for a friend, you should be all right. Or you would be if it were an other pointsman."

Eslingen tilted his head curiously. This was the first time anyone had mentioned Rathe since the day he'd been hired. "Stickler, is he?"

"You mean you didn't notice?" Denizard answered. "And stiff-necked about it." She glanced over his shoulder, checking the light. "Come on."

Caiazzo was waiting in the great hall, talking, low-voiced, to his steward. He nodded to the man as he saw the others approaching, and the steward bowed and backed away. Caiazzo looked at them, and nodded. "Good. I'm not expecting trouble, mind, but it's always well to be prepared."

"Any word?" Denizard asked, and the trader shook his head.

"Not since last night."

Last night's message had been a smudged slate, barely legible, delivered by a brewer's boy, that did nothing more than set a new time and place for the rendezvous. There had been no explanation of why the messenger had missed the previous meetings, or any apology—which could just be the limits of the medium, Eslingen thought, but in times like these, I don't think I'd like to count on it. He said, "Then maybe we should expect trouble."

Caiazzo shot him a glance. "I trust my people, Eslingen, don't forget it."

"It's not him I'm worried about," Eslingen answered, and the trader grunted.

"Your point. But there'll be three of us, plus the boat's crew. That should be ample."

"You're coming, Hanse?" Denizard asked, and the trader frowned at her.

"Yes. I'm getting a little tired of doing nothing, Aice." His tone brooked no argument. The magist sighed, and nodded. Caiazzo smiled, his good humor restored. "Let's be off, then."

Caiazzo's boat was waiting at the public dock at the end of the street, its crew, a steersman and a quartet of rowers, hunched over a dice game, their backs turned to the other, unattached boatmen, who ignored them just as studiously. The steersman looked up at Caiazzo's approach, and nudged his people. They sprang to their places, dice forgotten, and Caiazzo stepped easily down into the blunt-nosed craft. Eslingen followed more carefully—he was still not fully happy with boats—and Denizard stepped in after him, seating herself on the stern benches.

"Point of Hearts," Caiazzo said, to the steersman. "The public landing just east of the Chain."

The steersman nodded, and gestured for the bowman to loose the mooring rope. The barge lurched as the current caught it, and Eslingen sat with more haste than dignity. It lurched again, then steadied as the oarsmen found their stroke, and the soldier allowed himself to relax. Caiazzo was watching him, and smiled, his teeth showing very white in the winter-sun's silvered light.

"Not fond of water, Eslingen?"

The soldier shrugged, not knowing what answer the other wanted, but couldn't help remembering the astrologer's warning. He'd been right about the change of employment; Eslingen could only hope he'd be less right about travel by water. Caiazzo looked away again, fixing his eyes on the shimmer of light where the winter-sun was reflected from the current. Eslingen followed the look but could see nothing out of the ordinary, just the sparkle of silver on black water. The winter-sun itself was low in the sky, would set in a little more than an hour, and the brilliant pinpoint hung just above the roofs of the Hopes-point Bridge. And then they were in the bridge's shadow, the light cut off abruptly, and Eslingen caught himself looking hard for the bridge pillars. He found them quickly enough, the water foaming white around them, and the steersman leaned on the tiller, guiding the boat into the relative calm between them. Eslingen allowed himself a sigh, and Caiazzo looked at Denizard.

"I'm not convinced, Aice, that there's going to be much profit in this little jaunt. It may not be scientific, magist, but I've got a sick bad feeling about it."

"I know," Denizard said quietly. "So do I."

To Eslingen's surprise, Caiazzo laughed again. "Oh, that's wonderful. I expected you to contradict me, Aice, or at least tell me not to anticipate trouble. The last thing I needed was for a magist to confirm my fears."

"Well, that's all they are at the moment—the stars are chancy, but not actively bad," Denizard answered. "But I'd be lying if I said I was comfortable. And night meetings are never my favorite."

"The midday ones can be just as dangerous," Caiazzo murmured, and lapsed into a pensive silence. Denizard sighed, and folded her hands in the sleeves of her coat. Eslingen glanced from one to the other, and wondered if they were also remembering the old woman in her shop at the heart of the Court of the Thirty-two Knives. That had been broad daylight, and he'd been glad to leave alive. He jumped as water splashed over the gunwale, and then told himself not to be foolish. The boatmen knew their business, and besides, they were none of them born to drown.

They were turning in toward the bank now, the boat rocking hard as the oarsmen fought the current, and Eslingen braced himself against the side of the boat, twisting to look toward the shore. The houses of Point of Hearts stood tall against the dark sky, lights showing here and there in open doorways and unshuttered windows, and he thought he heard a snatch of music carried on the sudden breeze. But then it was gone, and the boat was sliding up to the low landing.

"Wait here unless I call," Caiazzo said to the steersman, and the man touched his cap in answer. The trader nodded and levered himself out of the boat without looking back. Eslingen made a face, distrusting the other man's mood, and hurried to follow.

"Where to?" he asked, and Caiazzo turned as Denizard pulled herself up onto the low wharf.

"Little Chain Market," Caiazzo said. "It's not far."

"But very empty, this time of night," Denizard said.

"Don't you think I know that?" Caiazzo snapped. "Why do you think I brought the pair of you?"

"Let's hope we're enough," the magist answered, and Caiazzo showed teeth in answer.

"It's what I pay you for."

Eslingen's mouth tightened—he hated that sort of challenge—but there was no point in protesting. Instead, he loosened his sword in its scabbard, the click of the metal loud in the quiet, and fell into step at Caiazzo's right. The magist flanked him on the left, her eyes wary.

It wasn't far to the Little Chain Market, as Caiazzo had said—but the street curved sharply, cutting off their view of the river. Eslingen made a face at that: they'd get no help from the boat's crew, unless they shouted, and that might be too late. Caiazzo stopped at the edge of the open square, staring across the empty cobbles. The market was closed, the stalls shuttered and locked, shop wagons drawn neatly into corners; the winter-sun had dropped below the line of the rooftops, and the shadows were deep in the corners. Eslingen scanned the darkness warily, but nothing moved among the closed stalls.

"Now what?" he asked.

"Now we wait," Caiazzo said, glancing around. "And hope he shows this time."

Eslingen grimaced again, letting his eyes adjust to the darkness. He could distinguish one patch of shadow from another now, could make out the shapes of the trestles piled in the mouth of an alley, but there was still nothing moving in the market. He heard something then, a faint sound, like feet scrabbling against the loose stones of the river streets. It could be a river rat, but he moved between it and Caiazzo anyway, cocking his head to listen. Caiazzo moved up beside him, and Eslingen glanced at him, wanting to warn him back, but the trader lifted a hand, enjoining silence. Then Eslingen heard it, too, a wordless sigh with a nasty, liquid note to it. He swore under his breath, and Caiazzo snapped, "Quiet."

The shuffling came again, this time more clearly human footsteps, dragging on the stones, and Caiazzo turned toward them. "Who's there?"

"For the love of Tyrseis, sieur, help me."

Caiazzo's eyes flickered to Denizard, who nodded.

"It's Malivai," she said, and it was Caiazzo's turn to swear.

"Help me," he said, and started toward the source of the sound. Eslingen went after him, his hand on his sword hilt.

Malivai—it had to be the messenger, a nondescript shape in a battered riding coat—was leaning against the arch of a doorway, one hand pressed tight against his ribs, the other braced against the stones. Caiazzo took his weight easily, for all the two men were of a height, and eased the man down onto the tongue of a wagon.

"Gods, Malivai, what's happened?" He was busy already, loosening the messenger's coat, one hand probing beneath the heavy linen.

"I'd gotten to Dhenin, almost to the city itself, I thought I was clear, but then they found me again." Malivai caught his breath as the probing hand touched something, and Caiazzo drew his hand away. Eslingen could see blood on the fingertips and made himself look away, across the empty market. There was no sign of whoever had attacked Malivai, but he doubted that would last much longer. Almost without thinking, he drew his sword, the blade catching the last faint light from the winter-sun.

"That's old," Caiazzo said. "When?"

"Three days ago." Malivai winced again. "I told you, I'd made it to Dhenin, thought I'd lost them, but then they found me again. I got away, but one of them got off a pistol shot, that's what you see there, and they've been close on my trail ever since. That's why I couldn't make the last meeting. I couldn't get clear of them."

Caiazzo nodded. "But you lost them."

Malivai shook his head, dark braids falling across his face. "I had lost them, I wouldn't've come here else, but when I tried to pass the Chain, they jumped me again. I got free, but that—" He touched his side, flinching. "—opened again. But you have to know. De Mailhac's betrayed you."

"Has she, now," Caiazzo said softly, but before he could say anything more, Eslingen heard the sound of soft boots against stone.

"Sir," he began, and Denizard broke in sharply.

"People coming, Hanse."

Eslingen could hear the sound of swords now, and reached left-handed for his knife. "And not to open up shop, either. They're carrying steel, and they don't care who knows it."

"They probably also don't give a damn about legal limits," Caiazzo said. He was smiling, a toothy, feral grin that made the hackles rise on Eslingen's neck. He had served with officers who'd had that look before; they were the sort who got one killed, or covered in glory. "I don't see that we have a choice, do you?"

"The boat," Denizard said, and Caiazzo shook his head.

"There isn't time, not with Malivai." He stooped, brought the messenger bodily to his feet, taking most of the other man's weight on his own shoulders. He drew his own long knife with his free hand, and edged Malivai toward the mouth of the street that led to the public landing. "How many were there, Mal?"

"Three, I think, maybe four." Malivai's voice was weaker than before, and Eslingen risked a glance over his shoulder. The messenger was leaning heavily on Caiazzo, who was bent sideways by his weight. They'd never make it back to the boat before the pursuers appeared, Eslingen knew, and stepped between them and the footsteps that were getting steadily louder. Denizard moved to join him, her own blade drawn, and Eslingen glanced sideways at her, hoping she knew some magist's tricks to even the odds.

A figure stepped out of the mouth of the street that led west to the Chain, and was quickly followed by two more. They all carried drawn swords, but their faces were muffled by heavy scarves, drawn close in spite of the lingering summer warmth. Eslingen shook his head, studying them, and lifted his sword. It wasn't bad odds, even with a wounded man to protect, and the bravos were obviously concerned with keeping their identities hidden—as well they might, attacking honest people in the streets. It was nice, for once, to have the law on his side, but why was there never a pointsman around when he needed one? He killed the giddy thought, born of the anticipation of battle, and lifted sword and dagger.

The first bravo rushed him, sword raised for a chopping blow. Eslingen ducked under the attack, and drove his dagger into the man's stomach. There was leather under the linen coat, and the blade slid sideways but caught on a lacing and tore into the man's side. In the same moment, Eslingen brought his sword across, hilt first, and slammed it into the bravo's face. The man dropped without a word, and Eslingen spun to face the second man, parrying awkwardly. Out of the corner of his eye, he could see Denizard and the third man exchanging thrusts, but his own opponent feinted deftly left and struck right, and the tip of his blade ripped Eslingen's sleeve before the soldier could dodge away. Eslingen parried the next attack with his sword, and, as the man lunged again, trying to catch that blade, aimed his dagger for the bravo's throat. It was an awkward blow, but the bravo's own momentum drove him forward onto the blade, and Eslingen twisted away, freeing himself and his blade, the bravo's blood hot on his hand. He turned toward Denizard, and saw her step into the second man's attack, lifting her knee into his groin. He staggered back, blade swinging wildly, and Caiazzo shouted, "Ferran, to me!"

That was enough for Denizard's attacker, who dropped his blade and ran. Eslingen crouched beside the dead man, wiping his hand on the skirt of the dead man's coat, and then searched quickly through his pockets. He found a purse, and pocketed it, but there was nothing else. He shook his head—he had been hoping to find tablets, a slate, a paper, something—and turned to the other man, but Denizard was there before him.

"This one's dead, too," she said, and Caiazzo smiled, not pleasantly. "Good. Anything on him?"

Denizard shook her head. "Just his purse, and from the weight of it, he wasn't paid in advance."

"Or this one was the banker," Eslingen said, and held out the purse he'd taken. "There's coin here."

"Interesting," Caiazzo said. "Bring it, let's see what we were worth." The boatmen appeared then, breathing hard, and Caiazzo swung to face them. "Ferran, help me with Malivai."

Eslingen wiped sword and dagger on the dead man's coat, and resheathed it, his fingers still sticky with the other's blood. Caiazzo, still supporting Malivai, turned toward the boat, and Denizard fell into step behind him.

"How bad is it?" she asked, and the trader shook his head.

"I've seen worse," he said, and the steersman came to help him, taking part of Malivai's weight. The oarsmen followed, stolid, not looking at the dead bodies still littering the cobbles, and Eslingen trailed behind them back to the boat, wondering just what he'd gotten himself into this time. Two men dead, and another hurt—even Caiazzo would have a hard time buying his way out of this one. And I, Eslingen thought, don't have his kind of influence to buy off my second dead man in as many weeks. He glanced at Caiazzo, but the trader's face was closed and angry, and he decided to keep his questions for later. Together, Caiazzo and Ferran helped Malivai down into the boat, settling him against the cushions, and Caiazzo bent again over the injured man. Denizard stepped down into the boat as the oarsmen prepared to cast off, and Eslingen hesitated on the bank. For an instant, he was tempted to run, to step back into the shadows and turn and run as far and as fast as he could, until he was well out of sight and on the road north again. Then the magist looked up at him, her face curious, and Eslingen shook the thought away. It wouldn't work, for one thing, he thought; and, for another, I've given my word here. And, most of all, I want to know what's going on. He climbed into the boat and seated himself beside Denizard, letting his hand trail in the cool water, washing the blood away.

The landing by Caiazzo's house was mercifully empty, and the boatmen vanished with the second sunset. Even so, Caiazzo and Ferran kept Malivai more or less upright on the short walk to the house—hiding an injured man from any prying neighbors' eyes, Eslingen knew—and the trader only seemed to relax again when the doors closed behind him.

"Help Malivai upstairs," he said to Ferran, and the steersman hesitated. "Aice will show you the way."

Denizard nodded and started up the stairs. Ferran followed, almost carrying the messenger, who sagged visibly in his grip, and the senior steward appeared in shirt and breeches to help them. Caiazzo looked back at Eslingen. "Get yourself cleaned up, and join us. I'll want you there."

Eslingen nodded, for the first time really seeing the rip in his sleeve. The shirt was ripped as well: both would be difficult to mend, and expensive to replace. He sighed, and headed down the hall to the servants' stair.

Candle and stand were waiting just inside his door, and he lit the taper from the lamp that burned constantly at the end of the hall before going back into his room. He shrugged out of his coat, swearing at the length of the tear—it ran from the edge of the cuff halfway up the shoulder on the outside of the arm, impossible to disguise—and swore again when he saw his shirt. It, too, was badly torn, and probably beyond saving. He crumpled it into a ball, and only then realized that the bravo's sword had touched him as well. A long scratch ran along his forearm, showing a few drops of blood already drying. He scowled at that, and fumbled in his clothes chest for a clean rag. He had no desire to ruin a second shirt with bloodstains.

There was a knock at the door then, and he lifted his head. "Come in."

One of the maidservants—Thouvenin, her name was, Anjevi Thouvenin, Eslingen remembered, and mustered a tired grin—stood in the half-open doorway, a steaming basin in her hand. "The steward said you'd want to wash."

She'd brought a length of bandage, too, Eslingen saw, and he took that gratefully, used it to clean the blood from the scratch. With her help, he laid a strip of cloth over the bit that was still bleeding and tied it in place, then eased himself into a clean shirt. He used the rest of the water to wash his face and hands—the right still felt sticky—and then shrugged himself into his second-best coat. "Do you know where Caiazzo is?" he asked, and the woman grinned.

"The other end of the hall. Don't worry, you'll see the lights."

She was as good as her word. At the far end of the house, a door stood open, spilling a wedge of candlelight across the floor. As Eslingen approached, he could hear voices, and then the steward came out, wiping his hands on an apron.

"Oh, Eslingen, good. He wants you."

"I dare say," Eslingen muttered, and stepped through the door. The room smelled of boiling herbs, a scent he recognized from the army physicians' tents, and he wasn't surprised to see a small pot simmering on the lit stove. Malivai lay in the great bed, propped up on pillows, a wide length of bandage wrapping his ribs. Above it, the skin was bruised and sore-looking, and Eslingen winced in sympathy. Caiazzo, sitting on the edge of the bed, looked up at the soldier's approach, but went on talking.

"—not as bad as we thought. Damn it, Mal, you've no right scaring us like that. Eslingen here just joined my household, what's he going to think of me?"

The man in the bed managed a smile, but he looked exhausted. Caiazzo glanced back at Eslingen. "Nothing's punctured, just a long cut along the bone, and it looks clean enough. Of course, if they were Ajanine, we don't really need to worry about poison, that's a Chadroni trick."

"If they were Ajanine," Eslingen said, "they wouldn't have run." He sounded more sour than he'd meant, and Caiazzo fixed him with a stare.

"And I dare say you would know."

"The wine's hot, Hanse," Denizard said, from the stove, and Caiazzo looked away.

"Bring a cup, then, please." He waited while the magist ladled a cup full of the steaming liquid—it smelled of wine and sugar and herbs and something vaguely bitter, probably one of the esoterics—and then helped Malivai take a cautious sip. "Better?"

"Some," the messenger answered, but Eslingen thought his voice sounded stronger.

"All right, then." Caiazzo glanced over his shoulder, beckoned to the others. "What's going on with de Mailhac?"

Malivai took a deep breath and then flinched, his face tightening in pain. Caiazzo fed him another sip of the wine, visibly curbing his impatience.

"Take your time."

Malivai nodded. "She—there's a magist at Mailhac, but not of your kind, Aicelin. He seems to have de Mailhac and her people under his command."

Denizard looked startled at that. "There was no magist there when I was."

"You've been there?" Eslingen asked, involuntarily. "This year, I mean?"

"At the end of Lepidas," Denizard answered, and shook her head. "And I didn't see a magist there then."

"Well, there's one there now," Malivai said. "And de Mailhac does what she's told."

Caiazzo frowned. "Why? And how did he manage that?" The messenger's eyes slid to Eslingen, and the trader sighed. "Eslingen—Philip Eslingen—is my knife, and he probably saved your life tonight. You can speak freely."

"It's the mine," Malivai said. "He—all I could get was that he promised to increase the takings from the mine, and she agreed to it. And he's been there ever since. And as best I can see, Hanse, it's him who calls the tune."

"And if he promised to increase the taking," Caiazzo said, "why haven't I seen an ounce of it this summer?"

Malivai shook his head. "He's not letting it leave the estate. They—he's keeping it, but he's not spending it, and I never saw any of it, no one did. The mine's guarded now, never like it used to be. I'm sorry, Hanse."

"For what?" Caiazzo said. "Start from the beginning, Mal."

"Sorry," Malivai said again. He took a cautious breath. "I got to the estate on the thirteenth of Sedeion, didn't go to the house, like you told me, but went to the stables, they're usually hiring there. Only this year they're not, the head hostler said, for all I could see they were short-handed. When I asked him about that, he said they'd spent too much on their time at court, and couldn't afford extra hands—"

"Court?" Caiazzo said, and Denizard shook her head.

"De Mailhac hasn't been in Astreiant, I'd stake my life on that."

"The Spring Balance," Malivai said. "The queen was on progress then, de Mailhac joined the court there." He took another slow breath. Caiazzo reached for the wine, but the messenger waved it away. "I'll sleep if I have much more, I have to finish first. So I asked if anyone else on the estate was hiring, said I wanted to be near my leman in Anedelle, and that I'd been able to summer on the estate before—I've kin there, they'll speak for me. And I think he would have hired me, but one of the stewards came out, and when he heard who I was, told me to get off the Mailhac lands. So I went down to Anedelle then, and asked what was going on at Mailhac, and nobody seemed to know, except that there was a magist there who had de Mailhac under his thumb. Nobody likes him in the household—he's had the maseigne selling off her goods and he's banned all clocks from the house, which is a grand nuisance to all concerned." He smiled then, the expression crooked on his worn face. "Then a man tried to knife me while I slept, and I've been one step ahead of them ever since."

"Banned clocks?" Denizard said. "Why?"

Malivai made an abortive gesture that might have become a shrug. "Some project of his, they think, but no one knows."

Denizard shook her head. "What sort of magist is he? Did you get a name, or whose badge he wears?"

"I never got a name—I don't think any of them knew—but he doesn't wear a badge," Malivai answered. "All I know is, in Anedelle they say he has de Mailhac completely cowed—she dances to his tune—and he seems to have control of the mine."

Caiazzo muttered something profane, fingers tightening on the wine cup. With an effort, he put it aside before he crushed it, and stood up. "All right, Mal, sleep. You should, given what I put in the wine. Philip, Aice, come with me."

He led them to his workroom, where someone had already lit a branch of candles. Almost absently, Denizard lit a second branch of six, and Eslingen watched the shadows chase each other across the face of the clock. It was a little past two, two hours past the second sundown, and he could feel the weight of the hours on the back of his neck.

"We have to tell someone, Hanse," Denizard said, and set the last candle in its place.

"Oh, really?" Caiazzo stopped pacing long enough to glare at her, resumed his stride in an instant. "And whom do you propose we tell? Tell what, for Bonfortune's sake? Officially, I don't own this estate, Aice, it's petty treason for a commoner."

Denizard leaned forward, planting both hands on the table. "Gold, Hanse, is the queen's metal, it and the royal house were born under the same stars. And right now, with the star change imminent, that link is going to be stronger than ever."

"I handle gold every day of my life—well, these last ten years," Caiazzo objected. "And I'm common as they come. That hasn't made any difference."

"That's coin gold," Denizard said. "It's not pure gold, they add other metals to it in the refining, precisely to keep it safe. But what comes out of the mine is pure, and it can become aurichalcum if you handle it right. That's queen's gold, Hanse, and they call it that for a reason. The tie between them, the queen and her metal, it's too strong. And that's too dangerous to just ignore." She smiled then, not without a certain sour humor. "And after the clock-night, I find banning clocks a very unsettling thing, don't you?"

"You can't think this magist had anything to do with that," Caiazzo said.

"I don't know how," Denizard admitted, "but I do know this is dangerous."

"And betraying ownership of an Ile'nord—hells, an Ajanine—estate isn't dangerous?" Caiazzo's voice was less certain than his words. He stopped at the far end of the room, scowling at the cold stove. Eslingen stared at him, wondering what to do. Malivai's news was too strange, too important not to let Rathe know about it, especially if Denizard was right about the gold, and there was a link between it and the queen, and the clocks and the magist. Caiazzo would not be happy—Caiazzo would be murderous, an inner voice corrected, and reasonably enough so. You promised him your loyalty—and I promised to tell Rathe if I ran into anything unusual, too, he told himself. It may not have anything to do with the kids, but it is important. It's too strange not to be important. He slanted another glance at Caiazzo, who still stood silent, staring into the shadowed corner beyond the stove. It would be a shame to lose his respect, Eslingen thought, not just for the revenge the trader was certain to try to exact, but because he liked the man. . . .

Denizard's voice broke through his reverie. "It's become political, Hanse. And that's a game you don't play."

Caiazzo dug the heels of his hands into his eyes. He stood there for a long moment, unmoving, then lowered them and turned back into the light. For an instant, he looked older than Eslingen would have thought possible. "All right," he said, softly. "All right. Eslingen—in the morning, I want you to go to Rathe—since he got you this job, maybe he'll give you a break on this one. Go to Rathe, tell him about this night's business."

"All of it?" Eslingen asked, startled—this was the last thing he'd expected from Caiazzo—and the trader nodded.

"Well, as much as you have to, which, knowing Rathe, will be most of it. It was clearly self-defense there in the square, and on my orders, so neither you nor I need to worry about that, but somebody's bound to be asking questions about those bodies." Caiazzo nodded slowly, as much to himself as to the others. "Yes, tell him what's been happening—my people set upon in the streets, my business interfered with. That should keep him busy. And maybe, just maybe, it'll help put a stop to whatever is going on with de Mailhac."

Rathe woke to the sound of knocking, gentle but persistent, and lay for a moment in the cool dawn light trying to place its source. It was someone at his door, he realized at last, and dragged himself out of his bed, groping for shirt and breeches. The knocking was still going on, a steady beat, not quite loud enough to wake the neighbors, but insistent. Rathe shivered, still only half awake, and reached for the knife that he had left hanging in its scabbard over the back of the chair.

"Who is it?" he called, and crossed to the door.

"It's Istre, Nico."

Rathe lifted the bar, and pulled open the heavy door. The magist looked as dishevelled as Rathe could ever remember seeing him, shadows heavy under his eyes, magist's robe discarded for a coat that didn't quite seem to fit across the shoulders. He hadn't shaved, either, though the fair stubble was hardly noticeable at first glance, and Rathe stepped back automatically. "What's wrong?"

"I've found it, Nico. I know what the children are being used for."

Rathe took a deep breath, feeling as though he'd been hit in the gut. "What?" he said, and b'Estorr stepped past him, reaching into his pocket to produced a small drawstring purse. He untied the strings, and poured a small triangle out onto the tabletop, where it lay gleaming in the early sunlight. Rathe stared at it for a moment. "Istre . . . "

b'Estorr nodded. "It's gold, Nico. Actually, it's coin aurichalcum. An impure form of true aurichalcum, more pure than most ordinary coins, but not nearly as pure as the real thing. Magists use it in their work."

He picked up the little wedge and handed it across. Rathe took it gingerly, turning it over in his fingers. The shortest end was curved, and there were letters running along that curve, as well as what looked like part of an embossed design in the center. He looked up sharply. "This looks like part of a coin."

b'Estorr nodded again. "It is. That's where most of us get it, from great crowns."

"Gods, I've never seen one," Rathe said, and looked at the wedge of metal with even more respect. The great crown was the largest of Chenedolle's coins, each one worth a hundred pillars—more than many people saw in their lifetime. "But what does this have to do with the children?"

b'Estorr dropped into the nearest chair. "Aurichalcum is gold, common gold, that's been mined in a particular process. Everyone knows that much, but not many people outside the university know how. The process itself is what makes it magistically active, and that process requires people, special people. To turn raw gold into aurichalcum, each step of the process must be performed by pure beings who have the proper zodiacal relationship to their task—which, in practice, means children or carefully trained and watched celibates, each of whom is chosen for the job according to her or his birth signs."

Rathe sank down on a stool opposite b'Estorr, set the piece of aurichalcum back on the table. "Children," he whispered. "Gods, but why? Who would be doing such a thing?"

b'Estorr shook his head. "That I can't tell you. It's crazy, it makes no sense to me at all, but that's what everything points to. It's the only thing these children could work together on. Someone has stolen them to process aurichalcum."

Rathe looked from the wedge of gold, bright in the rising sun, to b'Estorr. "If magists use it . . . "

b'Estorr spread his hands. "I know, Nico, I know, and I've been wracking my brains trying to think why, or who. Gods know, we're all limited by the sheer cost of coin aurichalcum, but that's nothing compared to the effort to process the stuff. It's false economy. And utterly mad."

"Stealing children's pretty mad, Istre," Rathe said, and the necromancer made a face. "Whoever's doing this is pretty crazy anyway. If the motive is crazy, well, it kind of fits, doesn't it?"

"So all we have to do," b'Estorr said dryly, "is find a gold mine. As I recall, there are gold mines aplenty in the Silklands, and in the Ile'nord, the western hills of Chenedolle, in southern Chadron, and in the Payshault, all of which are within reasonable striking distance of Astreiant."

Rathe shook his head. "No, it has to be someplace that has good roads—they were buying draft horses, not pack animals." If it was them, of course, a little voice added, but he shoved the thought away. It had to have been the astrologers who were buying the horses, or their allies; they couldn't afford for it not to be.

b'Estorr nodded. "All right, that probably rules out the Silklands. Anyone sensible would go by water. But the rest—how can you choose?"

"I know," Rathe said. "Does this connect with the clocks, Istre?"

"It could," b'Estorr answered. "Aurichalcum—especially the purer forms—well, it's not just politically potent. I suppose it would be possible to use it to turn the clocks, but why . . . "

He let his voice trail off, and Rathe nodded in morose agreement. There was a little silence, the only sound the rumble of an early wagon on the street below. The air that came through the half-open window was damp, and smelled of the distant river; Rathe cocked his head, and thought he could hear the chime of the tower clock at the head of the Hopes-point Bridge. "There haven't been any new disappearances in days," he said at last. "Does this mean they have all the kids they need?"

b'Estorr shrugged, got restlessly to his feet, and then stopped, the movement suspended, as though he'd simply needed to move and was now at a loss for something to do. "They could have. From the nativities I've seen, for the children who are missing, yes, I think most of the process is covered. But I don't know, Nico, I wish before Aidones that I did." He sighed heavily. "So what do we do now?"

Rathe threw up his hands. "I don't know. I'll go to Monteia—hells, I'll go to the surintendant, and I'll tell them this, and we'll all look at each other, and say, wonderful, what now? Aside from anything else, we don't have the right to pursue it, not outside the city, so we'd have to work with the local nobles, but since we don't even know where the children are—" He broke off, shaking his head, aware of the futility of his anger. b'Estorr had given him more information than they had been able to gather over the past few weeks, but it still wasn't enough. "I feel like a bastard asking this, after all you've done, but is there anything more you can do? Anything more you can tell us?"

b'Estorr crossed to the window, pushed the shutter open, and leaned out into the morning air. "When was the last disappearance?"

Rathe shook his head. "I'm not sure—five days ago, I think. I can check with the station. Does that matter?"

b'Estorr turned back to face him. "I don't know. And I hate having to keep saying that. But it might help. I can do some more research, see if anything shows itself—I'll certainly consult my colleagues. They'll need to know about it for the clocks, anyway."

Rathe nodded. "I appreciate it. Look, will you come with me to Monteia? You understand what's happening here better than I do."

"Of course," b'Estorr said, and scooped the wedge of gold back into its bag.

Neither man spoke as they made their way from Rathe's lodgings to the station at Point of Hopes. Rathe caught himself walking faster and faster, as though hurrying might help, might make up for how long it had taken them to figure out what was going on. b'Estorr's discovery was utterly vital, the first piece of information that made sense of the child-thefts. If only it hadn't come too late. Surely not, he told himself, and made himself slow his pace again. If nothing else, they could protect the children who hadn't been taken, first by arresting the hedge-astrologers and then by concentrating their efforts on the vulnerable ones. Asheri was one of those, but she had more sense than many a woman grown, and they would be able to deploy the full resources of the station to keep her safe. And surely, surely, knowing why the children had been stolen would help them find the missing ones.

The station courtyard was empty, none of the runners in sight there or in the stables. Rathe caught his breath—he had expected to find Asheri waiting, sitting in the early sun on the edge of the dry trough where she could get the best of the light for her sewing—and shoved open the main door. Jiemin, this morning's duty point, looked up, startled by the violence of his entrance.

"Nico . . . ?"

"Where's Asheri?" Rathe demanded, and Jiemin shook her head.

"I haven't seen her yet. It's early, Nico, she probably slept in."

"But I told her to be here by now," Monteia said, from the door of her workroom. She shut it behind her, shaking her head, and looked from Rathe to the necromancer. "What's up, Nico?"

Rathe ignored the question for a moment, crossed to look out the back door. The garden was empty even of laundry, and he turned back into the room, barely able to keep the fear at bay. "Istre thinks he knows why the children are being taken. Asheri—"

Monteia cut him off. "Why?"

b'Estorr said, "They all have stars that make them useful—appropriate—for processing aurichalcum."

Monteia frowned. "Queen's gold?"

b'Estorr nodded, his blue eyes grave. "And aurichalcum is dangerously powerful, especially now with the starchange approaching."

Monteia swore under her breath. "And Asheri?" she said, to Rathe.

"She said she knows her nativity to the minute," he answered, voice suddenly ragged, "but I don't. I never asked, and she never told me. Her sister might know."

"Go," Monteia said. "Both of you—please," she added tardily, to b'Estorr. "See if she's at home, find out what her stars are, and get her here where we can take care of her."

Rathe nodded, and was out the door almost before she'd stopped speaking, b'Estorr on his heels. Asheri lived on the southern edge of Point of Hopes, in the warrens east of the junction of the Customs Road and Fairs' Road. He had been there before, and led the way through the labyrinth of narrow streets, barely able to keep from running as he saw the peeling face of the clock that oversaw this corner of the city. It had been reset, though, since the clock-night: as they turned down the alley that led to a cluster of narrow houses, it struck the half hour, and its tones were echoed from the distant towers of Point of Dreams.

Asheri's house was no different from any of the half dozen that circled the well-house at the center of the open space, a plain building one room and a hallway wide, with a strip of muddy garden running beside and in front of the stone sill. A tall woman, unmistakably Asheri's kin, the sister she had lived with since their mother's death, had strung a line between two poles, and was hanging laundry, temporarily overshadowing a straggling patch of vegetables. Among the clothes already pinned to the line was the apron Asheri had worn the day before, and Rathe caught his breath again.

"She didn't burn them," he said, and heard b'Estorr swear.

The woman looked up at their approach, her eyes narrowing, but her hands never stopped moving on the wet cloth. Somewhere, in one of the other houses, Rathe thought, a child was wailing; even as he looked, he heard a voice exclaiming a rough endearment, and the crying took on a new, muffled rhythm, as though someone had picked up the child and was bouncing it.

"Mijan, where's Asheri?"

"Missing her already?" Mijan answered, and smiled. "You knew she was meant for better than running your errands. She's gone."

"Gone where?" Rathe demanded, and heard b'Estorr swear again.

Mijan set a much-mended skirt back in her basket, her expression suddenly wary, folded her arms across her thin chest. "To the embroiderers. Last evening at seven o'clock. You know that's what she wanted, more than anything, that's why she worked for your lot."

"She didn't have the fee," Rathe said bluntly, and Mijan shook her head.

"No more did she, but she won one of the lottery-places—you know, they hold four places a year for those who don't have the means."

"They hold those at the Spring Balance," Rathe said, through gritted teeth, "and the Fall Balance. Never at Midsummer, Mijan, you know that. And so did she."

Mijan was looking genuinely frightened now. "I know, I'm not stupid. But the woman—she was respectable, Rathe, a guildswoman to her fingertips—she said that one of the apprentices they'd chosen this spring couldn't continue in the place, was sick or something, the family was sick, and Asheri was at the top of the list, the next in line. She passed all the tests, you know, it was just her number wasn't quite high enough."

"Which house, Mijan, did you think to ask that? Which master?" Rathe heard his voice rising, didn't care. "You let her go, when children are disappearing every day?"

"That's precisely why I let her go," Mijan shouted back. "Do you think I haven't worried enough about her, running gods alone know where through every quarter of the city, when children are being stolen in broad daylight? She's a thousand times safer with the embroiderers than she ever was with your lot."

Rathe flinched, recognizing the truth of that, and b'Estorr put a hand on his shoulder. "If she's with the embroiderers, mistress. Asheri knows her nativity, I know that. May we get a copy?"

"Why?" Mijan looked from one man to the other. "Who in Demis's name are you? Nico I know, but you . . . "

Rathe took a breath, controlled the anger bred of fear and guilt. "His name's Istre b'Estorr, Mijan, he's with the university. A necromancer. And, no, we don't think any of them are dead, but he's been helping us, and we know why the children are being taken. And I'm very much afraid Asheri's one of them."

"She's with the embroiderers," Mijan whispered.

Rathe shook his head. "I devoutly hope so, but—it's a bad time for coincidence. I need her nativity—please, Mijan. You know I wanted—want—nothing more than for Asheri to find a place in the guild. Let me make sure she has the chance."

"She's there, I tell you," Mijan repeated, but her eyes were wet with sudden tears. "I did what you told us, we washed the clothes, and locked them away, she was wearing my second-best skirt—and furious she was, too, to think the masters would see her without her having the chance to take it in. I should've known, we never have luck." She shook her head, wiped a hand across her face with angry force. "Her chart's inside—you'll have to copy it, though, I won't let you take it away."

"Fine," Rathe said, still struggling with his anger. It wasn't so much Mijan he was angry at—how could she, how could any southriver housekeeper, pass up the chance to see a kinswoman decently established?—or even Asheri, for taking a chance, but the astrologers and their respectable-looking accomplice, for playing on the one source of hope children like her had. And that must have been how they lured the others away, he thought. The horoscopes, the questions the children asked, would have given the astrologers a very good idea of what they would have to offer to overcome the children's fears—give them a chance at their hearts' desire, and they were young enough to take the chance, even the cleverest, most wary ones. Like Asheri, he added, and Mijan reappeared in the doorway, a wooden tablet in her hand. She gave it to Rathe, who handed it to b'Estorr, trying to ignore Mijan's small noise of protest. b'Estorr studied it for a moment, then reached into his pocket for a flat-form orrery, adjusting the rings to the appropriate positions. His mouth tightened then, and he handed the tablet back to Mijan.

"It fits," he said. "It fits, Nico. She has the key stars, she's perfect for their operation."

"What?" Mijan cried, and Rathe took her by the shoulders, gently now.

"No one will hurt her, she's too valuable. We know why they took her, and some of where, and we will find her, I promise." He took a deep breath, hoping he could make that true. "Is there anyone who can stay with you?"

Mijan took a deep breath, swallowing her tears. "No. No need. I'll be fine. Just—find her, Rathe. They said, she'd won a place. It was so much what she wanted, they seemed all right, how could I think . . . ?" Her voice trailed off, and she shook herself hard. "I'll be all right," she said again, as much to convince herself as anyone, and looked back at Rathe. "And if she's with the embroiderers all this time, I will cut your heart out."

"If she is," Rathe answered, "I'll hand you the knife myself."

He turned away without waiting for an answer, knowing she didn't believe it any more than he did. b'Estorr fell into step beside him, stretching his long legs to keep up.

"What now?"

"The embroiderer's hall," Rathe answered. "Just in case. But I don't think she'll be there."

There was only a single master in evidence this early in the day, and she greeted them with a certain puzzlement. Rathe explained what they wanted, and even though he'd expected it, felt his heart sink as she shook her head.

"No, we haven't taken in any new lottery-prentices. We do redraw if someone drops out, but that hasn't happened in years—" She broke off as the two men turned away, Rathe calling his thanks over his shoulder.

"Back to Point of Hopes," he said, and b'Estorr touched his arm.

"The river's faster from here," he said. "University privilege."

They found a boatman more quickly than Rathe would have thought possible, but even so, he fidgeted unhappily until the boat drew up at the Rivermarket landing. Monteia was pacing the length of the main room as they burst through the door, but she stopped at once, seeing Rathe's face.

"Inside," she ordered, and jerked her head toward the workroom. Rathe started to follow, but b'Estorr caught his sleeve, handed him the orrery. Rathe took it, careful not to disturb the settings, and preceded the chief point into little room.

"Bad?" she asked, and shut the door behind them.

Rathe nodded. "They've taken her. They offered her a place in the embroiderers, the one thing she wanted badly enough to take chances for, and they've got her. And, Astree's Web, it's my fault. She would never have done this if I hadn't asked her—" He broke off then, knowing how pointless this was, but Monteia shook her head anyway.

"You don't know that, Nico. It's the time of year to have your stars read, and Asheri always was—is—a saving creature. Tell me what happened."

Rathe took a deep breath, and set the orrery on the worktable. Quickly, he ran through what Mijan had told him, finished with b'Estorr's analysis. "She's important to the process, he says, so they shouldn't hurt her. But, gods, we have to find her."

Monteia nodded, her expression remote. "I'll send to Fairs again, tell him what's happened today—I already told him to arrest any astrologers he found, and why, but I haven't heard anything yet. This should make him move a little faster, though." She shook her head. "It's times like these I wish Astreiant still had walls. I'll send people to ask at the gates and the inns along the main highway, see if anyone saw her or someone taking a child with them, but I can't say I've a lot of hope for it."

They hadn't found any of the other children this way, there was little likelihood Asheri would be any different. Rathe swallowed his anger, said, "There has to be something else we can do."

Monteia looked at him. "If you think of something, Nico, let me know."

"I'm sorry." Rathe shook his head. "She's a good kid—and it's my doing, Chief. This one's my responsibility."

Eslingen took the river way from Customs Point to Point of Hopes, the early sun warm on his back through the heavy fabric of his second-best coat. The weight of it, and the stains on the dark green linen, annoyed him unreasonably; if he was going to go to Rathe with this particularly questionable story, he would have preferred to look his best. Inside the station's wide main room, the duty point looked up at him, blankly at first, and then with recognition.

"Is Rathe around?" Eslingen said, before the woman could say something unfortunate, and she grinned.

"He's with the chief point now—Eslingen, isn't it? You can wait if you want, but it's a busy morning."

"Already?" Eslingen murmured, but turned away from the table before she had to answer. A fair-haired man in a dark red coat, shirt open at the throat, was sitting on the bench that stretched along one short wall, reading through a sheaf of broadsheets. Not the sort of person I'd've expected to see here, Eslingen thought, not a merchant but not a knife, either, and only then saw the anvil and star of the Starsmith pinned to the fair man's cuff. A poet or an astrologer, the soldier decided, or maybe a magist out of his robes, and he smiled. "Hope you don't mind," he said, and settled himself on the bench beside the fair-haired man, keeping a scrupulous distance between them.

The man looked up, his face unsmiling but not unwelcoming, and nodded. "Looking for Nico?"

Eslingen nodded. "A friend of his, are you?"

"I do some work for him from time to time."

Eslingen looked again at the badge on the man's cuff. "An astrologer?"

The man shook his head. "A necromancer, actually," he said, and offered his hand. "Istre b'Estorr. I'm at the university."

For a wild moment, Eslingen wondered how Rathe could have found out about the bodies already, and have had the foresight to call in a necromancer for something that wasn't even in his jurisdiction. He had never liked the idea of necromancers, no soldier did—no matter what the scholars said, he thought, some of those deaths had to be untimely. b'Estorr tipped his head to one side, and Eslingen shook himself, took the hand that was held out to him. "My name's Eslingen, Philip Eslingen. Late of Coindarel's Dragons."

"Oh. And currently Hanselin Caiazzo's knife," b'Estorr said.

Eslingen looked at him warily, wondering how in all hells he could have known that, wondering, too, what ghosts he might be carrying that the other could feel. b'Estorr smiled faintly, as though he'd guessed the thought.

"Nico mentioned you once, said he owed you a good turn. I'm glad to meet you. It's made a lot of people much easier to know that Caiazzo has a capable knife to back him again."

"So I heard," Eslingen said. "Are you working for Rathe now?"

b'Estorr nodded, the smile vanishing. "I'm afraid so—"

He broke off as the door to the workroom opened, and Rathe burst out again. "Monteia's sending to Fairs, we'll see if Claes can't find one of these damn astrologers, make him tell us what's going on—" He broke off, seeing Eslingen. "Philip. Sorry, what are you doing here?"

Eslingen looked back at him. "I need to talk to you—Caiazzo sent me—but if this is a bad time—what's happened?"

Rathe took an unsteady breath. "Asheri, one of our runners. She's disappeared—been stolen, like the others. And we know a large chunk of how, and why, but still not who, or where they're being taken."

"Gods," Eslingen said.

"So unless it's really important," Rathe went on, "you'll have to wait."

Eslingen hesitated. "It is important," he said at last, "but I think I can wait, at least until you've gotten this settled."

Rathe gave him a fleeting smile of thanks, looked at b'Estorr. "Is there any way we can narrow down the location of the mine? Something in the kids' stars, anything?"

Eslingen froze, his eyes widening. A mine and the missing children in the same breath, and a crazy magist in Mailhac. . . . He took a deep breath. "What's this about a mine?" Rathe turned on him, eyes angry, and Eslingen held up a hand. "What I was sent to say, it may be more important that I thought. What mine, Rathe?"

"The children who've been taken, they all have the right stars to work the process that turns gold into aurichalcum," the pointsman answered, impatiently. "It's the only thing we've found that binds them together, but now we have to figure out where that gold mine could be."

Eslingen swore. "Look, Rathe, last night Caiazzo met a man—" He broke off, shaking his head, tried to reorder his thoughts. "There's an estate in the Ajanes, Mailhac, it's called, the woman who ostensibly owns the title actually owes Caiazzo a lot of money, and she pays it out of the take of a gold mine that's part of the estate."

"Which explains where Caiazzo's cash comes from," Rathe said, but his eyes were wary. "And I hear he's had trouble with money this season."

Eslingen nodded. "The gold hasn't come in the way it should. And from what the messenger said, it won't be. There's a magist living on the estate, apparently he promised to increase the take, but that was just to get her confidence. According to Mal—the messenger, it's him, the magist, who's running everything, and keeping all the gold on the estate. The rumor was, he may be making use of it himself."

"Gods," the necromancer murmured, and Rathe waved him to silence.

Eslingen went on, "Caiazzo's man was attacked on his way here—that's what I was really sent here for, to tell you who'd left a pair of bodies in the Little Chain Market, and to claim self-defense, which it was. I was also supposed to tell you about the Ajanine situation, make it clear that, whatever de Mailhac thinks she's doing, Caiazzo has nothing to do with it." He shook his head. "But this . . . this is worse than any of us imagined. I don't want Caiazzo hanged for a high treason he's not committing. He's been going mad from the want of gold, it could be a disaster if he doesn't get it, but he doesn't want queen's gold, he wants spending gold."

"Caiazzo has a magist in his household, doesn't he?" Rathe said. "She must have suspected something when she heard the news."

"She did," Eslingen answered, "she mentioned aurichalcum, but she thought it was political. Something to do with the starchange and maybe with the clocks—which, as I said, is why I'm here."

"She would have needed to know the children's nativities to make the connection," b'Estorr said, and Rathe nodded.

"Yeah, I can see that. But, gods, now we know—" He broke off as the door to the workroom opened again, and Monteia stepped out, waving a sheet of paper to dry the ink.

"Know what?" she asked, and Rathe bared teeth in a feral grin.

"Where the children are."

"Where?"

"An estate called Mailhac, in the Ajanes." Quickly, Rathe outlined Eslingen's information. "It fits, Chief, and too well to be a coincidence. This has got to be where they are."

Monteia nodded thoughtfully. "A noble. That would explain how she could afford all these hired hands, or how this magist could, with a noble name to back him." She looked at Eslingen. "I suppose I believe you when you say Caiazzo's not involved."

"If he were," the soldier answered, "I wouldn't be here."

"True enough," Monteia said.

"We have to send someone after them," Rathe said, "and I want it to be me. Gods, if we move fast enough, Asheri's only been gone since last evening, we might be able to overtake them."

Monteia shook her head. "I can't send you, Nico, and it's not because I don't agree with you. We don't have the authority outside Astreiant, you know that. That's the queen's business."

"If we can convince her, or her ministers or whoever, intendants probably, to act in time," Rathe said, bitterly.

"Which is why I want you—and Master b'Estorr and Master Eslingen, if he's willing—to go to the surintendant," Monteia went on as though he hadn't spoken, though Eslingen suspected from the set of her lip that she was barely holding her own temper in check. "Tell him what we've found, and see what he can do."

Rathe nodded, tightly. "Sorry, Chief."

Eslingen sighed. "Caiazzo is simply going to love this."

"Caiazzo," Rathe said, "will appreciate not being hauled up on treason charges. Come on."

They took a low-flyer, and Rathe paid without demur. As they climbed out of the carriage outside the Tour, Eslingen glanced uncertainly up at the thick stone walls. It looked more like a fortress—more like the gatehouse it had once been, the strongest point in the city walls—than a court of justice, and he couldn't help wondering just how much of the old ways still prevailed within those walls, in spite of all the boasting. Caiazzo would not be pleased, he was sure of that, and wished for an instant that there had been time to contact the trader, ask what he wanted done. But Rathe was right, time was short, especially if there was to be any chance of overtaking this last victim. He took a deep breath, and followed the others into the dimly lit building.

Rathe spoke quietly to the first green-robed clerk he saw, and within minutes, they were ushered into the surintendant's room. Eslingen glanced around once, quickly, impressed in spite of himself by the delicately painted paneling, fruited vines climbing pale willow trellises, and the obviously expensive furniture. Then the man behind the desk cleared his throat, and Eslingen blinked, startled. The surintendant wore plain black, unrelieved by any lace, just the pale linen at collar and cuffs, and his thinning hair was cut unfashionably short. He raised one sandy eyebrow in chill query, and Eslingen found himself wondering whether the furniture or the clothes represented the man's real taste.

"We know what's happening to the children, sir," Rathe said, and Eslingen saw the older man blink.

"Then you had better sit down, hadn't you? Magist b'Estorr I know, primarily by reputation, but this gentleman?"

Eslingen met the cold stare calmly. "Philip Eslingen, lieutenant, late of Coindarel's Dragons, currently of the household of Hanselin Caiazzo."

"Indeed?" Fourie looked at Rathe, the hint of a smile on his thin lips.

"Not what you think, sir," Rathe answered, and no longer felt the triumph he had expected. It was a hollow victory, with Asheri lost. "When we determined that the one thing all the kids had in common was that they knew their stars to better than the quarter hour, I asked Istre to look at all of them together, to see if he could find something in common there—why these children, with these stars."

b'Estorr said, "What I found was that there was only one magistical process for which these nativities, and children, would be suitable. And that is the making of aurichalcum."

"Even Caiazzo isn't that stupid, or ambitious that way," Fourie said. His eyes narrowed. "Those damned hedge-astrologers, and you were right, Rathe, and I was wrong." He looked at Eslingen then. "Or was I?"

Eslingen took a long breath, choosing his words carefully. "Master Caiazzo has—interests—in an estate in the Ile'nord, in the Ajanes, more properly. And there's a gold mine on that estate."

"Which has been funding his sudden prosperity, I daresay," Fourie muttered. "Go on."

"The owner of the estate has taken in a magist," Eslingen said, "who seems to be keeping the gold for his own purposes, and is willing to kill to keep them secret." He gave an edited version of the previous night's events, stressing that Caiazzo had been waiting for an overdue payment. "Master Caiazzo thought it was just de Mailhac pushing to see how much she could get away with, she did that last year, too, or at worst that she'd overspent herself and didn't have the money to send, never something like this. As soon as he realized it involved politics, he sent me to the points."

"And that was the last piece we needed," Rathe said. "The children are at Mailhac, in the Ajanes."

Fourie leaned back in his chair, pressing his long fingers together at the tips. "It's never the easiest solution with you, is it, Rathe? An estate in the Ajanes, which means it falls under the rule of four quarters." He shook his head. "It'll take time to organize an expedition, a few days at least—"

"We don't have that much time," Rathe said. "Putting aside the kids, we don't know what he's mining the aurichalcum for, we could be standing on the edge of a disaster—"

b'Estorr cut in, his own voice uncharacteristically urgent. "The clocks—aurichalcum moves clocks, or it can, it has powers most of us don't even dream of, not in our nightmares. There's no time to be lost."

"There's no time left," Rathe said.

Fourie lifted a hand, and Rathe subsided reluctantly. "I have no authority outside Astreiant. No pointsman, adjunct point, or surintendant himself has that authority outside the city. Much as I'd like to, much as I desperately want to, I can't send you or anyone into the Ajanes. I don't have the power."

It was an impasse, Eslingen thought, and a bad one. He looked at Rathe, seeing the frustration barely held in check, saw the same anger, better hidden, in the magist's eyes. He said, slowly, certain he would regret it later, "Denizard—Caiazzo's household magist—she said Hanse would have to send someone north to deal with all of this. Admittedly, that was before we knew what was going on—" And Caiazzo still doesn't, he realized abruptly, would be furious when he was told. "—but I can't see that it'll change things. Someone will still have to deal with de Mailhac, and I don't see why that someone can't also deal with the magist and the children."

"He has the resources," Fourie said, with distaste. "And I'm sure a little good will from the judiciary wouldn't come amiss. Especially given the questionable nature of his involvement in this entire affair."

"The main thing is the children," Eslingen answered, and prayed he wasn't committing himself too deeply for Caiazzo to back him up. "Caiazzo has been made part of this without his knowledge and against his will. I know he'll want to put it right."

Fourie stared at him for a long moment, then reached for a sheet of paper. He dipped his pen in the silver inkwell and began to write, saying, "I'm not fond of relying on people like Caiazzo—or anyone outside the judiciary or the nobility, Lieutenant, not your master in particular. This should be a matter of the law. But, as you say, the children have to be our main concern." He looked at Rathe, his pen never pausing. "Rathe, I want you to go with him. Mind you, this is not an order, I cannot order you to do anything outside the city, but you're the best man I have."

"Of course I'll go," Rathe said, and Fourie nodded.

"b'Estorr I can't give any orders at all, but I imagine his talents would come in very useful."

b'Estorr looked at Eslingen. "If you'll have me, yes, I'll come." His mouth tightened. "I'd like to see the end of this."

"You'd be welcome," Eslingen answered, and meant it.

"I wish I could send a troop of the royal guard with you," Fourie went on, and lifted the sheet of paper, waving it to dry the ink, then reached for his seal and a stick of wax. "Unfortunately, there isn't time to arrange it. What I can do, have done, is send you with a letter authorizing you to call on the royal auxiliaries in the area." He glanced at another sheet of paper, looked at Eslingen with another of his thin smiles. "They're commanded by your old colonel, Lieutenant. It makes one wonder what Coindarel has done this time." He looked back at Rathe, held out the sheet of paper. "Use it if you need to, Nico. I hope you don't."

For an instant, Rathe could only stare at the letter. Whatever he had expected—and he wasn't at all sure what that had been; Fourie's temper was notoriously uncertain—this official carte blanche had not been it. If anything, he'd expected more pleasure at Caiazzo's inadvertent involvement, had half expected the surintendant to take the opportunity to try to trap the trader, to score a point on him at last. And I've been unjust, Rathe thought, abashed. The children have always been the main issue; Caiazzo can wait for another day. "Thank you," he said aloud, and took the paper, folding it carefully, protecting the heavy seal.

"Be off with you, then," Fourie said. "And bring those children home."

They took the river to Customs Point, a quick journey with the current, and Eslingen led the way to Caiazzo's house. The trader had been waiting for him in his workroom, the steward said, glancing warily at Eslingen's companions, but at the soldier's nod brought them up the stairs to the gallery. Caiazzo rose as the door opened, but checked when he saw Rathe and the magist.

"Oh, come, surely this is a little elaborate for a simple case of assault, and self-defense, at that."

"If it were just a simple case of assault," Rathe snapped, "I wouldn't be here. But in fact, you've given me the last piece of a very nasty puzzle."

The trader's face went still. "What are you talking about?"

Behind him, Denizard stirred, then was silent. Rathe said, "Your gold mine, Hanse—yes, Eslingen told me about it, and a damn good thing he did, too. You think it's just greed that kept your bought noble from sending you the coin you needed?"

Caiazzo reseated himself behind his desk, fixed Eslingen with a cold stare. "I had thought so, yes. It's not that unreasonable a thought, is it? But you're going to tell me there's more to it."

Denizard said, quietly, "We knew that, too, Hanse. There's the magist, and the clocks, to make things urgent."

"Which is why I sent to the points," Caiazzo answered. "This isn't business I want to handle."

"Except you're in it up to your neck already," Rathe said, "and you don't even know what it is." He looked at Denizard. "You must have some suspicions about all this."

The woman shrugged. "A gold mine, and a magist interested in it, keeping the take for himself? Coupled with clocks that strike when they shouldn't? It speaks of aurichalcum to me, which speaks of politics, though how he's making the stuff is beyond me. It's too much for one person to handle, even if you could find the people you needed—" She stopped abruptly, the color draining from her face, and Rathe nodded.

"Couple it with the missing children, and you get a nasty picture."

Caiazzo looked from the pointsman to his magist. "Is it possible?"

Denizard shook her head. "It's too many variables. Getting the right nativities would be hard enough—hells, just making sure you have total celibates handling the gold would be hard enough, I don't care how careful the guilds are, celibate means celibate."

"The nativities match the process," b'Estorr said, and Denizard looked at him.

"I know you. I've heard you lecture. You're sure?"

b'Estorr nodded, and she winced.

"Gods, then I suppose it is possible. But it's crazy."

"I don't know him," Caiazzo said, and Denizard shook herself.

"Sorry. His name's Istre b'Estorr, he's a necromancer. I'll vouch for him."

Caiazzo said something under his breath. Rathe leaned forward. "It was the hedge-astrologers, the ones working the fair without bond, that found the kids, and they were careful, did their work well. Most of the kids are under the age where sex becomes a serious curiosity, and every single one knew her or his nativity. You've been playing a political game for the first time in your life, Hanse, though it's not the one Fourie thought it was, but I don't really care. All I care about is getting the children back safely. The rest—doesn't exist, as far as I'm concerned."

Eslingen cleared his throat. "I understood that you'd be sending people to—rectify the situation, sir. I want to go. And so do they." He nodded toward Rathe and b'Estorr.

"And why in the names of all the gods don't they just send a royal regiment?" Caiazzo demanded. "No, don't tell me, too much time, too much money, and better to let some poor trader handle it. Gods, what a mess. Yes, Eslingen, I was planning to let you deal with this magist, you and Denizard, but under the circumstances, any assistance would be gratefully accepted."

"Doing it this way means you stand less chance of losing that land," Rathe snapped, and stopped, shaking his head. "Thanks, Hanse. I won't forget this."

"But everyone else will," Caiazzo said with a dark smile. He reached for a bell that stood on the edge of the table, rang it twice. "You'll need money and horses, I can get those from the caravan. Take Grevin and Ytier, they're good men in a fight, and you'll want men to help with the baggage. You can pass those two off as agents of mine, Aice, no one in Mailhac should have contacts in Astreiant, and Eslingen's just new to the household." He stood up as the steward appeared in the doorway.

"Sir?"

"We have a journey to arrange," Caiazzo said. "There's a pillar in it for you if everything's ready by first sunset."

To Rathe's amazement, the steward had everything in order by the time the neighborhood clock struck six. Caiazzo's servants, a pair of tall, greying men who had been soldiers and caravan guards in their younger days, accepted the sudden assignment phlegmatically enough—they were probably used to this sort of thing, Rathe thought. He had sent to Point of Hopes, both to warn Monteia of his departure and to send a runner for his clothes, and now that bundle was tied with the rest on the frame of a rather ill-tempered pack horse. There were two others, one of whom carried food and water, as well as a spare, plus the six riding animals: nearly twice as many horses as people, Rathe thought, and shook his head. He wasn't used to this sort of travel; he had spent most of his life in Astreiant, except for a trip to Dhenin, and then he'd gone by river. He had learned to ride as a boy from a neighbor who was an hostler at the local tavern, but the roads to the Ile'nord and the fields outside the city were two very different things. He sighed, looking at the horses, as Eslingen came up beside him.

"You do know how to ride, don't you?"

Rathe nodded. "Oh, don't worry, I won't disgrace you. Rouvalles isn't going to like this, if all these came out of his train."

"You know him, too?" Eslingen asked, and the pointsman shrugged.

"I've met him."

Eslingen nodded. "I daresay he isn't. But he'll have more time to find replacements than we have to find good mounts." He slipped a long-barreled pistol into a tube attached to his saddle, and looked back at Rathe, absently patting the horse's neck. "Does your friend the necromancer know how to ride?"

"You don't like him?"

Eslingen sighed. "I—most soldiers are a little wary of necromancers, that's all. It was a disappointment."

"Ah." Rathe turned his head to hide a grin. "Well, don't worry about him either. He's Chadroni, born and raised there. He rides."

The main door opened then, and Denizard and b'Estorr came down the short stairs. Denizard was carrying a small chest under her arm, which the taller of the servants, Grevin, Rathe thought, took from her and added to one of the piles of baggage. b'Estorr had sent to the university for his clothes as well, and carried a worn pair of saddlebags and a long leather case that could only contain swords. Eslingen lifted an eyebrow, seeing them, and Rathe grinned openly.

"Oh," he said, "didn't you know? Istre's a duellist when he has to be."

"And how do you reconcile that, necromancer?" Eslingen asked.

b'Estorr glanced at him. "If a fair duel is called, and you're killed, it's generally assumed it was your time. One can, after all, reject a duel."

"I see," Eslingen said. "Any fighting isn't likely to be polite, you know."

b'Estorr smiled, not nicely. "Duels aren't. At least, in Chadron they're not." He turned and began strapping the case expertly to his saddle.

"No," Eslingen said. "I would guess they're not."

They took advantage of the winter-sun that night, and the next three, the first night camping out by a field smelling sweetly of cut hay and grains. The next night they found farm lodging with an old soldier who now held a small patch of land to farm for himself. He was Chenedolliste, but he welcomed Eslingen as a brother. It was, Rathe reflected, only the ordinary folk of Chenedolle, those who had never carried pike nor musket, who were suspicious and resentful of the Leaguers who now served the queen. The soldiery saw only colleagues who, at one time or another, might well be facing them across a field, or might be at their back. It was all in circumstances, as the stars suggested. When Rathe asked if he'd seen any unusual travelers, someone riding hard, or wagons, the man shook his head without curiosity. He had his farm and paid little attention to anything beyond its edges; neither the children nor the clock-night had reached him. A farm woman north of Bederres, however, had heard the gossip, and said she'd seen a trio riding hard toward the Gap highway, and one of them had a child at his saddlebow. It wasn't much, but Rathe clung to it, afraid even to acknowledge his worst fear. If, somehow, they'd gotten it all wrong and the missing children were somewhere else, then he'd only made things worse.

They crossed into the Ile'nord on the morning of the fourth day, the landscape unmistakable when they reached it. Dame school classes taught every Astreiant school child that it was an inhospitable place: certainly it was no place for people who lived by farming and trade. The spine of the land broke through in a low, barren line of hills that rose to the northwest, seeming to get no closer no matter how far they rode. Those hills would grow, Rathe knew, shouldering up to the northwest to become the hills and mountains of Chadron. Somewhere among them was the gash that was the Chadroni Gap, impassable in winter, unless you had overwhelming incentive to get through it. The air here held more than a hint of the coming autumn, a sharpness that blew down from the foothills. Glad as they all were to be free of the city's heat, it made them all uncomfortably aware of time passing, and it was all Rathe could do not to demand they move faster. But they were already working the horses hard, didn't dare do more. When Eslingen signaled the next stop, drawing up under a line of trees that looked too orderly to have grown there without encouragement, he made himself relax, sitting slack in the saddle. He was managing well enough, but his muscles were still sore. If you keep on like this, he told himself firmly, you'll be no good to anyone once we get to Mailhac.

Denizard drew up next to Eslingen, pushing her sweat-damp hair back up under her cap. "You know these roads, maybe better than I do. What's the next town?"

Eslingen rested his hands on the pommel of the saddle and looked around him. "I'm not sure, it's been a while since I've taken this road north."

b'Estorr said, "Chaix, I think, it's been a few years, but as I recall, it's three days good riding from Astreiant. There's a good inn there," he added with a faint, almost wistful smile. Eslingen nodded.

"I know Chaix. We usually come at it from a different direction, it's a crossroads town, isn't it?"

"Complete with gallows," b'Estorr confirmed.

Eslingen rolled his eyes and moved away. "I'd like to give the horses a better rest than we've been able to, so let's say we stop at Chaix tonight."

Rathe sighed. The soldier was right, he knew that, and besides, he was stiffer than he'd realized from the days of riding and sleeping rough. His lodgings were modest enough, he thought, but at least he had a bed. "At least it'll give us a chance to get what news there might be about anyone else who's traveling north," he said.

It was just past first sunset when they reached Chaix, passing under an arched gate with a clock set into the keystone. The town had no walls, and the arch looked strange, almost forlorn, without the supporting wall to either side. The winter-sun was still high, casting pale silver shadows along the dusty street, and b'Estorr shaded his eyes, squinting at the signs that hung from the buildings lining the main road. "It's the Two Flags here, isn't it?" he asked, and Eslingen grinned.

"Always ones to hedge a bet, these folk. I like them." He nodded to a square of yellow light spilling from an open door. "Good beer, good wine. It's how you tell the border taverns. And last time I was here, it was clean, reasonably comfortable."

"That's how I remembered it," b'Estorr agreed. Denizard edged her horse restlessly away, scanning the buildings. The town seemed quiet enough, no one unduly surprised by their presence, but still, Rathe thought, they were enough of an oddity that the inhabitants should have noticed any strangers.

"All right, look," he said. "Eslingen, why don't you and I get rooms and order dinner. There's bound to be a temple of sorts here—I think it'd be better—smarter—if Istre and Aicelin handled any questions. My accent is a dead giveaway, and people don't answer questions for strangers they're wary of. But you two have the perfect standing to do so."

"The temple—such as it is—is down that cross street," Denizard said, rejoining them. She looked at b'Estorr. "Your altar or mine?"

Rathe looked where she had pointed. It was a small, round stone building, the design that usually signaled a pantheon or at least a shared temple, and he thought he understood the magist's attitude.

b'Estorr exhaled heavily. "Either way. It's a crossroads town, a trading town, so the primary deity may be Bonfortune."

"But death is so universal, isn't it?" Eslingen offered. But a smile took the sting from the words.

"And you're Chadroni, Istre," Denizard said. "Like Rathe, I've got the Astreiant accent, they may not trust me."

"Whereas everyone looks down on Chadroni, so they're more likely to talk with me," b'Estorr said with a sigh. "Right. Mine, then. You'll join me, though, I trust, Aice?"

She tilted her head. "Wouldn't miss it. We'll see you both at the tavern—Two Flags, right?" Eslingen pointed, and she peered at the sign, brightly painted in gaudy colors, gilt touching the edges of the banners and the carved ropes, and nodded. "Shouldn't be hard to find again."

The two moved off into the pewter twilight, and Rathe looked at Eslingen. "After you. You're the one who knows the town."

Eslingen grinned and dismounted, and Rathe trailed behind him into the inn yard, the two servants following with the horses. Chaix was a strange, narrow city, the buildings jammed close together, stables built directly against the walls of the neighboring houses. It was as though the whole city were modeled on the Court of the Thirty-two Knives, with its narrow streets and its buildings brushing up against one another, cutting off the sunlight and the river breezes. He knew he was prejudiced, tried to see the city with eyes other than an Astreianter's, but it was hard. The aromas were certainly different, heavier, richer, bordering on the exotic—at least, the less mundane ones, the ones that weren't common to every city with a population living in close proximity to one another. Eslingen, he noticed, was looking about him with a faint, almost supercilious smile.

"Nothing like your home?" Rathe asked, and regretted the words as soon as they were spoken. He was tired, and worried, and at the same time very much a stranger, almost as though the Ile'nord were still some other kingdom. To his relief, however, the soldier shook his head without taking offense.

"Entirely too much like, actually. Esling is very like this. And gods, do you know, I haven't missed it a bit?" He shook his head, his eyes momentarily distant.

"Is that why you joined the armies?" Rathe asked, maneuvering his way around a puddle of dubious origin. He caught the inn door as Eslingen flung it open.

"I imagine so. That, or remain in Esling with an uncertain future. And it's always been my determination to have an uncertain future of my own making." He grinned then, and moved forward to meet the landlady.

The Two Flags was as Eslingen had described it, neat, well appointed, but not fancy. Rathe let Eslingen handle the negotiations over the rate, uncomfortably aware of how out of his depth he was outside Astreiant's walls. He'd never been in the Ile'nord, and he certainly had never had an occasion to stay at an inn before, was accustomed only to patronizing the ground floor taverns, or occasionally breaking up unlicensed prostitution above floors. He found a corner table well away from the group of regulars, stolid women in dark wool, and sat watching the animated discussion. Finally, Eslingen joined him, carrying a pitcher and two mugs.

"All set," he said with a grin. "The others can get their own when they get here." He swung a long leg over the bench and sat down opposite Rathe.

Rathe eyed the pitcher. "Beer or wine?" he asked.

"Well, I know I said they served a decent wine, but then, I thought, what do I know about wine, really? I'm not Chenedolliste, what I think is good you might think is horse piss. So, I thought I had better stick with what I know is quality."

"Beer, then," Rathe said, resignedly.

"And damn fine beer, too. You'll enjoy it."

And it was good, Rathe had to admit. It carried the musty aroma of the hops that grew wild along the back fence of his garden, and was, he had to admit, ideal after a long day's riding. Eslingen drained his mug in a couple of long swallows and poured another; Rathe drank more carefully, too tired to risk a drunken night.

"How much further, do you think?" he asked.

Eslingen waved to a waiter, pointed to the board that displayed the evening's meal. "We're in the Ile'nord now. From what Caiazzo told us, my guess is that Mailhac is another day, day and a half away. Aicelin would know better than I." He seemed to guess the real question, said, reassuringly, "We've made good time, Nico."

"Good enough?" Rathe asked.

"If I knew that . . . " Eslingen shook his head.

A swirl of activity outside the open door of the Two Flags caught Rathe's eye, a tumbling knot of small figures, and he recognized it as a group of children. They were playing tag or some other rough game, and he realized with a shock how long it had been since he had seen such a sight in Astreiant. Only a few weeks, to be sure, but they'd been long weeks without the sound of children's laughter. One of the children, a boy, maybe four, maybe five, came running into the inn and buried his face in his mother's skirt. Rathe felt his heart tighten, and then the child's voice came clear.

"Janne hit me! You told her not to hit me, and she did."

A girl, a year or so older than the boy, appeared in the doorway, face mutinous. The mother rolled her eyes to the ceiling, then gestured to the girl. "Janne, what did I tell you about hitting your brother?"

"Little boys are fragile, and can get hurt more easily, but I didn't mean to! The little gargoyle ran into me."

"Well, both of you, be more careful in the future. Go on, and try not to kill each other."

The girl made a face, but darted away again. The boy sniffed a few minutes longer, was fed a slice of bread from his mother's plate, and headed out the door again. Rathe forced himself to relax, took another swallow of the beer.

"Lovely sight," Eslingen said, and Rathe looked at him, surprised.

He had not figured Eslingen as someone with much tolerance for children, let alone affection.

"You don't have any children, do you?" he asked, and Eslingen shook his head, looking slightly appalled.

"No. But when enough women have considered you, not as a suitable mate, but as a suitable father for their children, you develop a certain tolerance for them. You look at them, and think, well, yeah, I could do better than that." The fine lines at the corners of Eslingen's eyes tightened as he smiled in self-mockery. "It's probably just as well Devynck let me go. I think Adriana was planning some dynasty building. And the gods know, I've nothing to offer an heiress like herself in equal exchange for marriage, so it would be just for the fun of it, and the future generations of the Old Brown Dog."

Rathe nodded, but didn't know what to say. No one, to his knowledge, had ever viewed him in quite the light Eslingen was describing. And he wasn't even fully sure what he was feeling, faced with Eslingen's revelation. There was a small knot in him at the thought of Eslingen and Adriana; for some reason, he hadn't thought Eslingen favored women. Not that he'd any reason to think that, nor any reason for this small surge of what he strongly suspected was an irrational envy.

The light shifted then, and he looked up to see b'Estorr and Denizard in the doorway, stepping carefully through the pile of children now playing jacks on the stone outside the door. b'Estorr's expression was carefully neutral; Rathe had known him for a number of years now, and knew he wasn't sure he wanted to hear the magists' news.

Eslingen got up, fetched another pitcher and two more mugs. "You look like you need it," he said, then topped up his own mug. "And if you do, we're going to. What is it?"

Denizard dropped onto the bench beside Eslingen. "Nothing dire, hells, nothing we didn't expect, but it's a little hard to hear it. Over the past few weeks, the people here have heard what sounds like an army on the move—and these people know what army movements sound like. They were nervous, naturally enough, and went looking, but they didn't find much sign of them, just wagon tracks. But armies don't travel with so many wagons, so I understand."

"There's only a couple of people who say they saw anything," b'Estorr said. "And what they saw, well, they said it was eerie—wagon after wagon, maybe four or five at a time, heading north but skirting the town. Aside from the noise the wagons made, and the horses, it was quiet. No voices, no calling, no singing, no orders . . . just the wagons at twilight, and silence."

Rathe shivered in spite of himself, and b'Estorr shook his head at the image he had inadvertently conjured up. "Then, yesterday, some people saw a group of men riding hard, didn't stop here. One of them had a child with him on the saddlebow. A girl, they thought, from the hair."

"Asheri." Rathe dropped his head in his hands, splaying his fingers through his hair and tightening them, as though the pain would make him think more clearly.

"On the good side," b'Estorr went on, "the word is the Coindarel's men are camped by Anedelle. That's only two hours from Mailhac."

Rathe nodded, barely listening. It was a relief to know he was right, that they were on the right road, but it didn't take away the greater fear. Or the nagging certainty that none of this would have happened if he hadn't sent Asheri to the fair. He looked at Eslingen. "Is there any point in pressing on tonight?"

Eslingen made a face. "Given that we know where we're going, that we don't have to track these people, I would say yes, but the horses are tired, we're tired. If this rider suspects he's being followed, we might well ride into an attack."

Denizard nodded. "A lot of the people around here will be Mailhac tenants or their kin."

"How far is it to Mailhac from here?" b'Estorr asked.

"Just under a day," the other magist answered.

b'Estorr nodded, and reached for a pocket almanac. "I think we have time," he said, after a moment. "The moon isn't at its most favorable for the next few days, Asheri's stars make her valuable for several of the final steps, which is probably why they're hurrying, but they're also in opposition to the current positions."

"And if we press on tonight, we'll arrive there early tomorrow morning," Denizard said. "She'll know we hurried. We don't want to make de Mailhac suspicious. Arriving in the afternoon is likely to seem more normal to her."

"If anything does, these days," Eslingen muttered. "I say we risk it. We spend the night here, we get an early start, we're rested, the horses are rested, and we don't arouse de Mailhac's suspicions."

"And she's going to be wary enough of us, anyway," Rathe agreed. "Right, then, we'll spend the night." The decision made, he felt more helpless than ever, and he pushed himself away from the table. "If you don't mind, I think I'm going to turn in."

"Not a bad idea," Eslingen started to rise, stopped by a hand on his arm. He looked down at b'Estorr, who shook his head slightly, and Eslingen grimaced in comprehension. "We'll be up a little later. I want to check on the horses."

Rathe, who had missed the exchange, just nodded and headed back towards the stairs, grateful for Eslingen's understanding, anxious for a few moments to himself, to let the fears run wild and then to put them away, firmly, and for all. Tomorrow they would be at Mailhac. Then it was only a matter of time before everything was resolved.

11

The next morning dawned rainy, and the air smelled more than ever of the coming autumn. Rathe glared at drizzle beyond the tiny windows as he shaved and dressed, but got his impatience under control before he climbed down the creaking stairs to the main room. They would still reach Mailhac by the end of the day, and that was all that mattered. Eslingen was standing by one of the windows in the common room, looking out at the grey, wet sky. He shook his head, hearing the other's approach, but didn't turn.

"We may not make as good time today," he said mournfully. "Seidos's Horse, I hate wet travel."

"I suppose the weather had to break sometime," Rathe answered, more philosophically than he felt. He hoped the rain wasn't an omen, and dismissed the thought as being foolish beyond all permission. He accepted a cup of thick, smoky-smelling tea from the yawning waiter and joined Denizard at one of the square tables, wrapping his fingers around the warmed pottery.

"It couldn't have waited another day?" When there was no answer, Eslingen drew himself away from the window and sat back down opposite Rathe. "It could be worse," he said. "It could be snow."

Rathe just looked at him. Eslingen raised his hands in defense. "I've seen it, snow this time of year, and not that much further north than we are now. Miserable marching it was, too."

"Sounds like the Chadroni Gap, and from the sound of it, you were in one of the higher parts," b'Estorr said, from the doorway. He shook the rain from his cloak, hung it near the porcelain stove in one corner of the common room.

"Yes, well, that's not so very far north of here, is it?"

"There's north, and north," b'Estorr agreed with a shrug. He sat down at the table, wrapping his hands around a cup, and glanced at Rathe. "I couldn't have asked for better weather. If it's stormy at Mailhac, and I think it will be, from what they told me at the temple, there's not going to be any work done in the mine today."

Rathe allowed himself a breath of relief and gave the necromancer a nod of thanks. That was good news—it could only be good news: whatever delayed the magist's work gave them more time to find the children, and to free them before they had outlived their usefulness.

"How so?" Eslingen asked.

"The wind and rain carry too much corruption," b'Estorr answered, "and this magist has taken too much trouble this far to spoil it all by carelessness. It may not be a pleasant ride today, but that's all to the good."

Denizard made a noise that might have been disparagement or agreement. "Are we ready, then?"

Rathe nodded, stood up, setting aside his half-finished cup of tea. "I'd like to get there before nightfall. I want to see what this place looks like on first impression."

Eslingen lifted an eyebrow. "Spoken like a soldier."

Rathe looked at him, grinned. "I'm sure you meant it as a compliment."

As Rathe had feared, the riding was worse than the past few days had been. The dry dust of the roads had been turned overnight into a thin mud, and the wind blew chill from the northeast, driving the rain through the thin summer fabrics of their garments. When they hit the first of the true foothills, the pack horses began to labor, and they had to slow their pace to keep together on the narrow track. Eslingen swore softly and steadily as the horses' hooves slithered and caught on the rock-strewn mud, and the horses seemed to take confidence from the murmured words, dragging themselves and their riders up the ever-steeper roads. He was the only one who spoke; the others kept silent, faces tucked close to their chests, not wanting to get a mouthful of the cold rain. The first sunset was almost on them by the time they came opposite a massive boss of stone where the track tilted down again, curving out of sight around the side of the hill. Denizard pulled up beneath a stand of wind-twisted trees and let the others draw abreast. She took a breath and gestured.

"That's the Mailhac estate."

It was hard to see at first. Shadows already filled the narrow intervening valley, and the land itself was rough, all rocks and angles, the greyed green of the scrub fading into the brown grey of the outcrops. The main house fit into its surroundings almost uncannily well. It was an old place, the stone as grey as the land around it, and obviously built for the Ajanine wars, with stocky towers on each corner of a square central building. Some of the upper windows had been enlarged, the old arrow-slits broken out and filled with glass, but it still had the look of a fortress rather than a home. Rathe shook his head, staring at it. "Gods," he said quietly. "What a rotten place for children."

Denizard nodded. "It looks much better when it's not raining, I promise you, but—yes."

"They'll be expecting us," b'Estorr said, wiping the rain from his face, and Eslingen nodded.

"There's someone in the west tower, see? Now, I know this is rough country, but there's been peace in this corner of it for a while. I wonder what de Mailhac's expecting."

"Us, probably," Denizard said, and Rathe looked sharply at her.

"What do you mean? If they were warned, the children could be in serious danger, could be used as hostages—" He broke off as the magist shook her head.

"De Mailhac has to assume that Hanse will be sending someone to find out what's going on, that's all I meant. And it's in her interest to convince us that there's absolutely nothing wrong. That's what she did at the beginning of the summer, and I'm ashamed to say, I believed her." She beckoned to the nearest groom, who edged his horse a few steps closer. "When we get there, I want you two to stay with the horses—make whatever excuse you have to, but I want to be sure some of us can get away if we have to."

"Coindarel's camped at Anedelle?" Eslingen asked, and b'Estorr nodded.

"Near enough to make them nervous, anyway. They're not fond of soldiers in these parts."

Eslingen gave him a sour look. "We may be glad of them soon enough."

Rathe sighed, impatient again, and looked back at the house. The clouds seemed thinner now, though the rain seemed as heavy as ever, and the stones of the manor seemed strangely paler in the brighter light. "We're wasting time," he murmured, unable to stop himself, and Denizard gave him a sympathetic glance.

"Come on, then," she said, and touched heels to her horse.

By the time they reached the house, the rain had stopped. The household had been well warned of their approach, and servants appeared with torches to light them through the main gate. It had held a portcullis once, and Rathe, glancing to his right, saw Eslingen looking curiously at the remains of the machinery. They emerged into a narrow courtyard, the horses' hooves suddenly loud on the wet stones, and more servants came running to catch their bridles. Their own grooms slid down to join them, and took unobtrusive control of the pack horses. A woman stood in the doorway of the main house, the torchlight gleaming from the rich silk of her skirts: the landame of Mailhac had come herself to greet them.

Denizard swung herself down from her horse, and the others followed suit, trailed behind her toward the doorway. "Maseigne," she said, and de Mailhac nodded in answer.

"Magist, it's good to see you again. Welcome to my house. I trust all is well?"

You know it's not, Rathe thought, hearing a faint, breathless note in the woman's voice. She was a pretty woman about his own age, maybe a little older, with fine hands that she displayed to advantage against the dark green of her skirts. Her hair was red, unusually so, almost matching the torchlight, and her skin was correspondingly pale, seemed to take luster from the rich silk of her high collar. She was obviously one who liked her luxuries, Rathe thought; no wonder she'd taken Caiazzo's bargain.

"Master Caiazzo is concerned about some matters," Denizard said, bluntly, and Rathe saw the landame's smile falter. She recovered almost at once, but he guessed the others had seen as well.

"But where are my manners?" Denizard went on. "Maseigne, let me present Philip Eslingen, late lieutenant in the royal regiment, and now part of the household. Istre b'Estorr, who handles the northern trade for Master Caiazzo, and Nicolas Rathe, caravan-master."

"Gentlemen." De Mailhac inclined her head a calculated few inches.

"Lieutenant Eslingen speaks for Caiazzo as I do," Denizard said. "You'll forgive my bringing so large a party, but one of Hanselin's messengers was attacked while returning from Mailhac, so we had, we felt, reasonable fear of bandits in the hills."

"If that's the case, I think you were quite wise," de Mailhac said. "We'll certainly have no trouble housing your people, or your animals.

I'm extremely disturbed to hear about the messengers, though. I hope they're well."

"We have hopes," Denizard said, deliberately vague.

"I'm pleased to hear it. Come in, please. It's a vile night, I'm sorry you had to travel in such weather. And I know very well that Mailhac doesn't show to advantage in conditions like this. I hope you told your companions it's not normally this forbidding."

She kept up a constant stream of polite conversation as she led them into the great hall. A generous fire was burning in the massive fireplace, and Rathe moved closer to it, feeling the steam beginning to rise from his wet clothes. They were all thoroughly soaked, and de Mailhac gave orders for baths to be drawn. "I'll let you take the chill off—I've had my people lay fires in your rooms for you, and I've had wine sent up. It can only help, on a night like this. When you're ready, Magist Denizard, I hope you will all join me for dinner. We don't often have guests; I'm looking forward to a very pleasant evening."

"As are we, and thanks for your hospitality, maseigne. Hanselin told me to apologize for coming on you without warning, but as I'm sure you understand, the business of the gold has become urgent. Most urgent," Denizard amended with a smile that, as yet, had no teeth in it, but instead the promise of steel.

De Mailhac lifted her head slightly. "Of course. I do understand that his—business—is somewhat dependent on this estate. But we can discuss this at dinner, or after."

They had been given rooms suited to their status, Rathe saw, with some amusement. Denizard's was the largest, Eslingen's somewhat smaller, and he himself had been tucked into a much smaller room with b'Estorr. There was barely room for the tub between the hearth and the single large bed, and the necromancer laughed softly.

"I'd forgotten how they treat merchants here. It makes me almost homesick."

Rathe grunted, stripping out of his still-damp clothes. Their luggage, such as it was, was already waiting, and he reached for his own bag. De Mailhac's servants were regrettably efficient; he hoped that her guard were less so, and then shook that thought away. "Do you want the bath first, or shall I?"

"Go ahead."

Once bathed and dressed, they made their way to Denizard's room. It was indeed much larger, and the paneling was carved and painted with scenes from some local battle. A long mirror stood in one corner—obviously a new addition to the house, Rathe thought, and surveyed his reflection dubiously. He had brought his best coat, but it still sat badly on him, and the plain wool was creased from the days in the pack. Still, he thought, glancing at the others for reassurance, no one looked much better—Denizard's skirts were crumpled beneath the concealing magist's robe, and b'Estorr's stock had definitely seen better days. Then there was a soft knock at the door and Eslingen came in, elegant in a dark blue coat that set off his pale skin and jet hair to perfection. His linen looked at first glance as though it had been freshly ironed, and the skirts of his coat were arranged to hide the worst of the wrinkles. Rathe shook his head, impressed in spite of himself. Eslingen was going to go head to head with the nobility itself, and just might come out on top. No one speaks a language so precisely as one who isn't born to it.

"So," Denizard said. She gave her reflection a final critical glance, and adjusted her lace-edged cap. "Are we ready?"

"We'd better be," Rathe said. "How does she seem to you?"

"Nervous," Denizard said, with a small shake of her head. "Not terribly, but there's an undercurrent there. She's not best pleased to see us. That could just be because she knows Hanse is extremely irked, but I don't think so. She was a lot sharper last year—this spring, for that matter. You saw how she tried to come the aristocrat with that comment about his business?"

Rathe nodded.

"Normally she pulls that off a lot more convincingly. She's lacking a good deal of her usual ginger," Denizard said grimly, "and that makes me nervous." She took a breath. "Shall we go down?"

"Oh, let's," Eslingen murmured, bowing Denizard through the door.

A waiting servant led them from their rooms through the main hall to a smaller room that had been converted for dining. A fire burned in the hearth there, small but throwing enough heat to take the worst of the damp from the air, and de Mailhac stood by the hearth, the flames striking highlights from her skirt. She had changed her dress, but the fabric was still the same flattering shade of green, bodice and sleeves embroidered with scrolls of gold. The long table was set for six, Rathe saw, and the light from a dozen thick candles struck slivers of light from silver and glass. It was all a great deal less barbaric than he had expected from an Ajanine noble, he thought. Obviously, de Mailhac furnished her household from Chenedolle proper.

"Now I can bid you a proper welcome to Mailhac," de Mailhac said. "We may not be in Astreiant, but—I think—we set a table that won't disgrace us." She took a breath, though her smile did not dim. "There is another guest here at Mailhac whom you'll meet shortly, a magist like yourself, Aicelin—Yvonou Timenard. Perhaps you know him? Though I doubt he's of your college."

Denizard shook her head. "I've not traveled too far from Astreiant, I'm afraid, except on Hanselin's business. No, I don't know him, but I do look forward to meeting a colleague."

Rathe glanced at b'Estorr, but the necromancer's face was blank. Not a name he knew either, Rathe guessed, and looked back at de Mailhac.

The door opened then, and a man came in, a magist's dark robe hanging open over a respectable belly. He looked to be past his middle years, his thinning hair almost white, but his round face was unwrinkled, showed nothing but an almost childlike embarrassment.

"Maseigne, I understood you have other guests. Please do forgive my appalling tardiness—I hope you've not held dinner on my account." He trundled over to de Mailhac, looking a little like a child's clockwork toy, and came to a stop, looking expectantly up at her. She smiled faintly at him—she bettered his height by a good hand's breadth—and extended a hand to introduce him to the others.

"Yvonou, may I present Aicelin Denizard—also a magist, and an important member of Master Caiazzo's household. Aicelin, Yvonou Timenard, who has been good enough to join my household."

"Delighted to meet you," Timenard exclaimed, and clasped Denizard's hand with enthusiasm. Watching him, Rathe felt his heart sink. They had come so far, risked so much on what was really a chain of coincidence and guesses, and then to find this, that de Mailhac's mysterious magist was this child's toy of a man. . . . He bit back his fears. Looks could easily deceive, he knew that well enough, but even so it was hard to believe that Timenard was capable of anything as complicated as the theft of the children.

De Mailhac introduced the others then, and Timenard offered his hand to Eslingen as well, pronouncing himself pleased to meet another representative of their mutual acquaintance. He was perfectly polite to the other two, but his greeting was less effusive, marking their relative status to a nicety.

"Well, this is pleasant, maseigne and I have been our only company for the past several weeks, it's always nice to have new faces and fresh conversation—and from the capital, too, that's an unlooked for treat."

The door opened again, and de Mailhac nodded with what looked like relief to the servant who stood there. "Dinner is ready," she said. "Please, be seated."

They took their places, de Mailhac at the head of the table, Denizard at the foot, and a woman servant began to pour the wine. Timenard was seated at de Mailhac's right hand, Rathe saw, the position corresponding to Eslingen's, and took his own place opposite the magist.

"And how is the capital?" Timenard asked. "As exciting as always? We're so isolated here, we long for tales of the court, don't we, maseigne?"

"It's pleasant to have a change," de Mailhac agreed. Her hand on her wine glass was white-knuckled, Rathe observed. If she wasn't careful, she'd shatter the stem and that would draw attention, certainly unwanted. Timenard's eyes flicked sideways then, and Rathe thought he saw the ghost of a frown cross his round features. De Mailhac seemed to see it as well, and relaxed her grip on the glass. She took a hasty swallow, and set it down again, laying her hand flat on the table top. She wore no rings, Rathe saw, no jewelry at all, and that seemed odd.

"We're hardly at court, any of us," Denizard demurred, and Rathe thought he caught a gleam in Timenard's eye. Not triumph, he thought, but more satisfaction, as though the older magist had scored a point. No, of course none of them would have any dealings with the court, they were all of common birth, no better than merchant class, and rank seemed to matter here, to Timenard and to de Mailhac. It would matter to de Mailhac, seeing as it was a merchant-venturer who had gotten the better of her enough to secure the rights to her estate and the gold produced on it. But Timenard? There were astrologers at court, certainly, but aside from that, magists were not in great number in the queen's court. Was he ambitious? Or was he ambitious on behalf of one of the potential candidates, and grateful that none of their guests were likely to know much about the tangles of the succession? Or was it something else altogether?

"No, of course not," Timenard replied, sounding absurdly sad. "Not working for a trader, as you all do. But surely there is at least gossip you can share? Who's in favor, who isn't, who's brought a new color into favor?"

Denizard and b'Estorr exchanged looks. "I'm afraid we've been too busy this summer to pay much attention to anything beyond the great gossip. Everyone talks of the starchange, of course."

"And the missing children," Rathe said. He watched Timenard as he spoke, and thought he saw a ghost of something, a shrewd intelligence, maybe, flash in the pale eyes.

"Missing children?" de Mailhac repeated, her voice flat. "We've heard nothing of that."

"But we have, maseigne," Timenard said. "You remember, the man who came earlier this month, he mentioned something of the sort." He looked at Rathe, smiling. "Children of the common folk, he said, who had disappeared, or possibly run away. I'm afraid we didn't pay much attention, under the circumstances."

"And why would you?" Rathe said softly, fighting to control his anger. "The problem seems to be confined to Astreiant."

"Sad for the city, but yes," Timenard agreed.

Denizard shrugged, forced a smiled. "For anything else, I'm afraid we've been working too hard to take much notice. I'm sorry to be such an unentertaining guest, I feel as though I'm not earning my keep."

"Nothing of the sort," de Mailhac interposed quickly, before Timenard could say anything. The old magist looked absurdly disappointed, and his bottom lip, Rathe would have wagered, trembled as though he were about to cry. What in the name of all the gods are we dealing with here? he thought. Or did I get it all wrong? Is this simply a commercial deal gone wrong, nothing to do with the children? He pushed the thought down. The stories of the wagons passing by Chaix, of the three riders with a child, moving fast, the whole oddity of this evening—it all had to mean something.

De Mailhac turned to Denizard and Eslingen. "And how is Hanselin? We never get to see him here, only when I travel to the court at Astreiant."

"He's well enough, maseigne, though, as I said, troubled by the silence and, more importantly, the lack of any deliveries from Mailhac," Denizard said. Her voice was pleasant enough, but there were teeth behind the words. "He is not a man to cross, maseigne, I do beg you to believe that. And the two of you have an agreement, an oath of honor between you, that he should regret deeply were it to be broken." The magist lifted a shoulder in an elegant shrug.

De Mailhac glanced almost involuntarily at Timenard, and the round man leaned forward.

"Oh, dear, yes, that is fully understood, and very distressing it must be for Master Caiazzo to find his plans delayed. But . . . " Timenard spread his hands. "He must understand, the mines here at Mailhac are virtually played out. I have been doing everything in my power to help maseigne eke out what we can, but it's barely enough to support the estate itself, let alone such grand merchant plans as Caiazzo must have in train."

"Ah. And why not just tell Hanse that?" Denizard asked, still pleasantly. "I'm sure—something—could be worked out."

"But the people he sent . . . we sent them back to him with just that message, begging his patience and understanding. Are you saying he never received word?" Timenard blinked at her in what looked like genuine puzzlement.

Denizard turned a crust of bread between her fingers. "No," she said, choosing her words carefully. "Not precisely. As I told the maseigne when we arrived, only one messenger returned to Astreiant, and he was attacked and nearly killed on the road south."

De Mailhac and Timenard exchanged looks, and the magist laid his hand briefly on the noble's where it lay on the tablecloth. Rathe, watching closely, couldn't be sure if the magist meant to comfort or to warn her.

"But that's—dreadful," Timenard said. "What must he think of us, of matters here? He must surely think maseigne is trying to renege on—as you say—a pledge of honor, and that is not to be borne."

"After last summer . . . " Denizard said, and let the words hang in the air. "You can understand our concern."

Eslingen cleared his throat. "We understood that the mines did well enough for you to have spent the Spring Balance at court, maseigne. And that's not a cheap proposition."

Timenard's face flushed pink, his bright blue eyes wide and a little angry, and de Mailhac's eyes fell. The old magist frowned at her, and looked at Eslingen.

"I'm delighted Master Caiazzo's people are so well informed, but they don't, perhaps, know everything."

De Mailhac stirred, seemed about to speak, and Timenard turned to her, continuing earnestly, "Please, maseigne, you must let me explain to them, it's likely the only thing that will satisfy your associate."

De Mailhac lifted a hand in permission—or was it acquiescence? Rathe wondered—and Timenard gave her a half bow, turned to speak to Denizard. "As I said, we fully understand the constraints the lack of gold must place on Master Caiazzo, but, also as I said, it has been completely unavoidable. Yes, maseigne visited the court at the Spring Balance, but the reason will, I hope, appease you and Master Caiazzo."

Denizard inclined her head. "I hope so, too, Magist Timenard. I most sincerely hope so."

"Maseigne understands the obligation she is under to Caiazzo, rest assured of that, and it was because of this obligation that she attended the queen this spring past. There is, just to the east of this land, an open parcel on which, it is likely, are further deposits, enough to satisfy both Caiazzo and the requirements of managing an estate such as Mailhac. Maseigne petitioned the queen to extend Mailhac's seigneurial rights to that parcel."

"I see." Denizard sounded almost suspiciously demure. "And did Her Majesty grant this petition?"

"It's still under advisement," Timenard conceded, a trifle stiffly. "We expect a decision by the Fall Balance."

"That's rather late for the trading season, surely," Eslingen murmured in a tone of silken menace, and Rathe, despite himself, hid a smile. This was a very different Eslingen from the one who had been Devynck's knife.

"Entirely too late for bankers' comfort," b'Estorr agreed.

"But there seems to be little or nothing either Maseigne de Mailhac or Magist Timenard are capable of doing about it," Denizard said, and managed to make it a mild rebuke.

De Mailhac spread her hands. "I wish there were something I could do, Aicelin, truly. I know Hanselin to be an honorable man, and I have appreciated his forbearing these few months. If there were any way I could supply his needs—and my obligation—then please believe I would."

Denizard smiled gravely. "I have to, maseigne, and will certainly take your word to Caiazzo, though I'm sure you'll be willing to show me your plans in more detail—perhaps a visit to the mine, or to this new land, would be in order." This time, Rathe was sure he saw fear flare in the landame's eyes, but Denizard continued without hesitation. "In any case, I know he'll be relieved to hear of the possibility of redress."

"The mine itself is always dangerous ground, no one goes there," de Mailhac began, and Timenard cut her off, his voice riding over whatever else she would have said.

"But the miners are competent, maseigne. I'm sure something can be arranged."

De Mailhac's smile looked forced, but she murmured something that was obviously meant for agreement. The rest of the dinner passed in polite conversation, and when the foursome excused themselves, pleading the day's travel, the landame nodded and managed to look only mildly relieved. Timenard rose with them, his earlier good nature evidently restored by the rich red wine. He summoned servants to light them to their rooms, and wished them a cheerful good night from the bottom of the main staircase, but Rathe could feel his eyes on them as they climbed toward their rooms.

Once the servant had left, the four gathered again in Denizard's room, and Rathe prodded moodily at the dying fire. Outside the shuttered window, the wind was rising, soughing through the trees above the manor house.

"Someone's lying, in a big way," Denizard said after a moment, and b'Estorr nodded. He crossed to the window and pulled the shutters aside, staring out into the half light. The weather was breaking, Rathe saw over the other man's shoulder, the clouds were shredding to reveal patches of sky and what was left of the winter-sun's light. It was another hour or two to the second sunset, he thought, and realized with some surprise that he hadn't seen a clock in any of the rooms.

"Obviously, but they said so much, and so little, where's the exact lie?" Eslingen asked. "I don't believe the mines are played out, not the way that table was set and provisioned, not with gold about the only means of support for an estate like this—does this look like good farmland to any of you?"

"Well, one thing they're lying about," Rathe said, "is her stay at court. Or the reason for it." He got up, went to join b'Estorr at the window. "Look, I served the Judge-Advocate Foucquet when I was a boy, I've seen cases like this. There is no way either the law, or the queen, for that matter, would permit a petty Ile'nord ladyling"—his voice was savage—"to extend her rights to free land. And even if the law permitted it, Her Majesty wouldn't countenance it." He remembered standing behind Foucquet in the great hall of the Tour, watching the queen with adolescent awe. She was a tall woman anyway, and her anger at a southern noble who was seeking much the same kind of extension de Mailhac said she sought had only seemed to make her taller. Nobles, she said, could learn to live within their means, certainly within their lands. She would set no potential strife in motion by increasing holdings that had been sufficient and more than sufficient for generations. Free land was just that, and would remain so, for the use of people who farmed or herded for themselves alone, or their families.

Denizard nodded. "I agree. I doubt Her Majesty would extend de Mailhac's rights in any case, and certainly not over mining land, but I don't know how much it helps us." She looked at b'Estorr. "I don't suppose you recognized this Timenard?"

The necromancer shook his head. "I didn't see a badge, either."

"What exactly does that mean?" Eslingen asked, and b'Estorr looked at him.

"It could mean any number of things. The main one is, we can't tell what his training is—or was, since if he's making aurichalcum on this scale he's definitely stepped outside the bounds of any legitimate school. And that means we can't be sure what he's capable of."

"You know," Denizard said, slowly, "I think he was already here in the spring, when I was. He didn't wear a magist's robe then, and I didn't pay much attention to him—he certainly wasn't being introduced to the honored guests at that point. But I'm almost sure I saw him."

Eslingen grimaced. "Well, one thing's for certain, Malivai was right. It's him who calls the tune here now. It's subtle, but when it comes to it, he makes the decisions."

Rathe nodded. "And I think they were lying about not having heard about the children. She was, certainly, I'm sure she knew they were missing."

Denizard sighed. "I agree."

"I did wonder why you'd mentioned that," Eslingen said.

"I thought it would be more suspicious if we didn't," Rathe answered. "Timenard's agents must have warned him that the city was upset, common folk like me would be bound to have it on their minds, to the exclusion of more important matters.

Denizard grinned. "He does think well of himself, doesn't he? I haven't seen so many airs and graces since I was last at court myself—and I'll bet he's lower born than any of us."

Eslingen said slowly, "He's not what I was expecting, I must say. Are—do you really think he's behind all this?"

Now that it was said, Rathe was suddenly angry, and knew that the anger was masking his own uncertain fear. He swallowed hard, trying to still his instinctive response, said, "He calls the tune here, just like your messenger said. There's no gold, though there's enough money for them to live remarkably well, and de Mailhac, for one, didn't want us to go to the mine. That's enough—with everything else, that's enough for me."

"There's more than that," b'Estorr said, and turned away from the window at last. "Did you notice—did anyone see or hear a clock strike in this house since we've gotten here?"

Eslingen blinked. "Now that you mention it," he began, and in the same moment, Rathe shook his head.

"I was noticing that, actually. Why—?" He stopped then, remembering the clocks in Astreiant striking the wrong hours, too soon, too late, time and the world suddenly askew, at odds with each other. "You think he was responsible for the clock-night."

b'Estorr sighed. "I don't know if he did that. But aurichalcum is a potent metal—it's one of the few things in the world that's strong enough to affect a well-made clock. If he's mining and manipulating it in quantity, it would certainly throw off the household's timepieces. And I think it would ultimately be less suspicious to get rid of the clocks than to try to explain why they were running badly."

"There were clocks here last summer," Denizard said. "Handsome ones—an old one that had to be an heirloom, and a very nice modern case-clock up in the gallery, at least from what I saw. They weren't here this spring. I thought she'd just sold them for the money, but now . . ."

"What in Dis's name can he want with that much aurichalcum?" b'Estorr muttered, and no one answered.

After a moment, Rathe said, "I suppose our next step is to go to the mine, see if the kids are there."

"What we need to do," b'Estorr said, and kicked the edge of the hearth, "is to put paid to his plans, whatever they are. And the one sure way to do that is to pollute the mine."

Rathe looked at him. "I may not want to know this, but how do we do that?"

b'Estorr took a breath. "Oh, it's fairly easy. The mere presence of adults—worldly wise, probably inappropriately born—in the mine itself will taint the gold and spoil the whole process." There was a small silence, the fire hissing in the grate. Rathe stared at the coals, trying to imagine getting into a mine without being seen.

"What about the children?" he said aloud, and b'Estorr gave him an unhappy glance.

"If Timenard is mining aurichalcum, creating it in this kind of quantity—he's put his hands on a source of power that frightens me. It's the kind of power, at least in potential, that moves mountains, and I mean that literally. You saw what it was like at Wicked's, and his power will only have increased from then. The children are less important than stopping whatever it is he's doing, Nico. I'm sorry, but it's true."

Rathe shook his head, wanting to deny the other's words, but stopped by the note in the necromancer's voice, by his own memories. "We can't just leave them," he said, and Eslingen cleared his throat.

"We can't make any real plans until we know what conditions are like at the mine. We might be able to pollute it and get the children free at the same time."

b'Estorr said quietly, "Of course, the only problem then is that getting out of Mailhac, with or without eighty-five children, may be rather difficult."

"Are magists always given to understatement?" Eslingen asked.

Rathe shook his head. "Well, but something like this is what we have the sur's warrant for. We use it. We send for Coindarel's regiment."

"To, basically, attack an Ile'nord holding? Will he come?" Denizard asked, and Eslingen smiled, spoke before Rathe could reply.

"I think I can send a message with the warrant that will bring him. Coindarel has, I think, probably more quarterings than maseigne here."

"If you can, Philip," Rathe began, and Eslingen help up a hand.

"I can."

"So we're agreed, then," Rathe said, and looked at b'Estorr. "If we send for Coindarel now, we'll have—what, three, maybe four hours to do what we have to before he can get here with his troop. That should give you time to do what you need to do with the mine, and at the same time, give us a chance to get the kids into some temporary shelter."

b'Estorr nodded. "I think it will work. Assuming Coindarel comes."

"Oh, he will," Eslingen said.

Denizard handed him her writing kit, and Eslingen seated himself by the fire, balancing the wooden case on his lap. He wrote quickly, the pen scratching across the paper, and Rathe wondered just what he could say that would guarantee the prince-marshal's arrival. Eslingen had served with Coindarel, the pointsman told himself firmly. He would know what to say.

"Finished," Eslingen said at last, and folded the paper firmly, adding a blob of wax to seal it.

"I can send it with one of my people," Denizard said, and Rathe intercepted the note before she could take it.

"I'd better take it. I'm the caravan-master, remember? Who else would go check on the horses?"

He made his way down the side stairs and out into the courtyard, shadowed now as the winter-sun dropped toward the roof. The main gate was still open, he saw, but a pair of sturdy-looking men in half armor lounged against the inside arch of the gate. They looked lazy enough at the moment, but their back-and-breasts were well polished, swords and half-pikes ready for use, and Rathe nodded in their direction, hoping they would assume he was simply checking on the horses. No one challenged him, and he drew a sigh of relief as he ducked into the stable door. He stood for a moment in the sudden dark, the smell of hay and horses strong in his nose, and a voice said softly, "Rathe?"

He turned toward the speaker, and saw the taller of the two grooms standing in the door of one of the stalls. "Grevin."

The man stepped back, beckoning. "Over here. But keep your voice down, sir, the hostlers sleep in the hayloft."

Rathe nodded, and came to join them in the narrow space. They had made themselves a bed in the hay, he saw, and felt a brief pang of guilt that they wouldn't get to use it. "We need to get a message to Coindarel, at Anedelle, as quickly as possible. There are guards on the gate, though—"

"Not a problem," the other groom said with a grin that showed white in the darkness. "There's something very strange going on here, and the people don't like it. There's a back door that no one's ever bothered to show this magist of hers."

"Where?" Rathe demanded.

"By the kitchen," the groom answered. "It's right there, they say, but the magist doesn't concern himself with the servants' quarters."

And a good thing, too, Rathe thought. "Then the guards are his?" he asked, and Ytier nodded.

"That's what they say. I can't say I'm sorry to be leaving, all things considered."

"We won't be able to take the horses, though," Grevin said.

Ytier shrugged. "We can get mounts at any of the houses along here, if we pay enough. I know these people."

Rathe reached into his pocket, came up with the letter and his purse, and handed them both across. Ytier took them, weighing the purse briefly in his palm, and nodded.

"That should be enough. Even if it isn't, we can walk to Anedelle in a couple of hours."

"Good enough," Rathe said, and hoped it would be so. "Good luck," he added, and let himself back out into the courtyard.

Rathe crossed the courtyard again, acutely aware of the guards still lounging by the gate, but suppressed the desire to wave to them. Instead he went back into the hall and slipped quietly up the main stairway. As he reached the top, he heard footsteps, then voices, de Mailhac's and then the magist's, and dodged instinctively into the first doorway he saw. Caravan-master or not, he had no real desire to explain what he was doing out of his room at this hour, especially after he'd claimed the same exhaustion as the others. He found himself in a long room that smelled faintly of cold ash, and stood for a moment, head tilted to one side, as his eyes adjusted to the darkness. He could hear the footsteps, closer now, and then de Mailhac's voice, rising querulously as she approached the door.

"—I don't like this, not right now. They could spoil everything."

"I told you, and I'm telling you again, this means nothing." Timenard's voice was sharper than it had been at dinner, held more authority. It was also coming closer to the door, and Rathe glanced around the room, looking for a hiding place. Tapestries covered the wall to his left, and he put out his hand, testing the space between them and the wall itself. Not much, but maybe enough to hide him, he thought, and took a cautious step toward them, groping for the edge of the heavy fabric. He found it, and in the same moment felt the tapestry sway inward under his hand. There was a niche in the wall, one of the guard posts one still found in the oldest houses, and he slipped into it, letting the tapestry fall back into place over him.

"It's too late," Timenard went on. "Our plans are too far advanced—pull yourself together, maseigne, there's nothing they can do to stop us."

"I wish I were as confident as you," de Mailhac said, her voice suddenly louder. Rathe saw light through the gap between the tapestry and the wall, the wavering pallor of a single candle, and held his breath. The light dimmed, moving past him, and he heard the distinct double click as a latch snapped open.

"You should be," Timenard said. "You can be."

"But what are we going to do about them?" de Mailhac demanded, her voice fading again. Rathe tipped his head to one side, not daring to shift the tapestries, but didn't heard the latch close again. De Mailhac's voice came again, a little muffled, but still too close for comfort. "They are dangerous, Timenard."

"I don't deny it," the magist answered. His voice sounded closer, and Rathe grimaced, flattening his back against the stones of the wall. From the sound of it, Timenard was still in the room—standing in a doorway, maybe, Rathe thought, and that meant he himself was stuck behind the tapestries for a while longer. "And they will be dealt with, maseigne. Leave that to me. But now—"

"The list," de Mailhac interrupted him, her voice sounding less muffled, and Rathe heard the latch click closed again.

"List?" Timenard echoed, sounding startled.

"The list you wanted," de Mailhac answered. "You did say you wanted it?"

"Oh, yes," the magist said, and Rathe thought there was a fractional hesitation in the round man's voice, as though he'd forgotten ever mentioning a list. And don't I wish I could get a look at it myself, Rathe thought, but didn't move a muscle behind the concealing weight of the fabric. He saw the light swell again, caught a brief glimpse of the pinpoint of flame and the shadows of the two, tall and small, and then their footsteps had passed him, were receding down the long hall. Rathe allowed himself a deep breath, but didn't move immediately, listening for any sign of their return. There was nothing but silence; he counted to a hundred and then to a hundred again without hearing anything more.

He lifted the tapestry aside, stepped back out into the narrow room. It was as dark as before, and empty, but he hesitated, looking for the second door, the one he had heard open and close. There was no sign of it, just the main door, half open to the hall, and the blank paneled walls. Carved paneled walls, he corrected himself, and his interest sharpened. In Astreiant, carvings like that could hide any number of doors and compartments, and in spite of the situation, he couldn't repress a grin, remembering one of Mikael's friends, drunk and earnest, explaining how he'd found some rich merchant's private strongroom behind a similar set of carvings. His eyes were adjusted to the dark by now, and he could make out the pattern, a vine heavy with fruit. Experimentally, he ran his hand along the carved stem, counting clustered grapes, and jammed his thumb painfully against an iron loop like a trigger. He put his thumb in his mouth and used his other hand to work the latch, wincing at the noise.

The door opened onto what seemed to be a small workroom lit only by the winter-sun's light that seeped in through the gap in the shutters. It was enough to show the worktable and chair and the massive cases that held the estate's account books. They were locked, and he spared them only a single regretful glance, concentrating instead on the handful of papers scattered across the table top. He picked them up one by one, held them to the light to decipher the stilted handwriting—de Mailhac's? he wondered. The notes were unsigned, were little more than drafts for the account books or for a more complete letter, but enough of the names were familiar to let him make sort of sense of the whole. There were only a dozen names, or so it seemed, and he recognized four of them as Astreiant printers, and one other—the one who had received the largest amounts—as a woman who had a reputation as political agent in the city. The last sheet was a broadsheet, much creased, with a woodcut of the Starsmith hanging over a mountain and contorted verses that argued for a northern candidate for the succession. Rathe frowned at that—there were three northern candidates, Marselion, Sensaire, and Belvis—and only then realized that the first letters of each line spelled out Belvis's name. He made a face, and set the sheet back in its place. From the look of things, de Mailhac was definitely supporting Belvis's candidacy with money and more; he wondered, closing the door gently again behind him, if the palatine had any idea the lengths to which her supporters would go.

The hall seemed quiet now, the servants busy belowstairs, de Mailhac and Timenard long gone, and he slipped back into the main hallway. He made his way back to Denizard's room without encountering anyone, and tapped gently on the door. It opened at once, and Eslingen looked out at him, frown easing to a sudden grin.

"You took your time," he said, and Rathe stepped past him, closing the door behind them both.

"Problems?" Denizard asked, and the pointsman shook his head.

"No. The message is sent and I've got us a way out of the hall. But I had a chance to do a little snooping on my way back, and I think I know some of what's going on." Quickly, he explained what had happened, describing the papers he'd found. When he'd finished, Eslingen lifted an eyebrow.

"One could almost feel sorry for Maseigne de Belvis. Whether or not she knows what's going on, she'll lose any chance at the throne when this comes out."

b'Estorr shook his head. "It doesn't make sense. You don't go to all this trouble, manufacture aurichalcum illegally—Dis, steal eighty-five children in order to manufacture aurichalcum—for political gain. It would be like taking a caliver to a gnat."

"I saw the papers," Rathe said. "And I know those names, the printers, and I saw one of the sheets. That's part of it, Istre."

"De Mailhac's part, anyway," Denizard said, and the others looked at her. "De Mailhac is an Orsandi, they're related to Belvis by marriage, it would make sense for her to support that candidacy. It's a nasty thought, but suppose Timenard's duped her, too?"

"How do you mean?" Rathe said after a moment, not liking the sound of it.

"Suppose he has told her that whatever he's doing is for Belvis, to help Belvis, but that's just a cover?" Denizard shook her head. "I can't think of anything else that would make sense. Istre's right, aurichalcum's too potent to waste on mere politics, but I trust Nico's knowledge of Astreianter printers." A fleeting grin crossed her face. "I know to my cost it's encyclopedic."

"But if aurichalcum is queen's gold," Eslingen said slowly, "if it's linked to the monarch, why wouldn't you use it if you wanted to influence the succession?"

"It's too powerful," b'Estorr said again, and Denizard nodded.

"There are better, less dangerous ways to affect even a royal decision," she said. "With fewer chances of it blowing up in your face."

Eslingen nodded. "Which brings me to another thought, then, Aice. Is there any chance of us convincing maseigne she's been duped, and getting her—and more to the point, her household and presumably her guards—on our side?"

"I doubt she'd listen," Denizard said with regret. "She doesn't much like me—too common for her taste—and I don't have any real evidence. We don't even know what Timenard is really doing."

"Besides," Rathe said, "the guards are his."

"Lovely," Eslingen said. "So we're back to the original plan?"

Rathe nodded. "So now we wait for second sundown."

The brilliant diamond of the winter-sun was already below the edge of the trees, glinting through the gaps in the leaves. They watched in silence as it sank further, vanishing at last behind the shoulder of the hill. When it was well down, the four slipped down the stairs. As the grooms had said, the back door was easy enough to find, a small door at the end of a hall that led past the kitchen. It looked as though it would lead to a storeroom, and Rathe braced himself for disappointment as he tugged on the latch. It opened smoothly, without creaking, and a breath of damp air came in with it, bringing the smell of a midden. Rathe made a face, and stepped out into a narrow paved courtyard that was obviously used to store the kitchen's leavings. The iron gate at its end was open, and there were no guards in sight. He allowed himself a sigh of relief—for the first time, it seemed the stars might be favorable—and they went on out into the deepening night.

The wind was still strong, tearing the clouds of the day apart to let through bits of starlight. Rathe stopped, confused by the dark and the sighing trees, and Denizard pushed past him, a dark lantern ready in her hand.

"This way," she said, and the others followed.

She led them cautiously around the manor house, following some path that Rathe couldn't see, and brought them out at last beside a small stream. Now, at the height of the summer, it was more sound than water, the stream itself perhaps a foot wide, clattering over the rocks at the center of its bed, but Denizard's lantern showed higher banks where the spring floods had carved a deeper channel. Beyond the far bank, a path led uphill following the course of the stream, barely wide enough for a man and a pack pony to walk abreast. It rose steeply, without much regard for travellers' footing on the rocky ground, and Rathe heard Eslingen swear under his breath. Denizard heard him, too, and gave a grim smile.

"It's all uphill from here," she said, and the soldier swore again.

"How far?" Rathe asked, adjusting the sword he'd borrowed from b'Estorr, and the woman shrugged.

"According to the deed to the estate, a couple of miles, but it's always felt further to me. The road gets better about half a mile up—this is the path they use to bring the gold down, they don't want it to seem easy to strangers."

Rathe sighed at that and glanced up, wishing that the trees didn't cut off so much of the starlight. The waning moon was no help at all, had already set, and Denizard's dark lantern did little more than add to the darkness. Rathe looked away from it deliberately, stretching his eyes as though that would help him find his night sight more quickly somehow, and followed the others up the stony path. As Denizard had promised, it got easier as they climbed higher, widening until two horses could walk abreast, but even so it took most of their concentration to keep from slipping on the rocky track. It was well over an hour later when Eslingen, walking a little ahead of the others, stopped and held out a hand.

Denizard shuttered her lantern instantly. "What is it?" she murmured, her voice barely a breath above a whisper, and Eslingen waved her toward the woods.

"Guardpost," he murmured. "Only a couple of men, so it's not the real thing yet."

"Probably here to catch any of the children who try to make a run for it," Rathe whispered, and ducked behind b'Estorr into the shadow of a bush. He could see movement now, darker shadows among the trees, and then, as one turned, he saw the spark of a lit slow match bobbing at chest height. He held his breath, seeing that, fought the urge to duck, and the spark moved away again, vanished as the guard turned back to his post.

"Probably," Eslingen agreed, "but we can't afford a fight at this stage. We'll have to go around."

Denizard made a sound that might have been a sigh. "This way."

She led them up the slope to her left, climbing cautiously through the trees and rock until they could pass the guards unseen and unheard. The guards' interest seemed to be focussed on the mine; they stood facing uphill, turning only occasionally to glance back down the road toward Mailhac. They had a brazier with them, and a lantern, Rathe saw, and hoped it had ruined their night vision.

Even after they had passed the guardpost, Denizard did not return to the road but led them along the slope parallel to it, her boots silent in the thick carpet of dead leaves and debris. It was quiet enough, Rathe thought, following more cautiously, but the same soft cover hid all but the largest rocks and was dangerously slick in places, making the footing treacherous. He slipped once, and swore silently, pain shooting up from a wrenched toe, but that eased almost at once and he allowed himself a soft sigh of relief. All they would need now was for someone to get hurt.

Ahead, a light showed between the trees, a cool, diffuse light, and Eslingen stopped, tilting his head to one side. "Mage-fire?" he asked, his voice barely above a whisper, and b'Estorr nodded.

"I would say so. They'll have to work all hours to take advantage of the proper stars, and there's no better way to light this large a space."

"This way," Denizard said, and pointed to her left again. She led them further up the slope where the trees and brush were thicker, crouched at last behind a cluster of rocks and screening bushes. Rathe copied her, then reached aside to part the branches, staring down at the mine. It lay in a hollow, long since cleared, filled with the cool, shadowless light of the mage-fire like sunlight through fog. If anything, the area seemed surprisingly ordinary, the long run of the sluice lying crooked across the yard, the stone storehouse with its iron-bound door, the scattering of wooden shacks that must hold tools—ordinary indeed, Rathe thought, except for the children. A gang of twenty or more stood at the long table at the mouth of the sluice, picking listlessly through the rubble that covered its surface. Behind them, the mine entrance loomed, an empty hole framed with heavy timbers. The mage-light didn't penetrate its darkness, and Rathe suppressed a shiver at the sight, made himself look more carefully at the yard. There were more guards, of course, a trio—all armed with calivers and swords, though no armor—keeping a close eye on the laboring children, and at least five more scattered across the yard, two by the storehouse, the other three on the hillside to the right of the mine. He shook his head, watching the children work, their movements slow and uncoordinated.

"Why make them work at such an hour?" he asked.

"Taking advantage of a favorable conjunction," Denizard answered, almost absently, and Rathe nodded. He had known the answer, or could have guessed it, but he was glad to hear another voice.

b'Estorr reached for his pocket orrery, looked up to the sky to find the clock-stars among the scudding clouds, then held the little engine so that its rings were lit by the reflected glow of the mage-fire. He twisted one of the inner rings, and frowned as the metal refused to move. Denizard frowned, too, and b'Estorr pressed harder. This time, the orrery turned easily, and he checked the settings.

"Trouble?" Denizard asked, and b'Estorr glanced at her.

"It may just need oiling."

Denizard lifted an eyebrow at that, and b'Estorr sighed. "Or there's enough aurichalcum down there to affect it. But whatever it is, that conjunction is ending—it has to be within a degree or two to be effective. So the children should be let off any minute."

Eslingen nudged Rathe. "Look." He pointed to one of the guards, who had set down his caliver and was consulting a battered-looking almanac. A moment later, the man put a whistle to his lips, the shrill sound seeming to make the mage-fire shiver, and the children stopped what they were doing. One, too slow, too tired, kept going, pulling a chunk of rock from the table, and the closest guard cuffed him, hard, then tossed the rock away. Together he and the others began herding the children back toward the stone storehouse—which had to be the stronghouse for the mine, Rathe realized. What safer place to keep the children than in a place meant to be locked and defended? And how in the name of all the gods are we ever going to get them out of there? he thought. Or, for that matter, how are we going to get into the mine?

Eslingen seemed to have the same thought, and turned to look at the magists. "You expect to get in there?"

b'Estorr nodded. "We have to. It's the only way to be sure."

Eslingen slid back down, to sit on the dirt with his back against a rock, and Rathe saw the glint of white as he rolled his eyes. "The madness of magists," he muttered, and took a breath. "Right, then, I'll have to clear you a way, won't I?" He started to get to his feet, but Rathe put a hand on his arm.

"What did you have in mind?"

"Cause a distraction—draw off the guards and keep them busy while the magists do their work." Eslingen glanced around the rocky ground. "There's plenty of cover, and we've got four pistols between us. We should be able to hold them."

Rathe shook his head. "If you want to do that, and I think it will work, we have to free the kids first. Otherwise they can use them against us." He squinted through the trees toward the storehouse. The children had vanished inside, and now the guards were taking up their positions outside the door—only two of them, Rathe saw, but that was enough. "A distraction would be nice for that, too."

"We could probably provide that," Denizard said, and b'Estorr showed teeth in an angry smile.

"I'd like nothing better."

"Can the two of you handle the mine yourselves?" Rathe asked.

"Oh, yes," Denizard said. "Polluting the mine is really quite simple—I'm sure that's why the guards aren't at the entrance itself."

"It's just getting away from it that might be difficult," Eslingen muttered. He shook his head. "This is getting complicated."

"I don't think we have any alternative," Rathe answered. He looked at the magists. "All right. Give us time to get into position, and then—make noise or something. Draw off the guards. We'll release the kids, and then return the favor."

"Freeing the children will probably be a good enough distraction in itself," Eslingen said, and grimaced at Rathe's glare. "Well, it will be. And they have every incentive not to hurt them, which is more than I can say for us."

b'Estorr nodded. "As soon as we see the children leave, we'll head for the mine."

They were right, Rathe admitted, much as he hated the idea, and nodded shortly. "All right," he said again. "Let's go."

They made their way along the side of the hill, careful to stay well back in the shadow of the trees. The glow of the mage-fire was both a help and a hindrance, enough to light their way but deceptive in the lack of shadows. It seemed to take forever to reach the slope overlooking the stronghouse, and almost as long again to work their way cautiously down to the edge of the clearing. Rathe was sweating freely, certain that they had taken took long and that the magists would act before they were ready, but made himself stay behind Eslingen, matching the soldier's pace. At last, they reached the edge of the trees and stood peering out at the building.

"Two guards on the door," Eslingen said, his voice a mere breath of sound. "But the others have a clear view, damn it."

Rathe nodded, the weight of the pistol awkward in his belt. At least it was a flintlock, not the matchlocks the guards were carrying, but he wished he had more than one. He jumped as a crack like breaking wood sounded from the other side of the yard, and then realized that the magists were finally moving. The sound was repeated closer in, and the guards started toward it, leaping the stream and heading up the slope.

"There he goes," Eslingen said softly, and Rathe saw one of the two guards from the stronghouse move to join the others.

"I suppose it was too much to hope they'd both go," he muttered, and saw Eslingen smile.

"Be grateful for small favors," he said, and darted forward, pistol raised. He dropped the remaining guard with a single blow and dragged the unconscious figure out of sight while Rathe surveyed the building. There was only a single lock on the door, but it was a heavy one, and he didn't dare risk the noise trying to shoot it off. He took a step back, peering up into the darkness. There were, of course, no windows—why should there be, in a building designed to keep gold safe?—and he swore softly. Eslingen stepped up beside him, leveling the musket he'd taken from the guard, but Rathe pushed the barrel aside.

"I don't see that we have any choice," Eslingen said.

Rathe shook his head. "Oh, yes, we do. Keep an eye out, would you?" The soldier turned obediently to face the yard, shouldering the musket. Rathe pulled a small knife from his sleeve and set to work on the mechanics of the lock. It was not, he saw with considerable relief, a mage lock, and why should it be? Trouble was the last thing Timenard was expecting, his plan had been almost perfect. Not, Rathe thought, propitiatingly, that he had grown careless, or that Rathe thought him a fool. But the lock was a fairly straightforward affair for one born and bred in Astreiant's southriver. He felt the mechanism give, gave a small grunt of satisfaction, and wrenched the lock from the door. Eslingen gave him a slightly incredulous look.

"Did you learn that before or after you became a pointsman?" he asked. Rathe just bared his teeth at him, and plunged into the darkness. With a small sigh, Eslingen followed, striking a flint and lighting one of the lamps along the wall. There were three barred doors off the little entrance way, two to the right, a single one to the left, each with a grilled opening in the center. Rathe tapped quietly at one of the right-hand doors. There was no response from behind it, but there was a small scurry of noise from behind its neighbor. Then a face appeared in the small, barred window: Asheri. Rathe let his eyes flicker closed for an instant, then moved to investigate the lock.

She looked surprised when she saw Rathe, and then relieved. "I thought it would have to be you, Nico."

"I'm glad you had faith in me, Asheri love. Are the boys in the other room?" Rathe asked. This lock was more complex, better built than the one on the main door, and he could feel the knife point slipping on its works without making contact.

"Yes." She stuck her hand out the window, pointed to the door across the corridor. "Though why they think they have to separate us, I don't know."

"I wouldn't imagine the situation is conducive to misbehavior," Rathe agreed. "Ash, keep the other girls quiet for me while I try to get this door opened. Then get them out and away from here as quickly as you can."

"Would this help?" Eslingen said, from behind him, and held out a ring of keys. "It was hanging by the door."

Rathe took them gratefully, found the right key on the second try, and swung the door wide. The room was full of children, all girls, all in the crumpled clothes they'd worn when they'd been taken. Someone—Rathe doubted it was Timenard—had given them straw and blankets, but the improvised beds just made the room look more pathetic. They were all standing now, the largest group huddled together as though they were cold. A tall girl with dark brown hair and wearing a green dress stood near Asheri—she had to be Herisse Robion, Rathe thought, and was almost surprised to realized he had never seen her before.

"It's all right," he said aloud, and hoped he sounded soothing. "I'm from Point of Hopes, we've come to get you out of here. The doors are open and the guards are busy elsewhere. I want you to head back down the mountain—follow the stream, not the path, it'll take you to the road—as fast as you can."

Robion nodded, grabbed the nearest girl, and shoved her toward the door. "Come on, let's go."

The urgency in her voice seemed to reach even the most frightened, and they began to file out the door, slowly at first, then faster. Eslingen shook his head, looked at Rathe. "I'll cover them from the main door," he said, and turned away, the matchlock still at the ready.

Asheri said, "I'll stay with you, Nico."

Rathe shook his head, trying the next key in the lock. "No, get moving, we're not done yet." The lock snapped free at last, and he pulled open the door.

This room looked much like the other except that it was filled with boys watching warily, poised to run or attack. Asheri said, "It's all right, he's from Point of Hopes."

"Nicolas Rathe, adjunct point." It seemed foolish to introduce himself there in the darkened strongroom, but he hoped it would make them listen. "We've got the doors open. Head down the mountain as fast as you can—follow the stream, the girls are ahead of you."

"They've got guns," a voice said, and there was the sound of a slap. "Stupid. You want to stay here?"

"We've drawn off the guards," Rathe said, and hoped it would still be true. "Now, get moving. Asheri, go with them."

The boys began to move, Asheri with them, and Rathe made his way back to the doorway. He drew his pistol as the boys began to dart across the yard, heading for the downhill path and the stream, and joined Eslingen by the door.

"No sign of the guards?" he asked, and Eslingen shook his head. "Are you thinking this might have been the easy part?"

Rathe nodded, grim-faced. "I wonder how Istre and Denizard are doing."

"I haven't heard them in a while, so I guess they're at the mine." Eslingen drew back as the last boy shoved past them. "Maybe they need our help. I'm pretty impure. Do you suppose the less innocent a person is, the quicker the mine could be polluted?"

"Only one way to find out," Rathe answered, and in the same instant, heard a shout from the hillside.

"Damn kids, get them!"

Rathe swore, heard himself echoed by Eslingen. He could see the first of the guards scrambling down out of the trees clutching his musket, and lifted his own pistol, saw Eslingen level the musket he'd taken from the guard.

"Mine, I think," Eslingen said, and fired. The sound echoed in the greying darkness, bouncing off the rocky hills, and pulling the guards up short as though by a rope. They were out of range, and knew it, but the leader waved his arms, drawing his men back toward the yard.

"This is not a good spot for a pitched battle, Nico," Eslingen said, and set the now-empty musket neatly in the corner of the door.

"Even I can see that, but what choice did we have?" Rathe demanded.

"None, but now we have to think of something else."

"I'm open to suggestions," Rathe said.

"I'm glad to hear it." Eslingen said, and drew his pistol right-handed. "If we can make it to the mine itself, that'll give us some cover, and some time, right?"

"Right."

"Go." Eslingen said, drawing his sword, and he charged for the mine entrance. Rathe pounded after him, practically treading on his heels, knife in one hand, pistol in the other. He heard the snap of shots, and then the angry shout of the leader reminding his people they were out of range. Then they'd reached the entrance and plunged into the darkness. Rathe collapsed against the nearest wall, catching his breath, and peered out into the yard.

Outside, the guards stopped abruptly, unwilling to go in after them. And not unreasonably, Rathe thought, when all they have to do is wait for reinforcements. The mage-light seemed to stop a few yards in front of the entrance, casting almost no light into the mine itself. Rathe blinked, dazzled by the contrast, and wondered if there were magistical reasons to keep the mage-fire out of the mine itself. Everything felt ordinary enough, from the mud under his feet to the solid rock at his back, and he shrugged the thought away, looking at Eslingen. "Now what?" he asked, and hoped that, from all his soldiering, the other man might have some cache of ideas for handling what could rapidly become a siege situation. Before he could answer, however, both men caught sight of a light behind them, and Eslingen whirled, leveling his pistol by reflex.

"Easy," Rathe said, recognizing the footsteps. Denizard's dark lantern clicked open, throwing a fan of light across the rocky floor.

Denizard and b'Estorr stood behind the wedge of light. In the shadows, it was hard to see their expressions, but Rathe thought they looked sober, and the air teemed with the chill currents of b'Estorr's ghosts. He felt the hair on the nape of his neck rise and said, "Were you able to do anything?"

Denizard half nodded, half shrugged. "Oh, polluting the workings was no problem. But if Timenard has taken as much gold as I think he has, and if all that gold has been processed into aurichalcum . . . " She shook her head. "b'Estorr's right, it's too much just to be politics, but what in all hells would require that much gold?"

"Istre?" Rathe turned to the other magist.

"I don't know. I don't even want to hazard a guess. But whatever it is, Nico, whatever he's using it for or making with it, it will give him incredible power."

"This is all very interesting," Eslingen began from his place by the entrance, and stopped abruptly. They could all hear it now, a sudden confusion of voices and the sound of horses' hooves first on stones and the hard-packed ground of the yard, and then echoing on the bridge over the stream. Rathe swore again, and moved up to stand across the entrance from the soldier, peering cautiously out into the yard. The mage-light had changed, strengthened, was enough to throw shadows now, and Timenard, an oddly foreshortened figure on a magnificent sorrel horse, had reined in at the center of the yard, seemingly oblivious to the way the horse sidled and danced beneath him. It was truly a gorgeous creature, enough to draw Rathe's eye even under these circumstances, and he heard Eslingen give a soft whistle of admiration. The mage-light seemed to gleam from its pale coat and the brighter strands of its mane and tail, turning them to gold. Behind him, a child cried out, and then another, and half a dozen guards appeared at the head of the path, dragging four of the children. They fought back hysterically, shrieking at the tops of their lungs, but the guards dragged them inexorably over the bridge.

"Shut up," Timenard said, almost conversationally, and they were instantly silent. He had not looked back, but Rathe could feel the focus of his attention change, center on the mine and the dark entrance. He was sure Timenard couldn't see them, no one looking out from the waxing mage-light could see into that darkness, but the magist's eyes were fixed on the spot where he and Eslingen stood.

"And is this how you repay maseigne's hospitality?" Timenard went on. "We have very strict notions of correct behavior for guests here in the Ile'nord, you know. I strongly suggest you come out of there right now. Or these children will die for your rudeness." His tone had not changed in the slightest, as though he considered bad manners worthy of a capital punishment. Rathe scowled, torn between anger and a sudden deep fear, and he saw Eslingen stir.

"Oh, right," the soldier muttered, his eyes roving over the magist and the guards. "And how's he going to do that? I don't see any weapons on him, and his people have their hands full with the kids. . . . "

His voice trailed off, less confident than the words, and b'Estorr took a step forward. "He can do it," he said. "Dis Aidones, can't you feel it? He can certainly do it."

Denizard nodded, wordless, her face pale. The lantern trembled in her hand; she looked down at it, frowning, and braced her free hand against the rock of the wall.

Rathe could feel it himself now, a shifting in the air like the presence of b'Estorr's ghosts, or the tingle of an oncoming storm—and most of all like the clock-night, the unnatural, uncanny wrongness of it. He could feel the ghosts shy back from it, a cold current nipping his ankles before retreating toward the mine, and tasted dust and heat and something strangely metallic, like lightning gathering. The mage-light was stronger than ever, clustering into motes of light that swarmed like insects around Timenard and his horse, and Rathe was abruptly certain that the magist could do exactly what he'd threatened. He stepped fully into the entrance where the reflection of the light could reach him, and lifted a hand. "Timenard! Killing the children won't do you any good at this point. And you need them—"

Timenard made a dismissive gesture and the motes of light seemed to follow, a streak of pale gold in the thick air. "There are others, others more easily obtained than these. My work is too close to completion to be so easily thwarted, and I don't intend to argue with you. Come out now, all of you, or these children die. It's a simple equation."

He crooked his fingers, and the motes of light swerved and clustered, gathering around his hand. Rathe could hear a faint drone, a humming just at the edge of audibility, like the echo of a swarm of bees. "And what happens to us?" he called, struggling to find the words that might delay the magist, stave off whatever powers he called for even a moment longer. "Our deaths for theirs—I don't know—"

He broke off at the sound of hoofbeats from the Mailhac road. The guards swung, startled, and the biggest of the children wrenched himself half away before the man holding him could grab him again. Rathe swore under his breath, seeing that, and Eslingen cocked his pistol.

"It could be Coindarel," he began, and in the same instant de Mailhac and a good dozen of her household swept into the clearing. She was hardly dressed for riding, a battered traveling cloak thrown on over the silk dress she had worn to dinner, the embroidered skirt hiked awkwardly up so that she could ride astride, showing practical boots over delicate fancywork stockings.

"What in all hells have you brought down on us, magist?" she shouted. "There's a royal regiment on the Mailhac road, and the woods are full of your damned children."

Timenard ignored her, his eyes still fixed on the mine entrance, but Rathe heard the humming fade, felt the unnatural pressure ease a little. De Mailhac lifted her face to the skies, her hair tumbling unbound over her shoulders. "You stupid, ambitious bastard, you've finished us. We've lost, and all we have left is barely enough time to get away from here and over the Chadroni border."

Timenard sighed then, and swung in his saddle to face her, his voice still bizarrely calm. "Why should we flee? Why on earth should we flee? This royal regiment will arrive too late, maseigne, a week ago they would have been too late. My work is too far advanced now, they cannot keep me from its completion. Now. I'll need your men to help me rid the mine of these intruders." He turned back to the entrance, raised his voice again. "I'm reluctant to shed your blood in the mine itself, but I will do it. And I will kill these children."

De Mailhac swung herself down from her horse, skirts flying, and started across the yard toward Timenard. She carried a sword, Rathe saw, incongruous over the bright green silk, and there was a small pistol jammed into her sash. Clearly she intended to fight, and Rathe wondered if there was any way they could make use of that.

"We've lost our chance to influence the queen's choice, can't you see that?" she demanded. "We're discovered, and we've no hope of further gain—of any gain at all. Unless we flee, and now, we'll take Belvis down with us."

Timenard ignored her, lifted his hand, fingers crooked, and the air thickened again, the light coalescing into a swarm. Rathe swore under his breath, glanced wildly at the magists behind him.

"Isn't there something you can do?"

Denizard shook her head, and b'Estorr said, "I'm a necromancer, I don't even know what he's calling—"

"Timenard!" de Mailhac demanded. "We have to protect Belvis."

"Belvis is expendable," Timenard said, impatiently, as though to an importunate child. "Leave me alone, woman."

With an inarticulate cry of anger, de Mailhac drew her sword. Timenard flung his hand back, not even bothering to turn, and the swarming light shot from his fingers, struck the landame with a soundless snap. Her arm hung in the air, her whole figure tensed, frozen in mid-motion. Only her eyes still moved, burning with fury and fear. Not dead, then, Rathe thought, trying to make sense of what he'd seen, not a mortal blow after all, though who knows what it would have done to the kids—

Timenard sighed then, the motion of his shoulders obvious beneath his heavy robe, and swung himself down from his horse. As his feet touched the ground, the horse shimmered as though the air around it was warped by a furnace's heat. The strands of its mane and tail seemed to fuse, become a solid sheet, and then its neck curled down and its hind legs buckled. For a confused instant, Rathe thought it was reaching for nonexistent grass or trying to sit, but its head curled further, its neck bending impossibly until its nose was tucked under its belly. The strong outlines of its muscles were blurring, too, fading, its forelegs curling under, and its color ran like water, shifting from sorrel to true gold and then to something beyond gold, an unearthly, shadowless luster. The last ghost of the horse-shape fused and vanished, and in its place stood a set of nested spheres, impaled on a yard-long axis. Rathe shook his head, trying to deny what stood before him. He had seen the great orrery at the university, both as a boy and at the ceremony that had confirmed the true time, and he recognized the form of the thing. But where the university's orrery had been brass, solid and secure in its mechanical connections, this was delicate as filigree, the shapes of the rings and the planets outlined with a peculiar iridescence. It had to be made of aurichalcum—of pure aurichalcum, he corrected himself. Even the coin aurichalcum b'Estorr had shown him had lacked that unearthly color.

"Sweet Sofia," Denizard murmured, and made a warding gesture. b'Estorr took a step forward, towards the entrance, towards the orrery, then stopped, shaking his head. Denizard closed a hand around his arm, her fingers white-knuckled, but the necromancer didn't seem to feel her grip.

Rathe looked at them. "What is it? An orrery like that—what can it do?"

"Entirely too much," Denizard said, grimly.

b'Estorr nodded. "Something that size, with that much aurichalcum—made purely of aurichalcum . . . " He took a breath. "Instead of drawing its influence from the stars, it could, conceivably, reverse the process. Affect the stars themselves."

"It can't do that," Eslingen said, but the protest was automatic. "That's impossible."

"Not anymore," Denizard answered.

"I think we've seen it," b'Estorr said.

"The clocks?" Rathe asked, and the necromancer nodded.

"To forge something like that, something that powerful—we're lucky all it did was throw off all the clocks in Astreiant."

Timenard stooped, lifted the orrery in his gloved hands. It was huge, the largest sphere as large as his torso, but he carried it easily. The iridescence played briefly over his fingers, and faded. "You, in the mine. I hold here the power to reorder the world, to compel the stars themselves to change and to change the world with them, to bring down the powers that are now and set up new powers in their place. You yourselves are commoners all—surely you can see this can only be to your good. Who has been blamed for the disappearances of these children? Leaguers and commoners. Unfair, but the way of the world. I give you a new chance, a new choice. Come out of there and join me. I can give you a better world than the one you live in."

The words were like a spell, an almost palpable temptation. Rathe shook himself, made himself look past the magist toward the mine road and de Mailhac's people huddled in confusion. Coindarel was on his way, but even if he arrived in time, what could he do against the power of the orrery? The mage-light was fading again, replaced by the dimmer light of dawn, and against it the orrery glowed even brighter than before. Pure aurichalcum, Rathe thought, the words running through his mind like a tune he could not forget. Unpolluted by anything else, the purest form of gold.

"Come now," Timenard called again, "come out and join me."

Rathe could feel the words tugging at him, a subtle pressure against his knees, as though he stood in an invisible stream. Eslingen took a step forward, then shook himself, scowling, and took two steps back, deeper into the shadows.

"You see what I can offer you," Timenard crooned. "What I can make you. A better, more just world."

Rathe shook his head, took a step sideways and stumbled, almost tripped by the invisible current. "More just?" he called, hoping to create some delay until he, any of them, could think of something that might stop the magist. "Whose justice? Yours? And what about the law?"

"The law was set up by nobles to keep commoners like yourself in their places. Don't be a fool."

"I won't," Rathe said, but in spite of himself the current drew him forward. "I won't see a world that sets one man up over all others."

"You will have no choice," Timenard answered, and touched the orrery's outermost sphere. The air rang, as though with the aftereffects of music, though there had been no sound. Rathe took another step, and was suddenly aware of the pistol in his hand. It was loaded, and the ball was lead, he thought, lead which was the antithesis of gold to begin with, and which had been sitting in contact with the impure compound of gunpowder. He lifted it, bracing himself against the invisible current of Timenard's will, and took careful aim, not at the magist but at the orrery itself. He held his breath, and pulled the trigger. The priming powder caught, and then, half a heartbeat later, the pistol fired, the sound shockingly loud, shockingly profane, in the close air. The orrery seemed to sob aloud, a weirdly soundless groan that shook the ground under their feet. Rathe stumbled forward, going to his knees in the muddy ground. Behind him Eslingen cursed and leveled his own pistol, bracing himself against the nearest timber.

"Timenard—"

Behind him, b'Estorr cried, "No, don't, the gold's unstable."

Eslingen hesitated, and in the same moment they saw de Mailhac shake herself, as though the noise, the attack on the orrery, had freed her from her trance. She lunged blindly forward, continuing the move she had begun minutes before. Timenard tried to turn away, his eyes suddenly wide, mouth opening in the beginning of a horrified shout. Her sword pierced the orrery's spheres, dissolving as it thrust, and the orrery screamed again, a wail of tortured metal. And then de Mailhac's bare hand touched the axis. Timenard cried out then, his voice lost in the sudden yelling, and fire flashed beneath de Mailhac's hand. Light surged with it, so that for a moment the two stood locked, their shadows and the orrery's black at the heart of a ball of fire hotter than any furnace. The smoke came then, crashing back over the ball of light like an ocean wave, and then it, too, was gone. Where it had been, where Timenard and de Mailhac had been, there was nothing except pale ash and a handful of dull, twisted wires.

There was a moment of utter silence, even the children too stunned to cry out. Rathe's ears were ringing, and he could see the same shock on Eslingen's face, pale beneath the dark hair. The magelight was fading fast now, overtaken by the paler light of dawn, and Rathe shook himself hard.

"Give me your pistol," he said to Eslingen, but it was b'Estorr who handed him a weapon. Rathe cocked it quickly and stepped out into the yard, leveling the pistol at the nearest guard. Eslingen moved up to join him, his own pistol drawn, and the magists followed.

"Stand away from the children," Rathe ordered, and was glad to hear that his own voice was relatively calm. De Mailhac's people were still in shock, he saw, some already looking behind them toward the road; the guard leader glanced at them, and then at the spot where Timenard had stood. Rathe could see the indecision on his face, and pointed the pistol directly at him.

"Stand away," he said again. "Put down your arms, all of you, or I will fire."

Before the man could respond, hoofbeats sounded again on the track from Mailhac. Rathe heard Eslingen laugh softly, and one of de Mailhac's servants tugged injudiciously at her horse's reins, making the animal snort and sidle. Almost in the same instant, the first of Coindarel's regiment swept into view, the prince-marshal himself narrowly in the lead. Timenard's guard leader looked over his shoulder, his expression unchanging, but slowly lowered his musket. His men copied him, stepping away from the children they had been holding. Coindarel gestured to his men, who fanned out, surrounding both the mine guards and de Mailhac's party, and a white-haired sergeant swung down off his horse, holding out his hands to the children. There was another small figure at Coindarel's saddle-bow, Rathe saw, and an instant later realized it was Asheri. He allowed himself a long breath of relief, and Coindarel edged his horse up to the mine, half bowing in the saddle.

"My Philip, I never expected to see you under these circumstances," he said.

He had to be curious about the explosion, Rathe thought, but wasn't about to ask any commoner directly. He stilled a laugh, recognizing the hysteria in it.

"Nor are these circumstances I ever expected to see," Eslingen answered, and carefully uncocked his pistol before jamming it into his belt. "You made good time, sir."

"How could I resist your appeal?" Coindarel asked. He was as handsome as a prince-marshal should be, Rathe thought, if somewhat older. He realized that the other was looking at him then, and shook himself back to reality.

"You're the pointsman, I assume?" Coindarel went on. "Which makes you—unofficially, to be sure—responsible for these brats."

Rathe nodded, too relieved to be offended. They were going to be all right, he thought, the children were found, and they were going to come safe home at last.

"These can't be all of them, surely?" Coindarel stood in his stirrups, turning to survey the half dozen or so in the mine yard. A few more children were creeping out from among the trees. Rathe saw, and braced himself to the task of finding the rest. At least Asheri was safe, he thought, and was instantly ashamed.

"No. We—I sent the rest into the forest, down towards Mailhac. They've probably scattered, I told them to follow the stream, but we're going to have to find them, get them back to Astreiant. . . . "

"You don't have to do anything, pointsman," Coindarel said. "That's what we're here for." He looked around the yard again, and touched heels to his horse, sending it dancing sideways toward the pile of ash where the magist had stood. "But we seem to be missing someone, by all accounts. Where's Maseigne de Mailhac—or her pet magist, for that matter?"

Before Rathe could answer. Coindarel's horse shied, bounced sideways on bunched feet, away from the ashes. Coindarel swore, one arm instantly steadying Asheri, and brought the animal back under control with an effort. Rathe pointed to the pile of ash, the wires that had been the orrery just visible beneath it. "That's what's left of them," he said, and Coindarel lifted his head, eyes wide, looking suddenly like one of his own horses.

"I'm not at all sure I really want to know," he said at last. "At least, not yet. Not until we've found the children, maybe not until we're back in Astreiant."

Rathe shook his head. "No, Prince-marshal," he said. "You don't want to know."

Coindarel lifted an eyebrow, but visibly thought better of it. He wheeled his horse again and trotted back toward the rest of his troop, just coming into sight at the head of the path. There were more children with them, a good dozen, and Rathe allowed himself a long sigh. Coindarel's men would find them, the children would come to them, and everything would be all right. The sun was rising at last, a breeze rising with it, and the ashes stirred, releasing an odd, acrid smell, hot metal and something more. Rathe winced then, thinking of untimely deaths, and turned to b'Estorr.

"I know this was just. But I also know what Timenard was." He looked back at the pile of ash, the dull wires half buried in it. "And I don't want anyone troubled by his ghost."

"I can do that," b'Estorr answered, and Rathe nodded.

"Then, please. Do it." It was his right, as a pointsman and a servant of the judiciary, to ask that, or it would be if they had been in Astreiant and Timenard had died on the gallows. Rathe shook the doubt away. He had told the truth: Timenard's death had been deserved, and de Mailhac's with it; if nothing else, treason was a capital crime, and madness like Timenard's was worse than treason. He nodded again, and b'Estorr nodded back.

"You're right," he said, and reached into the pocket of his coat, bringing out his own orrery. The metal was tarnished, as though it, too, had been through the fire, and he blinked, startled.

"Mine, too," Denizard said, and held up a smaller, double-ringed disk. "Gods, if that—device—of his was powerful enough to do that just in its destruction . . . "

"Then Nico's right, and the ghost ought to be laid, for good and for all," Eslingen said.

"I agree," b'Estorr said, absently, adjusting the rings of his orrery. They moved smoothly now, Rathe saw, and shivered, remembering their earlier stubbornness. The necromancer checked the settings a final time, then unfastened his swordbelt, and used the scabbarded blade to draw a circle around the remains of the fire.

"Let me help," Denizard said, and b'Estorr nodded.

"If you'd set the wards?"

Denizard nodded back, and crouched to begin sketching symbols along the outside of the circle. b'Estorr reached past her, drew more symbols inside the circle, murmuring to himself in a language Rathe didn't recognize. He drew two more sets of symbols, consulting his orrery each time, and then looked down at Denizard.

"Ready?"

"Done," Denizard answered, and drew a final symbol in the dirt outside the circle. Rathe felt something give, as though the air itself had collapsed, leaving a space that was somehow outside proper time and space, and b'Estorr reached calmly into the center of the circle, inscribed a final symbol in the air above the pile of ash. There was a flash of light, gone almost before Rathe was sure he'd seen it, and the feeling of dislocation was gone with it.

"Seidos's Horse," Eslingen said, under his breath, and Rathe nodded.

b'Estorr slipped his orrery back into his pocket and held out a hand to help Denizard to her feet. "That's bound them, not that there was likely to be much left to trouble anyone. Power like that is called soul-destroying for a reason."

"Thanks," Rathe said, and wished he could think of something more.

"Mind you," b'Estorr went on, "if they want to use the mine again—whoever de Mailhac's heirs are, they're unlikely to turn down gold—I'd suggest putting up something a little more solid to mark the spot, otherwise it'll drive the horses crazy." He seemed to realize he was babbling, and stopped abruptly, shaking his head. Rathe touched his arm in sympathy, and looked back across the yard to where Coindarel and his men were still gathering the children. There were two more of them on the hill above, he realized, a boy and a girl, and he lifted his hand to wave them down. They saw the gesture, and started toward the others, and a third stepped from behind a tree, picking her way carefully over the stones after them. That must be close to half of them, Rathe thought, and all of them safe and sound, frightened, certainly, but unhurt. That was a better result than he had thought possible even a week ago, and he felt unexpected tears welling in his eyes. He blinked hard, impatient with himself, and Eslingen laid a hand on his shoulder.

"Seidos's Horse, we did it." He looked more closely then, and the cheerful voice softened. "You can take them home now, Nico."

Rathe smiled. "Well, Coindarel can," he said. "They're going home, that's the main thing." And that, he thought, was more than enough for any man.

Epilogue

It was a slow journey back to Astreiant, despite the wagons Coindarel commandeered from every farmstead he passed, but the news ran fast ahead of them. By the time they topped the last long hill that led down to the city, the steep slate roofs rising like a stone forest from the paler stones of the houses, the royal residence sitting on its artificial hill to the north as though it floated above the ordinary world, they could see the crowds gathering along the Horsegate Road. The first parents had already reached them, reclaiming their children with shouts and tears of joy. Coindarel slowed his troop to a walk and gave up all pretense at discipline by the time they'd reached the outlying houses. Rathe, riding with the first wagon, was buffeted by the crowds, women and men thrusting flowers toward him and shouting inaudible thanks, clutching at boots and stirrup leathers as though they couldn't otherwise be sure it was all real. They grabbed at the wagons, too, and a couple of Coindarel's sergeants moved cautiously to block them so that the horses could keep moving.

Rathe heard a shriek from the nearest wagon, turned sharply, his fear turning to relief as he saw Herisse Robion, her green suit sadly battered now, leaning over the wagon's side to wave to someone in the crowd. Rathe turned to look, and saw the butcher Mailet, and with him Trijntje Ollre, tears streaming down her face.

"Trijntje!" Herisse cried again, and Rathe touched heels to his horse, edging it through the crowd.

"Need help?" he asked, and the girl turned to him.

"Oh, let me down, make them stop, please, it's Trijntje, and Master Mailet, and everybody—"

Rathe glanced at the wagoner, who shook his head. "I'm sorry, sir, if I stop for her, I'll have to stop for all of them, and we'll never get them home."

He was right, Rathe knew, but the expression on Herisse's face was too much for him. The wagon wasn't moving very fast, barely at a walk, and he brought his horse alongside, matching the pace easily.

"Here," he said, and held out his arm. She scrambled over the wagon's side, skirt hiked awkwardly, and he caught her around the waist, dragging her half across his saddle-bow. She clung to him, and he swung the horse in the same moment, depositing her gracelessly but unbruised at Mailet's feet. The big man grabbed her by the shoulders, pulling her into a rough embrace, and then Trijntje called her name, and the two girls hung sobbing and laughing in each other's arms. Mailet shook his head, his own expression fond, and looked up at Rathe.

"I'm in your debt, Adjunct Point."

Rathe shook his head. "It's my job, Master Mailet—"

"And I'm still in your debt," Mailet answered, the choler already returning to his face, chin and lower lip jutting dangerously. "I insist."

Rathe laughed then, suddenly, and for the first time in weeks, genuinely happy. "Have it your way, master," he said, and nudged his horse forward.

At his side, Eslingen laughed, too. "You can't seem to get on with that one, Nico."

Rathe grinned. "I'd like to see his stars," he began, and saw a hand wave from the crowd. Devynck stood there, Adriana at her side, and he looked back to see Eslingen's smile widen to delight.

"Adriana, Sergeant," he called, and swung down off his horse, looping the rein over his wrist.

"You'll miss the celebration at the Pantheon," Rathe said, and the other man looked up at him.

"Oh, that's for Coindarel, you know that. Besides, I've been wanting to see them again." He started toward the two women without waiting for an answer, tugging the horse along with him.

Rathe shook his head—Eslingen was right, of course, the prince-marshal would take the credit, or, more precisely, would be given most of the credit, but he couldn't bring himself to care too deeply.

"Nico?" It was Asheri's voice, from the second wagon, and Rathe turned, brought his horse alongside her.

"Yes? I haven't seen Mijan yet, if that's what you wanted."

"And you won't, either," Asheri answered. "She'd never come to something like this, she's too sure the worst will have happened."

She sounded impatient, if anything, but Rathe remembered the tears in Mijan's eyes, the bitter answer to all her own and her sister's dreams. *We never have any luck,* she had said, *I should have known.* As if she'd guessed the thought, Asheri's face seemed to crumple.

"Take me home, Nico, please?"

Rathe nodded. "I'll take you home," he said, and held out his hand so she could scramble across.

Once they were free of the crowd, the streets were almost empty. It didn't take long to reach the Hopes-point Bridge. Asheri shifted against his back, muttered something, muffled by the cloth of his coat.

"What's that?"

"I don't think it's fair," Asheri said, and Rathe frowned.

"What's not, love?" He could hear bells chiming, and could smell a sudden sweet drift of incense from a household shrine.

"The prince-marshal getting all the credit. He sweeps in at the last minute, like a hero out of some really improbable romance, he doesn't even do any of the work, not like you did, Nico, and the others—and the whole city thinks he's the hero."

"Well, but he is," Rathe said, striving for a light tone. "By definition. Prince-marshals are always the heroes."

"I think," she said seriously, "we need some new stories, then."

Rathe shook his head. "Probably, but don't fret about it on my account, Ash. People know. They know it was the four of us, and that's fine. We're none of us heroes, nor would want to be. Except maybe Philip," he added, and was glad to surprise a gurgle of laughter from her.

"He does come the gentleman, doesn't he?" She sobered again. "But it's still not fair."

"I meant what I told Mailet," Rathe said, and realized that he did. "It's my job."

"Then you don't get paid enough," Asheri muttered.

They turned off Clock Street at last, and threaded their way through the narrow streets to the cul-de-sac where Mijan's house stood. The square around the well-house was empty, not even the sound of a child drifting from the surrounding houses, but Mijan herself was working in the little garden outside her front door, her back stubbornly to the road from the city. Another woman—a neighbor?

Rathe wondered—was standing with her, hands twisted in her mended apron. She looked up sharply at the sound of hoofbeats, though Mijan did not move, and then reached down to touch the other woman's shoulder. Mijan hunched her back, and didn't move. Rathe reined his horse to a stop—and he would have to return it to Caiazzo soon, he thought, or pay for stabling—and Asheri slid down from the saddle.

"Mijan?"

Mijan turned at the sound of her voice, scowling, and pushed herself up from the dry dirt. "How could you—?" she began, and Asheri's voice rose in what sounded like a habitual response.

"Don't *scold,* Mijan, I'm fine!"

Mijan shook her head, but Rathe could see the tears on her cheeks. She opened her arms then, and Asheri stepped into their shelter, into Mijan's fierce embrace, burying her head against her sister's chest. Mijan rested her chin on the girl's head. "Oh, Asheri," she said, and looked at Rathe. "I—thank you, Rathe. I thought sure—" She broke off again, and the other woman took a step forward.

"I said she'd be with the others," she said. She had an easy, comfortable voice, and an easy smile. "And I said you should have supper waiting."

Mijan loosened her hold on the girl, her mouth pulling down into her ready scowl. "I wasn't going to spend good coin on something that might not happen."

"Then it's a good thing I did," the other woman said. "Come along, Mijan, you're in no shape to cook—you shouldn't have to cook, either one of you, not after all this, and I've got supper on the stove, a whole chicken." She looked at Rathe, including him in her smile. "You should join us, Master Rathe—you'll not get better, though I say it who shouldn't."

Rathe returned her smile, but shook his head. "I have to report to Point of Hopes," he said, and backed the horse away.

"I'll be in tomorrow for work," Asheri called after him, and he saw Mijan's mouth tighten in an old disapproval. She said nothing, however, and Rathe lifted his hand in answer, kicking the horse into a slow trot.

The streets were getting more crowded as he made his way back toward Point of Hopes with people coming back from the Horsegate Road who hadn't bothered to go on to the Pantheon. A fair number carried pitchers of wine and beer, but they were happy drunks, and

Rathe couldn't quite bring himself to care. At Point of Hopes itself, the portcullis was open, and the courtyard was crowded, pointsmen and women for once mingling amicably with people from the surrounding houses. Someone had brought a hogshead into the yard, and the air smelled of spilled beer. Houssaye saw him first, and came to catch the horse's bridle.

"Nico! You're back, and well." His eyes darted to the gate, and back again. "Asheri?"

"With her sister," Rathe answered, and swung down off the horse at last. "I brought her there myself."

"Thank Astree and all the gods," Houssaye said. "I'll take care of the beast."

"Thanks," Rathe answered. He could see Monteia standing in the station's doorway, a mug of beer in her hand, and lifted his own hand in greeting.

She waved back, and beckoned him over. "Welcome back, Nico—a job well done, by all accounts."

Rathe blinked, startled, and Eslingen looked over the chief point's shoulder. "Aagte asked me to see the beer delivered—that's her gift, sort of an apology for thinking ill of the chief point here, I think."

And probably a way to get you away from Adriana, Rathe thought. He said, "So you've been telling the chief all about it, then?"

"Well, b'Estorr has, more like," Eslingen answered, and Rathe realized that the necromancer was standing just inside the station, a large pitcher in his hand. "I'm still not fully sure what happened."

Rathe grinned. "What about the astrologers?" he said to Monteia. "Did you finally get them?"

"Most of them, anyway," Monteia answered, and looked around the yard. "Come inside, it's quieter there."

It was darker, too, and Rathe settled himself on the edge of the duty desk with a sigh of relief. It was good to be back—good to be home, he amended, and couldn't stop himself from smiling.

"Between us, Claes and I and Manufactory made points on six of the astrologers," Monteia went on. "There were a couple more, but they seem to have gotten away, more's the pity. The thing is, they say they were hired to find the children by a woman called Domalein."

"Savine Domalein?" Rathe asked, and Monteia nodded.

"Known to us, certainly."

"Not to me," Eslingen said.

Rathe grinned. "She's a tout—a political tout, from the Ile'nord originally, runs three or four printers that we've had our eyes on. Her name was in de Mailhac's papers."

"Domalein told them she wanted the kids for runners," Monteia went on, "wanted kids whose stars would predispose them to supporting Belvis. Or at least that's their story. It was Domalein and a couple of her bravos who actually took the kids. Whether the astrologers believed it or not I'm not convinced, but she paid them well enough to make it worth their while to say they did."

b'Estorr shrugged, set his pitcher aside. "It would be hard to prove they didn't know, but they had to suspect something. The stars—there weren't enough patterns in the horoscopes to make that work, if you ask me."

"And I'd take it kindly if you'd tell that to the surintendant," Monteia answered. "He can tell you who to talk to in the Judiciary."

"Looking for a conviction, Chief Point?" the necromancer asked.

"Oh, yes," Monteia answered, and Rathe cut in hastily.

"What happened to Domalein?"

Monteia made a face. "Gone. Probably got out as soon as she heard we were looking for the astrologers, but at least we got to go through her house pretty thoroughly. She left in a hurry, didn't even stop to burn her papers, and we found plenty of letters from your Maseigne de Mailhac. She was paying for the whole thing, from the printers to the astrologers, and paying handsomely, too."

"Except that Timenard had something else in mind," Rathe said, suddenly sobered again. He was himself something of a Leveller by heritage and temperament, and Timenard had tried to draw on that, paint a vision of a world without queen or seigneury. An attractive thought, for a southriver rat, except that it would have been Timenard and only Timenard who ruled in their place.

b'Estorr touched him lightly on the shoulder. "It's a matter of balance, Nico. You can't compel the stars, not in the long run, no matter how much aurichalcum you have. He could have made things very difficult for a while, very painful, but in the long run, the natural order reasserts itself. We were its agents this time."

"Personally," Eslingen said, "I'd be happier without that sort of favor."

Rathe smiled again, made himself relax. He heard the tower clock strike, and then, a heartbeat later, the case-clock on the wall echoed it, beating out the hour. The true sun was sinking toward the horizon, the winter-sun still high in the sky, and he allowed himself a long sigh, tasting the familiar summer smells. He was home, the children were home and safe, and that was the end of it. He looked around, and Eslingen put a cool mug in his hand.

"Drink up," he said, and Rathe laughed, and let himself be led away to join the celebration.